Born with dragon's blood in their veins, two humans begin a daring quest to unite humans and dragons, overthrow a tyrannical king, and forge a future of freedom, while balancing the burdens of leadership and love in the perilous Kingdom of Sanara.

I0750886

THE CHILDREN OF CERAGON

Volume 2

of

Prophecies of the Dragon God

by

Terry Brewer

Presented by
CandleBeam Books
Riverton, Utah 84065

The Continent of Bardares

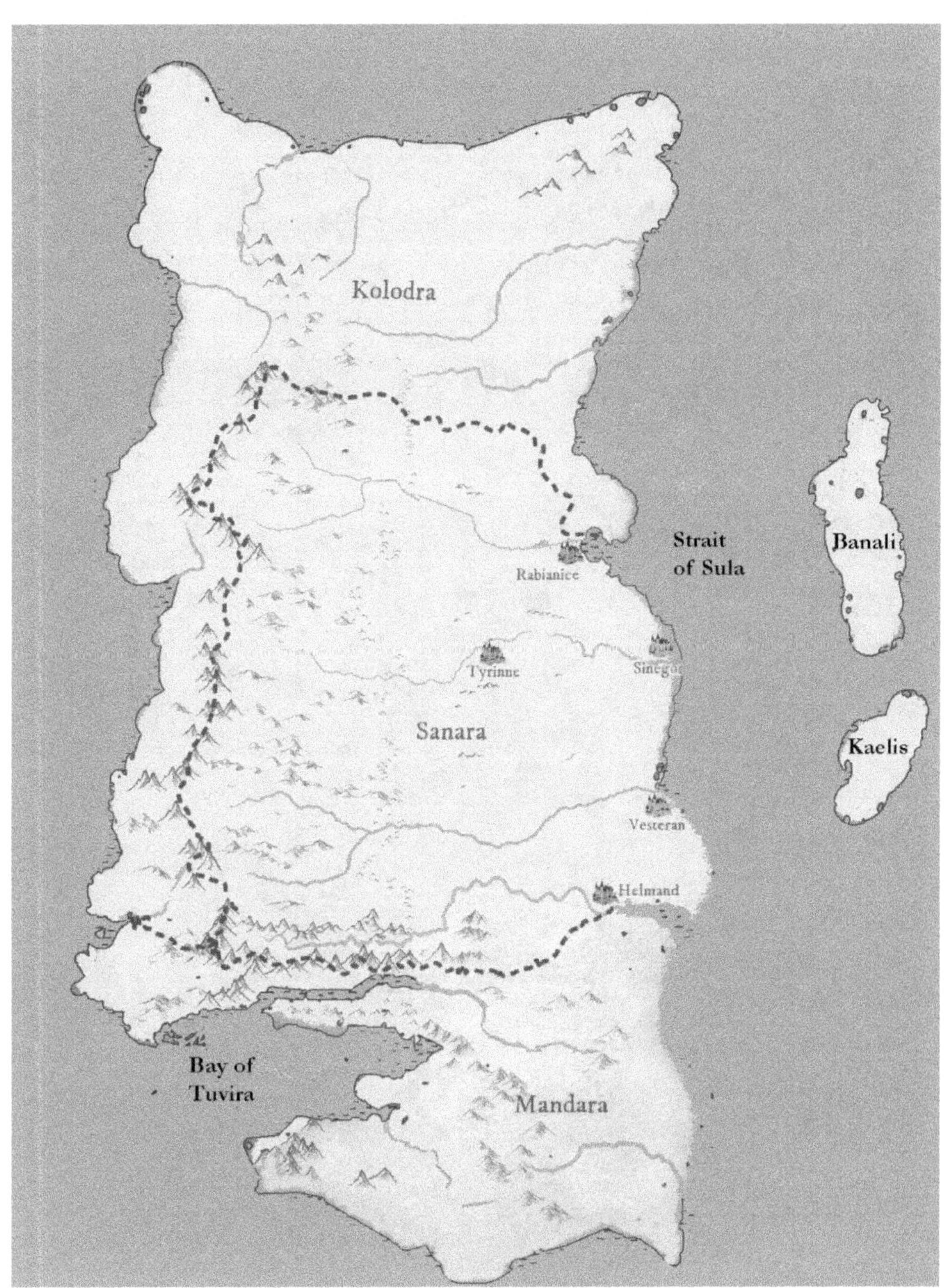

The Kingdom of Sanara

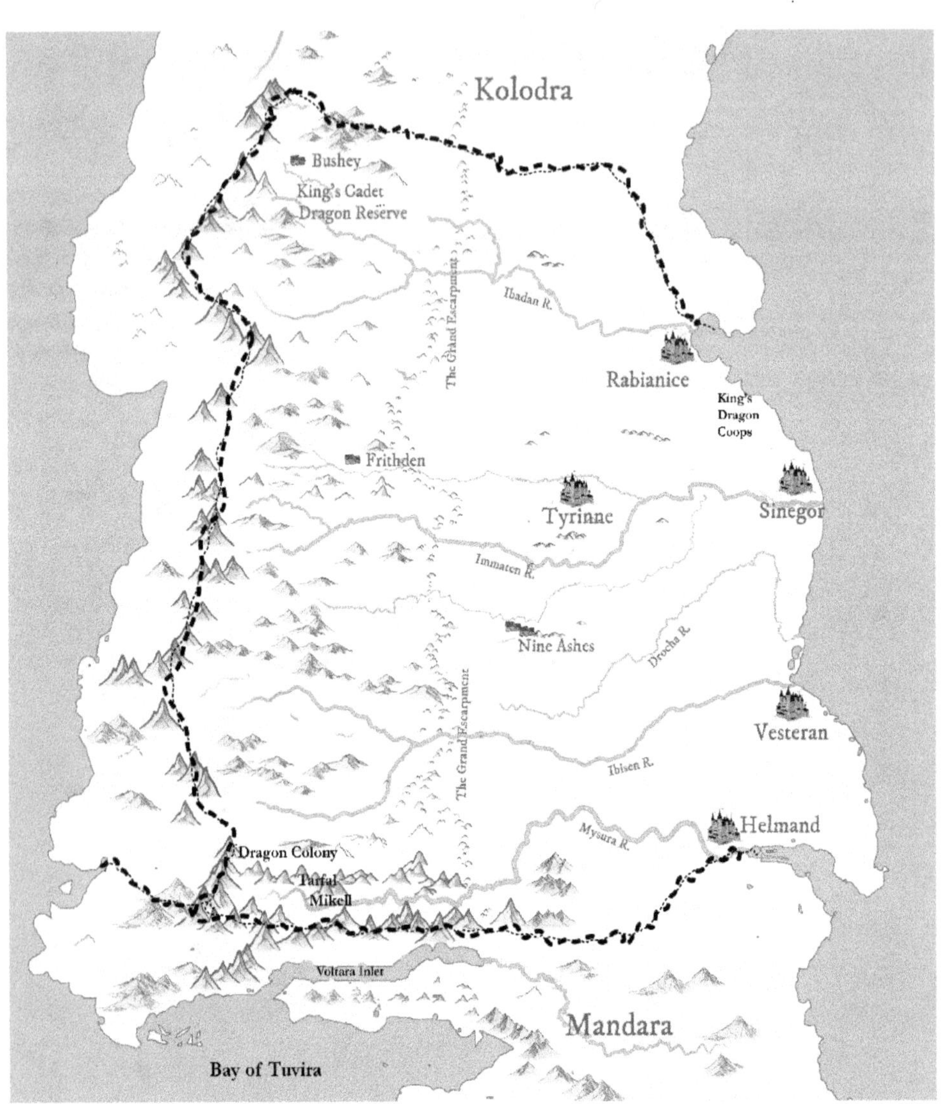
Kolodra
Bushey
King's Cadet
Dragon Reserve
Ibadan R.
The Grand Escarpment
Rabianice
King's
Dragon
Coops
Frithden
Tyrinne
Sinegor
Immaten R.
Nine Ashes
Drocha R.
The Grand Escarpment
Vesteran
Ibisen R.
Helmand
Mysura R.
Dragon Colony
Tarfal
Mikell
Voltara Inlet
Mandara
Bay of Tuvira

Contents

Chapter One

JARRAD DISMER

A man stood on the edge of the cliffs overlooking the East Sea in the quiet of a moonlit night. In his hand he held a dagger that gleamed softly in the starlight. His heart raced with a turbulent mixture of resolution and dread, with each shallow breath trembling in his chest. Below, the waves crashed relentlessly against the rocks, echoing his inner turmoil—a reflection of the weight of betrayals, secrets, choices and chance that had shattered his world.

The dagger was cold and uncompromising as it brushed against the skin of his throat. The need to bring an end to his anguish whispered in his mind as he paused. Staring into the abyss, he wondered whose body this blade should in truth claim: the king's? Brasa's? Or should he let his body fall to the dark waters below and end it all here?

***

Knowing his father, Barsom, held a place in King Valence's esteemed Grand Chamber of Advisors, Daven Ancaster had basked in pride. Their home was in the best and wealthiest part of Rabianice, the capital city of the kingdom known as Sanara. This meant that Daven's family occupied a top position in the highest social class, which allowed him to receive the best education, train to become a solicitor, and hire the finest tutors in martial arts, including swordsmanship, knife skills, crossbow use, and various forms of hand-to-hand combat. He humbly admitted that the combat skills he developed served him more than adequately in local tournaments and, once, when bandits attacked him.

What is more, given his standing in society, he could easily make himself a contender to replace his father in the Chamber when Barsom passed on or retired.

Shortly after coming of age, Daven married Kareim, the most wonderful woman in the world. By the end of their first year of marriage, Kareim bore their first child, a girl, whom they decided to name Elta, after his mother, who had died five years before. Daven genuinely believed he loved Kareim as much as any husband could ever love his wife, and he was as happy as he thought he could ever be.

After the old king's death, Barsom held the same position in the Chamber for Valence's son, King Deroth. This role implied that Barsom was among the select few who offered his wise counsel to assist the king in making decisions. He was always the member of the Chamber who cautioned the other eight members and the king against making rash, ill-considered, or seriously endangering changes from the way things were. Both kings kept him on mainly because Barsom played such an excellent 'Archos Partisan' when the other advisors started going off on some outlandish scheme.

Archos, the cruel-minded son of the gods Etmar and Rhetha, was ever a liar and a pretender, so it was only fitting that the role Barsom often played was to find fault with the council's unwise schemes and deliberations for governing the kingdom. Barsom's advice often set him apart from the others, as both kings usually followed the majority's plans. Particularly Deroth. But then, Deroth was rather prone to enacting laws after consulting only with his intelligence adjutant, Zaras Brasa, which often led to decisions that did not reflect the will of the majority or the complexities of the realm's issues.

Barsom's membership in the Chamber also meant that the old man was privy to all but the highest level of secrets in the realm. His position gave him power and responsibilities over important parts of the government. Unfortunately, that power was not always a good thing. More than once, Daven heard his father confess how the king forced him to make decisions abhorrent to his personal code of ethics, which was very sober, emphasizing personal honor and respect for others. Barsom confidentially shared stories about the secret police and their many visits under the Dragon Moon to those who had voiced even the smallest criticism of the king. He also told Daven about the prisons where innocent people entered and never returned.

Life changed one night when Barsom returned from a late chamber meeting, his forehead creased with worry, his face ashen. Daven noticed at once. "Father," he said, concern sharpening his voice, "are you unwell? You look dreadful."

Barsom managed a wan smile. "Is it that obvious?"

"I'll fetch the physician. Are you in pain?"

Barsom shook his head and moved past Daven, sinking heavily into an ornate, hand-carved armchair. "The pain I feel," he said quietly, "isn't something any doctor can cure."

Alarmed, Daven dragged over a matching chair and sat beside his father, searching his face. "Something happened at the meeting, didn't it? Was it Brasa again? I know how he torments you."

Barsom lifted his gaze to meet his son's. "You are perceptive, Daven. But this time, it's not his cruelty that wounds me. It's what he forced me to do." Daven's eyes widened. "Forced you? But you would never—" Barsom cut him off, anguish etched deep in his features. "But I have. Tonight, I condemned an innocent man, only to shield the king from blame." Daven stared, horrified. "Why, Father? How could you?" Barsom's voice trembled. "I traded that man's life for yours—and for your family's."

Our lives?" Daven's voice echoed, barely audible over a whisper.

Barsom nodded. "Brasa knows my reputation for honor, and he knows there's nothing I wouldn't do to keep you safe. That gives him—and the King—power over me. I'm nothing more than a pawn now, forced to obey or risk losing you."

Daven's fists clenched. "If your behavior continues, the people will turn on you as they have on the King and Brasa. They're the very spawn of Archos himself."

Barsom gave a bitter laugh. "Perhaps. But as long as I can protect you, I'll bear their hatred."

"And what will that cost you?" Daven asked, voice breaking. Barsom sighed. "The King will never release his hold on me. Our only hope is to leave this place."

"Leave? Where would we go?"

Barsom hesitated. "I don't know yet. We may have to flee the kingdom entirely. Would it surprise you to learn I've been quietly converting our assets into coins, jewels, and things easily carried or traded? Tomorrow, I'll show you where I've hidden them."

Daven shook his head. "I don't care about treasure. I care about you."

Barsom's eyes softened. "We may need those treasures to escape unnoticed. The King's Personal Guards watch me like hawks—those black-clad demons are as deadly as venom, and they miss nothing."

Daven swallowed hard. "What should I do?"

"For now, act as if nothing has changed. Don't alter your routine. Be prepared to depart promptly yet conceal any indication of it. If Brasa or the King suspects, our lives are forfeit."

"My family and I will be ready, Father. Just give the word."

Barsom pressed a trembling hand over his son's. "It's time you knew more about the shadows that haunt this kingdom."

Daven straightened. "What do you mean?"

Barsom glanced around, lowering his voice. "Are the servants gone for the night?"

"Yes, they all left an orai ago. I said farewell to old Arixell myself; he was the last, as always."

Satisfied, Barsom rose, locked the entry door, and beckoned Daven to follow. He led him up to his private office, locking that door behind them as well. Within the sanctuary of the soundproofed room, Barsom gestured for Daven to sit.

"From now on, we'll make a habit of locking ourselves in here to talk. I'll share with you what I learn in the Chamber and from the King—secrets and all. If there's something you must know, I'll tell you in full. In return, I want to hear about your life, your hopes, and your family. We must trust each other." A lump rose in Daven's throat. For the first time, he felt truly seen—not as a child, but as an equal, ready to share in his father's burdens.

As time passed, the two men found themselves regularly discussing the king, his secrets, and his confidants—sometimes in detail and with Daven asking many questions. Other times, Daven just nodded his head to show he understood. Barsom confirmed, as expected, that the character and personal attributes of both the old king and his son were exactly opposite that of his father. The worst part was how the current king repeatedly proved he cared little about most people in his kingdom. He was all about power, and at the heart of that power was his dragon army. All other matters were of secondary importance. Daven learned of whole villages of his fellow citizens being sacrificed to the Kingdom's own soldiers, dressed in enemy uniforms, solely because that would serve the King's propaganda and create broad support for his dragon army.

One day, just after High Sunstar, a messenger knocked on the Ancaster's door to pass word that the master of the house had been killed in a riding accident.

Daven fell against the door's frame in sheer anguish, with his knees barely managing to keep him from falling to the floor.

"How… how did this accident happen?" he managed to ask.

"Something caused the skell Barsom rode to bolt and trip over some large stones near the riding trail," the messenger explained. "It broke two legs and tossed Master Barsom against a rock wall. He died immediately from massive head wounds, and the skell needed to be destroyed."

"But Barsom's skell was extremely tame and never reacted in surprise to even the most severe provocation. What caused it to respond that way?"

"That we do not know. None of the nearby skells in the group reacted that way."

Certain that the accident was suspicious, Daven said nothing more but only asked where he could see his father's body.

Daven was given little time to grieve, for the king ordered him to take his father's place in some very sensitive border negotiations between three of the four major kingdoms on Badares: Sanara, Mandara, and Locarno. Accordingly, he was away from home for five sycles, which is thirty days.

The dreaded sweating disease devastated Daven's household while he was away. Within just three days, his wife, baby daughter, all his servants, and their families perished. After a full moon had risen and waned, Daven returned, accompanied only by his loyal chief steward, Arixell. He found that his entire household had been cremated and their ashes scattered upon the waters of the East Sea to prevent the further spread of the disease. He never even had the chance to say farewell.

What is more, his house had been burned to eliminate all traces of the sickness found there. Only the guest house and a remote outbuilding sometimes used for domestic beasts were spared because they had both remained locked up for the past three Kivans.

Daven's grief knew no limits. What else could happen to destroy the little remaining of his life?

The very next day, a nobleman, who was also a member of the chamber and a close friend of Barsom, revealed the truth to Daven: that Brasa had ordered Barsom's assassination with the knowledge and approval of the king. A hamaret thorn had been placed in Barsom's saddle in a place where it would eventually work its way through the leather and give the skell a suddenly agonizing sting. The nobleman informed Daven that he would be tortured for a week and then face the slowest death imaginable if he revealed the secret, and he had the authority to carry out this threat. In exchange for the information, Daven was forced to swear his support for the nobleman's candidacy as selectman of the chamber.

.

Why was my father murdered? Daven asked himself. Taking his place in the Chamber will inevitably seal my own fate.

Totally confused and grieving over the course of events, Daven spent orais, day after day, pondering what he should do.

***

One evening, he found himself standing on the edge of the Ladiad Cliffs, staring down into the swirling dark waters below. His right hand was lightly stroking the palm of his left with a finely honed edge of his Mandaran steel dagger. A thin trail of blood dutifully rose in the wake of the blade. Without question, the Royal Smithies of Mandara produced the finest steel weapons on the entire Badaren Continent. But why was it that they could produce such superior blades—so much better than the best smithies here in Sanara? He shook his head, pondering how easily he could have used this dagger in place of a razor for his morning's shave. Yet, that question seemed trivial now.

With a heavy, trembling sigh, he carefully pressed the tip of the dagger against his throat, feeling the steel bite into his skin. Carefully, he rotated the blade between thumb and forefinger—each movement deliberate and tense. A few agonizing seconds passed before he withdrew the knife, leaving a tiny crimson droplet blooming on his skin, glistening in the dim light.

Gripping the weapon firmly by the handle with the blade pointed downward, he raised it over his head and slammed its point with profound force into a branch of a nearby aldan tree. If only it were so easy to drive a dagger through the eyes of the present-day king!

The thought barely crossed his mind when the night sky vanished around him, replaced by daylight shining through an early morning mist. He threw up his arm to shield his eyes from the brilliant light and only lowered it when his eyes became accustomed to the change. But the landscape had changed, too. The cliffs were gone. Instead, he found himself in the midst of the most dazzling meadow he had ever seen. It stretched endlessly, bordered by landrin trees bursting with purple blossoms, while lush green-leafed lomas and aldans dotted the scene. Off in the distance, the unmistakable sound of a brook tumbling over stones reached his ears, and the air buzzed with the twitter of countless birds. Flowers of every hue clustered in small, vibrant groups, creating a tapestry of color.

There, in the center of the meadow, was a beautiful lady, with skin like bronze and hair like ebony. She was dressed in a crimson gown and bore a countenance that drew him in like a fuzzy-winged flit to a lighted candle. Instantly he realized there was only one being who could claim the form his eyes beheld. Without question, she was Lady Rhetha, wife of the Great Etmar and co-creator of the world upon which everyone dwelt.

Her eyes turned in his direction, and walking toward him, she voiced in almost musical tones, matching the natural environment that she crossed. "My son, Daven," she said, "do you really think your future can best be decided by the blade you bear in your hand?"

Daven's gaze darted between the golden brown of her eyes and the dagger still held in his fingers. He effortlessly pulled the knife out from the tree. Now seeming so incompatible with the environment surrounding him, it dropped to the ground with the loud metallic sound of steel bouncing off rock.

She smiled and nodded. "Your future is not to be determined by that or any other weapon. You must go to another part of the kingdom in secret and under a new identity. There you have work to do. From this time forth, you will no longer bear the name you were given at birth. Even in your memories, you will know yourself first as Jarrad Dismer." She pronounced the first name as 'D'yarrad,' with an emphasis on its first syllable. "The name Daven Ancaster will become nothing more than a distant echo in your mind. Yet, you will never forget your family, and your father will always be Barsom. They will remain a part of you, always. "You are already prepared for the journey. Justice can best be brought to the king if you fabricate your death and leave Rabianice immediately. I will give you a vision and instructions as to where you should go and what you should do. We may also have the opportunity of meeting once again."

With that, smiling, she reached out and ran her fingers through his hair, then turned about and walked away. Before she had taken ten steps, the image of her body had faded into the background of the meadow, and she was gone. He kept his gaze fixed on the meadow stretching before him, but in less than a minute, the scenery dissolved into mist. Suddenly, he was back near the edge of a cliff, as if the entire meeting had been a fleeting dream.

"Jarrad?" he said aloud to himself. "I like that name." Looking down at the rocky surface leading over to the cliff edge, he saw where his dagger lay, next to a gold coin with an image of the king's head. He picked both items up, and, sheathing the dagger, he glared at the coin. It was now a sharp reminder of what had just transpired. Thinking it somehow important, he placed the coin in a pocket, intending to store it later in a small chest where he stored meaningful items. In the future, he could pull it out and use it as a reminder of his visitation by a goddess.

***

Following the lady's instructions, Jarrad quickly converted as much of the last of his now-dead family's assets into coins and jewels as he could without raising suspicions. He then left a suicide note saying:

"I am unable to cope with the deaths of my wife and child, along with that of my father. So, I have given all my wealth to those I think best deserve it, and I intend to kill myself by jumping from the suicide cliffs of Ladiad into the Strait of Sula."

He rolled the note into a scroll, tied it with silver threads, and sealed it with his family crest. Last, using another silver thread, he attached the ring bearing his family crest to the scroll and left it where Arixell would be sure to find it in the morning, after Daven's apparent passing. He also left a note describing where Arixell could find a letter of recommendation and a documented financial annuity large enough to last until the end of his days.

During the night of his departure, he rode his favorite skell to the cliffs and left the reins loosely tied to a bush before scampering away. Using yet another name and wearing a hooded cloak to disguise his face, he had, on the previous day, purchased a wagon and two sturdy skells. These he retrieved from their hiding place in a thick forest on the outskirts of the city.

While in disguise, he had also taken a room in a lodging house on one of the less-travelled roads leading away from Rabianice, and that is where he spent the remainder of the night. Shortly after the rising of the sunstar. The next day, Jarrad collected all his financial resources from various locations, tucked them into hidden compartments in the wagon, and, following a vision of the route given to him by the Lady, turned his team of skells to the south.

It was a long trip, taking more than a Kivan, the term referring to thirty days, derived from the time required for the red moon, Kivan, to travel completely around the planet known to its people as Tamerel. Jarrad eventually crossed the southern border of Sanara near the city of Vesteran and entered the minor kingdom of Locarno. Fortunately, Locarno was a peaceful kingdom, which maintained its independence solely due to a three-way agreement between the major, and much more warlike, kingdoms on the continent of Badares: Sanara, Kolodra, and Mandara. Jarrad had personally helped to provide the language for that agreement, not so very long ago.

From Vesteran, Jarrad changed the wagon's direction from south to west, as directed by the map in his head, and, after a time, climbed a series of switchback turns, ascending into what was commonly called the uplands. A place of mountain ranges, river valleys, and killer beasts, the uplands were mostly remote from the lowlands, where eighty percent of the Badaren population lived. He found the narrow road on which he traveled, entering a wide and heavily forested valley and loosely following the Mysura River. The entire southern flank of the valley consisted of a chain of unimaginably tall mountains. Based on his studies of Badaren geography, he surmised those mountains to be those that followed the border between Sanara and Mandara. All the while, the road hugged the bottom of steep mountain slopes lining the northern side of the valley, above which the tops of snow-capped mountains, now and again, made their appearance. Eventually, Jarrad found himself in a small community by the name of Tarfal. The discovery of gold, silver, lead, and copper deposits in the nearby mountains led to the settlement of Tarfal only a year or two earlier.

Still following the lady's instructions, Jarrad purchased a little valley about one tondrin northwest of Tarfal. It was close enough to the village that he could leisurely walk there in half an orai, or ride in a fraction of that. Yet, surrounded by forest, he could build a private home The valley became his safe harbor, and, accordingly, he gave it the name of Harbor Valley.

Jarrad hired people to clear portions of his land, raised much of his food, and was able to obtain work as a teacher, an advisor on local questions of interest, a resource for people who could not read, and an informal arbiter of disputes. He soon found himself at the center of almost everything of consequence that went on in the valley, yet he had his privacy, and he loved it.

About a year after Jarrad's arrival in the valley, Deroth attacked Locarno. The attack occurred at a time when Mandara was engaged in an air and naval war with

Kolodra, making it possible for Sanara to conquer Locarno and absorb the little kingdom while Mandaran forces were distracted. Since the Mysura Valley was a part of Locarno, it too became a part of Sanara, but its remote location meant that the valley was largely left alone by the conquering kingdom's soldiers. A new magister was appointed for the valley, and new taxes were enforced, but the government mostly left the people alone now.

Many former residents of populated areas in Locarno, who did not like the prospect of living under the thumb of Sanaran soldiers in the lowlands, moved up into the mountain valleys and settled in places like Tarfal. Within a short time, the population of Tarfal grew from a few hundred to about twenty-five hundred residents. A nearby township named Mikkel, with a population of just over a thousand, was built when a thriving lumber industry started on the southern side of the valley. Farmers found the soil to be fertile on cleared forest land, and the growing season was long this far south.

Jarrad continued to serve the people around him and became familiar with everyone in the Mysura Valley.

***

Since the Valley was in the uplands, residents needed to be constantly on the alert for killer beasts. Jarrad, therefore, built himself a sturdy paddock, a fenced-off area large enough to hold his herd of thirty ellams. He lined it with hamaret thorns to keep predators from climbing over or through his barrier fence. Hamaret thorns were a wicked, yet natural way to protect livestock from even the largest predators. The individual thorns, each about the size of a thumb, were needle-sharp, as strong as iron nails, and coated in an acidic residue that burned any living tissue they came into contact with. Unfortunately, the only way to set up a hamaret fence was by manipulating the arm-length limbs into place with long-handled pincers and shears. It was no small effort for a man working alone, and today, Jarrad worked on this project by himself.

All at once, the open field surrounding Jarrad abruptly developed walls and a ceiling of stone, and the day disappeared except for reflected light coming from some unknown source. Jarrad found himself standing in a cavern of massive size with stone walls, ceiling, and floor. Gazing about, he marveled at the sheer size of the chamber. It could easily have accommodated well over five hundred people, and the city council building, the tallest structure in all the capital city of Rabianice, could have rested here without its bell tower even approaching the dome of rock above him.

The place was empty of life, except for himself. He called out, "Hello! Is anyone here?" The only response was an echo, which reverberated about him for at least a minute.

Then he heard a soft step. Turning in the direction of the sound, he saw the same beautiful woman he had met before, now dressed in a shimmering lavender gown of ornamented damask, appearing from out of a stone passage to approach him. While his eyes were drawn to her long black hair and creamy skin, he knew, whatever her appearance, that the woman was the Lady Rhetha, the goddess who had visited him two years before in his father's home.

She called him by name and said, "You have done well in following my instructions, and I am proud to see that you have become an important part of your new community. But I have a new task for you to perform, which is of greater importance. I need you to climb into the mountains and rescue someone who is in grave danger. While you are away, no beast shall dare threaten your livestock.

Jarrad tilted his head and in a soft voice replied, "How does one argue with a goddess?"

She returned his smile and said softly, "Argue?"

Before her departure, the lady added, "Remember well this cavern in which you stand. It exists in the mountains to the west of your home. I will give you instructions on how to find it, both by land and by air."

Surprised at this last comment, Jarrad thought, "Now, why would I want to find a place by air?

***

Jarrad soon found himself carefully filling a backpack with several odd things and taking a hike up into the rocky, sloped mountains, rising beyond his home.

Again, the Lady had given him precise directions, both on what to pack and where to go. She said that in a certain place he would find his future. She also told him that on this venture he would have no need to fear any killer beasts enroute, so apart from carrying a knife and a small hand ax, useful for many purposes, he went unarmed.

He meticulously followed her instructions and, after two days of hiking through extremely rugged terrain, found himself beneath a rocky overhang, six tondrins away from his home. There, he discovered the carcass of what he thought was a small, dead dragon. Only the dragon moved slightly. So, it was not dead, just on the verge of death. But… but… alive or dead, it should not be here! The king watches over his dragons like a mother watches over her newborn baby! How would a dragon, even one this small, ever get up here in the wildest of places without a whole team of dragon handlers standing nearby? What's more, the beast had no jewel in its neck!

Carefully, he looked all around the area at the bottom of the escarpment and found no cause for fear. Figuring this was what he was supposed to find, he watchfully approached the little creature, lifted its head, and gave it water to drink. When the dragon responded eagerly to the offering, he gave it more, a little at a time. When he thought it might be able to manage food, he gave it a few small chunks of raw meat—part of what the Lady had instructed him to bring. Over the next while, he fed the little dragon more pieces of his meat, a little at a time, and in so doing, he readily found the little beast to be a female. The dragon revived somewhat after a time and muttered a soft "Thank you."

Jarrad jerked back in surprise and blurted out, "You can talk!"

"Of course, I can!" the dragon said in a voice, which, though weak, reflected a tone of indignation. "If you can talk, why cannot I?"

Sighing heavily, Jarrad settled back on his knees and replied, with a shake of his head, "I admit, I can't think of a single reason why a dragon should not be able to talk."

He laughed inwardly at the absurdity of his situation and set about making a camp for the night. He cut kitka boughs to make two soft beds and spread blankets over each. He made a fire next to the rock face in such a way that its heat reflected out toward their beds, and when both were as comfortable as they could get, he sat back against the trunk of a tree.

While it slept, he examined the dragon carefully. When standing, her head, which seemed disproportionately large for her slender body, would barely reach his chest. Her long wings, he estimated, would stretch out to three or four strides on either side. Her scaly hide was a medium brown, reminiscent of tanned ellam skin, giving her an unexpectedly vulnerable appearance. Having seen numerous dragons over the years—though always from a distance—they had all appeared large and fierce. This one, however, looked barely capable of scaring a tree rat. She was likely just a fledgling.

After another orai passed, she opened her eyes and fixed her gaze on Jarrad. In an instant, the color of her skin shifted to match the speckled grey of the granite face behind her, blending seamlessly into the rocky backdrop. Jerking away in astonishment, Jarrad saw the little dragon instantly copy his move without hesitation.

"My, you are a bundle of surprises, little one," he said. "Do you have a name?"

"My name ... is Shaddra," the dragon said. "When you moved so quickly, you startled me. That is why I jumped. Is there something surprising in that?" Jarrad turned his head and rubbed the stubbled growth on his chin. "Hmm," he said. "Are you aware that your skin changed color when you first caught sight of me? It changed to match the color of the cliff face behind you. In fact, I would barely have been able to see you there at all if I had not seen your skin change and noticed the reflected firelight on your scales.

Shaddra's eyes widened in amazement, then slowly narrowed as her mind sought to wrap itself around this strange development. Within a minute, her eyes grew bright again, and she began to nod her head. "Unfortunately, I know so little about myself and the world around me. You have shown me that I can change my color, although I do not understand the reason for this change or what actions I took to cause it. But I will study it in my mind until I remember how I did it. Thank you for helping me gain this knowledge. In the meantime, may I ask your name?"

"My name is Da... I mean, Jarrad Dismer. I live in an isolated valley down below in, uh, that direction." He pointed down the slope to the east. "It wasn't easy to come up here."

"Then, why, Jarrad Dismer, did you, as you say, 'come up here'?"

"Oh, that is a long story."

"Since I am currently somewhat disabled, it appears that I have a lot of time to listen to long stories, or perhaps you have somewhere else to be?" With those words, the little dragon smiled.

"Well, my friend Shaddra, you possess a highly intelligent mind that supports your eloquent way of speaking."

"I would be glad to share my story with you if you will do the same for my benefit."

"Since my story is undoubtedly the shorter, I should go first," Shaddra said. "Then be my guest," replied Jarrad. "Though it may be short, I'm certain it will be very educational."

A good part of the night was thus spent in conversation between dragon and human as they related the histories that brought them to this forsaken spot in the Kukhala Mountains bordering the western side of Sanara.

As soon as she was again able to fly, Jarrad led her to his home and hid her away in his outbuilding. She had gained enough strength to fly but preferred to walk beside Jarrad on her four legs so that they could converse.

There, she built up her health, and they discussed ways that might improve her success at hunting. They discovered that she could change the color of her skin in many intricate ways, just by thinking about it. She could become invisible by matching the colors of her skin on the front side to the colors that lay behind her and vice versa. She could even hide her shadow somehow. How did she do that? The resulting effort helped improve Shaddra's success rate at hunting immensely.

Chapter Two

THE MIDWIFE'S APPRENTICE

Old Clara sat sipping tea at her table, pondering how to manage a particularly difficult problem she had discovered at her work this day, when suddenly the walls of her comfortable cottage seemed to blur and disappear. In place of a growing dusk peering through her window, she saw a bright sunstar shining overhead and felt its warmth. Instead of her stove and cupboards, she now saw grass, bushes, trees, and a little brook. She could hear the gurgling sound of the stream as it tumbled over rocks in its bed. Nothing remained of her house except herself and the table and chairs in her kitchen.

Disbelieving her own eyes, she set down her cup, rubbed her eyes, blinked a few times, and stood to better see around. Despite her disbelief, the scene before her did not go away. Rather, she saw a woman walk out from a nearby grove of trees and into what had been Clara's kitchen.

"Clara," the woman said, "may I sit and speak with you awhile?"

Her eyes widening in amazement, Clara dropped into as proper a curtsy as she could remember from her youth.

"I see you know who I am," said the woman, "but, please, there is no formality needed here. Please, let us have a little talk."

Not knowing what else to do, Clara rose and waved her arm toward an empty chair.

"I know you do not get many visitors," the woman said as she pulled out the chair and sat down. "I apologize for intruding."

Clara closely examined her visitor, as she, too, sat at the table. With one sweeping glance she noticed her visitor's deep brown hair and her simple but elegant green dress, which matched her eyes.

"I suppose, right now," Clara said, "I should be asking whether I am awake or dreaming. But, somehow, I already know the answer to that question."

"Oh, you are most assuredly awake," the woman said. "But I can understand your disbelief. Since you know who I am, you should know that the message I am about to give you is important to both you and Tamerel."

"Why am I so honored to be visited by Your Eminence?"

"You have, for so many years, been responsible for the birthing of young dragons. You know them, love them, and give them the best of care. You have an immense ability to love, and that is why I have come to visit with you. I have a favor to ask."

"For you, dear lady, I will offer anything that is in my power to give."

"Clara, I ask for nothing that will not be rewarded back to you many times over. In a very short time, you will have three visitors, strangers to you, who are in extraordinary danger. I have sent them because you are in a unique position to render them, and yourself, great service. Would you please listen to their plea and help them as only you are able?"

"I will consider it an honor to do what I can, dear lady," Clara said.

"That is good to hear. I will now depart so you can prepare for your visitors."

With those last words, the woman stood and walked back out into the grove of trees from whence she came. As her figure disappeared into the trees, the vision of the forest meadow melted away, and Clara sat staring again at the inside of her cottage.

Old Clara looked down at her teacup. Picking it up, she found the tea to be as hot as it was before the strange visitation. "The Goddess, Retha, has just visited me!" she said aloud as if trying to convince herself that it happened.

"And now, I am to have other visitors!" She knew the lady's word would happen soon, as she had said. "I must get ready for them!" she said in a firm, no-nonsense tone.

Just as the lady declared, Clara rarely had visitors of any kind, so she was not sure how to prepare. Quickly she tidied up her main room and set a fresh pot of tea to boil. Last, Clara washed and dried her teacup and set out three more matching cups. Clara might not have many visitors, but she would be ready to welcome these. The tea was hardly ready when Clara heard a knock on her door.

She took a deep breath, realizing she had no idea what to expect on the other side. When she opened the door, she found three people—a man and a woman, slightly older than she in their late fifties, and a child of about fifteen—all standing on the landing in front of her home. Clara immediately noticed the redness in all their eyes as if they had been crying.

"I beg your pardon, Lady Ramendi," said the man stiffly. "I am Doctor Tiimos Keiron, and these are my wife, Runa, and daughter, Eleth. May we beg a few minutes to speak with you?"

"Yes, yes, you may, but I can only offer my kitchen table and chairs for your comfort. I use the adjacent room as a work area."

"Lady Ramendi..." the man began after everyone had been seated.

"Oh, please, call me Clara. Everyone does."

"As you wish, Clara, and you may call us Tiimos and Runa. We have come at the request of... someone important. Someone who said you would be expecting us...?" He spoke those last words as if he expected Clara to be completely surprised by their visit.

"Yes..." Clara said, still not believing she had seen and heard the woman in the meadow, "I know the one of whom you speak."

Tiimos' whole body seemed to relax, and he continued, appearing quite relieved, "Then let me give you a little background as to why we are here. About fifteen years ago, I treated a pregnant woman for a horrible disease. That woman lived long enough to have her baby but died soon after. The woman and her husband were close friends of ours, and we were devastated. Soon after the baby's birth, the husband, named Boda, came to us saying that both he and his newborn girl were in grave danger. He asked if we would be willing to adopt the little girl because he was certain that he would soon be killed and the baby, too, if she were discovered. He also warned us that if anyone discovered the girl's identity, we would all face the same danger. His words were difficult to believe, but we loved our friend dearly and agreed to adopt the girl. Less than a Kivan later, we learned that our friend had been killed... murdered... by the king's agents.

Runa had been ill for several Kivans, and none of our friends or relatives had seen her, which was convenient. That made it possible for us to say that she had been in her last Kivans of pregnancy, and we had been too worried, because of her age, for her to undertake any outside activity. Everyone believed the baby girl was ours, and we only told Eleth who her real parents were a few years ago when she was old enough to understand.

"For fifteen years, we have raised and loved Eleth as our own and always been careful to keep her secret close to our hearts. We love her dearly, and, to us, she is our girl. But we learned yesterday that we are all in danger from those same agents of the king who killed Boda. They have discovered Eleth's identity, and though we have no idea why the king would concern himself with a little girl, we will not take any chances."

"Oh, you poor people," Clara said. "I cannot imagine having to live with the burden you carry and the pain you must be feeling today."

"The lady told us...," Runa said abruptly, with anguish written all over her face. "I mean..."

"Don't worry yourselves," Clara said. "As I mentioned, I know of the one who gave you the message."

She sighed with relief and continued, "She told us we must leave the kingdom today. She also warned us that attempting to take Eleth with us would lead to our discovery. She told us that you are the one who can save Eleth's life and give her the love that our little girl needs. Without her, the two of us can escape to Kolodra."

Clara looked over at the girl who sat quietly between her parents. "I... admit that this request is a surprise. The lady did not tell me what the nature of your entreaty would be. However, I must admit that although my work is enjoyable, it can sometimes be quite challenging for me. You see, I have many children, but they are all dragons."

This time the Keirons expressed common looks of surprise. "Dragons!" They all cried out at once.

"Yes, I work with dragons, and I do need an apprentice. It is not dangerous if she can keep secrets. If young Eleth can be discreet and is up to doing the work, I will assign her to the best of her ability; I would welcome her into my home. I do have a spare bedroom. I would care for her as my own until she is of age or can take over my job.

"Be warned, however, if she cannot meet those conditions, I would have to find another place for her to live."

Tiimos and Runa looked at each other with faces showing deep concern, but little Eleth's eyes shone brightly with curiosity and excitement as she looked directly into Clara's eyes and said, "When my parents told me earlier today that we must be separated, I cried for a long time. I must admit I was afraid of coming here—at least until now. Whatever the reason may be for the lady's news, I know I belong here."

Runa spoke up again, saying, "We have been giving Eleth chores to perform since she was four. Since the very beginning, she has absorbed knowledge about everything around her at an unbelievable rate and worked extremely hard, even for her age."

At this, Tiimos laughed and said, "She has already learned practically everything I know as a doctor, and mostly just by watching what I do. That includes how to perform surgeries. She watched me when I worked, and at other times, we practiced together using recently killed ellams, bound for the butcher's shop. She has the hands of a surgeon."

"Please stop talking about me like that," Eleth said, looking at her parents. "I just like to learn things."

"We apologize for talking about you this way," said Runa, "but Clara does need to know about you before she can make a knowledgeable decision regarding your future."

"I guess you're right," Eleth said. "I do not want to be separated from you, but I saw and heard the lady, too. Coming here is the right thing; I know it. I also know that I will see you again... sometime."

"We have packed Eleth's things into three boxes," Runa said, "which are in the carriage outside. Tiimos and I must be leaving right away to meet the guide who will help us cross the border. We hope this will not be too much of an inconvenience for you. We are all putting much faith into the words of the Lady."

"Yes," Clara agreed. "Indeed, we are doing that very thing."

After the Keirons left Clara's home, Eleth remained seated at the kitchen table. From across that table, Clara carefully examined the dark-redheaded girl who now stared despondently at the door through which everything she had ever known in her life departed only minutes before. She wondered how the girl could bear this kind of grief. Was there anything that might help her get through this lonely upcoming night?

"Eleth," Clara said, "tomorrow you will have your first chance to see a dragon. Are you curious about what dragons are like?"

The girl's golden-brown pupils perked and jumped to the corners of her eyes to stare at Clara. Once her head caught up with her eyes, she said excitedly, "Dragons! I get to see dragons!"

"Not only will you see them, but you will also work with and for them. I expect you will learn to love them soon enough."

"Like you do?" Eleth asked with a smile stretching across her face.

Clara's eyes took on a distant look of their own, and she nodded. "Yes, something tells me you will."

"But what is a dragon really like?"

"Oh, my, you are an impatient one."

"Please tell me! If you don't tell me, my mind will make up all kinds of wild images when I go to bed, and I won't get any sleep at all.

"Hmm. Have you ever seen a karam?"

"No, but I've been told about them, and I've seen many drawings. They're a kind of fierce killer beast. So, what about karams?"

"Dragons remind me of karams because they move quietly and smoothly like the killer beast. They are amazingly quick for their size and stronger than you would think. I also like the way a dragon's tail tends to curl or swish or flick in a sleepy feline sort of way to show its mood, just as with a karam.

"Really? I'd almost want to pet one."

"Ahh," Clara said, widening her eyes and ending the exclamation with a deep intake of breath. "I think… it would be safer to pet a karam."

***

Two sycles later, Clara, her satchel of midwife's tools slung over her back, moved steadily through the entrance of the dragon caves, her young apprentice close at her heels. As she passed, she barely nodded to the two sentries standing guard. They knew her well—no words were needed. No need to verify her identification tattoos. Her face was familiar here; as the head midwife, she had come and gone from these nurseries nearly every day for the past thirty years. Though Eleth had only been with her for a dozen days, the guards had quickly come to recognize her, too.

"Hurry, Eleth," she said to the girl, whose pace slowed every time they passed the new young guard named Jazen. "There's no time to flirt."

Eleth, grasping a small box and casually swinging an unlit oil lantern, hastened her steps and caught up. "Sorry," she said. "I don't know why, but my heart beats in my ears every time I look at him."

Old Clara paused and put an arm around the girl's shoulders. "I know why. It is something we shall have to talk over very soon. You are growing up, child. There are things you must be told. Since you are, technically, now orphaned and have no mother to tell you, I suppose the duty falls to me. This afternoon, if all goes well with this hatching, you and I shall go to the river with a picnic basket, and I will tell you many things."

The girl's eyes brightened. "What sort of things?"

The aged midwife smiled. "Matters of life and death and how both come to be."

"I've assisted my father for many years, Mistress. I already know the basics of procreation."

"Maybe so; however, there are still important aspects of life in the Coops that you need to learn. But hasten now, child. We have work to do. You just hold tight onto that precious casket under your arm and do not drop it."

"Drop the jewel?" the girl said defensively. "You know I never would! Do you not trust me, Mistress?"

Old Clara smiled. "If I didn't trust you, girl, you would not be the one carrying that box. Now pick up your skirts and keep up with me."

The girl nodded and dutifully followed the old woman inside the cave.

Clara liked Eleth. The girl was showing outstanding promise. Yesterday, they candled siris dragon eggs. Eleth was gentle, patient, a quick learner, and thoroughly enchanted with the tiny, wriggling embryos the candlelight revealed. Clara was glad about this news. Her dear old eyes were not as sharp as they used to be, but she still had a few good years in her to continue her work. If Eleth proved trustworthy, the midwife would let her in on the great secret.

They followed a tunnel for some distance. It was softly lit by oil torches set in sconces along the walls. Still, these underworld labyrinths were dim, and additional illumination was needed. The old woman took the lantern from her apprentice, lit it, and handed it back.

"Mind you hold this so we both can see. I'm too old to stumble. At my age, if I fall, some very dear part of me might get broken."

"I'll be mindful, Mistress," the girl replied and held the lantern where it would best help Clara. "I can see without it."

Clara looked at Eleth with a squint in her eye and continued on her way.

Within several minutes, they came into the first birthing cave, the biggest and most important of the four. Its ceiling rose more than a landrin above them, and its walls stood more than three landrins apart on all sides. Overhead shafts supplied light and ventilation.

Here the mighty firedrakes were born. The place was filled with the nests of some thirty huge brooding hens, sitting upon their eggs like majesties upon thrones. They softly crooned to their unborn, while mewlings of the latest hatchlings, singing back to their mothers, wafted through the air. Anyone who believed, as the king did, that dragons were dumb beasts, having no heart or feelings, had never been to the dragon birthing caves and listened to this, Old Clara thought. These were lullabies as tender and loving as those passed between any human mother and child. But they were, moreover, sad. The aged midwife understood all too well why that was the case.

One might think a cave filled with so many large creatures would be a filthy, smelly place. It was not so. Under Clara's direction, the nurseries were kept immaculate. Nest straw was replaced regularly by the coopers: teams of men and their boy apprentices in charge of cleaning the nurseries and feeding the brooding hens. Other female apprentices, like Eleth, under the care of other midwives than Clara, fastidiously attended to the dragons' hygiene, bathing the dragons every sycle and applying sweet oil to their scales. These midwives and coopers held important jobs in the realm, as they were the keepers of the king's flocks. Nevertheless, only Clara was given responsibility for the hatchings.

Several young coopers waved at Clara and Eleth as they passed by, and the women waved back, Eleth blushing. Her apprentice was stunning, the midwife mused. She caught the eye of every young man they passed and, no doubt, some of the older men, too. *I will need to teach her what to do with her beauty and warn her of its power before it gets her in trouble.* Clara thought. *The girl is nearly of age. She needs to know the facts of life and must learn she may never partake of them.*

Clara remembered she had once been lithe and young and caught the second glance of many a guard or cooper. But that was long ago, and, in her chosen profession, such beauty came to naught. The king's midwives were not permitted to wed nor have children; their duties must be undivided. So it was; the dragon hatchlings were Clara's children, and she their godmother, every single one.

The moment the two women entered the firedrake coop, a hush fell. Every dragon turned its head to gaze at Clara and the girl who followed behind. Such an event had never happened before. Yes, the hens knew her as a friend, but usually, she came and went unobtrusively about her duties without much notice. For some reason, she became the center of attention today.

"Good morning, friends?" she called softly. The hens returned her salutation with pleasant nods. This exchange seemed to break whatever caused the silence. The hens looked away, returning to nuzzling their hatchlings and crooning to their unborn eggs.

"Hmm," Clara murmured to herself, hurrying on, "how very odd."

It was quite warm in the nurseries. These coops were kept at incubation temperatures, a little higher than comfortable for humans, and it was not long until a human here broke into a sweat. The dragons produced sweat too, but the scent of it was not unpleasant, at least not to Clara. Something akin to the salty wind from the sea was how she thought of it. Its odor permeated in this and all the other caverns here. The old woman stopped, drew in a big whiff of it, and closed her eyes with as much pleasure as if she were smelling a rose. *Such sweet, gentle beasts at heart,* she thought. *Even the firedrakes. They would not fight if it weren't for the jewel. I do love them so.*

"Mistress?" Eleth's voice interrupted the old woman's reverie. "You said we must hurry. Why do we linger?"

Clara opened her eyes. "I use my nose to test the water, child," she said. "I can tell good fortune or bad before it happens, just by the smell."

"Can you really?" the girl asked and sniffed the air about her. "Yes, I can smell something, but I don't know what it is."

"Is that so?" Clara said with a strange look in her eyes.

"What do you smell here, Eleth? Is it fair or foul?"

"Fair," the Eleth answered, "but there is something strange about it."

"Yes, it is fair, young one, and indeed, something is amiss. You may have caught it."

"Caught what?"

"I don't know. Something. But I think it will be a good day."

"Will you teach me to do that?" Eleth implored.

Clara raised one of her fingers in response. "I can teach you many things, child, about both dragons and men, but I cannot teach you that. That, you must learn for yourself. And you will when you have cared for them as long as I have. Perhaps you have already started. Let's be on our way. Today, our business is not here with the firedrakes but in the coop of the messengers. Shaydem is waiting for us. Her egg will hatch this morning, and we mustn't be late."

That said, they hurried on.

At the far end of the vast nursery, they came to another tunnel, winding deeper into the womb of the mountain. At its end was a second cavern, less elegant than the first and oddly shaped, its ceiling lower to the ground.

This was the coop of the draft dragons. Here, the lullabies were just as tender but of a deeper, more alto resonance. The draft hens were no prima donnas, as were the firedrake brooders. Their bodies were oversized and heavy-bodied with stout, muscular hind legs and longer forelegs. They had a solid bone structure rather than hollow as did the flying dragons. Like all dragons, these had four strong toes at the end of their forelegs, with thickly padded paws and heavy-duty claws on the ends of their paws. Since they were wingless, draft dragon infants would never need to fly, bred as they were for heavy labor and leading infantry charges.

They were far from defenseless. Each draft dragon had four stout horns, two on their heads and two on their tails. The two deadly short horns, located on top of the forehead, pointed forward, ideally situated for a lethal upthrust of the head. Around their thickly muscled necks, and just behind the head, grew a bony, protective, dish-shaped neck plate. It extended two handspans up and away from the neck and slanted back at an angle so as not to interfere with the front horns and to act as a shield for the vital parts of the body. The tail was as long as the body and could swing accurately to any position above or to the side of the it. The other two horns, each a handspan in length, were located on the tail; pointing out and slightly up, they made the tail a viciously barbed whip.

When not in battle, draft dragons would spend their entire time under chain and harness, rooting up trees for the clearing of forests, hauling stones from the quarries, or pulling the large draft wagons filled with troops, supplies, or the many types of siege weapons used to fight the king's never-ending wars.

Again, as soon as the dragons saw Clara enter the room, silence fell. There was no feeling of animosity, but rather, a kind of unspoken deference. It made her uncomfortable. She hurried on through the nursery without a word, the eye of every hen following her.

The two women hastened down yet a different tunnel until they reached a third nursery. The ceiling of this cavern soared so high that one could look up and not see the roof. Here were hatched the swift air warriors of the King's Dragon Forces. These lethal raptors were the exact opposite of the draft dragons—sleek, light-framed, long-winged, and built for flight. Siris dragon hatchlings would each one day carry a single knight, their lord and master, until the end of their days, which, sadly, were few. There were no old siris dragons. Most died in battle within two or three years of their first seeing service.

As Clara and Eleth passed through the siris nursery, the same phenomenon as before repeated itself. Every hen grew silent; every eye keened her way.

What are they trying to tell me? Clara wondered. *Has something gone wrong? Is there some unseen threat in the nurseries? Are they, or is she, in danger?* "No," she told herself. The scent was yet fair, not foul. But what in the name of the Great Firedrake was going on?

Perhaps they have heard that one of their sons has died, she thought. *Perhaps one of the coopers or guards has said something to set them on edge.*

It had to be hard, Clara reflected, raising a hatchling only to have it taken from you and knowing it was going to be trained for slavery or war. This agony would cause any mother to suffer. Although the old midwife tried to keep from the hens the awful truth of what was happening to their broods after they left the nurseries, she was sure they knew. They knew the future for their offspring was bleak; only lives of danger or arduous toil and abuse lay in store for them.

Yes, the hens knew, and because they knew, their lullabies were bitter and often brought tears to the old woman's eyes.

If only she could ease their pain! But it was difficult to say words of comfort when the old woman had seen the draft dragons chained and whipped and the war wagons returning, piled with the bloody, ruined bodies of the wounded on their way to the Houses of the Medics. Worse, she had listened in the inns as the dragonriders, both men and women, bragged of their battle exploits, describing in detail how their dragons were gored, scorched, or dismembered, yet they lived to tell the tale.

From what she overheard, Clara had a pretty fair idea of how the king used his dragons in battle. The smaller siris dragons, being swifter and more maneuverable than the big firedrakes, were employed for swift-strike, up-close, one-on-one combat. They could dip, soar, and strike like veps and carry riders armed with swords and projectile weapons. They could send three or four streaking balls of fire, aimed at precisely placed soft targets, in a day.

The firedrakes, on the other hand, were larger and more muscular, hence more powerful, and more difficult to kill. Slower on the wing than their siris dragon cousins, firedrakes were used for both air and ground fighting. Their candle, as it was called, could send a blasting inferno some fifty strides, but only to a limit of seven or eight strikes in a day. A firedrake knight must learn to take that into account and use his mount's fire reserves with restraint and judgment. Still, a lone firedrake could easily wipe out a dozen men or more with a single discharge, and when the fire was gone, the dragon could still engage the enemy with its sheer bulk as well as with tooth and claw.

The knights were protected from injury by their mounts, but the dragon steeds they controlled through the jewel often faced each other, nose-to-nose, with no protection save for their natural armor, individual strength, and skill. With their long, sinuous necks, they struck at each other, tearing scale and flesh from wherever they could land a strike. Hook-tipped wings also drew blood, and, often, the two beasts rose on their powerful haunches and clawed at each other like a pair of rampant karams, raking gashes in each other's breasts, while their dark, purple blood wet the soil until one or the other fell.

Despite all this horror, Clara knew dying was not what darkened the dreams of the firedrakes or their mothers. It was guilt. No one accepted death with greater grace than dragons. It was the natural course of things. But the monstrous, hideous evil of being forced to kill their kind was what dragged the dragon soul to its lowest depths, and it was all because of the jewel—the jewel that allowed humans to control them, the jewel Clara embedded in their necks at birth.

Chapter Three

DAUGHTER OF THE GREAT CERAGON

Aided by the glow from the lantern, the old woman and her apprentice shuffled on through the dim corridors, arriving at the tunnel leading to the last nursery in the stone honeycomb of the birthing coops. Though she bore love for all of those she cared for, these were her favorites; these were the intelligent ones, the messengers.

Messengers were petite as dragons go, usually about the size of a draft skell or a large yolka, not counting their wings. These hatchlings would grow to become carriers of communications, military secrets, and couriers in all sorts of subterfuge. The king had to know what was happening at all times. His solution was to entrust riders of messenger dragons with coded intelligence concerning the many intrigues, battles, and businesses of the realm. Accordingly, messenger dragons soared the skies from dusk to dawn. Though often sent out riderless, they were still enslaved to the soldiers holding the counterpart jewels that commanded their actions. Despite their protective armor, most messengers met their fate riddled with crossbow bolts, shot down by the opposition, or swiftly dispatched by those who would claim their precious jewels.

Clara loved the messengers for their cleverness and bravery. She also found them the easiest with which to communicate. The fact that dragons could speak was a well-kept secret among their kind. They did it by forming words in their throats without moving their mouths; hence, they kept even their riders from learning the secret. The messenger hens were exceptionally intuitive and always the first ones to figure things out. Clara had learned to be incredibly careful with her words and thoughts around the messenger hens, as these bright little biddies seemed to pick up on everything and would want to discuss it.

If anyone were to discover that Clara could speak with dragons, her actions would be construed as treason, and the sentence for treachery to the king was death by dragon fire. The thing Clara feared most was having to face one of her children, knowing it knew and loved her as she loved it, and yet it would be forced to kill her.

The jewel. Everything revolved around the jewel.

Clara stopped just inside the messenger's coop. Again, the same thing happened as in all the other coops. At the first sight of Clara, the dragons fell silent and continued to stare.

Clara looked about carefully to make sure there were no humans in the coop. Satisfied, she called sweetly, "Hello, mothers. Where is our soon-to-be mother? Where is Shaydem? Ah, there you are, looking proud and ready, as a good mother should. How are you today, my dear friend?"

An older hen, the iridescent green of a rooster nurmekka's tail, chirped at her from its nest. "Here, Clara. Proud I am, but not so well as I would like."

"Oh? What is the matter?" Clara asked concernedly.

"Time," the hen answered with a wry smile. "I am losing a battle with time."

"Ha, I join you in that!" Clara said, dismissing the complaint with a laugh. "I am sorry. A good midwife I may be, but I cannot stopper the sands of the oraiglass."

"Nor would I expect you to," Shaydem clucked. "But come see. My hatchling has been peeping from inside its shell all morning. It wants out."

"Yes, yes, it comes, it comes," all the other hens clucked, craning their necks from their nests to see. "A new one comes. Tell us, Clara, how does the egg?"

"Let us have a look," Clara said. "Come, girl," she added to Eleth. "Put down the box and hold the lantern above the egg for me so I can see."

Slinging off the large satchel from her shoulder and letting it slip to the ground, Clara moved close to the nest, while Eleth stood over her, watching with interest as the old midwife bent to her task. Shaydem rattled her scales, rose, and moved aside, revealing a single, smooth, cream-colored sphere, as round and luminous as the moon. They heard a small clucking sound coming from inside. When Clara thoroughly inspected the egg, she discovered a hairline fracture in one end.

"Oh, we are just in time, Eleth!" the midwife said. "Get the jewel."

Eleth leaned in for a closer look.

"We must implant the jewel within a few minutes after birth, or the hatchling's brain won't adequately accept it," the midwife instructed. "Watch me carefully and see how I do this. Someday it will be your task."

"What do you mean?" Eleth asked.

"I mean, you are my apprentice," Clara answered. "I am training you to take over for me when I can no longer work."

The girl shook her head. "I know that. I mean the part about the hatchling's brain not accepting the jewel."

Clara hesitated. That was a delicate matter, one she would rather not discuss in front of the hens.

Interestingly, Shaydem supplied the answer. "She means, from the time the hatchling first opens its eyes and senses the world, its brain begins making associations and connections about where it is, what is happening, and who it is. From the first, it understands it is a being unto itself, a creature that can move and breathe and feel, and think, independently at its own will. It knows, inherently it is free. Free to learn. Free to do. The longer it enjoys this freedom, the more it will be retained in memory, even after the Jewel of Obedience is implanted. Those hatchlings whose jewels are not immediately implanted may later, when difficult things are asked of them, revert to the independence they felt at infancy and rebel. If they rebel, they must be destroyed. It is a serious inconvenience to their masters and, for the king, a costly one. Time and funds have been spent on the raising of a hatchling to adulthood and the training it receives. Humans do not like to lose a useful dragon. The king does not like having an investment fail to make its intended return. It creates a very unhappy situation."

How it hurt to hear the hen explaining the sad reality of dragon life to Eleth in such frank, unflinching terms! *How like a dragon*, Clara thought, sadly, *to understand it all so perfectly and yet bear it so bravely.*

"In spite of your blood, little apprentice, you have much to learn," Shaydem continued. "You are fortunate to have a master teacher like the one you have. This egg will become my seventeenth hatchling, and Clara has attended every one. Watch well, and listen, for she is the best of them all at what she does."

Clara looked a little surprised by Shaydem's words but said nothing. It was not the first time she had heard reference to Eleth's blood. What was that about? In fact, Clara was surprised that the dragons had spoken freely with Eleth nearby. They had never trusted anyone but Clara, not even her former apprentices.

Eleth nodded and exchanged a smile with her mentor. "I know she is the best," the girl said shyly.

"I know not how it is in the other nurseries, girl," Shaydem went on, "but here, with the messengers, you must learn something more than hatching skills. To be welcome here, you must learn discretion. We like to know things, good or evil, and are not afraid to talk about them. You must keep what we discuss here today to yourself. The conversation that is about to take place cannot go beyond these walls. Do you understand that underling?"

Clara observed the intense gazes of Shaydem and the other hens directed at Eleth and wondered, "What is stirring the hens today?" *If they were to look at me like that, I would wither like a moonstool in the sun!*

Eleth did not understand the veiled threat. But Clara knew full well that if she broke the trust with which the hens were commissioning her, the consequences would be lethal. The secret that dragons could speak to humans, save for one or two trusted individuals was strictly kept by the dragons. Once an untrusted guard and midwife overheard a dragon speaking in the human tongue. Within a day, both the midwife and the guard were brutally attacked and torn apart by the hens. Dragons do not care for the taste of human flesh, but, in this case, they left neither knucklebone nor lock of hair to stand as evidence of their deed. To the world, the two humans had just disappeared. Since then, the dragons had spoken only around Clara, never revealing their voices to any other humans until Eleth arrived.

Clara stood very slowly and turned to face the rows of sharp-eyed stares. "I sense, my friends," she began carefully, "you are about to talk of things my young apprentice is not ready to hear. Perhaps, for her own good, we should ask her to leave."

"No, no! Let me stay. Please, Mistress, let me stay!" Eleth begged, suddenly passionate. "I now have no one in the world but you, dear Clara. And I have no other wish but to grow up following in your footsteps. Please, do not send me away. I promise I will be faithful to whatever you ask me to do. I can keep secrets if that is what you want. In the two sycles I have been here, I have come to love these dragons almost as much as you do. Please, let me see this new life come into the world. Please, Mistress. Let me stay."

Her enthusiastic plea surprised both her mentor and the roomful of brooders. The hens exchanged enchanted looks and clucked softly among themselves.

"Stay, *Daughter of Ceragon*," Shaydem said. "But know you must keep this confidence on pain of death. If you betray Clara, I will kill you myself."

Eleth paled but answered, "As you say, let it be so."

All eyes turned on the old midwife.

"Clara stood with an odd look on her face. "Daughter of Ceragon?" she said quietly. "I haven't heard this term before."

"It is an endearment that we dragons choose to use sparingly."

"Very well," Clara said, still looking at Shaydem curiously. She straightened her dear old back that kept letting her know how far from youth she had come. "Now tell me, friends, what is this all about? It is obvious you old biddies have been pecking at seeds of gossip in the wind. Let us have it out in the open. What is astir?"

Perched on the edge of the nesting box above her egg, Shaydem shifted her weight and settled into a more comfortable position.

She began by saying, "I, like you, dear Clara, am getting old. I think this will be my last hatchling. I feel my years drying up. Once my egg count diminishes, I will be used for nothing but stew and will be sent to the butcher. My last duty to the king will be to feed his armies."

"Oh, dear Shaydem, I beg you, say no such sad tidings!" Clara cried.

But another hen said, "Clara. You are aware that we all know what she speaks is the truth. So be still and listen. And know this. Every one of us here..." All the hens exchanged looks and nodded affirmation. "We support her in her plea. We will keep the secret."

"Very well, Shaydem, let's hear this plea of yours," Clara said, swallowing the lump in her throat and fighting back a biting pang of regret. Clara was almost certain about the request the old hen was about to make, and she doubted her ability to fulfill it. She would most certainly have to say no.

"I plead," the hen proceeded delicately, "*that you help my hatchling take flight*."

Clara gasped, her eyes opening wide upon hearing the coded phrase. The dragon's request was not what she expected! She had expected Shaydem to ask her to falsify the laying reports and pretend the old hen was still fertile, delaying her butchery and allowing her the more graceful, natural death of old age. That was the way every dragon *ought* to die, as far as Clara was concerned, not in the cruel duties of the king's service.

But the old hen had not said anything about lying on a report; she had purposely uttered the words, "Help *my hatchling take flight.*"

So that was it! That was the scent she had smelled all morning. Word of *the flight* had somehow gotten out. This was to be a dangerous conversation, and the hatching even more perilous still.

Clara looked slowly from Shaydem toward the other hens. Each leaned eagerly forward from its nest, awaiting the midwife's answer.

"I don't know what you're talking about," Clara mumbled, knowing full well that they knew she was lying. "Help your hatchling take flight? Why would you ask me that? It's not my duty to fledge the dragonlings. You know that."

Shaydem snapped, "Save your breath if that's your answer," and then lowered her voice. "It is no good dodging the question, Clara. We all know about *the flight*."

"Hush, I pray you!" Clara said, her face paling and her finger going to her lips. "A cooper may overhear..."

"No. There are no coopers or guards about at the moment," another hen assured her. "You checked for that when you came in, and we have made sure of it, too. Several of us are even now keeping watch for any who may come our way. You may proceed without fear in that regard."

"What is this about a flight?" Eleth asked, mystified.

Shaydem turned to her. "Your mistress has been sneaking eggs out of the nurseries for more than twenty years without anyone knowing," she said. "She has been raising them in secret and setting them free... without jewels!"

Clara reddened. The truth was out. Trust the messenger hens to be the ones to discover it. "How long have you known?" she asked the old hen.

"Just since yesterday."

"How did you find out?"

"At the breeding that morning. A young male whispered what he knew of it to the hen he mated, and she told it to us."

"And you spread it throughout all the nurseries."

Shaydem shrugged. "News travels."

Clara raised an eyebrow. "And here I thought messenger dragons were known for their discretion."

"We were discreet," Shaydem defended herself hotly. "We only told the dragons."

"Humph," Clara muttered sourly. "That makes me feel so much better!" "Well," she added, "that explains why the hens in all the other nurseries looked so intently at me this morning."

"Yes. They liked you before, Clara. Now, they worship you. We must talk. We want to know how you did it. Humans are stupid, no offense intended..."

"Not all," Clara interrupted.

"True, but most are," Shaydem qualified, "present company excepted. Now, we understand how you were able to sneak an egg out in your satchel and get past the coopers and guards. But how did you keep the mothers from knowing about it? That must have been a trick!"

Clara sighed. "I suppose you must hear it all. Very well, it was simple, really. Whenever I attended to a stillborn egg, I removed it from the mother's sight as quickly as possible to save her pain, as is my duty. But instead of disposing of it, I kept it. At the next opportunity, after determining from candling that a viable embryo was in its early stages, I distracted the mother and switched the eggs. I had only a two-sycle limit before the dead egg became unusable, but that was enough. Later, the mother would think she had hatched a stillborn, but in truth, her egg was home with me, safe and warm, tucked in a quilt in a coal bucket beside my stove."

"That," Shaydem cried, "is genius."

"As I live a tondrin from the nearest neighbor and rarely have visitors, it wasn't difficult to keep the egg secret. I raised each hatchling until it was old enough to fledge. When it grew strong enough, I took it out for practice short flights, tossing it from my roof and, later, trees and cliffs, until it had the strength to fly greater distances."

The old woman's face took on a dreamy look; a gentle smile sat upon her face. "The night of its release, which is *the flight*, I take the young one out to the top of the mountain just as the sunstar is setting and point its nose to the stars that are appearing. 'Look there,' I tell it, turning its face to the southwest. There is the Great Firedrake, 'Ceragon,' the father to whom all dragons return when they die. See his strong, long neck and supple, arching back as he rises and flies across the sky? Look at him, young one. Look hard! You will see no jewel on his neck. He is free, and so should all his offspring, dragonets, and dragonells. You, too, are free now to go your way. Fly south and west to the unexplored lands, and follow the direction in which your father in the stars directs you. Find a place where no king rules. There, establish your rookery and wait, as more will soon join you. Farewell, my love. Be brave and happy. Above all, remember the kindness your mother, Clara, has shown you, and then be kind to others, as is your nature."

Clara's story ended, and the nursery was silent for a long time.

Finally, she said, "Now, you must tell me, Shaydem, exactly what the male said. Tell me, word for word, what he said to the hen at the breedings."

"Excuse me, please," Eleth interrupted. "What are *the breedings*?"

Clara answered briskly, for she was impatient to have her questions answered. "As it now stands," she explained, "the King controls every aspect of a dragon's life. It is trained to do whatever task it is given; it is forced to slave, fight, and kill, and even its privacy and pleasure of mating are usurped and controlled by the throne. The best female dragons are kept for one purpose: breeding and laying.

No other females are allowed to breed. As for male dragons, only a select number are brought to the hens for breeding on a strictly controlled schedule. Careful tallies are kept of dragon casualties so that the breeding schedules can be adjusted to maintain a balance in the population."

"In our natural state," Shaydem continued, "dragons mate for life. It goes against our nature to breed whenever and with whomever the humans decide. Worse, it causes our hearts to grow hardened. We do not enjoy breeding, and we do not allow ourselves to bond emotionally during it. It is only one of the terrible travesties the king commits against us."

"That surprises me," Eleth ventured. "I always knew dragons were expensive, so I assumed they were also well treated."

The dragons immediately bristled.

"Is that what you think?" Shaydem snapped. The scales on her back rose. "Are you blind, child? Are you, in truth, a *Daughter of the Great Ceragon*? Do you have any idea of your destiny?"

"Forgive her," Clara jumped in, defending her apprentice's naiveté. "She is too young to understand such things as war and politics and social injustice. Give me time. I will teach her better." *And what is this about destiny*? she thought.

The old hen gave a little huff but, out of respect for Clara, did not pursue a further reprimand.

Clara gazed thoughtfully at this display, but all she could say was, "Please, Shaydem, continue your tale!" as she returned to the topic that deeply touched her heart. "This male at the breeding—what did he say? Tell me about my hatchlings. Did he see any of them? Did any make it to freedom? Are they alive? Are they well?"

The old hen smoothed her ruffled scales and answered with civility, considering the offense. Messenger dragons were slow to forgive a slight, however unintended. "This male had just returned from a diplomatic courier mission, carrying messages to a very remote place, and his route took him far beyond the king's borders and away from common travel routes. On his way home, he passed over high mountains covered with snow. The mountains carry the clouds on their shoulders, but there are green valleys. No humans are known to live in this place. It was there the male found your dragons."

Clara clasped her hands together and cried breathlessly, "Oh! what news! Pray, go on, dear friend! Do go on!"

Shaydem complied. "Seeing a small group of them below, the male swooped down to see if they were friends or foes. He was surprised to see they were neither;

in fact, they wore no jewels of any kingdom! They were very friendly and kindly invited him to stay with them for a day or two to rest and eat, which he did. Amazed at all he beheld, the male asked to hear their history, and they seemed eager to tell it.

"The oldest of them were young adults, some of whom had families, while the others ranged in age from younglings to newly fledged. Their numbers, they said, started small, but every season, a few newly fledged dragons would come winging their way toward them. They were constantly on watch for this, and the moment one was spotted, some dragons greeted it and lovingly welcomed it into the flock. There are now well over a hundred dragons, as some have bred and begun raising their broods, and some of the offspring from these broods have fledged, mated, and started their broods in turn. The male said these dragons were living in giant caverns beside a valley, hidden from men. They were quite happy there. The weather can often be harsh, but the valley is protected from the worst by the exceedingly high mountains that surround it.

"To what kingdom do you belong?" the messenger asked them, his eyes wary. "Whom do you serve?"

"None," they replied in unison, their voices resolute. "We are free."

"Then what do you call yourselves?" he pressed. "What kinship binds you?"

"We are free dragons," they answered. "In spirit, we are children of Ceragon, the Great Firedrake—our father, as he is yours, as he is to all dragons everywhere. But our mother is not dragonkind. She is human. Her name is Clara. We call ourselves the offspring of Clara."

At this, Clara gasped softly. Tears traced paths down her weathered cheeks. "They said that? They remember me?"

Shaydem's eyes sparkled with laughter. "Remember you? They love you! When they learned their guest was from your kingdom, they urgently asked if he knew you."

"He nodded, recalling. 'Of course,' he told them. 'You cared for him after his hatching, and, as far as he knew, you were well.' Hearing that brought such joy among the free dragons, more than words can say."

Leaning in, Shaydem lowered her voice to a whisper in Clara's ear. "The male also spoke of a young human boy, about the same age as your apprentice. The free dragons have found him. Just as we call Eleth a Daughter of Ceragon, they call the boy a Son of Ceragon. There is great significance in their arrival at the same time."

Clara drew back, startled. She considered a moment, then whispered, "A boy? What could this mean? You called Eleth a Daughter of Ceragon; now there is a Son of Ceragon? I have never heard these titles. Are you saying they have a destiny?"

Shaydem shook her head gently. "I cannot speak of it now, but know this: the girl beside you is more than she seems."

Clara stood in silence, thoughtful. Then, in a clearer voice, she said, "I feel guilty, you know, for not having freed any draft dragon hatchlings. They can't fly, you see. They'd never get far."

"Do not worry," the old hen reassured her. "The draft hens understand. They trust that your work will one day bring freedom to all dragons. As for your 'children,' put your mind at ease. They are well, and their numbers grow. Still, the King would not be pleased, Clara. Your end would be neither swift nor merciful."

"Why, Mistress?" Eleth asked, distressed. "Why risk so much?"

Clara looked up at her through tear-filled lashes and shrugged. "Because I love them," she said quietly. "It's wrong for one creature to dominate another, to force them against their nature, or to use them for selfish ends. If the king ever catches me, I'll tell him so to his face!"

The hens chuckled fondly, gazing at the old midwife with gentle affection.

"Oh, my brave mistress," Eleth whispered, wrapping an arm around Clara's thin shoulders. "It is an honor to know you."

Shaydem cleared her throat, drawing all attention. "This is my plea, Clara. Take my egg, as you have the others. You saved them—save mine. I'll go gladly to the butcher's block if only I know one of my brood made it to freedom."

A loud squeak came from the egg. It rocked in its nest, then grew still.

"See?" the old hen said. "Even the egg implores you! What say you? We all await your answer!"

Every hen leaned closer. Eleth held her breath.

Clara smiled through her tears. "I've never been able to say no—not really. So, I won't start now. Yes! Of course, I will."

A chorus of croons arose as every hen lifted its head, singing to the cavern roof like wolves howling at a full moon. When the echoes faded, they began to sing in earnest.

Dragons rarely sing, and when they do, it is sacred. There were no words—only reverence, a sound like wind over distant seas, calling from far-off shores.

When the song ended, not a single eye—dragon or human—remained dry in that cave.

Clara straightened, wiping her cheeks. "Eleth," she said gently, "if we're discovered, it will mean your life as well as mine. Are you willing to risk everything for a dragon egg?"

Eleth's eyes shone. "I already have! Perhaps it is my destiny."

"Then let's get this one hatched," Clara said, determination in her voice. "Shaydem, care for it well. For two weeks, it is yours to nurture and love. When the time comes, I—not the king's taskmasters—will come for your hatchling."

"But how will you get him past the guards?" Shaydem asked anxiously.

Clara offered a wry smile. "I have a potion. It will make the hatchling appear sickly, near death. I'll tell the guards I'm taking it home to tend him—no one questions the midwife. Later, I'll say he died. But you'll know better. You'll know he's free."

"Oh, kind friend!" Shaydem exclaimed.

"Brave, brave Clara!" the other hens joined in, their voices full of hope.

The old woman smiled, hiding the blush on her cheeks behind her hands. Well! This day had turned out to be quite different from normal—a wonderful one, just as the scent of it foretold. Nevertheless, Clara knew the battle had just begun. Every moment, every day of her continued treachery would spell danger. And yet, the burden had suddenly become much lighter. The hens would help her now. There need be no more deceit between them. That was a relief. Eleth was proving to be an eager, capable apprentice, someone she could trust to take over when her dear bones had insisted, at last, on seeking their rest. Best of all, she had learned her children were well and free. Suddenly, it might be possible that all the vain hopes she had kept to herself all these years—that one day humans and dragons would share the earth in friendship—could come true! A day of peace and justice would be a long time coming, but it could happen! Who knew? One day, the dragons would have their justice; perhaps the king himself would be forced to wear a jewel!

The egg suddenly cracked, and a tiny, sharp snout poked through. The old midwife laughed and turned to her duties with the egg.

As she worked, her thoughts came back to the phrase "*Daughter of Ceragon?*" *There are yet some secrets the hens were not willing to share. But why Eleth? Does the girl know what they mean? And now there is a boy? That is not important for the time being. It has been a good day. But Eleth and I must talk.*

Let ripening age tug at her weakened leg as it would; she did not care. Today, her heart felt young enough to fly.

As Clara and Eleth worked their way back through the tunnels, Clara again noticed how adroit the young girl was in the dark. *"Hmm,"* she thought.

"Eleth, dear," Clara said, "there are a few lanterns on the left side at the top of this stair. Would you pick one up to give us some more light?"

"Yes, Clara, I'll pick one up, but they're on the right side, not the left."

Clara was familiar with the coops and was aware that the lantern storage area was located on the right side of the path, at the top of the stairs. It was also far enough ahead that the light from their single little lamp did not reach anywhere near it. The stairs were dark from bottom to top. How was it that Eleth could see so well in the dark?

When they reached Clara's cottage, she kindled a fire in the stove and gestured for Eleth to join her at the small kitchen table. The cozy space filled with the promise of warmth as Clara set a kettle of water to boil.

"Eleth," Clara began, her voice gentle, "you've been helping me for two sycles now, and I couldn't ask for a better companion." She smiled kindly. "I think we make a good team." Clara hesitated, glancing at Eleth with curiosity. "There's something I've been meaning to ask you, though, and please, only answer if you're comfortable. Earlier, I heard Shaydem call you 'Daughter of Ceragon.' Why would she call you that?"

Eleth looked down, twisting her hands in her lap. "Clara, I don't know how Shaydem knew," she admitted quietly. "Before today, I'd only heard that name once. When I was ten, my father—Tiimos—sat me down for a private talk. He told me he wasn't my birth father. My real parents died when I was a baby, and the Keirons adopted me. He said I should never share this story unless I trusted someone with my life, because that's precisely what it would mean. I trust you, Clara. That's why I want to tell you what he said."

Clara's eyes softened. "Why do you trust me so much when we've only known each other for half a Kivan?"

Eleth managed a small smile. "Because Shaydem trusts you. And that's enough for me."

Clara reached across the table, covering Eleth's hand with her own. "I'm honored. Please, tell me your story."

Eleth took a deep breath. "Tiimos told me my mother—Careen Morkath—fell gravely ill before I was born. He called it 'dragon disease.'"

Clara gasped softly, her hand flying to her mouth. "Dragon disease? I've never heard of anyone surviving that."

"Tiimos said that, while he was caring for my mother, my father experienced a vision—a meadow appeared in our house, and a beautiful woman told him that both my mother and her unborn child—me—would die unless he killed a young dragon and brought back its heart's blood to her." Eleth's voice wavered. "Then the vision vanished."

Clara listened, eyes wide. "Did he believe her?"

"He did," Eleth replied. "He risked everything to sneak into one of the king's dragon reserves—the place where young dragons are kept before they fledge. Somehow, he killed a young female dragon and brought its heart's blood home. My mother drank it, and she recovered—long enough to give birth to me. Tiimos was there to see it happen. But she died not long after."

"Oh, Eleth…" Clara's voice was full of sympathy.

"It's all right. I never really knew her or my father. But someone saw what he'd done, and the king's men hunted him down. Before they caught him, he entrusted me to Tiimos and Runa Keiron." Eleth's voice grew steadier. "I thought they were my real parents, until Tiimos finally told me the truth. That's when he explained the blood my mother drank made me a Daughter of the Great Ceragon."

Did he know what that meant?" Clara asked.

Eleth shook her head. "No. He didn't know. But I've noticed things—things that make me different. I've always kept them secret."

Clara leaned in, her curiosity aroused. "What sort of things?"

"I can see clearly for tondrins, even in the dark. I can spot a fly's wings moving at a distance, like the wings of a seabird. I can smell the difference between a human and a dragon from several landrins away. I'm stronger than anyone else my age. I remember everything I see and do, and I learn quickly. My hearing is… extraordinary. For example, earlier today, I heard everything Shaydem said about a 'Son of Ceragon'—even though she spoke quietly in your ear."

Clara's eyes widened. "Shaydem was right. You are more than you appear."

"There's more," Eleth added quietly. "The dragons—when they're together, they speak in their language. I can hear it, though I don't understand what they say."

Clara's jaw dropped. "They can speak to each other?"

Eleth nodded. "They can. But I think I'm the only human who can hear them."

Clara let out a slow breath. "I always suspected they had their own language, but I was never able to catch them at it. Eleth, you must keep these gifts secret. I promise your secrets are safe with me, but you mustn't trust anyone else—not even the dragons—unless you are sure it's safe. For now, keep listening and learning. Perhaps you'll discover what it truly means to be a Daughter of Ceragon."

Clara smiled, her eyes shining with wonder and concern. "You're full of surprises, dear. I can't help but think there's a reason for all of this, a purpose only the gods understand. I'll have to ponder what you've told me."

She paused, then let out a long, heartfelt sigh and reached for the kettle. "Now—after all that—would you like some tea, Eleth?"

Chapter Four

SON OF THE GREAT CERAGON

One year prior to the day that Eleth came to stay with Clara, Alton Fletcher stood next to a cluster of saplings in a position where he could best see the targets of the village's archery range, set up a short way from his home in Frithden. In the red light of a half-full Dragon Moon, he could barely make out the shape of his son, Axel, standing at the step-off line—the line where the bowman stood to loose his arrows at the various targets downrange. The place where Alton stood lay much closer to the targets than the step-off line, so even in the darkness, he had a clear view of the target Axel was using. Alton watched his son in awe. Axel should not have been able to see the target at the distance where it now stood. But the young man did. The bow the lad held had a draw weight of twelve stone. There was little likelihood that anyone else in the district, Alton included, could even string a bow with that kind of draw weight, let alone hit anything at such a distance.

Nevertheless, Axel was firing five arrows, using his own unique style, in the time it would have taken Alton to shoot two. The minimal light should have prevented the young man from seeing well enough to hit anything, especially a target barely a handspan in width and three hundred twenty strides away. Yet the archer who was loosing arrows repeatedly across the distance of eight landrins and striking the skellseye every time was only fifteen years old!

Yes, it had been barely more than fifteen years since the day when Alton stood atop a boulder and made the most amazing shot of his entire life at a hirvior standing at a distance of two hundred fifty strides in full light. Now, here was Axel making repeated accurate shots across a distance that was one-third greater than that, and he was doing so in the dark!

Alton knew Axel to be an exceptional child from before his birth. As the boy grew up, evidence accrued daily of how remarkable Axel was. Alton never mentioned to the boy the things he noticed: his extraordinary sight and hearing, his physical strength, and now his ability to see in the dark. The youngster had already mastered every task that could be performed in Alton's shop and was producing bows of the finest quality. He had even invented a new kind of bow, which he called a 'steelbow.'

Axel also carried many of the traits of his mother, Lyssa. He was honest, persistent, sensitive, and caring, and the hair, falling over his ears, was the same yellow-blond color that Alton had loved on his cherished wife.

The fletcher's heart burst with pride, knowing that this young man, his son, would eventually fulfill some meaningful destiny. Otherwise, why would the Lady of the Meadow have appeared and revealed a way for the child to live when he should surely have died? Oh, Enok, you were so much more than a small-town herd doctor, and you were so right about him. There must have been something special in the blood that Lyssa drank. Alton himself had killed the dragon that gave up the blood, which extended Lyssa's life long enough to ensure Axel's birth. But it must have done so much more.

He roughly wiped a tear from his eye. Lyssa, my Lyssa, he thought with a sigh, what a son we have!

A hand rested on Alton's shoulder, and he turned to look into the eyes of his father, Erland.

"Son," the old man said, "I think the time has come. Shall we take the boy into the shop and make it official?"

"Shouldn't we wait until morning, when the whole family can be present?"

"Keila is already there and has prepared the place for the ceremony. She said that doing it tonight would make the event even more solemn and memorable for her grandson. You should see what she has prepared. There must be a dozen candles burning to light up the shop's back wall with an auspicious glow, the fireplace is roaring merrily, and she has placed wreaths of caledra all around the place. The shop now smells like the village council hall on Founding Day."

Alton laughed quietly and said, "I suppose the decision is made then. I'll call Axel to head on in."

As Axel approached the shop with his Da beside him, he noticed a strange light emanating from the windows and asked his father what was happening inside. "We are going to be holding a special ceremony there.

"A what?"

"A ceremony for someone who has earned a tremendous honor."

At two and one-half strides tall, Axel stood about a finger's length above his father. He looked down into his Da's eyes and saw a glint of pride in them but could not read any more meaning than that.

"Will you allow me to hold your bow for a few minutes?" Alton asked.

"But, why...?" The look in his father's eyes told Axel that he needed to surrender the bow for a time. Axel trusted his father, so he handed it over.

Alton opened the shop door for his son, then led him past the workbenches over to the fireplace at the back end of the shop. There, he turned to stand beside Erland Fletcher and looked back at Axel. A small forest of lighted candles set a halo of light about the two men, who now stood in a dignified manner before the hearth. The sweet, earthy scent of caledra leaves in several wreaths hanging on the walls deepened a sense of the solemnity of the event.

Axel noticed his Grand Ma'am standing against the side wall. Yes, he thought she would be the one to place these decorations here. Grand Ma'am could always turn an event into a celebration.

The boy stopped several steps in front of the two men and was about to ask what this gathering was all about when a solemn voice, emanating from the elder Fletcher, announced, "Axel Fletcher, come kneel before the masters of your trade."

Axel recalled the last time he was commanded to kneel before these two great men. It was then that they commissioned him as an apprentice member of the 'Knights of the Strelice' and pledged to never reveal the secret process he would be learning about in the making of the 'power bow.' So, this ceremony must have something to do with the Knights.

Erland Fletcher's voice then continued, saying, "Forty years ago, in the year 1415, Wittham Fletcher first perfected the process for making the 'power bow' and so became the first 'Master' bowyer. Two years later, I started working for Wittham in this very shop. Eight years later, in 1425, Wittham deemed me worthy of the title of Master Bowyer. Alton began working in this shop when he was eight. I declared Alton a master four years after the master's death. You, Axel, also began working in this shop when you were eight, but it has taken you only a remarkable seven years to obtain a skill level not only equivalent to that of your Da and Grand Da but, indeed, a step higher. You are the inventor of the incredible Steelbow. Therefore, despite your tender age, I declare that you will now be known as a Master Bowyer and Fletcher with specialization in both the power bow and the steelbow. I only wish Wittham had lived to see this proud day."

Alton handed his father the bow Axel had given him. Erland held the bow up high and pronounced, "Here, I hold the masterwork you created and show it proudly as proof of your skill level."

Erland brought the bow back down and returned it to Alton's hands.

"Axel Fletcher, you are aware of the secret Knights of the Strelice and their purpose. Tonight, I am empowered to ordain you to full Guardianship in the Knights, not just as one who wields a power bow, but as a Master Bowyer. This I do upon your renewing your oath in the name of the gods, Etmar and Rhetha, who watch down on us from the sunstar, that you will keep the secret of the power bow and its fashioning, along with that of the steelbow you invented. Do you swear and pledge to only sell or transfer the power bows and steelbows you make, along with knowledge of their fashioning, to fellow guardians of the Secret Knights, whom you will recognize by their possession of keywords?

"Yes, I do," Axel pledged.

Then, Erland lifted a delicately carved ivory plaque, the size of a coin, from a nearby workbench and held it above his head in both hands. "This token," he declared, "is of a likeness to similar tokens granted to me and your Da when we were raised to the designation of Master and were given the right to train both apprentices and journeymen in our field. I give this token to you in honor of your proficiency.

"Axel, son of my son, I now present this Strelice pendant to you. This token is the single most important object you will ever own. Keep it hidden from sight, except for identifying yourself to a fellow Sentinel."

He lowered the plaque and held it out toward Axel, who reached to take hold. But the old man did not relinquish his grip. Instead, while the plaque was held in their four hands, Erland said, "The symbol on this plaque is the 'strelice.' It was used by the first bowyers and fletchers in our history to identify themselves as such. But recognition of the symbol faded away as the use of bows gave way to the dominance of the crossbow. Our family has resurrected the symbol to represent mastery of the power bow and its superiority over the crossbow.

"The purpose of the Knights is to guard the secret of our new bows while inducting into our fellowship those whom we deem trustworthy to serve one singular goal—the overthrow of the Tyrant of Sanara, King Deroth and his dragonrider army. Know the truth, my dear young master: if the king ever learns of the knights' existence, our lives, the lives of the Society's guardians, and all our families are forfeit. Deroth executes his murders without taking any prisoners or leaving any witnesses behind.

Axel looked up into the eyes of his Da and Grand Da. "You have both told me enough about your experiences for me to fully understand why my family created the Knights. I pledge to support the principles of its founding with all the power of my being."

Erland released his grip on the token, leaving it in his grandson's hands. He then stepped back, saying, "You are truly worthy to bear the name of 'Master.'"

Alton returned the bow to his son, then started to applaud. Immediately Erland and Keila joined in, and they stepped forward to participate in the congratulations.

Placing one hand on Axel's shoulders, the old man reached down with the other to draw the boy to his feet and said to everyone in the room, "This day commemorates my grandson's becoming a man two years early. He deserves a day away from the shop as a reward for his skill, hard work, and contribution to the family business. What say you all?"

A cheer rang out from the others. "Go ahead and celebrate, Axel," said Alton with a broad grin spread across his face and a merry laugh, "because the next day we will expect you to work all the harder!"

Axel's eyes rolled, and he replied, "I'm already slaving away in this shop to show you older folk how to get things done. There won't be any change."

That brought on a general laugh from everyone in the room, reminding Axel how he respected his family and truly felt loved by them.

***

Two days later, Axel Fletcher and his best friend, Jemmy Sandor, were celebrating Axel's awarded day away from the shop by marching down the large foothill leading to their homes in Frithden. It had taken the two boys most of the morning to scale the nearby mountain summit that had been their goal for the day, and now, on their return journey, it was well past high sun. The going was slow on the route up to the low-lying peak, but they made excellent speed on the way down. The ridgeline they were currently descending was largely devoid of trees, giving the boys a broad view of the valley below and the distant line of mountains marking the southern and eastern boundaries of their world. At the end of their day's adventure, the small village in which they had been born and raised stood out among the cleared fields and forests on the valley floor. While the village was yet a tondrin away, they knew they would arrive at their homes in Frithden to find well-deserved rest and refreshment within an orai.

No matter where one treks in the uplands, there is the ever-present danger of meeting a killer beast on the hunt. But this hike took them perilously close to the Ghanara-Dan forest, where killer beasts chose to dwell in formidable numbers. As was their habit, both youngsters were armed and prepared should they meet any kind of killer beast on their way. Axel carried his powerful steelbow, made from layers of different treated woods and ellam horn, one he had made himself. Jemmy sported a spear nearly three strides in length, half again as tall as he. Both were experienced with their weapons of choice.

"You should have taken the shot, Axel," Jemmy said, with a frustrated tone in his voice. "The world would be better off with fewer sengels to worry about."

"You know it was no threat, Jemmy. I don't kill for fun."

Jemmy rolled his eyes. "Sure, it was no threat to you. All the killer beasts avoid you like you were a dragon. But it would love to set its claws into any other person who might come up here."

"It left you alone, didn't it?" said Axel, with a silly grin on his face.

"Yes, but only because I was next to you. Face it, Axel, you've got something that all the killer beasts are afraid of."

"If I have something like that, why aren't other animals afraid of me? You saw how I was almost gored by that yolka a few sycles back."

Jemmy shook his head and laughed. "That yolka didn't live long enough to make a second try, so how could we know what it thought?"

"It attacked me once. It would have done it again if I gave it the opportunity."
"Which you didn't, so you can't prove your point," Jemmy said. "Besides, a yolka is a food beast. It's a dangerous one, sure, but not a killer beast. It's only the killer beasts that run away from you." He furrowed his brow and struck his friend's shoulder out of frustration. "Admit it, Axel, there's something different about you. You can shoot an arrow farther and more accurately than any man in the village, even your Da, and all the killer beasts run away from you. What is it?"

"Maybe it's because I work harder than everybody else and stink more as a result?"

"Oh, look at me, everyone," Jemmy said in an indifferent voice as he rolled his eyes again. "I'm laughing so hard.

"Aw, Axel," he continued, this time with more animation in his voice. "You can do better than that! I know you still won't tell me anything true, but you can think up something better than what you just tried to feed me."

"I guess I can never fool you, Jemmy, my friend. Speaking of food, I'm hungry."

"I am too. Is your granny going to have something ready for us when we get back?"

"I saw a pile of moonstools on the kitchen table, and my grand ma'am was pulling the feathers from one of the fattest kiplans we had in our yard. Those are signs of a kiplan stew and dumpling meal waiting for us when we reach home."

The thought alone made their mouths water.

The fact that he was different from other boys his age was nothing new to Axel. Rarely would anyone approach the subject with him, such as Jemmy just did, but Axel was not blind to what happened around him. That sengel had been hidden on that high branch and was waiting for prey. Yet, as soon as the wind shifted and brought the scent of the two boys in its direction, it leapt from the branch and ran away, just as Jemmy had described and just as if it were truly being chased by a dragon. Axel did not know the reason, but he had a suspicion. It most likely had something to do with the unusual circumstances of his birth.

On the edge of his vision, Axel saw a black smudge, like a spatter of tiny ink spots, rise into the sky over the far eastern mountains and blinked his eyes to make sure it was real. There it was, still and traveling fast. "Jemmy!" he shouted, "Look over there!" He started running, running as fast as his legs would move him.

Jemmy paused, looking confused, before rushing to stay as close as possible behind his friend. "What do you see, Axel?" he cried out as he scrambled around rocks and clumps of scrub. "What am I supposed to look at?"

The smudge was moving faster, much faster than the boys could go. By the time they reached the next viewpoint on the ridgeline, the ink spots appeared more like a distant flock of birds, and it had covered half the distance from the eastern mountains. That meant it had flown at twenty times their speed.

Axel called back to Jemmy without stopping. "It's those dark spots on the eastern horizon. They can be nothing less than a flight of dragons!"

Jemmy couldn't see the spots, but he knew his friend well. If Axel said there were dragons on the horizon, then dragons there were.

Little by little, the spots became a cloud of individual black dots with wings, and even Jemmy could see them. "Gods above," he exclaimed as he valiantly tried to keep up with Axel.

When the cloud got closer still, Axel counted aloud, even as he ran. "Eighteen, nineteen, twenty. Twenty dragons are heading directly for Frithden," he shouted back over his shoulder, "and we can't do a thing about it!"

The boys ran further on, losing sight of the eastern horizon when they detoured around a large patch of conifers blocking their way. Axel, who had outpaced Jemmy by a hundred strides, stopped at a point on the hillside with a clear view. He was still more than half a tondrin away from Frithden.

Jemmy, a long moment behind, halted close by, breathing heavily, and tried to follow the direction of Axel's intense gaze. There, Jemmy saw dragons, a lot of them, beginning to circle above the village.

Axel counted again, then said, "There are seventeen firedrakes and three siris dragons."

They could see villagers below on the streets looking up, then rushing into some of the buildings, either to seek shelter or to warn others of the danger. No one down there had time even to think about what the dragons might do before some began diving on the village, and the descending dragons started breathing out brilliant orange-red fireballs! They attacked, not in a random way, but at specific parts of the little town, using some kind of pattern to envelop the entire village, and each dragon expelled multiple shots of fire at defenseless homes and businesses. People came running out into the streets, only to be engulfed by new fireballs. A few villagers ran toward the forest, but two siris dragons hunted them down before they even came close. One person held a bow and managed to get two wild shots off before being struck down.

Axel saw every vile attack, and each panicked scream from the people below rose to penetrate his ears. His face stiffened in rage from the assault on his senses. He placed an arrow on his bow and stood ready to draw and shoot should any opportunity to target a dragon come up. Regretfully, he only had broadhead arrows in his quiver, and they would be near useless against a dragon's armor. But the dragons all stayed over the village—too far for even a low-chance shot—so the arrowheads made no difference.

As the first wave ascended away from the village, the remaining dragons came down to strike the buildings missed by the first wave. That first wave was already back up at altitude and readying another attack run.

Axel discerned that this wave would strike his house. Both his eyes and his mouth opened in shock as he watched one of the dragons hit the three small buildings with a blast of fire, leaving them all in an angry inferno. But there... over there, was another bowman on the street. Even at such a distance, Axel could tell that this bowman was his father, Alton. He saw an arrow leave Alton's bow, seemingly heading nowhere, until a large firedrake crossed its path. The arrow struck directly into the soft tissue under the dragon's chin. It penetrated deeply and killed the dragon instantly. Axel saw the beast crash into a row of burning houses. "Da got that one," he said in a matter-of-fact way.

Then another firedrake came upon his father, who was prepared to loose another arrow. This dragon's rider deliberately set a path to avoid exposing his beast to a chin shot. What was Da going to do?

Alton's second shot missed the dragon, but it struck the rider, causing him to fall from the beast and become entangled in a long tether. That dragon immediately turned away and flew back along its original course.

The rider on a third dragon flying nearby saw how accurately the man's arrows had flown, and he banked his dragon desperately to turn and evade the next shot. His effort proved unsuccessful. The third arrow from Alton's bow struck a shiny red object on the brown-colored dragon's neck and seemed to bounce off. When the dragon peeled sharply to the other side, its rider was thrown abruptly from the saddle, causing his safety harness to snap like a piece of thread. Axel smiled in approval of that shot.

The fourth time, however, Alton's luck ran out. A siris dragon flew in fast and low, directly down the street behind Axel's father. With Alton facing the wrong way, Axel knew what would happen next. "Look out behind you!" he shouted, knowing that Alton would never hear it.

The siris dragon came in close and shot a small fireball directly onto Alton's back. Axel watched in terror as his father burst into flames. The fire whirled about his body, spiraling into the air. In ten heartbeats, the man became a charred pile of ash.

Axel dropped to his knees in shock. His father was dead; his home was a literal inferno, as was everything in and around it. The precision targeting of the dragon firebolts had now turned the entire village into a firestorm that sent pillars of flame twirling two landrins into the air, destroying every home, barn, and workshop. All structures in the village were built of wood, and whatever was not directly targeted soon caught fire from the adjacent buildings. In a matter of half an orai, nothing remained unburned, and no one had escaped. That meant Da, Grand Da, and Grand Ma'am were all dead—and just as he said, he had not been able to do a thing about it.

Jemmy was also on his knees, crying softly. "They're gone... they're all gone," he said in a whimper.

Axel stood and, with some trouble, pulled Jemmy up from his knees. "We have to go down there," he said, "and see if we can save someone."

Just then, he heard a thunk sound from somewhere further up the hill. Instantly recognizing the sound for what it was and the precise direction it came from, Axel turned without conscious thought, drew his bow, and loosed an arrow in one smooth motion. In the same instant, he felt something pull at his cloak just under his arm. Axel followed the flight of his arrow until it struck its intended target—a soldier wearing the light-blue uniform of Kolodra, standing about two landrins up the hill. The soldier, who was holding a spent crossbow, plainly received a mortal wound, but he would take some time dying. No further attention was required in that direction.

"Hey, Jemmy, did you see that guy up there...?" He turned back toward Jemmy, only to see him spitting up blood. The feathers from a crossbow bolt were just visible, protruding from his chest.

Axel shouted a long "Nooooo!" as he threw down his bow and wrapped his arms around his friend to catch him as he fell. Gently, he laid Jemmy down on his back and looked into his open eyes. There was life in him yet, though Axel knew the boy had but seconds.

Jemmy returned Axel's look and coughed out some more blood, which sprayed across Axel's cloak and oozed down the side of the boy's mouth.

"Axel..." Jemmy said in a rough, grainy voice. "You're my best friend and like a brother. Now, you're all that's left." He closed his eyes while he coughed again and then looked up into Axel's eyes. "It's up to you to find justice for our families... for my folks and... for your Pa and grand folks. You can bring peace to our people by... finding their murderers. Kill them! Promise me you'll kill them!"

Axel had already promised himself, so he didn't need to promise Jemmy, but he nodded and said, "I... will."

Jemmy nodded back; then Axel saw his friend's eyes cloud over and become still. Jemmy never stopped staring into Axel's eyes until he was no longer there.

Anger filled Axel's body. He used one hand to close Jemmy's eyes, then raising his head to the sky, he said with trembling, curled lips, "Jemmy, I promise they will all pay for their crimes!"

Still holding Jemmy in his arms, Axel let out a long, loud wailing cry. He turned again to look up the hill at Jemmy's killer, only to see him climbing onto the back of a siris dragon and flying away.

That one will die soon, he thought. But who were the other murderers, and who ordered them to come here to do their bidding? He stared again toward what remained of the once-thriving community, and, breathing heavily, he cried aloud to the spirits of those who now lay dead before him. "I give my oath to kill those responsible for destroying my village!" He then raised his voice to shout, "...and slaughtering all those who are dear to me!" Looking back at Jemmy, he quietly said, "All of them!"

When somewhat recovered, he turned his friend over and saw the point of the crossbow quarrel just sticking out of Jemmy's back. He put the fingers of his glove around the metal broadhead and, gripping it firmly, managed to pull it through with only a moderate effort and gently lay his friend on the ground. That quarrel could be used to track down its owner.

Axel saw the dragons begin to reform up in the sky, except for a few, which still circled the village. One flew perilously close to his position and even looked down in his direction. Standing, Axel placed a new arrow onto his bow, waited, and watched, knowing if that dragon came any closer, he would shoot it out of the sky.

The group of dragons rebuilt their formation and started flying away. They had destroyed their target; no need to hang around. But no... one stayed behind—the dark-brown-colored one that Da had tried to kill. It was flying erratically and had no rider, but it was coming straight for Axel. Lowering his eyebrows and clenching his jaw in pure anger, he swore by Etmar's staff and drew back on his bow, aiming for the eye. If that beast continued coming this way, Axel would shoot it down or die trying.

Before Axel could loose his arrow, the dragon abruptly dropped and landed hard, down the hill from Axel a couple of landrins away. It struck hind feet first, but its forelegs collapsed under its weight. Bouncing and turning a complete somersault in the air, it tore into the dirt and came to a stop with the noise of a giant tree crashing to the ground. Giant clouds of dust billowed into the air so that Axel could barely see. Not dropping his guard, Axel opened his mouth in astonishment and strained with eyes as big as kiplan eggs to see what lay before him.

The dust took its time to settle, but eventually some things became more distinct. Barely twenty strides away, the enormous dragon lay on its side directly in front of him. He noticed that the dragon's eyes were closed, but they slowly opened after a moment and blinked. With a small move of its head, it looked directly at him, and Axel detected a look of surprise on its face, eyes wide open, its mouth dropped, and face muscles lax. Still not moving from his defensive stance, he wondered how a dragon could even have a surprised look on its face. Apart from the large teeth growing out of the sides of its mouth, it hardly looked fierce at all.

Its head reminded Axel of a skell's head, though significantly larger than that of a skell. Its body was not covered with all kinds of spiny horns and fins, as he had imagined dragons in the past. Rather, the dragon's hide consisted of smooth overlapping scales, much like a snake. Axel's mental image of a dragon was a beast covered in all kinds of pointy protrusions. But except for its pointed ears and the points on its exposed canines, he could see no other points anywhere on this dragon.

Though surely in immense pain, the dragon shook its head slowly in a kind of wonder of its own. Axel could tell that it would not be getting up, but he jumped noticeably when the beast started talking in a weak and faraway voice. Alton stepped down the hill toward the dragon and approached within a few strides.

"I smelled you," the dragon said, "but never would I have suspected to find a human here, especially a youngling like you! You have a light but definite dragon smell, and you are... human?" There was a distinct element of wonder and awe in the dragon's voice. "Indeed," it said in confirmation, "there must be something special about you!"

Axel relaxed his bow and just stared with his mouth open. "You can talk!" he said in a near shout.

"Of course, I can talk!" the dragon said in a weak, indignant whisper. "Does that cause you great difficulty?"

There was no way to answer that question, except for "But your mouth does not move when you talk."

Still lying on its side, the dragon lifted its head and said, "Dragons speak by shaping words deep in our throats. What does that matter so long as you understand my words?"

"I suppose not much," said Axel. "Nevertheless, it remains somewhat discomfiting."

The dragon turned its long neck to see the still-burning wreckage of the village.

"Was this village your home?" it asked, looking back at Axel.

Axel nodded, a slow response.

"I deeply regret that the jewel has forced me to be a part of your home's destruction. My masters have compelled me to perform despicable acts like this many times. Your people fought a competent defense but were surprised and outmatched."

The dragon paused a moment as if in thought. "Nevertheless, one village archer's arrow struck my jewel. It was an incredibly lucky shot, or he must have been a man of amazing skill with a bow."

"He was my father," Axel said in a low tone. "No one in the village comes even close to matching him when using a bow... except maybe me." There was no pride in the words he spoke last. Axel said, "But the jewel on your neck is so small that he probably wouldn't have seen it from that distance, and hitting it would be pure luck." Axel was already in possession of two red jewels, like the one in this dragon's neck, so he knew something about them. Axel's jewels were cut from the necks of dragons killed by his Da and given to Axel some eleven years before.

"Whether intentional or not," said the dragon, "the strike disoriented me so that I could not maintain my equilibrium. He... was a big man, yes? With long reddish hair and sideburns?" The boy confirmed the description with a nod. "Alas, while he has killed me, he was in turn killed by one of my companions. I saw that."

The boy turned his head and wiped away a tear. Nevertheless, with new resolve, Axel looked back to speak again to the dragon, "How can he have killed you when here you are? And what's so special about that jewel?"

"All dragons are controlled by the jewels they wear. But your father's arrow struck mine and partially dislodged it. It broke the jewel's control over me and caused me to throw my rider. Unfortunately, at least for my rider, I threw him from me so forcefully that his safety line snapped, and he fell to his death. I will also likely die at any time, for a dragon cannot be separated from his jewel and still live.

"One benefit, however, is that this mishap freed me from the chains of silence and obedience, which controlled me. I do not have much time left, youngling. If you please, what is your name?"

"Axel Fletcher?"

"That is a solid name and carries with it your father's strength and courage. You did not move at all when I performed this ungraceful landing so near to you. Unfortunately, you must change your name, lest the king's forces trace you to the outlaw Fletcher and destroy you, too."

"Why would the king do that? These dragonriders wore the uniforms of Kolodra. Everyone knows that light-blue color. And why would the Kolodrans want to kill my father?"

"These dragonriders are killers working for King Deroth of Sanara. They wore Kolodran uniforms to throw the blame for this butchery on King Branton. Their real purpose was to kill your father, who had been declared an outlaw, and now, it seems, they will seek to destroy you, too.

"There is something special about you," the dragon continued. "I know of no human who has ever smelled like a dragon before. That is why I sought you out."

Axel's sense of smell was better than any human he knew, but he had never realized that his scent was anything like that of a dragon. "I smell like a dragon, and you could smell me from up there in the sky?"

"Why, yes, if close enough."

The dragon paused before speaking in a noticeably weakening voice. "I ask a boon of you, Axel. Nay, there must be two. They will be my last, I guarantee. The first is large, and I ask it because you are so special."

"Why should I help you, dragon?"

"Because you would gain true revenge for your people and stop the slaughter that the slavers force dragons to inflict on both humankind and other dragons.

"I ask you to do whatever you can to destroy the power that enables the jewels to control dragons. I do not know how you can accomplish this task, but I believe you are the one that the gods have foreordained to do it. In return, if you can do this, I guarantee that dragon attacks on humans will most likely cease.

"The second request will seem easier to do but may endanger your life. Please, would you consider cutting the remainder of the jewel and its setting from my neck so that I may die completely free? After taking the jewel, you must hide it where no one can find it, for the king's flying officers will surely return to retrieve it. Lastly, you should hide yourself, Son of Fletcher."

"I'm only fifteen years old," Axel said. "You can't ask me to do these kinds of things. If it is my fate to free the dragons, I won't avoid it; but how can you or anyone else determine that I am the person who should, or even could, accomplish such a wonder?

"The dragon said, 'I am asking you to take on this quest because, as you see, there is no one else I could ever ask to do such a thing.' "But also, I know you are different and special. You are a son of the Great Ceragon, and great is the prophecy concerning your future. It means that in your heart, you are a dragon, too. You are also the child of the Archer. You have shown no fear today. You keep your weeping inside, and I do not know how you can stand it. Finally, let's face it; you smell like a dragon—at least to another dragon."

"I don't know about that," Axel responded, "but I can complete the task my father started. Are you prepared, Dragon?"

After receiving a slow nod, Axel drew out his knife and walked around behind the dragon to the location where his father's arrow had struck. There he found a jewel, the size of a pebble, protruding slightly from the dragon's neck, being held in place only by an exposed metal setting stuck deep in the dragon's flesh, possibly even to the spine. He found he could grab both the jewel and the setting solidly with his left hand. He pulled hard, and the setting came out far enough to expose its roots, still implanted into the fibers and nerves of the spine. The dragon stiffened but otherwise did not move. With a quick slice of the knife at the base of the setting, the whole thing came free. Instantly, the dragon sighed, relaxed, and moved no more.

When Axel came around to the front where lay the dragon's head, he saw that the dragon was dead, but he could also see something on its face that might be interpreted as a smile.

Axel placed his arrow back into his quiver, along with the crossbow quarrel and the red stone. Hanging the bow on his pack, he lifted Jemmy's body to his arms—an action that he performed without much effort. He carried his friend down to the Frithden village cemetery half a tondrin away. There he walked past the several rows of rough-cut stone markers and laid Jemmy in the shade of a tall loma tree.

The cemetery lay only a short distance from the village, so Axel turned in that direction and began to search around the still-burning shells and skeletons of homes. For the next several orais, he looked for any sign of life, for any sign of hope. Intense heat from the fires limited his course to the centers of smoke-filled streets, now heavily strewn with glowing rubble.

He jumped when he heard the bleating of a coshil, a medium-sized farm animal often kept for its meat and for the creamy milk it produced. It came out from behind a burned-out wagon and looked about as if trying to find the barn or yard where it had been kept. This one was very tame and walked right up to Axel. Like many other coshils kept for milking, it had its short but very sharp horns removed when it was young. Axel rubbed the little animal behind the rounded stubs of his horns and said, "It looks like you and I are the only survivors of this massacre. I'm sorry, but I don't have anything to feed you."

As Axel went about his search of the village, the little coshil followed behind at a discreet distance. The fire had burned or was in the process of consuming everything of any use, but Axel eventually found a tin washtub that would work for his purpose and a shovelhead with a handle, which was little more than charcoal. The tool would be usable if he could find a piece of durable wood that could fit into the socket of the shovel blade. He searched for a while but did not find anything that would be suitable for his needs. Nevertheless, he had an idea.

He ran all the way back to the place where Jemmy died. The coshil followed behind for a distance but stopped in a field of still-standing green hay to feed.

Once back at the spot where all this day's sorrows had begun, Axel looked around. There were Jemmy's spear and his still-drying blood. The view of his village down the hill was so different than this morning. There was also the impossible-to-miss carcass of the dragon. He remembered the whole experience again as if living through it, and his throat choked up so much he could hardly breathe.

After a few minutes, he began to get better control of himself. There was a job to do. He picked up Jemmy's spear and ran back down to where he left the metal tub and the shovelhead. With some work, he managed to fit the butt end of the spear into the socket of the shovel and pound it tight with a rock. The repaired shovel's handle was rather long, but the tool served well enough for Axel's purposes.

He started with his Da and what few other piles of ash and burned remains he could identify as once being human. These he carried to the cemetery in the washtub one at a time, ignoring the horrible smells of burned flesh. They were the people caught out in the open. Most had been burned beyond recognition, their forms shrunken and twisted by the relentless heat, while a few were only partially charred. Among the scattered bodies, two were still recognizable as villagers he knew.

He buried all the bodies he found, except for his Da and Jemmy, in the cemetery, carefully marking each spot with stones from the walls that surrounded the village's fields. He located only seventeen of the roughly three hundred residents of the town. Their graves did not need to be deep, for his Grand Da told him badly burned bodies would not attract animals. He was a dragonrider once and should know.

Axel dug two deep graves out in the forest: one for his father and a second for his best friend. He thought about burying his father next to his mother's grave. But knowing that the king's men would be returning soon, he did not want anyone to dig up those he loved most to search for clues as to what happened.

While placing his father's thoroughly charred body into the grave, Axel noticed the remains of Alton's right hand tightly closed into a fist. Alton always used a three-fingered grip on his bowstrings, and that required an open hand while battling the dragons. Why did he close his hand into a fist? Acting on a hunch, Axel painstakingly pried open the hand to discover a brass talisman—the one given to Alton by his wife, Lyssa, on her deathbed.

Axel shuddered when he saw it and sat back on his haunches, finding the mere act of breathing to be unbearably painful. He stared at the talisman dangling from the black stump, which no longer bore any resemblance to his father's hand, the same hand that had tussled Axel's hair every morning at breakfast. Never could Axel recall seeing his father without that golden sunstar hanging from his neck; at least, not until now. But Alton knew he was about to die and covered it with his fist, hoping to protect it from dragon fire. He succeeded in that. Undoubtedly, Alton's last thoughts were of his beloved Lyssa.

Carefully pulling the necklace free, the young man discovered the brass chain to be undamaged. Thinking it only proper, he placed it around his neck. He wondered whether Alton realized when he clasped the little sunstar in his hand that this talisman would be the only physical inheritance he would leave to his son.

Axel piled no stones over Jemmy and his Da but disguised the graves and carefully marked the spots in a way that only he could know. He would look for more of the villager's remains after the king's men had done whatever they would do here.

Kneeling beside the two graves, he tried to contemplate all that had happened this day. For the most part, he had gone about his grisly work today soberly, matter-of-factly. But now his heart burned as if the dragons had targeted it, and his tears couldn't drown out the pain. In the light of a setting sunstar, Axel realized that all he had and all that he had known was rising into the air along with the thick smoke, which still billowed from the smoldering village.

Chapter Five

SHADDRA

Axel knelt by the graves of his father and best friend for more than an orai before he heard the voice. All kinds of thoughts were jumbled in his mind—sorrow for his loss, frustrations at his inability to help his father or anyone else in the village, the shock of watching his best friend die in his arms, and the strange words of a dragon, which shouldn't have been able to speak at all. Most of all, he pondered what he should do now.

"Hello," said a voice from out of the red haze of a setting sunstar,

Axel quickly grabbed his bow, which already had an arrow nocked to its string, and jumped to his feet. He looked out into the forest in the direction from which the voice had come. Was it someone from the village? The voice sounded like it came from a mature woman. Was she able to escape to the trees?

"I realize this is not a very good time to disturb you," the voice said clearly from somewhere nearby, "but I wondered if we might talk."

"Who are you... and where are you? Come out where I can see you!" Axel shouted.

"My name is Shaddra, and I am standing right in front of you."

Axel's eyes scanned the forest for a sight of anyone who might be there. He saw no one.

"You don't need to worry that you can't see me," the voice continued. "I will show myself soon enough. We need to talk a little before I do."

Axel stiffened and continued to point his arrow in the direction of the sound. "I don't understand," Axel said with a wary look on his face. "Why would you want to hide? Pardon me if I sound rude, but I'm not used to speaking to thin air. Why is it you won't show yourself?"

"I saw how capably you use that bow and thought it safer to remain out of sight for now. At least until we come to an understanding of the situation we find ourselves in."

Axel gave an exasperated huff. "Just tell me, are you an enemy? A dragonrider?"

"I am neither unless you choose to make me an enemy."

"All right, I'll accept that," Axel said. "What do you want to talk about?"

"Perhaps we should begin with introductions. I told *you* my name. May I ask yours?"

"I'm Axel Fletcher. Shaddra is a name I've never heard before. Is that your first name or your family name?"

"Shaddra is my *only* name. Now, I have a question for you. That dragon you killed; I heard him call you *Son of the Great Ceragon*. How, exactly, did you come by this honor?"

Shaddra's words caused Axel to take a step back in surprise. "You were close enough to hear that?" he asked with a note of doubt in his voice.

The voice suddenly took on a more urgent tone. "That is not important now. Yes, I overheard much of what was said. Now, answer the question!"

"I don't know what a *Son of Ceragon* is, let alone why he called me that!" Axel snapped. "What's so important about it?"

"Hmmm," the voice said thoughtfully. "Let us explore that thought for a moment, shall we? Here is what I have observed. You heard a crossbow being fired from two landrins away and reacted so fast that you turned, drawing your bow as you did, and struck down your enemy, seemingly without aiming, all before the bolt from the crossbow tore through a fold in your cloak."

With widening eyes, Axel said, "The bolt pierced my cloak?" He looked down and was surprised to see two holes, chest high, in his cloak.

"That bolt missed you by less than a thumb's distance. If you had not turned when you did, *you* would have been killed instead of Jemmy. I suppose Jemmy would have been killed by a second shot from the assassin because *you* would not have been there to protect him."

"How do you know...?"

"Think back to when you were looking down on the village; you heard the cries of those people as they tried to flee from danger, even though you were more than half a tondrin away. You saw your father and recognized his face and features from that same distance. Can all humans see and hear so well?"

"I don't think that..."

"You also saw the arrow launched by your father and witnessed it strike the jewel on the dragon's neck. That jewel was less than half the size of a kiplan egg, yet you saw it from half a tondrin away! Can other humans do the same?"

"I haven't thought about it much... but I guess not."

"I saw you pick up your friend and carry him in your arms for more than half a ton—that's two thousand strides without a rest. Later, you ran that same half tondrin distance at full speed up the hill from the village and then ran back down with only a brief stop at the top. What is more, you were not even winded by the effort. Can other humans do that?"

"I... I don't..."

"Can you see in the dark?"

Axel had enough of this. "All right, who are you, and how do you know these things?"

"I know them because... I... am... a dragon, and a special one at that."

Oh, not another dragon, Axel thought. Then he realized that if this creature *were* a dragon as it claimed, it could have killed him easily. Why was he still alive? Strangely, he did not feel threatened in any way. So, what did this dragon want from him?

"Can all dragons talk?" he asked.

"If you can talk, then why cannot we? Does that bother you?"

"I guess not. It's just a bit of a surprise. Okay, you're a dragon, and you can talk, and you're special. Special in what way?"

"I am a messenger dragon—a female messenger dragon."

"I've heard of those; they're smaller than the others, aren't they?"

"Very true. But I am also special in another way."

"So, once again, what is special about you?" Axel asked, getting a little put off with this whole thing.

He barely finished speaking those words before a dragon, the size of the largest skell, miraculously appeared less than ten strides in front of him. Axel jumped back in surprise, tripped, and only managed to keep himself from striking the ground hard by twisting and using his arms to catch his fall. He quickly jumped back to his feet, dusted himself off, and studied the creature before him.

She was only a fraction the size of a full-grown firedrake, yet from ear to foot, she stood a full arm's length taller than Axel himself. He had never seen a dragon so small, nor so near, and wondered if she might be only a fledgling. Her scales were a shifting mosaic of colors, mirroring the shrubs and rocky landscape behind her, but tinged with a subtle gray. Axel realized she must have been in plain sight all along, camouflaged so perfectly that she was nearly invisible—until she chose otherwise. Only when she wished to be seen did she dull her colors, like a sorcerer casting off a cloak. As he watched, her coloring softened and brightened, gradually settling into a warm, golden buff reminiscent of his father's prized skell. In the fading light of the sunstar, her scales flashed and glimmered, catching the rays like hammered flakes of gold.

Miraculous! Axel thought with an astonished grin, scarcely able to believe his eyes. He found himself enchanted, as if he could not get enough of staring. Although Axel realized that he might be considered rude according to dragon etiquette, he still could not draw his eyes away. He felt compelled to examine every inch of this marvelous beast in closer detail.

She had a gentle snout, ending in what could almost be called a beak, with long, pointed ears rising a handspan above each side of her forehead. Just behind the ears and sides of her face was a ribbed, fan-shaped circlet of bone and scaly hide, as if made to funnel sound to her ears but also sturdy enough to protect the head from blows. The dragon's bright green eyes were staring back at him with curiosity equal to his own as she slanted her head from side to side, examining him from every hair on his head to the mud on his boots.

The dragon appeared completely at ease, lounging comfortably on her haunches with her long neck gracefully arched. Her sinuous, snake-like tail was coiled about her, occasionally flicking with a mind of its own. Axel observed that her four legs each bore long-fingered hands, featuring three substantial fingers and a tiny thumb. All her fingers and thumbs culminated in wickedly pointed claws. The middle finger on each hand was wider and much thicker than the others, to help support the dragon's body weight when on the ground, he guessed. The dragon kept its wings folded close to her body, making it difficult to determine the length of her wings, but he estimated they would easily reach twenty or more strides from wingtip to wingtip when stretched out.

She was, indeed, a magnificent creature, but of all her features, what most caught Axel's attention was her face, which seemed capable of almost human expression. The look on her features now was neither menacing nor fierce but pleasant and respectful. So gentle was it, in form, that he felt his fear recede and his anger soften, so much so that he almost forgot he was talking to an enemy. That realization slammed back to him like a sudden, bitter wind, piercing his heart. He stiffened his stance and hardened the grip on his bow.

"I see you're a dragon who can do magic. I admit I'm impressed, but I must be honest and say, beautiful and mysterious though you are, demon, I hate you! You have killed my family and best friend and destroyed my village!"

"I did not!" the dragon said firmly. "You watched the attack. No messenger dragons took part. What's more, the firedrakes and siris dragons who did were slaves of the king. I am a free dragon and have never harmed a human in my life!

If you need proof, look at my neck! I carry no jewel!" The dragon turned its head and showed the back of its neck. Sure enough, the surface of the neck appeared as nothing but smooth scales.

"I thought... I thought all dragons had jewels in their necks. Why is it that you have none?"

"A very kindly human saved me from that fate. Now, I belong to a free dragon colony."

"You said you are named Shaddra... right?"

The dragon nodded its head and said, "And I do not do magic. If jewels do not control them, all messenger dragons can change their colors to look like their background. In such a case, I would appear invisible to you if I stood still. If I moved, you might see a strange blur that could easily be explained away. Fortunately, the king and his troops have not learned this secret."

"Hmm," Axel said, "I suppose that is good to know. But why have you come to me? Just to ask a bunch of questions?"

"Yes... I suppose so. I had to ascertain who you are."

"Okay, who am I?"

"As you have already been told, I believe you are a *Son of Ceragon*, perhaps even *The* Son *of Ceragon*."

"I've heard that term somewhere before today. What does it mean?"

"It means you were born with dragon blood in your veins. It means that, on the outside, you are human, but, inside, at least a part of you—a major part—is a dragon. So many of the things you have done today could not have been done by any other human, even ones who are fully grown, and besides... you do smell like a dragon."

"I don't know if I would call that a compliment," Axel said.

"I do not think other humans can smell a dragon's scent, but dragons can, and so can killer beasts. You live on the verges and near the Ghanara-dan. Have you ever been attacked by such a beast?"

"I've encountered many killer beasts, and some have come awfully close to me. But they always run away. I thought they got spooked somehow."

"Yes, they got spooked... by you. The killer beasts are all deathly afraid of dragons, and they know the smell of dragons from their very births."

"Okay, so let's suppose I am this *Son of Ceragon* or whatever; what... does... that... mean?" He spoke the last part of the sentence in a firm, impatient voice and with crisp pauses between each pair of words.

"There is an old foretelling, passed down among dragons…"

Axel perked up. "A foretelling? *A*… foretelling… is a prophecy!"

The dragon looked at him curiously. "Yes, in the human language, a foretelling is a prophecy. I am surprised you know the word."

Wrinkling his brow, Axel said, "All right then. So, what is this proph… er, foretelling about?

"The foretelling tells us that *the Son* and *the Daughter of the Great Ceragon*, together, will bring freedom and wisdom to both the dragons and the humans of Tamerel."

"Etmar's fire! You mean there's a Daughter *of Ceragon*, too? Hey, I think you've got the wrong person here, Shaddra," Axel said with a shake of his head. "The dragons, which destroyed my village, may have been slaves, but my family and friends would still be alive if it weren't for them. That's not something easily forgotten."

"So, what do you intend to do now?" asked Shaddra. "If you stay here, you will be slaughtered by the dragons and men who will certainly be coming tomorrow morning."

"What makes you so certain they will kill me? I was born and raised in this country, and I know a great deal about dragons. I know how to survive, and I might even be able to get some revenge."

"Hmm," said Shaddra thoughtfully. "You already know about dragons?"

Axel let an exasperated breath of air blow out between his teeth. "Um," he muttered, "not everything, but you might say that dragons have played a big role in my family history."

The dragon cocked her head to one side in thought for a moment and said, "If you are indeed certain that you can survive the coming day, as you say, then I have an idea. Tomorrow morning more of the king's dragons will come here so that their riders can look for the jewels embedded in the slain dragons and carried by the dead riders. Let me suggest that, tonight, you look for those jewels, the ones you do not yet have in your possession. You must find them before the dragons return. One jewel will be found on the neck of the dragon that fell into the burning buildings, and the last ones will be on the two dragonriders who fell from their mounts. Each of the jewels is worth more to the king than ten villages the size of yours."

"The dragonriders wear their jewels on chains hung around their necks. If you can find the bodies, then you should also find their jewels. It is already dark, but I think you will still be able to see what you are doing as you search. Remember to keep the matching pairs, carried by dragon and rider, together. Meanwhile, I will fetch some friends, though I won't be able to get them here until this time tomorrow, or perhaps the day after. If you are still alive then, as you claim you will be, it will be another sign that you are indeed one of the two humans who are predicted to come. We will take you to meet a man who may answer many of your questions and help you discover your destiny."

"A man? You'll take me to see a human?"

"Of course! You are not the only human I have the opportunity to know."

"Oh, why not, then?" Axel said with a hint of sarcasm in his voice and a shrug of his shoulders. "What else have I got to do?"

Axel saw the dragon smile at him. "Look for us here at your cemetery." It gave a nod, opened its long kitak-like wings, and took off almost vertically into the air with great sweeping flaps. In a moment, it disappeared over the trees.

Axel didn't know why he trusted this strange little dragon—whose lips never moved when she spoke—but he did.

Bowing his head, Axel rubbed his brow with the fingers of his right hand. Abruptly, a memory came from out of nowhere and settled into his brain. "It is the prophecy…," he said in a whisper, "the, uh, foretelling the Lady told me about. It must be. Did she really call me '*The Son of… Ceragon*'? Yes, just like the dragons did… and I told her that I was the son of Alton Fletcher. He chuckled. So, who in the world is Ceragon? I guess I'm going to find out."

Finding the fallen dragon was not difficult, even in the dark. Axel remembered where it landed. Getting to the jewel proved to be more of a problem. The dragon fell at an angle into one of the largest collections of buildings in the village and slid over and through their debris for quite a distance. The falling beast slid into the burning buildings and flattened everything in its way. The charred and burned remnants were pushed up in front of the sliding corpse, and the dragon's head and neck were somewhere underneath the pile it created.

The first dead dragonrider lay out on the nearby dirt roadway. She had been scraped off her saddle by the wreckage of the buildings struck by her crashing mount. Axel easily walked over and removed the simple chain holding the woman's command jewel, and he held the brilliant red object in his hand. As he did, his hand trembled. Heedful that this object was the tool used to enslave a massive, yet beautiful, creature and force it to kill, he tucked it away in his pouch.

Then he stopped to look at the pale face of death below him. Grand Da told him what it was like to be a soldier, how most were conscripted, and how they had no choice when given orders. But the brown dragon clearly said all these riders were people who loved killing. What's more, they came specifically to kill his Da.

Axel promised Jemmy he would destroy everyone responsible for the raid on his village. He again swore that he would never rest until that promise was fulfilled.

Speaking of dragons, he thought, looking over at the enormous dragon body, I need to find that one's head and neck. He started following the line made by the dragon's spine, beginning at the tail, passing over the back, and disappearing into the rubble at the point marked by the rear end of the saddle.

"I guess I start digging," Axel said aloud and lifted the makeshift shovel he, fortunately, thought to bring along. He reached the jewel after nearly an orai's worth of removing partially burned planks and beams and shoveling hot coals and ashes. He also vigilantly searched for any signs of human remains. The charred and still smoking material here was less than a stride in depth, but it still managed to give him several painful burns on his arms and hands. As he expected, he found the jewel undamaged. The dragon's scaly hide was not hot, and neither was the jewel. He was genuinely surprised that he could not pull this jewel out by hand, unlike the other one in his possession. He was forced to cut the stone out from the thickly scaled hide.

Recalling that this dragon had been brought down by a spectacular shot to the soft tissue beneath its chin, Axel reflected that it hadn't just been a long shot—it had been a truly remarkable one. He remembered how his Da always preferred to craft and use bows with draw weights that only he could handle. With a short laugh, Axel thought back to the times he would sneak Da's new bows out to the practice range set up just beyond their home. Shaking his head, he remembered how he'd never wanted to spoil his Da's image of himself as the best archer around.

Digging deeper under the dragon's head, he found the spot where the arrow should have been found but discovered it was completely burned to ash, down to the scaly hide it had penetrated.

The dragon's scales had shifted enough to completely obscure the entry wound, and any associated blood had been burned away. *"Hmm,"* he thought. *There was no way that he could retrieve the bodkin arrowhead. But then, the king's men would have enormous trouble even finding this wound. If they did, they might think the arrow was pulled out before it could burn. Even if found, all bodkins were generic in this kingdom. There would be little likelihood that it would offer any hope of a traceback to its creator without the shaft and its fletching.*

Using the shovel, he did his best to restore the still smoldering beams and ash to make it appear that no attempt had been made to dig here. *Let the king's men wonder how Da brought this beast down.*

Running through his memory from the attack, Axel determined the approximate spot where he might find the second dragonrider. That rider fell, not in the village, but upon a hillside about six landrins away. He located the man's body in a thick clump of scrub aldan, which proved to be only a temporary obstacle to reaching the dragonrider's gemstone. No arrow had brought this man down, so all he needed to do was to remove the jewel from his neck.

Reaching into the pouch at his side with one hand, he could easily feel and count the four jewels it held. Axel took his new finds over to a rock just beyond the edge of where the village used to stand and where the two jewels given to him by his Da nine years before were lying concealed. The large rock had a small hidden cavity about the size of a human head and was, once, perfect for hiding small things that should not be found by anyone. On this visit, he emptied the cache of its contents and added them to the pouch. Now, it contained a total of six shiny, red gems—four with pointed silver settings and two with silver chains. He wondered how much death was associated with these jewels. He also wondered if any more were yet to die because of them.

Remembering to keep the jewel pairs together, he tied the chains of the necklaces to the corresponding jewels he took from the dragons. He saw that the dragon's jewel setting was broken where it should have contacted the jewel. The break must have been what brought that dragon down.

Now that all the jewels were found and retrieved, it was time for Axel to locate a place to spend the rest of the night and get some sleep. He also needed a fortified hideout where he could watch for incoming dragons and keep himself safe from the dangers they would bring.

***

The first of the king's dragons appeared over the ghostly smoking ash and charcoal remains of Frithden about two orais after the rising of the sunstar. Axel watched the brown siris dragon fly a slow circle just above the tilled fields surrounding what once was a village. It never touched down, but its rider closely scanned both the air and ground that he sailed over. After making a second circle, the siris dragon returned in the direction from which it originally came.

Axel took this opportunity to extricate himself from the hiding place he had fashioned in one end of a large, densely packed slash pile, consisting of the leafy branches and other trimmings left over from a recent forest clearing operation by some of the villagers. The stack stood four strides tall, eight strides wide, and ran the entire length of the road from the village to the cemetery. After the field next to the road had been cleared of trees during the previous summer, logs usable for lumber were carted off to the mill, while branches, leafy trimmings, and other debris were tossed onto the slash pile to dry for a full year. Villagers were to have used these scraps to keep household fireplaces hot throughout the coming winter. Axel looked over at the smoking skeleton of Frithden and thought how the village's tumbled-down fireplaces would never be used again.

After refilling a waterskin in a brooklet not far distant, Axel relieved himself into the stream, then scurried back to his hideout. There, he once more checked the stack for any indication that it contained anything other than wood trimmings. As he climbed back inside, he turned to shift a thick branch with his shoulder, carefully placing it to block and hide the entrance to his hideaway. Three small peepholes gave Axel views of the cemetery, the main street of the village, and much of the sky above.

Barely half an orai had passed since Axel settled in when a formation of dragons appeared once again over the shattered remains of the village—their second arrival in as many days. The formation quickly dissolved as individual dragons peeled away from the group, fanning out to search the land surrounding the village. Some swooped low, gliding above the ruins at heights of only twenty or thirty strides, while others skimmed the treetops of the encircling forests, with some flying perilously close to the ground. Axel realized that these dragons—and their riders—must be the same ones who had attacked Frithden the day before. Watching them, Axel felt as though his village was being violated all over again, and a fresh wave of hatred flared hot within his heart.

The aerial search lasted a long time, but eventually several dragons landed, and their riders jumped off to search through the wreckage of the little town. A few landed near the fallen dragon, killed by Axel's father. Their riders were searching the dragon and the two dead riders for their jewels.

A siris dragon settled down in the cemetery. This one was different from the first he had seen; it was as black as if dipped in an inkwell. It was quickly followed by two firedrakes, one of which was carrying two riders. The four riders descended from their mounts and walked directly over to the fresh graves. Two of the men wore fine civilian attire, while the other two wore military uniforms. He recognized one of those in civilian clothes as the King's Magister for Frithden, Vaylo Tansor, a man of sixty years. The sight of the magister, despised by everyone in the town, made Axel grind his teeth. His presence here confirmed there were plenty of reasons for that hate.

Axel's hideaway in the slash pile lay three landrins distant from the edge of the cemetery, too far away for a normal human to hear what was spoken, but his acute dragon hearing helped him to hear and understand the invader's conversations perfectly well.

"It appears someone may have survived this execution," one of them said. "These graves did not dig themselves." That man, decked in a black, ornately decorated, thigh-length doublet showing beneath an open black velvet cloak, addressed another wearing a gray Sanaran officer's uniform.

"Set out a team to look for the Fletcher's shop," said the elegantly dressed man, "and any bows they find are to be brought to me immediately. Magister Tansor, you will go with them to point out where that workshop is located."

The brown dragon was correct, Axel thought. *All this destruction happened because the king wanted to kill my Da.* The order to find bows from his family's shop made Axel reflect on the situation. Not all bows made in the shop were power bows—what the Kingsmen called 'strongbows,' or the newer 'steelbows.' Da never sold such a bow to a stranger—only to people he knew very well. Axel understood Da and Grand Da especially strove to keep the bows from falling into the hands of the king's magisters. There would be no such bow found by these people.

"Yes, Adjutant Brasa. It shall be done," the officer replied and turned, along with the magister, to return to his dragon.

"Wait," the man in black called out. "I want a dragon or two to check out that slash pile for escapees. At the slightest smell of a human, I want them to turn the pile into a wall of flame."

Axel's eyes widened in shock at hearing the words, but he did not move. The dying dragon, back on the hill where Jemmy was killed, said Axel had a scent like a dragon, not a human, and so did the messenger dragon he met at the cemetery. His life might very well depend on those words being true.

The high officer then gave commands to a second officer to have the men exhume every fresh grave and search for anything that might help explain what happened here.

On a signal from the officer on the ground, two more firedrakes descended to the cemetery. After a quick consultation, the two new arrivals retrieved shovels from somewhere and started desecrating the graves Axel had dug only the night before.

The sound of large wings settling nearby alerted Axel that new dragons had joined those already on the ground. These landed somewhere out of his view. Axel couldn't tell how many dragons were in this new addition, but there were definitely more than a few. He could hear the riders giving commands to their mounts to spread out along the line of debris in the huge slash pile and flush out anyone hiding within.

A few minutes later, Axel was startled to see a colossal dragon's face materialize in front of one of his peepholes, its nostrils flaring as it sniffed the air. At one point, the creature drove its face directly toward the spyhole Axel used to observe the cemetery. It looked straight into the spot where Axel sat, and he could feel the heat of its breath as it snuffled inquisitively. Suddenly, the dragon's eyes widened in recognition or surprise. Its body tensed briefly, then erupted into frantic action as it began tearing away the limbs and branches concealing Axel's hideout.

"Ho there, beast!" the dragon's rider cried out. "Stop that! What do you think you're doing?" The dragon immediately obeyed.

"Did it smell human in there?" a commanding voice shouted from behind the dragon. The cemetery was out of sight due to the bulk of the dragon's body.

"I don't think so, Sir," the rider shouted back. "It's not giving the sign for smelling a human, but something has its attention. "Perhaps we've got a terana or a bush kota hiding in there."

Meanwhile, the dragon had leaned its head into the pile again as if attracted by something there. Axel again saw the huge eye staring into his peephole.

"Stop that fumbling around," the rider exclaimed to his mount. "It's human flesh we want." He grabbed hold of the jewel at his neck and said, "Hear me! Find me human flesh." The dragon suddenly stiffened, obediently returned to poking its nose around the woodpile near Axel's peephole, and then slowly moved on.

"Sorry about that, sir! I'm certain it was just distracted by some kind of creature in the slash pile."

"If you can't keep your beast under control, we may have to send the both of you back for remedial training," the unseen speaker called out in a firm voice. "See that the beast obeys!"

Axel's hideout had partially collapsed when the dragon pulled at its top cover, but the hideaway was not in danger of being discovered, so he rubbed his hand across his face to wipe away some of the sweat that had flowed down his face in rivulets while the altercation was commanding his attention. Then, he again strained to see what was happening around him. More dragons landed, while others took off into the air. Soldiers came and went, carrying word of their discoveries. An officer jumped off a dragon and hurried to assume a position of attention near Adjutant Brasa, where Axel heard the man in black ask, "Yes, Officer Bilton, what is your report?"

"Sir, I led a team investigating the area round the corpse of a brown dragon lying on a nearby hill. The jewel has been removed from its neck. There are significant traces of human blood in two places, near to the dragon's remains. There are also siris dragon tracks not far from one of those locations. We assume that is the place where Officer Haskan received his mortal arrow strike."

Axel had two conflicting attitudes toward the death of that man. The first was that the murderer got what he deserved. He felt the second attitude more deeply in his chest. He was the first person Axel had ever killed. That thought was like a vise clamping down on his heart.

"Adjutant Brasa," one officer said in a loud voice. "We have exhumed all the new graves and found nothing of interest to do with the bodies. They all appeared to have died in the fire. Should we just leave what's left of them as they are before we go or rebury them?"

"Put them all back," said the officer. "They stink horribly. I don't want to be smelling that over the remainder of my stay here."

A few minutes after that, another officer stood to report. "Sir, someone has already been here and stolen the gemstones from the dead dragons and riders in the area. We have also not been able to determine what brought either dragon down. If the one in the village was hit by a quarrel, then any part not penetrating the beast would possibly have been destroyed by the fire."

"Archos' bloody excrement!" the man in black shouted and, grabbing the officer by the top edge of his armor, pulled the man's face over until they were staring eye to eye. "The king will have our gizzards for losing those jewels!"

"But how could any villager from a place like this even know the jewels were there?"

"It seems that question is now moot," said Brasa. "The jewels are gone, and the king will have our heads if they are not found."

"Hopefully, the thief will be foolish enough to try selling them. There's no place in the kingdom that could be done without our knowing."

"We have no way of knowing whether the thief is a peasant or a Kolodran spy. So, I want you to set up search teams to scour every square handspan of this valley until you find those gems!"

"But Adjutant Brasa, the dragons have already searched both the village and everything around for a distance of two tondrins."

"Then do it all again and search out eight tondrins. Should the missing villagers remain unfound, you will return daily to scour the forests for them. The sooner you locate them, the easier it will be for you."

The king's soldiers stayed until the setting of the sunstar prevented any more of a search effort. Periodically, dragons would land near the cemetery, and their riders would give reports to the man called Brasa. Axel estimated the time based on the movement of shadows within his limited view from the slash pile. He missed hearing the comforting hourly tolls of the bell in what was once the village council hall. A rumbling in his stomach grew so loud he became worried that some passing soldier might hear it.

Eventually, Commander Brasa ordered the dragons to reform above the shell of the village and return to their base.

While Axel watched them leave, he felt the burning inside him flare again. This time the fire was not directed at the dragons so much as the humans who rode them. The faces of Magister Tansor and Adjutant Brasa stood out particularly strongly in his mind.

***

Sometime after the departure of the dragons, Axel carefully lifted the thick branches covering his hiding place and climbed out, constantly watching the skies above for any return of dragons. The sky was now dark, but he had no difficulty in seeing everything around him. He decided to resume his search of the village to determine whether anything of importance had been missed by the flames and not removed by the soldiers. After some hours of fruitless wandering, he decided to return to the cemetery. He had discovered the remains of a few villagers, but nearly all were in places still too hot to comfortably remove or trapped under large blackened and fallen beams too heavy to be lifted without an extended effort. He marked the location of these bodies in his mind for future retrieval and decided to return to the cemetery.

The rise of the sunstar was not far off, while Axel walked the short distance back to where he first met the messenger dragon. Of a sudden, he heard a voice coming from somewhere ahead.

"Hello," the voice said.

"I suppose that is you, Shaddra," Axel said in response, squinting his eyes trying to see where the dragon stood.

"Axel, I'm sorry to approach you like this again. I just wanted to ensure you wouldn't shoot me just because I surprised you," Shaddra said gently.

"What makes you think I wouldn't shoot you out of spite?" Axel retorted, his tone guarded.

"Oh, I see," Shaddra replied with a faint smile. "I suppose I'll have to take my chances."

A few moments later, she reappeared a short distance in front of him, settling back on her haunches as she had before. This time, her hide shimmered with a bluish hue, startling Axel and causing his eyes to widen in surprise. Without a doubt, she truly could change her color.

She quickly added, "I will be joining two of my friends shortly."

"And why didn't they come with you?" Axel asked.

"I suppose they did not want to be shot by that bow of yours either," Shaddra said with a definite smirk on her face. He wondered how a dragon could show an expression like that.

"Okay, I guess I am a bit jumpy right now."

"That is quite understandable. I suggest that you remain a bit jumpy for a while yet."

Shaddra looked up into the sky in a general westerly direction. "I see that my friends are making a timely entrance."

Axel turned in the same direction and saw two black shadows against the starlit black sky.

"You see them, do you not?" Shaddra asked.

"Yes, I see two dragons approaching," Axel replied, "a firedrake and a siris dragon, I believe."

"No other human," the messenger dragon said, "apart from the *Daughter of Ceragon*, whoever she might be, would be able to see what you see. That, plus your other skills, makes *you* special—much more special than I am."

The two dragons, guided by the still bright coals and the dark smoke from the village, flew directly in, circled over their heads, and landed a safe distance away. Axel could not help but feel nervous at their approach.

"You are sure these are friendly dragons?" Axel asked, looking at Shaddra. "They're not wearing jewels?"

"Hukken! Torkar!" Shaddra said in a voice akin to a shout. "Come join us. Axel here wants to make certain you are not the king's slaves. Will you bare your necks to him?"

Again, Axel was amazed that, apart from an open mouth showing many sharp teeth, her face did not move to form the words. Instead, they seemed to come from deep in her throat.

"If he remains a landrin off, I will," said the firedrake in a deep bass voice.

The siris dragon looked sternly over at the firedrake and then turned back to face Axel.

"I heard what you said to him, siris dragon!" Axel called out.

All three dragons quickly turned their heads to stare at Axel. He stepped back slightly and spoke in a quiet voice. "I mean... I heard you saying something in a high-pitched voice, but I don't know *what* you said, if... you know what I mean."

Shaddra visibly smiled at his words. She turned a much more severe face to her friends. "That is one more foretelling, which is fulfilled in him. As I have told you, he is *the Son of the Great Ceragon*."

"Do you swear that you witnessed all the other foretellings you spoke of being actually fulfilled in him?" the siris dragon asked.

"Are you saying," Shaddra said in a huffy voice, "that I must have him repeat all the things I witnessed, just for your personal conviction? You heard what he just said; will you accept my word for the other things or not?"

"Yes, yes, you know we will. We always have. Is it not so? You are like a big sister to us," the firedrake said in his deep voice, but a voice that had a slight bleat of a coshil to it. Axel would never have imagined a firedrake speaking in such a way—that is, once he got over the whole speaking thing first.

"I'm more like a *second mother*, and you know it," Shaddra pointed out with emphasis.

Axel could not help but giggle inside at their little exchange, especially since Shaddra was only one-quarter the size of the siris dragon and just over one-tenth the size of the firedrake.

Shaddra turned her head toward Axel to say, "I apologize for our rudeness. Uncle Jarrad would be quick to make a teaching point about that. I should have made introductions before getting into anything else," she said. She pointed in the direction of the siris dragon, who now came forward. "May I present Council Leader Hukken?"

The mossy-green-colored siris dragon easily stood three strides tall at the shoulder, and its long neck went up from there. Axel thought it strange that the dragon did not look fierce or even scary—just curious. His face showed immense interest in the human youngling, but he did not smile.

Hukken stopped and bowed his head low—low enough that Axel could easily see that no jewel adorned his neck. "I am pleased to meet the *Son of the Great Ceragon*," he said upon rising. "However, I am worried about the portents you bring."

"I assure you," Axel said, "you are no more worried than I. You see my village before you. Is this likely to happen to other villages? How am I to fulfill my promises?"

"I will not ask about your promises," Hukken said with a half-smile on his face, "at least for now. However, there may come a time when we will hold a fascinating conversation."

Shaddra took this moment to continue her introductions. "Axel, may I also present Assistant Council Leader Torkar?" At this point, the firedrake stepped forward and bowed his head. Axel again noted the absence of a jewel, as with the other dragons. This one topped the siris dragon by a stride in height and by at least double in its weight. This firedrake was the gray color of anyu bark, complete with streaks of black and reddish yellow.

Both Hukken and Torkar were each covered in a thick layer of overlapping scales, had tails extending close to twice the length of their bodies, and had four large, formidable teeth protruding from their mouths when closed, two facing up and two facing down. They managed a wide variety of expressions in their faces, despite the teeth. As with Shaddra, the sides of their bodies were covered by wings, the length of which Axel could not even begin to imagine.

"Hukken and Torkar," Shaddra said, "are the heads of the council that governs the Free Dragon Colony in all matters not brought before the Colony as a whole."

"I think I understand that. They're like the headman of a village council, except there are two of them."

Shaddra pursed her lips in a very human way and said, "That definition will do for now. Our purpose here is to decide whether to help you or let you make your own fate."

"I think I know *your* vote..." Axel said, then looked over at the messenger dragon with his eyebrows curled together. "Uh, you do have a vote, don't you?"

Shaddra grinned and chuckled a bit. "I certainly have influence."

"Shaddra," Hukken interjected, "I say we accept your suggestion of taking him to meet Jarrad. Jarrad will give us the advice we need."

"I agree," said Torkar with a wily smile, "*if* the youngling will behave himself properly."

Shaddra lowered her head and stared over at the firedrake. "You would prefer we give him a leash and a muzzle, Torkar? He probably has the bite of a chuda."

"Of course, we do not want a leash, but we truly know nothing about him!"

"You should be afraid of me!" roared out Axel, "because I do have the bite of a chuda!"

The dragons looked at him and then at each other. Torkar suddenly broke out laughing and said, "Nice try, youngling, but that is not believable!"

Every one of the dragons broke out laughing at this one, even Hukken.

"Hey," Axel said, "Jarrad is a human name. Is he the human you referred to a while ago?"

"Yes, he is human," she said with a smile. "Do you agree to come with us to meet him then?"

"I will come, as long as I can return soon to bury the remains of my friends and family."

"That should be workable, but the king's men may yet return to investigate this place. We will arrange to keep a watch here, and, after a time, you may come back to complete your task..."

"Wait another moment!" Axel suddenly said with a strong element of panic in his voice. "Are you telling me that I should ride with you on the back of a dragon?"

"You could walk if you choose," Shaddra pointed out, "but that would take a Kivan or two. Tell me, which do you prefer?"

"But... I don't know how to ride!" Axel said, backing away.

"We are not exactly used to it, either. However, we know how to fly, and we will not let you fall. Jarrad has not fallen once."

"And... how many times has he flown with you?"

"Oh... once," Shaddra said in a timid voice.

"Once?" Axel shouted, dropping his jaw in disbelief.

Altogether, the three dragons broke out again into loud guffaws, and it took a moment or so before their laughter gradually died down.

Shaddra grimaced a little, looking at Axel's still gaping mouth, and said, "I am sorry, Axel; it was just a bit of dragon humor. Jarrad has ridden many of the free dragons on numerous occasions. I do have to admit it was worth a little lie to see your face. I promise I will never lie to you again."

She spoke the last sentence in total seriousness, but Axel still had trouble with the fact that her lips did not move. *How can you tell if dragons are lying to you*, he thought, *if their lips don't move?*

"When do we leave?" Axel asked.

Shaddra looked up at the sky and said, "The journey will take more than a day. If we leave right away and make no stops, we can reach our destination just after the setting of the sunstar tomorrow."

"As you wish," Axel said, "but you need to show me how to do this."

"I will take you as a rider this time," Shaddra said. "First you come to the left side of me and say, 'May I mount?'"

"Why do I say that?"

"It's because Jarrad says we dragons should require it of anyone who wants to ride us."

"Has this Jarrad a reason for having you go through this ritual?"

"Yes, he says that dragons have always been required to let humans mount them when told. Now, among the free dragons, things are different. We own our backs, and we decide who will ride us and who will not."

"Interesting. Okay, I get your permission. What do I do next?"

"Just step here and here and hold on tight as you would on a skell without any saddle or reins."

Axel laughed and said, "That means wrap your arms around the neck and pray you don't fall off."

"That will work," Shaddra said.

Rolling his eyes, Axel ritualistically asked for permission and followed her instructions on how to mount. She took off in a gentle rise as soon as she ascertained his grip around her neck was tight. The other dragons followed quickly behind.

The ground quickly fell away from beneath them, and the world around them whirled about with a mind of its own, causing Axel to grip Shaddra's neck even harder.

"Ooooh!" shouted Axel into the wind. "It's a good thing I haven't eaten anything today!"

Chapter Six

UNCLE JARRAD

The queasiness in Axel's stomach did not last long, and he found that the fear of falling was manageable—most of the time. Accordingly, he let his curiosity guide where he concentrated his gaze. At first, he looked back at the ruins of his life left behind. The village was not particularly big when it was whole; now, as he stared down at the patch of ruin known as Frithden, it seemed even smaller, almost insignificant in the vast expanse of ground beneath him.

He knew that this moment was, quite literally, the day his life was to change forever—but a change to what? He shook his head and felt hollowness inside as the dark smudge behind him, identifying the center of his life to that time, disappeared when the dragons were surrounded by fog.

The fog penetrated everything he wore, bringing chilling cold to every bone. Suddenly, he realized, *"It's a cloud!" We're flying through a cloud!*

Then, Shaddra and the others rose above the fog, and Axel saw flat layers of other clouds in the sky. *So, this is what clouds look like from above!* He wondered if they were all flat like this. No... he'd seen many clouds, which towered like bumpy pillows climbing to unimaginable heights and changing their shapes as he watched. These clouds were not like them. Dragons seemed to fly over these flat clouds without effort, but could the dragons fly over those huge billowing clouds?

He looked over at the other two dragons and noticed how smoothly the beat of their wings propelled them through the air. On the ground, even the firedrake was somewhat clumsy... out of place anyway. Up here, the small group of dragons felt completely at ease. Up here, they were not fearsome beasts carrying death in every part of their bodies but streamlined birds, streaking like arrows in flight.

He felt the chilly wind blowing swiftly against his face but then realized it was not the wind that was moving. It was his face moving against the air. How strange was that? And it was harder to breathe up here. He had to take deeper, more prolonged breaths to compensate. He wondered why that was so.

When the sunstar rose, the light reflecting from the cloud tops was nearly blinding. It forced Axel to keep his eyes looking toward the west until the clouds beneath began to scatter and reveal the incredible stretch of land below. Off to the east he saw the ridgeline marking the top of the Taiken escarpment, stretching from as far as he could see behind him to as far as he could see before the little group of dragons. To the distant west, a long, long line of very tall mountains formed the border of the uplands on that side. That would certainly be the Kuhala mountain range.

Up ahead, he saw that they were going to cross a mountain range, and a tall one at that. Many of the peaks still had snow on them, although it was the beginning of the season of growth. He had learned by practical experience that higher altitudes tend to be colder than those down below, especially at night. He was thankful he had worn his cloak—it was too cold up here, even with the cloak. Feeling confident enough to release his hold on the dragon's neck for an instant, he yanked up his hood, tied the strings at his neck to tighten it around his head, and used two additional ties to keep the cloak close to his body.

Late in the day, they left the white-capped peaks behind, and the sky grew darker. Axel looked over his left shoulder and saw Kivan resting above the misty sheets of clouds. The moon was full and bright, giving off enough light to turn the clouds below into wispy pink shrouds. But the cloud layers ended where they bumped into the range of snowy mountain peaks. The sight helped him determine the dragons were still flying in a south and west direction. Judging by the ease he found in taking a breath, they were flying at a lower altitude.

Time passed, and more clouds came and gradually disappeared. Down below, he could make out the tortuous, serpentine lines of rivers, large and small, and the valleys surrounding them. At the call from one of the dragons, the group settled to the ground in a grassy clearing near a clear stream. Shaddra spoke to Axel over her shoulder. "We are stopping for only a short while. Get down, stretch your legs, and do whatever else you need to do, but stay close. We will be leaving shortly."

Indeed, the rest was brief. Shaddra called him back less than half an orai after their landing. Again, the dragons and their single passenger rose from the ground and turned their noses to the south. The sight of the ground dropping away beneath them was breathtaking for Axel, but he supposed it to be commonplace to the dragons.

Before them, now, lay a small range of mountains in the distance, and protruding above them, the tops of yet another distant line of mountain peaks appeared—snow-capped and formidable and much higher than the range just behind him.

Upon nearing the closer range of mountains, the dragons again ascended to surmount the obstacle. This time Axel knew what to expect and, wrapping his cloak more tightly about him, worked to control his breathing. Again, the orais passed, and the night began to fade.

On the far side of these mountains, a long valley made an appearance. Down through its center ran a river of substantial size. From horizon to horizon, the forest covered most of the ground below, apart from the tops of the mountain divides. He could clearly determine which parts of the forest were deep Ghanara-dan, which were the more open verges, and where lay the less dangerous upland ground surrounding them.

He estimated they had been flying for more than a full day and knew that he was in desperate need of sleep and was going to be extremely sore in many places when they finally landed. It had been a long time since he had ridden even a skell, so his body was completely out of practice in the skills that would have been helpful for this ride. He could feel knots forming in several key muscles, and his backside was surely going to be bruised.

Ever since leaving Frithden, he saw little indication of human habitation or activity below, apart from a few lights in the distance. Only in this valley did he spot something, which must have been a road, hugging the northern side of a large cliff-like ridge of land or rock, effectively dividing the valley from its northern rim of mountains. His eyes moved along the road, westward, until he saw in the distance what must be a village, or maybe two, and some cultivated fields, situated on the upper end of the long valley. He guessed it to be larger than Frithden, though certainly more remote.

Frithden was loosely surrounded by a few villages, some close to the same size, but mostly smaller and, usually, quite a bit smaller. All of these villages were located within five to twenty tondrins of Frithden, yet the people of Frithden still considered them neighbors. Here, no other settlements were to be seen anywhere in the entire valley.

Axel heard a high-pitched call coming from one of the dragons and answering calls from the others. He wasn't certain which one started the discussion, but he did notice that Hukken, the siris dragon, suddenly sped up. Axel thought the group had been traveling at a very rapid rate of speed, based on how fast the wind hit his face and how fast the ground passed by underneath, but the siris dragon moved away like the group was standing still. At first, he wondered where it was going, but after thinking about the subject, he assumed the dragon was going ahead to their destination to announce their upcoming visit.

Sure enough, the remaining two dragons approached the village, but staying some distance away, they circled to the opposite side and gradually descended. The mountain slopes on this side of the river were covered in Ghanara-dan forest, while the valley, which was their apparent destination, was blanketed with the lighter green of the verges. Humans were unlikely to go into any part of these forests. But, ahead, there were two clearings, a small one and a much larger one, the second large enough to be called a mead. They lay two tondrins beyond the settlement, where he saw a single dwelling in the large clearing along with a substantial outbuilding. Next to the outbuilding lay two paddocks, one obviously for skells and another for ellams. As was the common practice in this kind of country, linear fences of hamaret thorns surrounded the paddocks to keep out killer beasts. A significant part of the larger meadow consisted of planted fields.

The dragons continued flying at a low level until they dropped quickly down to the edge of the larger clearing. Fear streaked through Axel's body, and he instinctively threw his arms tightly around Shaddra's neck.

"My word, Axel!" Shaddra said after coming to a stop. "That is a good way to kill us both. If I had been aware that you intended to attempt to strangle me, I would have arranged for you to ride Torkar. You would think twice before doing that to him!"

"I'm sorry, Shaddra," Axel said. "If you ever drop like that again, please give me some warning. I'll do better, I swear."

Axel quickly slid off Shaddra's back once the messenger dragon was firmly on the ground and standing still. He welcomed the feel of something solid beneath his feet again. He looked around and saw Hukken, next to the forest's edge, standing beside a man who carried a lantern. Even in the darkness, Axel could tell the man was tall, of a size equal to Axel himself, and was once very dark-haired but now showed some gray on his temples and in streaks interspersed throughout. His skin was also dark in color. He was dressed in a simple tunic and breeches and wore strange-looking shoes without buckles or ties. Despite the man's age, he stood straight and gave the impression of being rather fit.

Not knowing what else to do, Axel started walking over to where the man stood. When Axel came within half a landrin of him, the man called out in a loud voice, "So *you're* the one causing all this stir!"

Axel continued walking until stopping just a little more than a stride away. "My name is Axel Fletcher, and I suppose I am the cause, though not by intention."

"My name is Jarrad Dismer, but you may call me Jarrad. I understand you've had a very difficult few days, what with seeing your family and friends killed right in front of you as just the beginning. When was the last time you had anything to eat or drink?"

Axel had to think about this. "Um," he said with a grimace, "I last ate two days before yesterday, prior to the rise of the sunstar, and I have a water flask. It's... been empty for a while."

"I suppose you haven't slept in that time either."

"No, sir, I haven't."

"Let me have a quick word with Shaddra," Jarrad said. "After that, I'll take you where you can get some food and a place to sleep."

"Please give Shaddra and her friends my thanks for saving my life."

"As you wish."

The man walked over to Shaddra, accompanied by Hukken. There, he and the three dragons held a five-minute conference. When Jarrad backed away from the group, the three dragons rose in unison, almost straight up into the air, causing a sudden windstorm all about. Waving a hand at the departing dragons, he sighed noticeably and turned back to Axel.

Jarrad headed straight for an opening in the thick forest and beckoned Axel to follow. When he approached the man, Axel waited for the questions to begin but was surprised when the man said, "Shaddra gave me an overview of what has happened to you over the last few days. You suffered more in that amount of time than anything I could have imagined, and I have an excellent imagination. I'm deeply sorry for your loss."

"There's really not much I can say about it right now," Axel said in a little too crisp of a tone.

"I can see why you would be angry at anyone or anything you've come across. As for now, it appears we need to get you some food first and... a bath. You smell like smoke, and I see ash and blood on your cloak, even in this light. I think there is something much worse that you would like to wash off.

"Somehow, I thought you would need it, so I have a hot bath waiting for you. If you like, I can even give you your meal while you are in the bath."

Axel had been totally overwhelmed this day by all the events and news he'd come across. But now, he seriously thought he had discovered a mind reader.

The walk to Jarrad's house took only fifteen minutes. Jarrad intentionally did not walk fast for Axel's sake, which he appreciated. Axel could tell that Jarrad's natural gait was fast and long-strided, even though he must have been aged somewhere in his early fifties.

The house was constructed of wood, like most homes in the kingdom, but it boasted a large and distinctive design that set it apart. Its many windows, fitted with real glass, gleamed in the sunlight. A broad porch, crafted from flat stones embedded in the earth, extended to the side of the door. On it, two inviting chairs and a small wooden table were arranged, offering a cozy retreat shaded by the canopy of nearby trees during the day. Jarrad led Axel through the door and directly into some kind of room, which had the sole purpose of letting you choose which of four other doors to go through next.

"Uh, Mr. Dismer, could you direct me to the outbuilding? Things are getting a little urgent here."

Mr. Dismer laughed and said, "I thought I asked you to call me Jarrad?"

"Uh, yes, I recall you did."

"Then remember it. The term 'Mr. Dismer' makes me feel old." He showed Axel to a door in the corner of the entry room. "I suggest you go in there and see if you can figure things out. I've been experimenting and have created an indoor waste removal system."

"What! You brought it indoors? What kind of a foolish thing is that?"

"Just go in and check it out," Jarrad said, pointing at the door. "If you don't like it, we'll make some other arrangements."

Axel appeared after a while and said, "All right, where does the water come from, and where does it go?"

"That's the beauty of it. Water from the nearby stream is piped in from some distance up the hill. I shaped the clay pipes and baked them hard myself. They fit together well enough so that they don't leak, and they shoot a large volume of water underneath the... throne, and it whisks away all the waste in seconds. It all flows out through similar pipes, which empty into the stream about five landrins downstream from here. The stream is large enough to absorb the waste as well, just as if it were coming from a yolka crossing over the water down there, and the watercourse enters the Mysura River downstream from the two towns in the valley, so other people are not affected."

"Wow," Axel said with his head cocked in thought. "It might work here, but you'd never get it to work in a big village or township."

Jarrad then opened another one of the doors and announced, "This is what I call my bath room."

Axel followed Jarrad into a room where an iron stove and a long metal tub waited, along with several large pots of water boiling near the edge of the scorching stove. A large barrel stood on a pedestal next to the tub. Axel watched Jarrad pull a wooden plug from a bunghole in the barrel to start a stream of apparently cold water pouring into the bath. As the water flowed, he also dumped water from the pots. Stirring the water with a small paddle, he periodically assessed the temperature by dipping a finger and, later, a hand into the water. When the water reached the right level, Jarrad used light taps from a small mallet to pound the plug back into the bung.

"There you go. If the water is too cold, the remaining pots on the stove are within reach. If too hot, pull out the plug in the barrel. I'll go get your food."

Axel tested the water, which was just slightly on the too-hot side. Not caring about the temperature, he stripped and gingerly stepped into the water. It took a moment or two to get the rest of his body in, but once in, he smiled and collapsed into the most relaxed shape he'd been in for at least three days. He lost track of the time, but the water was still warm when Jarrad brought the food. Laying a wooden plank across the tub, he set out bread, fresh from the oven earlier that day; cheese; and... yes... kiplan stew, lots of it. It only took a glance for him to tell that it was a different recipe from the one used by his Grand Ma'am, but it still brought memories of both Grand Ma'am and Jemmy. He would have stopped everything else and brooded about his family, but a very deep hunger overcame everything that prevented him from digging into this meal. It was wonderful.

Lastly, Jarrad brought in a large glass of wine. Axel wrinkled his nose at seeing this and confessed he preferred beer or ale and was not much of a wine drinker. "I don't do well with the sour taste, and anything with a high alcohol content causes my dragon senses to weaken until the alcohol inside me is gone."

"In that case," Jarrad responded, "I believe you will find this wine to your satisfaction. I made it for myself to match my personal preferences. Try it and see if I am wrong."

Axel did as requested and found the wine to be sweet, juicy, delicious, and clearly low on alcohol content. It was one more piece of evidence that the old man could read minds.

***

Three orais later, Axel woke suddenly and immediately realized the bed in which he lay was not his own. All the events of the day ran through his head, and he saw it all again: the deaths of his Da and Jemmy, the firestorm rising into the sky higher than the tallest trees. One thing, however, stood out more than anything else from the day. One thing beat into his chest more than he could bear. He had killed a man.

It made no difference that the soldier had just murdered his best friend. It made no difference that he saw his father roasted alive only a few minutes before and other soldiers, just like that one, murder everyone he knew. The soldier's death consumed his thoughts, causing him to feel nauseated.

When Axel next woke up, the angle of the sunstar told him it was sometime in the afternoon. The clothes he had been wearing, including the cloak, were all missing, and a different set of clothes was waiting for him at the foot of the bed. The only clothing of his own that remained was his boots and the underclothes he still wore. A voice came from beyond the door to the room. "Your clothes are being washed," Jarrad said. "If you'll hand me your dirty underthings, I'll add them in. You're pretty tall, but you look like you'll fit into some of my larger things, so I set out a few of my extra clothes."

As he dressed in clean garments from the skin out, Axel noticed how the clothes were a tight fit but would do for now.

"A little tight in some places and a little loose in others." Axel responded as he stepped through the door. "They'll do fine until I can find something better."

"You are a growing young man and have muscles in places I can only dream of. From the looks of you, if you bend over too fast, you might rip out some seams in that tunic. How old are you anyway?"

"I'm fifteen, but my sixteenth birthday is only two Kivans away."

"You know, I remember when I was young enough to count the Kivans until my next birthday," Jarrad said. "It seems a long time ago now."

"Now, look, Mister... uh... Jarrad," Axel blurted out. "I need to change the subject. I realize that you and your dragons in the dragon meadow have saved me from certain death, but I've been answering question after question since first meeting the dragons. I need to have some questions answered, too, like, Why am I here?"

"You need to know that, in the first place, the dragons aren't mine. They are free dragons who have escaped from slavery to the king. I just happen to be their friend and advisor.

"I know you have as many questions as I do," Jarrad said. "What say we make a deal? You ask me a question, and I will ask you a question after answering yours. Does that sound fair?"

"Okay. Why am I here?"

"Let me see," Jarrad said, rubbing his chin. The gesture reminded Axel of a mannerism his father used to have. "*You* are here for at least two reasons," Jarrad continued. "The first is, as you noticed, to save you from being killed by the King's Dragon Forces; the second is to find out what is special about you. You *are* special. You know that already."

"Okay, I'm a little different from others. What's so special about that?"

"The answer to that is found in how you respond to my next question."

"Really, how's that?" Axel asked with a genuine, quizzical look on his face.

"Have you ever heard the term '*Son of Ceragon*' before yesterday?"

"Yes, my father said that the lady in the Meadow called me by that name before I was even born, and when I was five years old, she told me directly."

Jarrad's face suddenly jerked with surprise, and his mouth dropped half a thumb. "Have you and your father both spoken with the lady?"

"Not at the same time. When the lady appeared to my father, she primarily shared information about my mother. The lady knew my ma was sick. She wanted him to kill a dragon and bring its blood to my Ma to drink, which he did, and she did. But she died anyway, a while after having me. I never... really... knew her."

Completely oblivious to the look on Jarrad's face, Axel said, "When I was five, the lady appeared to me. She called me by that name and said there was a prophecy about me that I would learn someday and that I had some important things to do. She didn't stay long enough to tell me what they were."

"How long before your birth did your mother drink the blood?"

"Wait, I think I deserve a question answered in here somewhere," Axel said impatiently.

"Please answer the question. After that, I'll give you a few chances to ask some of your own."

"All right. I don't know for sure, but they had to suddenly move from Nine Ashes to Frithden after my Ma drank the dragon blood. Da said he killed the dragon early in the Season of Growth, and I was born in the eighth Kivan of the year. I guess that means at least four Kivans passed before I was born, and it could have been more than that."

"Plenty of time, then, for the dragon's blood to integrate itself into every part of your mother's unborn child—you. The blood became you, and... *you* became the... blood?" Jarrad inhaled deeply and blew cheeks full of air out between his lips as he thought. "That would make you neither man nor dragon."

Axel looked at Jarrad quizzically and said, "I don't understand what you're saying, but it sounds rather ominous."

"Okay, now my turn. You said I could ask more than one, so... what relationship do you have with the free dragons, and how did that all begin?"

"Oh, so you're getting to the meat of things. Let's talk about that over a late breakfast."

They went into the kitchen, where Jarrad grabbed several pieces of wood and heated the stove, while Axel sat down at the table. Axel watched Jarrad crack a bunch of kiplan eggs into a bowl, grab a block of cheese, and shave some into the same bowl where he'd broken the eggs. Reaching for a white ballroot on a shelf, he cut half of it into small pieces and did the same to some small moonstools and to a red-colored fruit, or maybe a vegetable, that looked a lot like a globefruit on the outside, but the insides were nothing like a globefruit. Finally, all the mixed ingredients were placed on a greased flat iron pan on the stove.

Axel watched Jarrad's work with fascination. "What in Etmar's name are you doing?" he asked.

"I'm making eggs for breakfast. This is a new recipe I picked up not long ago. And *you* would probably be advised to watch your language. Not a good idea to offend any of the gods in your situation."

"They seem to be favoring me so far," Axel said with a grin.

"Can you really say that after what you've seen?"

"Uh, it's always been a fault of mine to talk without thinking first."

"I think it's a common fault among those who happen to be fifteen years of age," Jarrad said with a chuckle. "Here, try some of this." He cut some bread and placed several pieces on a plate in front of Axel. Next to that, he added a large amount of the egg mixture and sprinkled a little salt on top. Axel used a spoon to try a sample.

"It's good. What do you call it?"

"I haven't found a name for it as of yet. It's delicious without a name.

"I gather you want to know who I am and why I am hanging around a bunch of dragons." Jarrad asked.

"I guess that sums it up."

Jarrad scooped the remainder of the egg mixture onto a plate for himself, sat down, and began. "It's a long story, but I guess we have some time this afternoon. I was born in the city of Rabianice. I'm sure you know the details, but just for emphasis, I point out that Rabianice is the capital city of Sanara. I emphasize this because my father was initially a member of King Valence's personal Grand Chamber of Advisors and later served King Deroth, Valence's son.

Jarrad continued to tell the tale as he had experienced it, up to where his father took him into his confidence. "The worst part," he said, "was how the king repeatedly proved how he wasn't concerned about the people in his kingdom. He was all about power, and at the heart of that power was his dragon army. Everything else was secondary. I learned of whole villages of his people being sacrificed to his soldiers, who were dressed in enemy uniforms, solely because that would serve his propaganda and increase support for his dragon army. The son may have used the same trick with your village."

"He did," Axel said. "The dragon I killed told me so."

"Ah, then you already know about that."

Jarrad then continued his story, telling Axel about the death of his family, about his contemplating suicide, and about the appearance of the lady.

"You...? You saw the lady?" Axel cried out in excitement. "I knew there had to be others, besides my Da and me, who saw her!"

"You might be surprised at how many others have seen the lady. Not that it's common, and I don't know from any personal revelation, but I believe she does get around to the places she needs to be."

"Where did you see her? Wait... you're not going to count that as another question, are you?"

Jarrad started laughing, and it took him a moment to slow down. Near the end, Axel sort of joined in to show that it really was just meant as a joke.

"Don't worry about that for now, young man," Jarrad said, still shaking his head over what he felt was so funny. "Without questions, a person would never learn anything."

"My memory of the time before and after I met the lady is carved in stone, so I will never forget any part of it. I was at home in my bedroom and had a dagger in my hand, contemplating whose body it should be given the opportunity to adorn, when my bedroom disappeared, and suddenly, I was in the middle of the most dazzling meadow or garden I had ever seen. I could hear the babbling of a brook and the twitter of birds. I saw flowers of many hues, mostly clumped together in little groupings of the same features. And there, in the center, was a beautiful lady with skin like bronze and black hair like ebony. She was dressed in a crimson gown and bore a countenance that drew me in like a flit to a candle.

"I won't tell you the details of our conversation, though I remember every word of it still, for it is still burned upon my soul. I will tell you some of what we discussed and more later if the proper occasion should arise."

"All right then, what *will* you tell me?" Axel asked, shifting around in his seat as if unable to find comfort in any position.

Jarrad coughed in a way suggesting he did not know where to begin. "I, uh, I can say she told me that my future was not to be determined by the blade in my hand. She said that I had work to do in another part of the kingdom, where I must go in secret and with a new identity. She emphasized that I could help bring justice to the king if I faked my death and left Rabianice immediately. She would provide me with a vision showing me where I should go.

"I followed her instructions and converted as much of my now-dead family's assets into coin as I could without raising suspicions. I then left a suicide letter and departed for the southland.

"I followed a vision of the route, given to me by the Lady. That vision is still embedded in my mind some twenty-seven years later. It was a long trip, taking more than a Kivan, and it brought me here to the isolated township of Tarfal. Back then the town had only been settled for a year or two, and Mikell would not start up for another year.

"Still following the lady's instructions, I purchased this valley, a tondrin outside of Tarfal, and built this house. I was close enough to Tarfal that I could ride to town any time I wanted; yet surrounded by this forest, my home was, and still is, private. This little valley became my safe harbor, and that's why I call it Harbor Valley."

"You were honest in saying that it would take a long time to explain who you are," Axel said, "but what is the nature of your relationship with the dragons?"

"Unfortunately, that story is also quite lengthy. Back in Rabianice, the lady informed me that on a certain day, I was to carefully fill a backpack with some odd things and take a hike into the woods. She gave me precise directions and said that in a certain place I would find my future. Recognizing the importance of following her instructions exactly, I complied with her request and ended up about six tondrins from here. There, I discovered what appeared to be a tiny dragon lying dead on a patch of grass. Only the dragon wasn't dead, just on the verge of death. Figuring this was what I was supposed to find, I gave her water and chunks of raw meat I had brought with me. She revived some and muttered a soft thank you.'

"'You can talk!' I remember blurting out.

"Of course, I can!" the dragon said. 'If you can talk, why can't I?'"

"It was Shaddra!" exclaimed Axel. "It's just the kind of thing she would say."

"Excellent guess. After a while, I was able to get her story about how she ended up on that mountainside. It seems she was freed as barely a fledgling from the king's breeding pens by a special person she called Mother Clara. Clara said to fly south and west to find refuge, but unfortunately, Shaddra had never been taught to hunt or take care of herself in the wild. She tried many times to take small game but usually failed. For that reason, she was up on that mountain starving to death.

"As soon as she was again able to walk and fly, I led her to my home and hid her away in my outbuilding. There, she built up her strength, and we discussed ways that might improve her success at hunting. By accident, we discovered that she could change the color of her skin in many intricate ways, just by thinking about it. She could become invisible by matching the colors of her skin on the front side to the colors that lay behind her and vice versa. She could even hide her shadow somehow. That certainly helped improve her success rate at hunting.

"The Lady had also shown me a place, high in the rocky crags of the mountains, where dragons—indeed, many dragons—could build a home. It was undetectable from above and below. Shaddra and I surmised from this evidence that more dragons would be coming with Clara's assistance and that we'd better be ready for them. Sure enough, six Kivans later she found a very confused siris dragon flying circles over the mountains."

"That had to be Hukken," Axel said with a firm nodding of his head. "And, next, she found Torkar, right?"

"That is also an exceptionally good guess," Axel replied. After that, she and her new friends began finding other dragons, struggling to fly over these tall mountains, at a rate of three to six a year. Clara sent representatives of all the dragon species, except draft dragons, and of both sexes. They were all guided to the mountain retreat, which they began to call the Free Colony, and they were taught by other dragons how to hunt for teranas, bush kota, kota, and even yolkas if the dragon was big enough. As the first ones matured, they tended to pair off and start families. Now, thirty years later, we have a colony of over one hundred dragons, with a wide variety of ages.

"I learned how to ride on the backs of dragons. Some of them have taken me up to see the Colony as it is now. It is well hidden, comfortable, at least for dragons, and has many alcoves where dragon families can set up lodging.

"Nearly all the dragons are my friends now, and I get visits from some of them two or three times a week. To avoid detection by humans, they always arrive at night and land in the clearing where you and I first met. I've rigged up a long rope and a bell so they can announce their arrivals."

"Now, that brings us back to you," Jarrad said, looking directly at Axel. "Shaddra told me all that you went through yesterday, for which, as I said, I am deeply sorry. But, if it is all right with you, I would like to hear the story from you. I need to make certain I don't miss anything important."

Axel was not in the mood to describe all that happened over the previous days, but he figured Jarrad deserved to get the whole story. Axel told the tale without leaving anything out.

When Axel mentioned his search for the jewels, Jarrad stopped him and asked, "I suppose you have more than one of these jewels?"

Axel grimaced and nodded his head.

"Oh, you really are in trouble. And you have them with you here?"

"I couldn't leave them back in Frithden. Who knows when I might ever get back there?"

"I suggest you find a hiding place for them out in the forest at the first opportunity. They need to stay secret."

"I'm guessing that after you found the jewels, Shaddra brought you over the mountains, here to me?"

"Yes, that's what happened."

"You know," Jarrad said, "Shaddra is convinced you are the *Son of Ceragon*, whatever that means. The term is apparently significant, and we need to discover precisely what it portends."

He stopped talking and just thought for a moment. It was a long moment, after which he looked over at Axel and said, "I think the real question we need to answer, for now, is what are we going to do with you?"

Jarrad placed a hand on Axel's shoulder and looked him in the eyes. "Shaddra happened to mention some of the extraordinary talents that she observed in you. But what other kind of skills do you have?"

"I can do a little of everything. I think very logically, but I have had little in the way of any formal schooling. My education consists solely of what my grand-ma'am was able to teach me. I can read, write, and cipher. However, I consider myself a fletcher and a bowyer, just like my Da. According to him, I'm pretty good at it."

"That is quite a bow you brought with you. It appears to bend backwards, and I've never seen a quiver like that. Where did you get them?"

"I... made them," Axel responded with a bit of a question in his voice. "I made the quiver using a design of my Da. The bow is my design, and I usually make my own arrows, but these are just some extras my Da made. The process to make this bow required about five Kivans from beginning to end."

"Shaddra said you were rather good with that thing. I use a crossbow, and yes, I know they are illegal, but would you mind if I gave your bow a try?"

"Oh, I'd like to see that," Axel said with a giggle and a big smirk on his face.

"You think that's funny?" Jarrad said with an offended look on his face. "I saw you only have broadheads, but I do have a bow and some bodkins we can use for practice. There is a target range outside. Let me see what I can do with your bow."

"I just want to see you string it."

"What! You're saying I can't string a bow used by a fifteen-year-old youngling? I may be more than three times your age, but don't discount my strength. You grab your bow, and I'll get the arrows."

When they stepped out of the house, Axel stopped to get his bearings. He looked up at the mountains surrounding them on three sides and at the encircling forest. Small clumps of trees poked up here and there, and some cultivated plots were set near two wooden structures. The clearing surrounding the structures was just under a half tondrin in diameter. Two medium-sized streams flowed along the sides of the meadow, meeting near a road heading out of the clearing. "Let me see," he said. "We came here through that little opening in the forest, so the dragon meadow must be over that way."

"The... what?"

"The dragon meadow. You know, the clearing where you said the dragons land."

"Ah... yes, and that road, over there, goes to Tarfal. There is a good place to try out the bow over this way."

They wandered to a clearly marked archery range. At one end there was an area with a bench obviously intended as a place to lay out equipment: crossbows, bows, arrows, whatever; and a clear lane was set out with marked distances of one and two landrins. A large target was set up at the two landrin marker, with a red-painted circle of about one span in width serving as the skellseye.

"Why is it so close?" Axel asked.

"You don't think that a two-landrin distance is appropriate for a bowshot? "Just for fun, let's start with this and go from there."

Axel handed the bow over to Jarrad. It had a string in position to slide along the body up to the notch at the top.

Jarrad put his foot through the space between the bow stock and the string, intending to bend the bow across his knee.

"Wait, stop," Axel said. "You could break either the bow or some of your bones by doing that. Most likely it would be your bones."

"But I've always strung a bow this way," Jarrad protested.

"Use this bowstringer instead," Axel said, handing Jarrad a piece of rawhide about a thumb in width and a stride and a half long. "I'll show you how."

Axel removed the bowstring from the bow and slid one loop of the string onto the bow's upper limb, pulling it down past the indentations used for nocking. He properly nocked the other end of the string in place on the lower limb. "This bowstringer," he said, "is made from chuda hide and is very strong. Now watch."

There was a large loop on one end of the stringer, about a handspan in length, and a little pocket sewn into the other end. Axel simply put the pocket over the nocked lower limb, then placed the loop over the bow *and* the string on the upper limb.

He stepped on the middle of the stringer, which was dangling near the ground, pulled up the bow's grip, and slid the string over and into the upper nock with his right hand. After that, the bow stringer was easily removed. The entire process took less than fifteen seconds to complete. Axel, then, showed how the bow was unstrung by reversing the process.

"Okay," he said, handing the bow and stringer over to Jarrad. "Now, you try."

Jarrad placed the bowstring and the stringer in place as he had seen Axel do, stepped on the middle of the dangling bowstringer, and pulled up on the handle. He struggled for a while but found that the bow bent only slightly.

"All right, all right," he said. "What's the trick? "I followed all your instructions, but the bow isn't bending."

"Oh, it bends. I'll show you." Axel took the bow back from Jarrad, leaving everything in place, and stepped on the middle of the dangling stringer. He proceeded to pull up on the handle and slide the bowstring in place with almost no apparent effort.

"Did you really do what I just saw you do?" Jarrad said, with his head cocked a little to one side and his eyes narrowed. "There is a trick, is there not?"

"I'm sorry, but what you saw is what I did. Here," Axel said, removing the stringer and passing the, now, strung bow back to Jarrad. "Let's see you hit the target."

Jarrad placed an arrow onto the bow and tried to draw back its string. He was able to move the string only about a thumb's distance. "Arggggh!" he shouted and loosed the string. The arrow flew about one-half of the way down the course.

I pulled that string only a thumb's distance, but it still shot the arrow over a landrin downrange!"

"What is the draw weight of the bow you normally shoot?"

"It's five stones," Jarrad replied.

"Oh, I see now why you had a problem," Axel said, shaking his head and grinning broadly enough to show his teeth."

"All right," Jarrad said with a strong huff in his voice and fire in his eyes. "So, what is the weight of this bow?"

"This bow has a draw weight of twelve stones."

Jarrad's mouth fell, and his eyes flared wide open in shock. "I have enough trouble with five stones, yet you can shoot a bow like that?"

"Why would I bother carrying this if I couldn't shoot it?"

Still shaking his head, Jarrad said, "I think I'd better let you show me what *you* and this bow can do."

Axel took back the bow and, picking up one of Jarrad's arrows, looked at it closely. He shook his head and sighed heavily, then placed the arrow on the side opposite from that used by Jarrad.

"Why are you loading it like that?" Jarrad said. "It's backwards."

"Will you please just let me do it my way?" Axel said, finishing the sentence with a quick puff of air from his nose.

"Oh, please do it your way. It's something I want to see," Jarrad said, clearly expressing his irritation at Axel's words.

When Axel drew back the bow—an action he performed with astonishing ease—Jarrad noticed something remarkable: Axel didn't just pull the string to his ear; he did so using only the thumb and forefinger of his gloved right hand. Even more surprising, the arrow itself was steadied by the thumb and forefinger of the left hand gripping the bow. With a fluid motion, Axel released the arrow. It flew straight and true, striking the target dead center and burying itself up to the feathers.

"That was amazing!" Jarrad said. "And you drew back with your thumb and first finger, not three fingers!"

"Using the thumb and first finger of the left hand holds the arrow more firmly, which is especially useful when riding a skell or when running or bouncing on a skell. It also reduces vibration on release. The arrow's flight is more accurate that way. Placing the arrow on the right side of the bow has several advantages, one being I can reload a new arrow after a shot much quicker and easier. That's why I carry a waist quiver on my right side and not one designed for over the shoulder.

"Hey, look at my arrow," Jarrad exclaimed. "Am I even going to be able to pull that out?"

"Don't worry," Axel said, "it will come out."

"How far can you shoot that thing accurately?"

Axel grinned at Jarrad and said, "Let's see." He turned and started pacing back, finally stopping at two hundred and forty strides away from where they started."

"I was going to ask if you *really* thought you could hit a target at six landrins, but I think I'll just shut up and watch. However, I can barely see the center mark."

Axel loaded another arrow with his right hand, drew, and loosed in one swift motion.

"You didn't even aim!" Jarrad said in shock. "I lost track of the arrow, but something tells me you hit the target dead center. I've got to see this! He started off at a run towards the target. Axel followed closely behind.

When they reached the target, Jarrad was a little out of breath, but Axel stood calmly as if he had walked the distance. Just as Jarrad had predicted, the arrow struck the target in the center, only half a thumb away from Axel's first arrow, but this time it had penetrated to about half the arrow's length.

Jarrad slowly shook his head and said, "I made this target with three layers of densely packed straw mats, each a span in thickness and separated with chuda hide. No arrow was supposed to go through. That bow of yours, not to mention your arm, has a powerful punch. There definitely *is* something special about you!"

Axel grabbed his second arrow and calmly pulled it out of the target. Afterward, he did the same with the first. He showed a little strain in so doing, but it came out as he had predicted.

Jarrad rolled his eyes, sighed, and turned back to the house.

"Why did you shake your head when you picked up the first arrow?" Jarrad asked.

"I make my arrows out of specially treated landrin wood. Among other things, that keeps the arrow from wobbling and makes for a straighter flight."

"Among other things?"

"Occasionally, an arrow made from some other kind of wood will shatter near the nock when loosed on this bow."

"Oh, I see how that might happen."

As the two walked together, Jarrad said, "I suppose we still must figure out what to do with you. You said you usually make your own arrows?"

Axel nodded and said, "Yes, I make a special kind of arrow for this type of bow and more traditional arrows for use with bows belonging to other people."

"So, you're both a fletcher and a bowyer?"

"Yes, that's me."

"I assume you have nowhere else to go. No close relatives or friends to take you in?"

"No."

"And the king's soldiers will be looking all over the kingdom for you. That's not a good thing, but apparently, they have no description of you, not even your age."

"The dragon I killed yesterday said I should change my name."

"He did?" Jarrad said in amazement.

"Yes, that dragon force was sent specifically to kill my father."

"Let me think on this for a moment, then."

As they approached the house, Jarrad paused, turning to face Axel. "Axel," he began, "how would you like to stay here and live with me?"

Axel stopped in his tracks, surprise flickering across his face. "I… I'm not sure what to say."

Jarrad smiled warmly. "We could say you're my nephew. You've apprenticed as a fletcher and a bowyer, and now you're looking to start your own shop. No one here has your skills, especially if you can craft bows like the one you're carrying. You'd fit in perfectly."

Axel hesitated. "But you barely know me. Why would you make such an offer after only a day?"

Jarrad's expression turned thoughtful. "First, I like you. I've a feeling we could become great friends. Second, Shaddra spoke highly of you, and her judgment means a lot to me. Third, given our pasts, I can't help but think the gods meant for you to come here. I can help you with your destiny, and you can help me with mine. And lastly, though they don't know it yet, the people of this valley need someone like you."

Axel frowned. "Need me? How could that be?"

Jarrad gestured toward the land around them. "Let me tell you about Tarfal and the Mysura Valley. Tarfal has about twenty-five hundred people, and it started thirty years ago after a big mineral strike in the hills. The valley is surrounded by dense forests, filled with rare southern trees. That led to a booming lumber business and the founding of Mikell, a village that's grown into a township southeast of here with over a thousand people."

He continued, "Once the forest was cleared, farmers discovered the soil was fertile, and the long growing season brought even more people. When I first arrived, this valley was part of the small, peaceful Kingdom of Locarno. But twenty-six years ago, King Deroth conquered Locarno, wiped out its aristocracy, and absorbed the land into his kingdom. Many refugees came here with nothing and rebuilt their lives from scratch."

Jarrad's voice softened. "We call ourselves Mysurans, after the river and valley, and we value our independence. But our biggest challenge here has always been the beasts—deadly creatures, more numerous than anywhere else in the kingdom. People are often at risk, whether working in the forest or just traveling. We lose one or two people per Kivan to these beasts. Crossbows are rare and frowned upon by the king, and traditional bows are too weak, so we mostly rely on spears. But that means waiting until the danger is right in front of us… It's not ideal."

He nodded toward Axel's bow. "If you can make weapons like that, you'd be doing more than just selling—you'd be saving lives. And not just here. We have strong ties with Blatten, a town across the Kulu range. They face the same dangers and would welcome your craft."

Jarrad paused, searching Axel's face. "You'd find both purpose and profit here. So, tell me, what tools and materials would you need to set up your workshop?"

Blinking off the shocked look on his face, Axel said, "I, uh, would need a spring lathe, a grinder, and some common carpenter tools."

"Hmm, we can get the carpenter tools readily enough, but we'll have to send away for the lathe. There's a stream running close to the house. What if we built you a workshop over there?" Jarrad pointed to a line of trees, which appeared to border a stream bordering the little valley. "We can even experiment with some ideas I have on using waterpower to help run some of your tools."

"Waterpower?"

"You'll see what I mean when we get the workshop made."

Axel's eyes widened in surprise, and his mouth dropped. "A workshop?"

"Isn't that what I said? Is there any way to build good bows in something less than seven Kivans?" Jarrad asked.

"I recently discovered a new glue made from Landrin blossoms, and it has a drying process much shorter than the traditional fish glue. That has dropped the required drying time down to two Kivans. I can now make basic power bows in just a little more than that amount of time. They will work very well for five years of active use; more, if properly cared for. If they're built correctly, they are powerful and accurate.

"If there is an abundance of ironwood in this area, I can make steelbows, like this one. They take longer but are much more durable and powerful than the power bows, and they weigh less."

"Ironwood? How can you make a bow out of ironwood? It's full of knots, and it's so brittle I can break a branch, a half-span in thickness, over my knee and not even get bruised."

"You don't understand," Axel said through gritted teeth. "A steelbow is made from very dry landrin wood and some other materials, primarily helmwood. Once the landrin wood is properly shaped into a riser, or 'handle' as you would know it, I glue on specially shaped pieces of helmwood and other materials to make the limbs. Then the whole thing is given a unique "ironwood bath" to ingrain tiny steel threads into the wood of the bow, and especially into the parts made from helmwood. The steel threads strengthen the limbs, which allows me to build a lighter bow without losing any strength. I can also make the bow stronger if I don't mind adding a little weight. There are some other steps involved, but you get the idea.

"I developed the procedure by adding the ironwood bath to a process discovered by the fletcher my grand da worked for all those years ago. He invented what we call 'power bows.' It's kind of the family secret and the reason why our bows have always been so much stronger than those made by other bowyers. I'm only telling you this secret now because I trust you and I think we have common goals. I may tell you more about that secret in the future, if you're interested and it proves useful to the goals we both seem to share."

But Jarrad's mind seemed to be stuck on a single idea. "Steel threads? And you've got these steel threads in that bow of yours?"

"Yes, of course."

"And you can make a lot of these steelbows in a short time?"

"No. But I can make many power bows in a short time. They will do what you want."

Jarrad began to show a bright gleam in his eyes. "Are power bows as strong as the one you carry?"

"No. As I said, this one has a draw weight of about twelve stones. But I can make basic power bows with draw weights anywhere from two to nine stones. However, you must remember it will take a lot of practice and muscular conditioning for a person to easily use bows of four stones or greater."

"My young friend, there are plenty of landrin trees around here and ironwood, too. There are also plenty of strong men. If you could quickly make quality bows, you would become wealthy and a pillar of this community."

"Is that a good idea if I'm trying to hide from the king?"

Jarrad said, "As long as you don't show off like what I just saw you do, you will be just one bowman among many in this township and the kingdom." "The local king's magister ran off about a year ago and is not likely to return, so he won't be a problem. You'll help protect people from killer beasts and arm this community against the kind of attack you saw two days ago. Does that sound like it is worth the effort?"

"I would sure be doing what I know how to do and what I do best."

"Then it's settled. Oh, and you really do need a new name. Any preferences?"

"I... no. No, I don't."

"Okay, let's see... Axel. Axel... Daimon! I knew someone with that last name, and I liked her, or, uh, this person, a lot. What do you think of Axel Daimon?"

"I like Fletcher better, but that one will do."

"Good! Let's get started! We'll need to travel to a big city to pick up your tools... and mail a letter to me announcing your forthcoming arrival!"

"What? How are you going to do that? We're in the middle of nowhere here."

"Oh, we can do it because we have friends. Let's start by piling wood for a fire over there in that pit. We won't light it until this evening, but we will need to build a big one."

Jarrad and Axel lit the fire when the sunstar started to fall behind the mountains. Less than an orai later, as darkness settled in, a bell hanging on the outbuilding began to ring.

"Wow," Axel said, "whichever dragon came was as silent as an owl."

The two walked out to the dragon landing area and discovered, to no surprise, that it was Shaddra. Jarrad explained how they needed to travel to Helmand, a big city on the coast, to buy supplies. They would need to spend a day there and return that evening.

"Hukken would do anything you ask, Uncle Jarrad," Shaddra said. "Would tomorrow evening be a good time?"

"My friends, you are too accommodating," Jarrad said. "If it isn't an inconvenience, we would be glad to accept your offer."

"Does this, perhaps, mean that young Axel will be staying awhile?" Shaddra asked with a sly smile on her face.

"Yes, it does," Jared responded, showing his smile, "and maybe he will stay for longer than just a while."

"I like that idea," the dragon said. "I very much want to get to know him better." She took off, as usual, straight up in the air. Though it was very dark this night, with Kivan not yet showing her face, Axel watched Shaddra's flight until she leveled off and turned to the west.

Jarrad put his hand on Axel's shoulder and said, "It should take about three orais to fly to the forest outside of Helmand, where we won't be seen. We will stay at an inn for the night, get our shopping done during the day, mail the letter, and return the following evening. You said you could write. It would not be a good idea to have this letter in my handwriting."

"Yes," Axel answered, "My grandma'am taught me. I think I can write well enough to make the letter look genuine. But you'd better tell me what to say."

Chapter Seven

MASTER OF SANARA

Deroth, King of Sanara strode briskly up to the high seat in the Grand Chamber of Advisors. There he stopped and placed his hands on his hips with arms akimbo. He scanned his eyes slowly across the faces of the nine Grand Advisors of the Chamber. He kept them there for longer than necessary before he announced, "Be seated."

The nine Grand Advisors promptly took their seats behind the large conference table in the room, but they remained rigid, sitting in a military-style "Attention!" position. Only their eyes moved.

The King did not stir but again scanned his eyes across the nine solicitors. This time his eyes stopped at each person as if giving him time to examine his heart and measure it against some unknown standard of weight on the other end of a balance beam.

"I regret to announce," Deroth said in a loud and grave voice, "that a remote village in the Irlan province, by the name of Frithden, has been attacked by dragon forces from Kolodra. The village was completely surprised and unable to defend itself. Accordingly, it and its population of more than three hundred villagers were completely destroyed. The only good news we have received is that the king's magister, who was assigned to Frithden, happened to be visiting friends in Tyrinne, along with his retinue, when the tragedy occurred and thereby missed being included among the casualties. I hereby demand that all advisors having charge of the various ministries use your offices to disseminate this news to the entire population of Sanara. Have them make certain that town and village defenses are up to standard.

"You need to know this is evidence that Kolodra, in coordination with Mandara, is attempting to weaken the Kingdom of Sanara. Our spies have witnessed the massing of Kolodran troops and dragons. Kolodra has increased the breeding of dragons of war and is raising money to buy more jewels from the Sullyalil priests. Our agents have also found indications of increased dragon breeding in Mandara. Such activity can only mean that Kings Altrince of Mandara and Branton of Kolodra are planning a combined assault on Sanara sometime within the next five to ten years.

"I regret this means we are now forced into doing the same as our enemies. We must increase the production of dragons and raise money ourselves to purchase more jewels! Both tasks are difficult to accomplish, so I command you to turn the minds of your departments toward how those problems can be resolved.

"Are there any questions?"

No hand or voice was raised from the nine.

"In that case, I dismiss you, but I request that you submit reports of your actions within the next week."

Members of the council rose and began filing out of the room, exchanging quiet whispers as they did. Two of the advisors remained behind.

One of these was High Commander Kalow, who oversaw the kingdom's armed forces. The other was Intelligence Adjutant Brasa, who directed all intelligence and disinformation services in the kingdom.

Once the room's guards closed and secured the doors behind them, the king strode to the end of the table where they sat and said, "Okay, gentlemen, give me your reports regarding the Frithden raid. You first, Kalow."

The Commander, bald, slightly overweight, and dressed in an immaculate grey uniform, said, "Our Special Missions Force attacked Frithden, dressed in Kolodran Dragonrider uniforms as planned and according to schedule. Their specific instructions were to destroy the village and its occupants, with special attention to killing Alton Fletcher and his family. The force was given a description of Fletcher and warned of his skill with a bow. They also clearly knew the location of the Fletcher home within the village. That information was provided by the village magister."

"What were the results?" Deroth queried.

"The village was destroyed, and Fletcher, along with his family, was killed. But unfortunately, that didn't happen until after Fletcher downed two of our dragons.

Both dragons and their riders were slain. A third rider was struck and killed, but the dragon returned to the compound along with its jewels."

Deroth's face flushed bright red, and he erupted in foaming anger. "You mean you let this man, who had already killed two of my children, murder two more... along with three flying officers?"

"Unfortunately," continued Kalow, trying to hide his unease, "the man possessed a powerful bow and had an uncanny ability to use it effectively. No archer in the entire kingdom could match his skill! But we confirmed he was killed by a fireball attack from a siris dragon."

"What about the man's workshop? You were to spare the workshop so we could examine the nature of this fletcher's powerful bows."

"The dragons spared the workshop as directed, sire," the commander said in a weaker voice, "but the firestorm burning the village engulfed the shop, destroying it and its contents completely, except for part of a single charred bow. So far. We have not been able to determine any major difference between it and other bows produced in the Kingdom."

Deroth glared down at the commander, and his upper lip curled noticeably. "Do you have anything else to report?"

"We also lost Flying Officer Haskan," the commander said with beads of sweat running down his bald head, "who was the special group sharpshooter tasked with eliminating any villager not already killed by the dragons. He was using a crossbow as his primary weapon and was killed by means of a standard bowshot."

"He wasn't another one of Fletcher's victims?" the king said, with a deep frown.

"No, his location was too far away from where Fletcher stood."

"Was the second bowman also dispatched?"

"We don't know, Sire. No one in the Special Force saw who delivered the killing arrow."

"Brasa!" the king shouted. "Can you add anything to what Kalow has reported?"

"Yes, Sire! Brasa responded confidently, looking the king directly in the eyes. We sent Special Force ground operatives back to Frithden, or rather what was left of it, to scour the area in search of the missing jewels. I can report there is evidence that one, and possibly two, villagers escaped the firestorm."

"How do you know this?" Deroth queried.

"The four jewels from the downed dragons and riders have been confirmed as lost. All four of them were cut from the dragons or taken from an officer by an escapee. Also, the person responsible for killing Officer Haskan was outside of the village at the time of the attack. We have found tracks and a blood spot indicating there were originally two at that place. Haskan killed or seriously wounded one, but the second individual must have been able to return a bowshot. It was accurate enough to strike Haskan but not kill immediately. Haskan was later found dead, dangling from his harness, when his siris dragon returned from duty. The person or people who took the jewels may have sought them simply for their monetary value on the underground market or have taken them specifically to give or sell to our enemies.

"The person shot by Officer Haskan on the hill may have survived his wounds. We say this because someone dug seventeen graves in the local cemetery after the attack. All the bodies in those newly dug graves were victims of either fire or smoke. None were victims of a crossbow.

"As for finding the one or ones who escaped, the only factual evidence we have is the arrow, which killed Officer Haskan. It is a hunting-type arrow, rather than a quarrel for a crossbow, well-crafted and with some distinguishing marks that may help it be traced. The rear portion of the arrow was turned slightly thicker than the front, very much like a crossbow quarrel, but longer, of course. We will send it to the most knowledgeable fletchers in the realm and see if it can provide any leads. Although it took us fifteen years, the arrow ultimately served as the evidence that led us to Fletcher and revealed that he had developed a bow with power comparable to that of a crossbow. We found that arrow outside of the Reserve, stuck in a tree next to the Tekla River."

"Yes, yes, Brasa," Deroth said with a wicked grin. "As the spirit of this Fletcher person learned to his dismay, I can always count on you for the detail work that locates an enemy. I only wish you were also able to learn the identities of those who helped Fletcher back fifteen years ago. There had to be someone."

"Alas, sire, that information has still eluded us."

Deroth placed his hands behind his back, turned, and paced to and fro behind his two advisors. They did not move their heads to look at him. After a moment, he stopped just to the side of Brasa and said, "Where do you stand regarding discovering who incited the mob that forced our magister in the Mysura Valley to flee with little more than the clothes on his back?"

"I must say," Brasa replied with a slow shake of his head, "that the townships of Tarfal and Mikell are very tightly knit communities, and I have not been able to place any agents into their ranks. Those people immediately recognize anyone who is not from that valley, and newcomers are closely watched until either leaving the valley or proving dependable. Four of my agents have returned from the Valley, claiming that suspicious neighbors and prying officials have made their lives miserable."

"Hmph! Then let's not even bother with finding the real culprits," Deroth muttered with a frown and a slight twitch of a lip. "Find a way to eliminate those people—all of them. Kill the people and remove the towns from the map. After Frithden, it's a little too soon for a direct attack. Find another way to do it and make certain that no evidence can trace the cause back to us."

Chapter Eight

NEW MAN IN TOWN

Five evenings after the attack on Frithden, Jarrad and Axel traveled to Helmand on the backs of dragons. They landed in the dark about half a tondrin outside the city. The place was a forested area that was so dark Jarrad had difficulty keeping from bumping into trees.

Axel had an excellent sense of direction and knew the route to travel based on what he had seen from the air. He could also see in the dark. Before venturing from the landing spot, he took careful note of their surroundings so the two humans could find this place on the following night for a rendezvous with the dragons. The problem with Jared's night blindness was solved when Axel found a long stick and, giving one end to Jarrad, was able to lead the way into Helmand.

Once in town, there was enough visibility from lighted windows and a few streetlamps for Jarrad to locate an inn he knew. The owner did not seem to mind the lateness of the orai, but they missed the evening meal. Happily, they were able to grab something to eat from a nearby tavern.

The next morning, after a quick breakfast at the inn, the first stop was at a shipping company, which provided a wagon and driver to carry all the things to be purchased during the day. After securing the wagon, they started running down the items on Axel's list of required tools and finding the shops selling those items—things like mallets, saws, draw shaves, wood chisels, rasps, files, and such. Axel was amazed that Jarrad chose to buy only new, quality tools from the best shops and purchased many tools on just the possibility they might be used. Axel shuddered at the cost.

"Do you really have to buy three of everything?" Axel asked Jarrad. "That's going to cost a whole bunch of money, and there's only going to be me working in this shop."

"Don't worry about how much we spend," Jarrad assured him. "I can easily afford everything on this list and many things you didn't bother to add. Also, even though you see your business as starting out small, you may find a need for expansion much sooner than you expect."

Axel had no idea what was meant by the phrase 'things he didn't bother to add' until Jarrad turned into a clothier's store. Jarrad looked closely at Axel, who was wearing the set of now-clean clothes he had worn the day of Frithden's destruction. "You need to portray the image of someone who has always lived in a city and has come from a family that would never have settled in a place like Frithden. No one who meets you must ever think you originally came from there. Look around as we walk on these streets. Remember what it is like. Learn as much as you can. Copy the way people move and speak here."

Jarrad purchased several outfits of varying materials for Axel. Some were durable work clothes, others for everyday wear, and still others were for more dressy situations. Several pairs of shoes and boots were added to the pile of things. Everything fit perfectly. Another surprise came when Jarrad started buying even more of the same clothing, this time in larger sizes. When Axel asked about these, Jarrad laughed and responded, "You are big for your age, but I think you're going to grow some yet. You'll need these pretty soon, and you won't find them in the Valley."

"Are we done yet?" Axel asked in exasperation.

Jarrad looked up at the mop of hair covering Axel's head and smiled. We have two or three more stops to make, and we are through with our shopping.

Just under an orai later, Axel ran his hand through the hair that remained on his head and frowned. "This feels all wrong," he complained.

"You must remember," Jarrad said, grinning widely, "that you are no longer a simple villager, nor just a boy, but a young businessman, and you have an image to project. People need to think of you as older than you are and have confidence in you."

"And short hair will do that?"

"Believe me, after a couple of weeks you'll never want to go back to long hair."

"I'll believe that when it happens."

The last shopping stop was at a tool and machinery business that specialized in more complex devices. Together, they selected a quality spring lathe. Jarrad saw a grinding stone, which he insisted was just what Axel's business needed, and he purchased it too.

By the time they finished with that store, the wagon was full. "Now, we'll go to the shipping agent," Jarrad said, "and have these things crated and readied for transport to Tarfal."

As the daylight orais waned, they made certain to post the letter Axel had written and found another inn for a meal. When darkness fell, Axel, again, took the lead and found the agreed-upon meeting place. The dragons were there waiting for them.

"This is what I call service," Jarrad said to Shaddra. "It's pleasant to have dependable transportation at your convenience."

Shaddra just rolled her eyes and said, "Remember, dragons used to eat humans. I hear their flesh was rather salty, but I am sure we could acquire the taste again."

Axel burst out into roaring laughter, while Jarrad just shook his head and grinned.

***

Axel's letter reached the Mysura Community Council Building, the designated delivery point for all mail in the Tarfal area, seven days later. Jarrad stopped by that afternoon to pick up his mail and, upon finding the letter, proceeded to open it there in the public building, right in front of several people he was well-acquainted with from the township.

"I'll be," he said in a moderate but happy, resounding voice to an audience that seemed to pick up that something new was happening. "My sister's son is going to come here to stay with me. You know, my sister and I had discussed the possibility of him coming to stay with me someday, and now it is actually happening. He is a master fletcher and a bow maker; young but highly qualified. All of you will really like him." Before the setting of the sunstar, everyone in Tarfal, and likely the entire valley, knew Jarrad's nephew would be coming to town.

The wagonload of tools and supplies packed in large crates arrived ten days later. The delivery was addressed to Axel Daimon in care of Jarrad Dismer. With the tools and supplies also came a skell. It was a splendid and sturdy breed that Jarrad and Axel picked out when in Helmand. However, the skell did not arrive at the same time as the wagon. Instead, Jarrad had paid the shipping company to send an extra wagon driver, who happened to detach the skell about ten tondrins east of Tarfal and ride it on trails bypassing the populated areas so that no member of the community saw its arrival at the Dismer property. On the delivery wagon's return trip, the second driver just hid in one of the now emptied crates as the wagon passed through Tarfal.

The next arrival to the township was none other than Axel Daimon. He had taken the new skell back along the same trails by which it had come and turned west upon striking the main road. After entering Tarfal, Axel rode up to the easy-to-find Council Hall and asked the people there if they could direct him to where his Uncle Jarrad Dismer lived. Thereafter, Jarrad really became Uncle Jarrad, and Axel began to feel another thread of affinity with the dragons.

While waiting for the arrival of the wagon, Axel very gently asked Shaddra if one of the dragons could help him make the trip back to Frithden. Shaddra asked why and was told he needed to take care of his family and friends. Three nights later, Shaddra flew him over the mountains and stayed to help him dig the graves for 298 people, who once lived in a village known as Frithden. Grand Da and Grand Ma'am were buried next to Alton and Jemmy out in the forest. The task kept them busy for six days.

Axel thought about also moving the remains of the mother he never knew over to join the husband she cherished but decided that by now she and Da had already found each other in the Halls of the Gods and decided to let her stay where she lay.

Through the trials of those few days, Axel and Shaddra created a most incredible friendship.

***

Axel and Jarrad were having breakfast the day after Axel's "arrival" in Tarfal when Jarrad said, "Two agents of the king and a half dozen soldiers came into town yesterday asking whether any strangers have appeared in town over the last few weeks."

Axel's face blanched, and sweat appeared on his forehead. "So, what did people say?"

"You need to understand that people here in the valley have no love for the king. Besides, they know that you are my nephew and, hence, no stranger. Everyone the agents talked to gave variations of the same answer: They knew of no strangers appearing in the towns. It was extremely fortunate that the dragons brought you here. You are safe in the confines of the Upper Mysura Valley."

Axel's face visibly relaxed with relief. "In that case, I owe you—and them—a great deal of thanks."

Jarrad waved a hand dismissively. "No need. I have no love for the King myself. Besides, you're starting to grow on me. You're… intriguing, Axel. No one's ever made me feel quite like this before."

Axel flushed, uncertain. "Well, thank you, then. I mean it."

Jarrad smiled. "You're welcome."

Then, with a sudden shift, Jarrad asked, "By the way, have you hidden your jewels yet?"

Axel blinked in surprise. "What? Uh… no, not in the forest or anything. I just buried them out in the old outbuilding."

Jarrad frowned. "That's hardly secure if someone's truly after them."

Axel hesitated, then nodded. "You're right. I should find a better spot."

Jarrad studied him for a moment, then arched an eyebrow. "Tell me, Axel, what do you really know about the Jewels?"

Axel's expression darkened. "Enough to know they've brought death—too many deaths. People, and dragons as well."

Jarrad set his teacup down and stared thoughtfully into space. "I've spoken with the dragons. They've shared some things about the Jewels with me."

"Like what?" Axel asked, leaning forward.

"They always come in pairs," Jarrad replied. "One is the master—called the Bechar. The other is the slave, the Minqar."

Axel's eyes widened. "My gran da told me a little about that. He served as a dragonrider for the king."

"Did he, now?"

"I'd forgotten most of what he said until Shaddra reminded me back in Frithden."

"And what else did your GranDa teach you about dragons?" Jarrad prompted.

"A lot, actually. He made sure I learned the Code of Orders for a Flying Officer."

Jarrad's curiosity was piqued. "What's that?"

Axel recited, "The first five orders are: one—Find me. Two—Present me. Three—Protect me. Four—Take me. Five—Attack."

Jarrad leaned in, curiosity evident. "Interesting. Could you clarify what each command signifies?" "Gran da never really went into a lot of detail about them, but I figured out that 'Find me' means come stand on my right side so I can mount you. 'Present me,' means to stand for inspection. 'Protect me' means to protect the rider using the specific techniques to be given next. 'Take me' means to take the rider somewhere. Finally, 'attack' means to direct an attack at a specified target using the techniques that will be provided next.

"Just think, you've replaced all of that with 'Let me mount,'" Axel concluded, "and the dragon does the rest."

"Not exactly," Jarrad said. "Sometimes, it's more like a negotiation process."

"Oh. That makes sense."

***

A few sycles after Axel's first appearance in town, the Tarfal township feted him with a community-wide party on the open ground next to the Council Building. The Upper Mysura Valley was a mundane place with little to excite people, so even small events inspired celebration. Since Axel was starting an important business, he was treated just as if he were an adult. The chairman of the community council personally introduced him to every member of the council and their families. He met the people running the larger businesses and danced with their daughters, several of whom looked him over carefully. There was food and music and plenty to drink. Axel was not used to drinking strong beverages, so he carefully accounted for every glass that was handed to him. It was a smart move. By the time the event was winding down, there were many, even members of the council, who were going to make it home only with the assistance of others.

The next day, Jarrad and Axel returned to planning for Axel's new workshop and business. Work started within a sycle after that, and the building went up quickly. The construction used beams, planks, and wooden shingles, all purchased from the local sawmill, and local carpenters from the town did most of the work. The building included an office area, with a comfortable desk and planning table, and a large open workshop with six fully equipped worktables and some machinery, which included a lathe and grinder.

On Jarrad's suggestion, they built the workshop close to a small, nearby stream but outside the flood zone. The major sawmill operation in Mikell recently brought in the concept of using waterpower to make saw blades move up and down swiftly. The new power source resulted in the straight and rapid cutting of logs into usable lumber. That operation gave Jarrad an idea as to how to speed up Axel's production of bows and arrows. Jarrad bought parts, including blades, from the sawmill and built a water wheel and smaller sawmill on his land. It was close enough to the new workshop to support its woodcutting needs but far enough away so that the noise was not distracting. He also connected the water wheel, by means of wooden gears, to the workshop, so it could turn the new lathe and grinder.

The shop was finished within two Kivans, but the diversion dam, the sluice canal, the water wheel, and its support building required yet another two. As soon as they could, Axel and Jarrad started hiring local people to supply the new business with the materials required in the making of bows and arrows. There was a need for ellam, yolka, or kota horns, which were used for nocks and bracing the "limbs," or, more specifically, the ends of the two arms of the bows being assembled. Fortunately, these horns did not need to be procured from their original four-footed owners. The butchers and hunters of the city had simply been throwing them away as trash for many years. Axel hired local children to search through rubbish heaps around the town for fresh horns at a copper button for each four-horn set. The "button" was the lowest denomination coin in the realm, its value being set at one-tenth that of a "full copper trone" or just a "copper," which was the most common coin in use.

Furthermore, with Jarrad's guidance, Axel purchased kiplan and sorset feathers from the butchers, steel arrowheads from the metalsmiths, bowstrings spun from long, shaggy ellam hair by housewives on their spinning wheels, and misch wax from the owners of misch hives.

Late in the year, the new businessman hired lumbermen and wagons to locate fallen landrin trees before the winter weather halted travel into the forests. They were accompanied by Axel, who went along to point out which trees met his requirements. Jarrad was there, too, just to learn something new.

"Okay, Axel," Jarrad said, "I know that after releasing seeds into the wind, landrin trees die, and their underground roots wither away quickly, causing the tree to fall. So, which of the fallen trees are right to use in bow-making? The ones that haven't rotted all look the same to me."

"Fallen landrins won't start rotting for about a year," Axel explained. "The wood continues to dry out over the year and will be perfect for making both longbows and arrows in the last Kivan of that year. The challenging part will be finding longer sections of trunk without protruding branches. Don't worry, I know how to pick out the right trees from the wrong."

They came back from the forest, accompanied by six landrin logs. Each measured about three strides in length and a single stride in thickness; one of the logs would be used to make arrows only.

The evening of their wood-cutting excursion into the forest, having cleaned up from their outing and eaten a satisfying meal, Uncle Jarrad and his new nephew, Axel, were resting on comfortable chairs set out in front of the former's cabin home. The red moon, Kivan, was just rising over the ridgeline to the east. Both were wearing faces that were nearly full. The sky was dark, but the meadow surrounding the cabin was still clearly visible in the red light.

"Can you give me an idea as to how many bows you can make from the five sections of wood we brought in?" Jarrad asked.

"No way to be certain," Axel responded, "but they were all free from the branches that create knots. Bows can't be constructed from wood containing knots. I'm thinking we'll cut close to a hundred blanks from each log. The only way to get the precise number is to go ahead and make the cuts. Remember, I've always started out before by splitting the logs into pie-shaped sections. That wastes some of the wood. I have no idea whether cutting the logs, rather than splitting, will result in more useable blanks."

Jarrad became silent, and his face darkened significantly. Axel noticed right off and said, "All right, what's bothering you now?"

"There are two things I have on my mind. The first is a question regarding your skills. It's a personal question, so I wouldn't be shocked if you don't answer.

Axel sat straight up in his chair and looked over at his new friend with eyes full of curiosity and concern. "Give me a try," he said. "How can I tell if it is too personal without knowing what it is?"

Jarrad also sat up straight and took a deep breath, exhaling the air slowly as if hesitant to ask the question at all. "With all these abilities you've received, courtesy of your dragon blood, can you tell how much of who you are has come from your birth parents and how much is a direct result of what has been gifted to you?"

Axel was completely surprised by the question. "I—I'm afraid I truly don't understand the question."

Jarrad grimaced and shook his head. "It's a bit difficult to express what's really on my mind. Take, for example, your skill with a bow. You are amazingly strong and skilled. Did you have to work to develop that skill, or did it just come to you?

"In other words, am I some kind of a god or just a human being?"

"Ouch. Putting it that way does come to the point. I really don't want to cause offense."

Pinching his lips together, Axel turned his mind inward and thought. "The fact is," he said after a moment, "I don't know how to answer the question. I never obtained anything without working for it. I started as an apprentice in my Da's shop when I was eight. Rarely would there be a day when I didn't work ten orais a day, either in the shop or at my grand ma'am's knee learning to read, write, cipher, and know the mysteries of the gods. I spent another one to two orais each day practicing with a bow or other weapons. I worked hard for what I achieved and progressed little by little. My progression in all these things was certainly faster than with other young people, and perhaps it went farther due to my dragon blood. I've never tried to boast of it or use my skills to demonstrate any superiority."

"That appears to answer my first question," Jarrad said, bearing a broad smile on his face. "Thank you."

"So, what else do you have on that devious mind of yours?"

"Me devious? I would never…"

Axel placed a fist to his mouth and coughed loudly, then lowered his fist to reveal a knowing grin.

"Okay," Jarrad said, "I've been thinking about your father's special warnings concerning the jewels and Shaddra's words saying there are always two jewels in a matched set. I recently spoke with her, again, about them. As I told you before, she called one of the stones 'Bechar' and the other was the... 'Minqar.' The Bechar is the controller, and it is shaped long and cube-like. It is usually worn on a short necklace draped around the neck of the dragonrider. You found two of those in Frithden.

"The Minqar is the acceptor or receiver. You have four of them in your possession. A dragon wears a Minqar on its neck from the time of birth and therefore soon learns it must obey commands given by the person holding the associated Bechar."

"How does Shaddra know all this stuff?" Axel asked.

"You'd be surprised by what Shaddra knows." She's a perfect spy because she can, literally, blend in anywhere. She also speaks with other dragons."

"You mean she speaks with dragons who wear jewels? I thought their jewels would keep them from that."

"Yes, dragons rarely talk to humans, anyway, but if they tried, I'm sure their regular speech would be controlled. Nevertheless, they have a way of talking that humans cannot hear. For some reason, that kind of speech isn't controlled."

Nodding his head, Axel said, "I've heard them talking in voices pitched too high for most humans to hear. I call it their "high speech.""

"I have recently learned," Jarrad said, "that Shaddra has been able to use the high speech you describe to learn many things, which are important for us."

"Do you know what happens when a dragonrider is killed?" Axel asked.

"No. Cannot say that I do."

"As I said, my GranDa was a dragonrider. I remember him saying once that, if a rider is killed, he will usually fall off the dragon and be caught by a tether of strong line attached to the dragon's saddle. Occasonally, the forces were powerful enough that the line simply snapped. I saw it happen in Frithden. But that's supposed to be rare. The dragons were always given a command through the jewel stating that if they lose their rider, they are responsible for retrieving both themselves and the body of their rider back to the headquarters of the King's Dragon Forces at all costs. Grand da said they could be vicious in defending a dead rider."

"Frithden showed us that the king's forces go out of their way to retrieve lost jewels," Jarrad said. "I suppose they can be used again if you have a new baby dragon and two slightly used jewels."

"Guess so. What, then, is the question you're building up to here?" Axel asked in a frustrated tone.

"This question has two parts. The first is, what happens if the bechar, as you called it, gets destroyed?"

Axel curled his lip in surprise. "How would I know?"

"Has Shaddra told you what gives the bechar such power over the minqar and, hence, over a dragon?"

"No. Of course not."

Rubbing the stubble on his chin, Jarrad paused for a moment in thought and then continued. "But there must be a reason, some kind of power that a bechar uses to make the minqar enslave a dragon. Hence, my second question … what would happen if we destroyed one of the Bechars?"

"Wait a moment," Axel said in a plaintive voice. "My Da told me to hang onto these jewels."

He told you to hang onto the minqars he gave you. He never said anything about any bechar."

"But Shaddra did. She said...."

"Shaddra was worried about two things: first, your safety, and second, keeping the secret that you have any jewels at all!"

"What do you want?"

"I think we should destroy the bechar from one of your matched sets and see what happens to its Minqar. We are never going to use it, and we certainly don't want anyone else doing it either!"

"You have a point. Do we tell the dragons?"

"Only after it's done."

"As you wish, Uncle Jarrad. We'll give it a try on one jewel, and that's it. Right?"

"Correct. Meet me in the workshop."

At this, Axel left the house and went to the outbuilding to retrieve two of his jewels: a matched Bechar and Minqar. He met Jarrad in the shop after digging them up from beneath the dirt floor.

Jarrad took the Bechar and placed it on the head of an anvil. He followed the action by picking up a very heavy steel mallet. "Ok," he said. "Are you sure you're willing to let me do this? They are, technically, your jewels now and worth a fortune."

"Unfortunately, I do not value lives in the same way that I value money. Bash that thing to the Halls of Archos!"

Jarrad hesitantly approached the anvil. He wanted to look away but knew that could cause a miss or a glancing blow. He had to strike home, so he watched what he did.

Afterward, the two men stared at the pieces left behind by the mallet. They did not spray all over but stayed together where the jewel once stood in its whole form. The pieces were fine, like sand, and of a uniform size. Interestingly, they were no longer red but white or even clear.

Axel reached for the Minqar and stared in wonder. Even as the pieces of its bechar were no longer red, it, too, was now clear and sparkly.

Jarrad whispered in a shaky voice, "Do you suppose we've destroyed whatever power this thing once had?"

"I think what you think is right. But we will never know until we can try it on a real dragon. Hey, I'm going after the other set."

"Are you sure you...?"

Axel was gone before Jarrad could finish his sentence.

When Axel returned, he carried the other matched pair of jewels. They smashed the bechar this time and obtained precisely the same result as before. Now, they had four minqars, but two of them were a deep red, while the other two were white and as clear as glass. Even if there was still some kind of power in these white jewels, they could never again be used for the nefarious purpose for which they were created.

***

A loud ringing sounded from a bell posted on the side of one of the barns.

"It seems we have visitors," Axel said. "Should I grab a lantern for you?"

"You know," his uncle replied, "after all the hiking we did today, I was just in the mood for another little stroll. Yes, please. Bring a lamp."

The walk to "Dragon Meadow," as Axel had dubbed it during his first visit, took less than fifteen minutes to cover the ten landrins from the house. When Uncle Jarrad and Axel emerged from the forest trail into the meadow, they saw that the name was well chosen. There, standing proudly, were three dragons—remarkably familiar to the humans—Shaddra, Hukken, and Torkar.

"Uh-oh," Jarrad murmured to Axel. "Looks like they're ganging up on us."

"Hello, my friends," he said in a louder voice. "To what honor do we owe this visit?"

Torkar looked seriously at Jarrad and said, "You may not feel so honored once we tell you our purpose."

Axel and Jarrad gave each other quizzical looks. Turning their eyes back up to the dragons, Jarrad asked, "And who is going to be the spokesp... dragon, representing this august group?"

"It seems I have been outvoted," Hukken said, "and, therefore, I am representing the others. There has been extensive discussion among the free dragons, along with many expressions of dissatisfaction regarding the fact that the Colony has existed for thirty years without any representation from draft dragons.

"Hukken," Jarrad said, "you know draft dragons have only small, nonfunctional wings. They cannot fly, so Mother Clara hasn't been able to help any draft dragons *take flight*. Has it not been only three sycles since you received the last arrival—a siris dragon, wasn't she?"

"We surely realize," Hukken continued, "that Mother Clara has done all she can to send us more free dragons. But we believe the situation has changed enough that an attempt to bring out a draft dragon or two is now possible."

"How has the situation changed?" Jarrad said, with surprise on his face.

"Why, we now have the *Son of the Great Ceragon* living among us, and the *Daughter of the Great Ceragon* is with Clara; there is great portent in these events."

"What?" Jarrad exclaimed. "There is a *Daughter of Ceragon*, too?"

"Um," Axel said, looking at Jarrad with a grimace on his face, "I probably should have told you about that." He turned to the dragon and asked, "Hukken, how do you know that the *Daughter of Ceragon* is with Clara?"

The new siris dragon brought news that, before she fledged, she had lived with the *Daughter of Ceragon* in Clara's home."

"Okay, Axel," Jarrad asked with a firm set to his jaw, "how did *you* first learn about this Daughter?"

Shaddra answered Jarrad's question. "I told him. I told him there is a foretelling among dragons about a *son* and a *Daughter of Ceragon*, who will bring freedom and justice to both the dragons and the humans of Tamerel."

"But how could a newly fledged dragon know about the foretelling?"

"Uncle Jarrad," Shaddra answered, "the young siris dragon did *not* know about it. But she kept talking about this human youngling, named Eleth, who was so special and smelled like a dragon. The rest of us were able to figure it out."

"All right. I accept there is a *Daughter of Ceragon*," Uncle Jarrad muttered. "How does this relate to having draft dragons take flight?"

At this point, Torkar, who was fighting not to blurt out something, managed to lose control. "The actual words of the foretelling, as given by the great Ceragon, himself," he growled with a tinge of frustration in his voice, "are that 'the *Son* and *Daughter of Ceragon* shall guide the *family* of free dragons and bring freedom and justice to both the dragons and the humans of Tamerel, else no one shall!' Every dragon knows we just cannot be a true family of free dragons unless *all* the progeny of the *Great Ceragon* are represented! Now, is it clear?"

"What do you say to that?" Axel asked, looking directly at Uncle Jarrad.

"What else could I have said?"

"Well, something else, Uncle Jarrad." Stepping into the house, Axel bowed his head and rubbed his forehead hard with his fingers. "You could have said, 'We'll think about it,' or 'Try getting back in touch in a Kivan or two.' No... *you* had to say, 'All right. Axel and I will find a way.' How, exactly, are we going to do that? Do you know what those few words you said really mean?"

"You know, I think you'd better learn how to give your elders more respect!" Jarrad said, only partly in jest.

"Etmar's Fire! Not when you commit us to do the impossible!" Axel said, continuing his rant. "Have you ever seen what a blast of dragon fire can do? I suppose we're just going to dance over to Mother Clara's place and carry back a couple of draft dragons on board a flying dragon ship? I don't know what draft dragons look like, but I hear they're quite big. How are we going to get them past the King's Dragon Army? They're everywhere. I used to see dragons in the skies over Frithden all the time, and I've seen them here, too—a few times, way up." He drew a deep breath and exhaled quickly. "I take more notice of them, now."

"Six Kivans ago, you were full of fire regarding how you would take revenge for your family's murder. Now, your fire has sputtered out."

"I guess I've had time to think about what I'm up against."

Jarrad, bearing a tiny smile, looked over at Axel and tried to communicate his sympathy. He saw that Axel, clearly, had not yet developed an understanding of his life's purpose. "Are you a believer in foretellings?" he asked.

"What?" Axel glared back at Jarrad, taken entirely aback. "Foretellings? What kind of foretellings?"

"Any kind."

"Frankly, the only foretelling I know of is the one the dragons told us about."

"Is that so? Axel, what about the one that foretold your birth?"

"As I said, that's part of the foretelling we got from the dragons."

"No, that talks about your destiny. What about the one foretelling of your birth? Where did you learn that one?"

"My birth?" Axel stared into space and tried to think. "The only story I know about my birth is the one my Da told me."

"And where did he get that story?"

"He... experienced it; he was there."

"Oh, so he just up and got this idea to venture into the King's Dragon Reserve because he was bored?"

"No, you *know* the story. He went because my ma had the dragon disease and the Lady... in the meadow... She... uh..." Axel plopped down into a kitchen chair and covered his face with his hands. "Foretellings... come from the gods, don't they?" He spoke the obvious from between his fingers. "You're saying that I'm into this business up to my neck and I don't have any choice, right?"

"You always have a choice. It's just that you must live with the consequences of your choices."

"And what are the consequences if I choose to forget about dragons and foretellings and just be a fletcher?"

"I think it highly likely you will meet your end at the claws of dragons because you were not around to free them. What's more, you would be fully aware that you had the assignment, no, the responsibility to make things right and didn't."

"What happens if I accept this *Son of Ceragon* role, as described in the foretelling?"

"Then you may win honor, power, glory... and revenge. There is also a particularly good chance you may still die at the claws of dragons. But think of the adventure!"

"Axel banged his head against the back of his chair several times and said, "Why did I ask you?"

"Dear Axel," Jarrad said, with a knowing smile on his face, "most children grow up with little choice but to follow the path determined either by their parent's economic situation, their station in life, or by the whim of the king. The gods have bestowed upon you not just a choice, but also a vast opportunity. True, it's a very dangerous opportunity, with no guarantee of success. It will, no doubt, require you to go through pain and suffering, but there is no growth without pain. At this time, you are like a seed planted in uncertain ground, and *you* will be the one who decides whether to let the ground destroy you or to climb your way out of the dirt and become one of the most amazing trees ever."

"That's what I'm worried about."

"What do you mean?"

"This tree attracts a lot of attention. It's been only a few Kivans since I helped bury three hundred people who are dead because of me. Can you promise that as I gain all this glory, other people, and dragons, too, aren't going to be paying for it?"

"Ahh," Jarrad said, "so... that's it." He paused to think, sucking in his lower lip as he did. Moving his head to make his eyes look straight into Axel's, he said. "Remember, Axel, I saw the Lady, just like your da. As was the case with your da's vision, her visit with me wasn't about me, but about *you* and the dragons. There is a reason *you* are here with me and the free dragons. That reason is that y*ou* are the person selected by the gods to change the world. Your family and friends who died are not dead because of you. They are dead because of the king and the monsters who helped him."

Now, it was Axel's turn to chew on his lip as he thought over the matter.

After a moment, Jarrad interrupted the silence by saying, "Are you not even curious?"

"Curious? Curious about what?"

"The free dragons say the *Daughter of Ceragon* is living with Mother Clara. As the one and only S*on of Ceragon*, aren't you curious to know more about who this girl is?"

"I don't have time, right now, to get interested in girls."

"I didn't say *girls*," Jarrad said in exasperation. "I said '*girl*,' as in *one* girl. The one who, for whatever reason, must have some things in common with you! Wouldn't you like to know what those things are?"

Axel could not help the beginnings of a smile forming on his face. "She's probably ugly."

"For a *son of Ceragon*, you didn't turn out too badly, Axel. You should give her the benefit of the doubt. Oh, but, Axel, it doesn't matter if she's ugly or the prettiest thing you've ever seen; you two have a job you were born to do together! We very much need to pay this little miss a visit."

"A what? You're serious?"

"Of course, I'm serious! We need to pay both Mother Clara and your girlfriend a visit."

"She's not my girlfriend, and you know it."

"Maybe not, but we have business with both these women. The dragons will give us transportation, which is a good thing because I haven't the vaguest idea where Clara lives. It's also good thing that, since your arrival here, you have had plenty of opportunities to ride various dragons in an assortment of conditions and be able to handle this long trip. I hear you've even been practicing archery from the back of the dragons."

Axel's face turned red. "Well, yes. Some of the younger dragons were bored, and we've just been having some fun together doing trick shots and stuff. You should see us. It's harder than shooting from a skell, but I've adapted."

Jarrad simply smirked and said, "I don't see any harm in that kind of play as long as you remember where your real work is performed."

They met with Shaddra the following evening.

"I wondered how long it would take for you two geniuses to come up with the obvious," Shaddra chided.

"I must confess," Jarrad said, "that the problem was not in determining our course of action but in overcoming objections." He looked over at Axel, who only glowered back. "Anyway, I understand that no dragon has ever attempted to make a return trip to Clara's house. Do you dragons remember the route well enough to get there, based on only one one-way trip each, and *that* was undertaken many years ago?"

"When we took flight, every one of us dreamed of going back to see her again. The route is firmly etched in our memories. However, each of us followed a different path to arrive here. There will be some agreement regarding much of the distance , particularly in those sections that are well-known and frequently traveled by our group.. As for the rest, we will just select a leader and go."

"Then, I suppose our task is to get Axel and me to Clara's place and back as safely as possible. What would you suggest?"

"I suggest that you fly on two dragons," Shaddra said, "Hukken and me. With Kivan nearly full, we should fly when it is not in the night sky to minimize the chance of meeting any of the king's dragons, which would mean three Kivans from tonight. The distance is great, and I do not fly as swiftly as Hukken. We will have to fly at night and spend our days on the ground in hidden camps."

"Why not fly on two siris dragons?" Axel asked."

"I proposed this option to the council and was outvoted. All agreed that I could provide certain skills that are more important than speed. I became convinced their decision was correct."

"It seems you have planned our whole trip for us," Jarrad said with a laugh.

"Yes, we have planned the trip. But what happens once you enter Clara's home is up to you."

Jarrad appeared a little apprehensive over Shaddra's words. "Do the free dragons want to have some kind of input as to what we discuss?"

"You know what we want. We trust you to find a way to make it happen." Looking straight at Axel, she added, "There will be time to discuss other matters to bring up with Mother Clara, I'm certain. This journey will be a source of enlightenment to us all."

Axel pursed his lips but said nothing.

Chapter Nine

FINDING CLARA

The time passed quickly as Jarrad and Axel dedicated themselves to finishing the setup of their modest sawmill in Harbor Valley. Over the course of about three Kivans, they hired local helpers, learned the ins and outs of running the operation, and gradually expanded their team. In a valuable addition to their fledgling enterprise, they even managed to recruit two experienced workers away from the Mikell sawmill at a reasonable cost.

These new hires taught Axel how to operate a compact, mobile overhead crane to pick up the heavy logs and position them on the saw for cutting. The crane also made it easy to transfer pallets of cut blanks to a covered storage area, where the wood could be kept safe until ready for finishing. The team's efficient cutting process quickly resulted in over four hundred stacked and stored blanks, surpassing their initial expectations.

After interviewing about thirty applicants from the nearby towns, Axel brought on two strapping young folks, both close to his age, to serve as apprentices. One was a young man and, breaking with tradition, the other a young woman. The apprentices would not be paid, but they would learn the valuable skills of bow and arrow making, which would one day make them professionals.

It did not take long for the people in both Tarfal and Mikell to learn that Axel was planning to make quality bows that could be purchased by anyone in the valley for reasonable prices. A sort of "bow fever" took hold, and soon, every male over twelve was clamoring to get one. Many women wanted bows, too. The prospective owners were also demanding lessons on how to use the weapons accurately. Accordingly, Axel began planning to have lessons on the proper use and shooting of bows. Some people already had basic knowledge, and a few, such as the hunters, could manage the new bows very well after minimal instruction. Axel found he needed to offer different classes to match the skills of his clientele, along with bows of different draw weights to match the age, skill level, and gender of the archers in training. Fees for the classes were set low to match what people could afford to pay. They would begin as soon as Jarrad and Axel returned from Clara's place, assuming they did return.

***

Just after the sunstar set on the targeted day of departure, Axel and Jarrad heaved on their packs. Not knowing what dangers or special needs might confront them, Axel packed his bow and a bag full of both broadhead and bodkin arrows. These arrows, however, were constructed with completely dissimilar materials and designs from those Axel planned to sell to the people of the Mysura Valley. Should any fall into the wrong hands, there would be nothing in the way of evidence to trace these arrows back to either the Valley or himself. Jarrad grabbed a crossbow and a bag of quarrels. A crossbow was a powerful weapon he could use well.

Their walk to the Dragon Meadow was, as usual, short. Though both were normally quite talkative, they did remain silent. Rather, they pondered the enormity of what they were trying to do. On the outside, the meeting seemed like nothing more than a long-distance social call. However, it could lead, in a figurative sense, to the joining of the *Son* and *Daughter of Ceragon* and to the ultimate fulfillment of the foretelling, which had inspired dragons for centuries, especially those who were enslaved.

Both walked with heads down, lost in thought.

Suddenly Axel stopped. Jarrad walked on a step or two before realizing that he had lost the young man. He, too, stopped and turned to cast a questioning eye at Axel.

Axel was still looking downward and shaking his head. "Are you as scared as I am about this?"

"You picked a very bad time to bring this up."

"Sorry, but I felt it was a subject worth discussing before we jump on two dragons to go out and face a whole army of enemy dragons."

Jarrad just pursed his lips, deep in thought for a moment. "My fear regarding this excursion exists at several levels," he said quietly. "Much of it centers on expectations. First—I fear that I won't be able to live up to what you, Shaddra, and all the free dragons are hoping for. Second, I fear what kind of expectations are going to rise among the women, especially once we finally meet those two important people, whose influence could shape the future not just of Sanara but of Badares and maybe even Tamerel. And third," he added with a wry smile, "I wonder if we're going to end up skewered on the end of some dragon's roasting spit."

Axel took a big sigh and started walking again, "Etmar bless me, and I thought I had it bad."

The dragons appeared on the far horizon exactly on time. As expected, there were two: Hukken and Shaddra. Timing their arrival to just when darkness enveloped the last glow of the sunstar, the two dragons glided gently onto the meadow and stopped, with a quick uplift of their heads and the dropping of their tails and hind legs. They stood there for a moment, while still beating their wings, and dropped their forequarters gently to the ground.

"Greetings to you, Dragons of the Free Colony," Jarrad said, with a huge smile spread across his face and his arms spread wide out to match. "We are about to depart on an amazing adventure!"

"Greetings, in turn, to our human friends," Hukken acknowledged. "If you want to be formal about this, Jarrad, I can match you as far as you want to go."

"Don't worry," Axel said, with a big grin of his own, "he'll come down from this high in a little while and be his natural self."

"Ahh, Hukken," Jarrad said, now with a grimace. "This is a remarkable occasion, is it not? We are going to do countless things on this trip that have never been done before."

Here, Axel broke in and said in mockery, "I think dying has been tried before, and so far, no one has recommended it."

"You pessimist. I think the odds are exceptionally good that we will come out of this unscathed. Look at our strengths: we have two archers, one a dead shot and the other close to excellent on a good day; two of the wisest dragons in the kingdom, one of whom can breathe firebolts; and we can fly at night, when all the king's forces are afraid of unseen monsters."

"Yes," Shaddra chimed in, "and all they have is two thousand fully trained and armed dragons of war. They stand not a chance."

Axel choked down his laughter this time but would not be able to withstand another one like that.

"Ahem," Jarrad coughed to get attention and said, "Fortunately, the vast majority of the king's dragons will be patrolling along the kingdom's frontiers rather than the interior." He stuck his tongue out at Shaddra.

That was all Axel could take. He fell to his knees, bellowing raucous laughter.

Jarrad took a long, slow look at Axel and thought, *I hope this laughter lifts his spirits and takes his mind off the burdensome responsibility he has. This project is going to succeed or fail based on what actions the son and the Daughter choose to take, and their ability to work together and communicate effectively will be crucial in determining the outcome. Axel should concentrate on other things than fear.* He paused for a moment, plastered a smile on his face, and said quietly, but loud enough for the others to hear. "Fear will kill us. Laughter will make us more relaxed and more aware of our responsibilities. Laugh away, Axel, and help us to learn how to laugh like you."

The dragons explained their planned route before taking off, citing major landmarks along the way. Axel got lost almost immediately, for his knowledge of geography was nil. But Jarrad pulled out some maps that showed the kingdom and its major features. He laid them out on the ground for all to see. "Based on what you dragons are saying," Jarrad said. "I believe we will skirt the eastern edge of the Kudra Mountains here. That is the rocky mountain range just to the north of us but still in the southwestern part of the kingdom. The three large rivers you speak of are the Mysura, the Ibisen, and the Immaten. Each of these rivers is an accumulation of many smaller rivers. The tributaries flowing from the Kulu Mountains in the south, the Kuhala Mountains in the west, and the Mateva Mountains in the north make the Ibisen the longest and largest river in the kingdom.

"After the Ibisen, the next major river to the north is the Immaten. It is formed from several tributaries coming out of the Mateva Mountains on the south, the Kuhala on the west, and the Zakutcha Mountains on the north. I'm certain that the big city you dragons saw in the northeast was Rabianice. I lived there many years ago. I'm not familiar with the other landmarks you mentioned.

"From what I understand, you are saying our journey will cover about two hundred fifty tondrins, as the dragon flies, and go straight across the middle of the kingdom, in a diagonal line, almost to the coast. Fortunately, nearly the entire flight will be across heavily forested and largely unpopulated areas.

"Don't look so sullen, Axel. When I came here from Rabianice, I traveled by skell and wagon. It took me more than a Kivan to get here, partly because the distance was half again longer by road than what we'll fly. Even flying low to avoid detection by the king's dragonriders, flying only at night, and landing for two rest stops each night along the way, we should get to Clara's place before the first light of the third day. At least I hope that's how long it will take."

"Do you want to approach Clara in the daylight?" Axel asked.

Jarrad blew a quiet whistle while he thought. "No, she will most likely be going to work that day. Besides, our visit would be highly visible during the daylight."

Hukken asked, "How shall we watch out for danger along the way?"

"What if first, as I said, we fly low to stay out of sight from the ground? Second, let's give Axel a special job—he'll keep his eyes on the sky, watching for any sign of dragons. He won't need to worry about anything else during the flight; just hold on and stay alert."

"Thanks to the new saddles, I won't even have to hold on," Axel said with a sly grin. "I'll be tied on. Where did you find those saddles, anyway, Shaddra?"

"Axel, as you grow up, you will need to learn that some questions are better not asked."

He put two fingers over his mouth to hide his responding grin. The only place to find dragon saddles was in a King's Dragon Force camp. Axel would like to have seen how she stole them. Jarrad was the one who invented the new saddle belts to replace the commonly used tether line.

"I guess everything else we have already discussed or included in our plans," Jarrad said. "Let's mount up and get going."

Five minutes later, the two dragons and their riders lifted gradually into the air and turned north.

That night's flight was uneventful. They stopped twice at streams for both humans and dragons to drink, refill water flasks, and splash cold water over sleepy faces. The two dragons seemed mostly unaffected by the effort so far, even after doing most of the work.

Axel was still amazed to see that dragons drink water, and, no, it did not put out the fire in Hukken's belly. It made him wonder just what the internal structure of a dragon was like. How, exactly, were the fire and water compatible?

Before first light, they dropped down into a thick area of outer forest, and the two menfolk set out blankets to soften the ground while they slept. At Axel's suggestion, some were painted on one side with harda sap to keep ground moisture from seeping through or to protect from rain when necessary. The dragons found open areas, trampled down any restricting vegetation, and, after turning around several times to find the most comfortable positions, settled in to sleep.

When Axel woke sometime after midday, he found himself lying in the shade of a big anyu tree. He felt a strong hunger in his belly, so he reached into his pack to pull out some dried meat stored there. Looking over at the still sleeping dragons, he knew they would be hungry when they woke and decided to do something about it. He grabbed his bow and quiver, strung the bow, placed the quiver on his hip, and ventured out into the forest. He had no fear of getting lost. His mind automatically recorded every step he took.

Just two or three landrins from the makeshift camp, he saw a karam poised behind a dense bush on a hill, waiting for an unsuspecting victim to pass below. The wind shifted just slightly, but enough that the karam was able to catch Axel's scent. It immediately leapt from its hiding place and scampered away at full speed. Only its long, spotted tail could be seen swinging about above the low undergrowth as it fled.

Axel merely shook his head and started walking along the animal trail he found beneath the karam's perch. He needed to travel only a few hundred strides before locating a kota trying to hide in a patch of scrub aldan. He raised his bow and launched an arrow in one swift movement, and the kota dropped dead before it slumped to the ground.

Axel cleaned the kota and picked it up over his shoulder by the horns to keep its blood from soiling his clothes and walked back to the dragon camp. The whole excursion had taken less than an orai and the others were still asleep. The smell of fresh meat, however, served to wake the two dragons as soon as Axel walked into the camp.

"What have you there, young Master Daimon?" asked Hukken.

"Why, I have breakfast for two dragons, who have served us well this day. We have some stores for you in our packs, but I thought you would like something fresh."

The two dragons looked at each other and then back at Axel. "Thank you, Axel," Shaddra said. "It is very thoughtful."

By this time Jarrad was awake and smiling. "How nice of you Axel. I'll take a plate of eggs with the yolks runny. You know how I like them."

Axel bent down and, picking up one of the packs they had brought, threw it at Jarrad. "There's some smoked meat in here. Enjoy!"

"Young people!" Jarrad muttered, feigning a frown. "When are they ever going to learn proper respect for their elders?"

"In your case, Uncle Jarrad," Axel said with an artificial grin, "you may have to wait a long, long, long time." He coughed and, replacing his artificial grin with a real one, chuckled.

Jarrad grinned back and joined in on the chuckle. He then shrugged and reached into the pack for the smoked meat.

***

The second night started out much the same as the first. Axel made note of the various landmarks described by the dragons as they passed by underneath or off to the side. The most obvious ones were the great rivers: the Mysura, which they crossed over upon starting out; the Ibisen; and ahead, he could see the Immaten. But there was something else. He blinked twice and looked again.

"Dragons!" he shouted. "On the horizon straight ahead and just to the left!"

At once, Hukken and Shaddra dove down to treetop level and glided into a valley just big enough to hold the party.

"Could you see how many?" Shaddra asked as Axel slid off her back.

"I'm pretty sure there were three. They appeared to be flying in this direction, but I think they'll pass by on our left."

Hukken tried to peer through the dense forest. "The trees are too thick here. We need to keep track of them."

Looking about, Axel saw a nearby landrin tree. He ran over to it, jumped up to catch the lowest bough, and started climbing. The boughs were strong enough to support his weight almost to their top. He climbed until he could poke his head out of the foliage and searched the sky for dragons.

"I see them!" he shouted down to the others. "There are three, all firedrakes, and they are going to pass close by. You'd better find yourselves a tree to hide under. Hukken, you're so big; are you going to be all right?"

"Yes, Master Axel, I just broke off enough of these branches to make a hole my size!"

"I should have known it would be that easy," Axel shouted down. "Okay, they are getting a little too close now. Let's keep things quiet."

Three or four minutes later, a flight of three dragons and their riders passed by about eight landrins to the west—close enough to be seen by the entire party on the ground. But the firedrakes were at a moderate altitude, and their attention seemed to be directed toward something further to the west.

Axel, with his head ducked down into the topmost branches, watched until the flight was thirty or forty landrins to the south before popping up for one last look around the night sky and climbing down.

"I thought the king's dragons never flew at night!" he said to the others.

"You folks can all see in the dark," Jarrad said, "but I've been totally blind during our flight. What do they expect to find?"

Shaddra pointed out that, while enslaved dragons could see at night, they could only respond to very precise instructions from their masters as to where to fly and what to look for.

"There is a human road over there," Hukken said, "where the king's dragons flew. They are most likely following it since it would be visible even on a dark night like tonight. They could use it as a guide."

Jarrad suddenly exclaimed in a loud voice, "I've got it! They must have been looking for something on the road! Recently, the king increased taxes on the transportation of food and other supplies across provincial lines. He raised them a lot, so people started moving their goods at night to avoid the tax collectors. Those dragons were out searching the roads for smugglers!"

"How did you know that?" Axel asked.

"Oh, I keep my ear to the ground in the village," Jarrad responded. "Even people in the Valley know a lot about what's happening in this kingdom."

"I feel bad for the smugglers," Axel said, "but their plight should be good for us. If we stay away from the roads, the dark night will hide us well."

"There is another possibility," Jarrad said with a deep frown.

"What's that?" Axel asked, calling down from the tree.

"It's possible the dragonriders have learned dragons can see in the dark and are giving their dragons some leeway as to where they fly at night."

"Can they do that and still retain control?"

"I don't know," Jarrad said.

"So, is the way clear now?" he asked Axel, as the young man dropped from the bottom branch of the Landrin.

"I took a careful look around when I was up there and saw no danger, but that can change quickly."

Jarrad patted Hukken on the leg, which was all he could reach when the siris dragon was standing, and moved to the ladder, which ascended to the siris dragon's saddle. After asking permission, he started climbing. At the top, he said, "I think we'd better stop wasting time and start moving."

Hukken was the first to leap into the air, with Jarrad holding on tightly to the saddle harness, even though he was belted in.

The group approached the place the dragons remembered as Clara's cottage about four orais later, about six orais after the setting of the sunstar. In pre-mission planning, they had decided to undertake this last part of the journey cautiously. The Dragon Breeding Caves were nearby and would be guarded heavily. They also knew that Rabianice, the capital city of the entire kingdom, was only a short flight away. Even though they were traveling at night, who knew what other surprises would pop up on their little journey?

After maneuvering at treetop height for the last orai of the flight, the dragons located Clara's cottage and circled it to give Axel a clear point of reference. To avoid attracting attention, the dragons moved off into a thickly forested area about forty landrins away and landed in a narrow opening next to an isolated stream. Their timing was perfect. First, daylight was only about an orai away. As before, they were all exhausted, and everyone went to sleep right off. They did not even bother posting a watch.

***

Axel, as was becoming his habit, woke up first and immediately set off on a hunt. When he returned an orai later, everyone was awake. He could feel the anxiety in the air, especially that emanating from the dragons.

"I see you are all awake to honor my return," he said. "After all, I do come bearing gifts!" He plopped two freshly killed and cleaned bush kota on the ground.

"Axel," Shaddra said, looking at him with sad eyes, "we do appreciate your efforts to provide a meal for us; there really is no way for us to hunt here ourselves. But Hukken and I are too nervous to eat anything right now. This is the most important day in our lives, and our insides just do not feel well at present."

"You know you are quite wrong there," came a voice from behind the two dragons. "Today is not the most important day in your lives." Jarrad stepped forward to stand looking up at the dragons. "That day occurred in this very place a little less than thirty years ago. It was the day a certain woman set you free.

"Why did you come here to visit Clara? Was it to renew old acquaintances? Yes, I suppose that is part of the reason—but only a small part. You are here to do what Mother Clara did for you. You have come to save two small dragons, probably not yet even hatched, from the unimaginable evil of slavery! It should not be a day of apprehension but one of joy in what you are about to accomplish!

"There is a chance that, just maybe, it will be the beginning of the *Foretelling* coming true. Because *you* are here, you will have a role in making it come true. Please eat and maintain your strength, as this day may demand much from both of you."

The two dragons cocked their heads and turned to look at each other. Their faces brightened up, and broad smiles formed on their faces. They nodded at each other and turned to Axel.

"Suddenly," Hukken said, "I find myself quite hungry, Master Axel. You are very considerate in procuring a fresh meal for us."

A short while after the sunstar slipped below the horizon, Axel and Jarrad set off toward the cottage. The two dragons followed at a respectful distance on foot, their scales glinting in the twilight, but paused about two landrins from the house.

"We'll wait here," Shaddra said, her voice low and melodic. "If you need to send us any word, we'll be listening."

Axel and Jarrad nodded in acknowledgment, then turned and continued along the path. After they'd walked about three landrins closer to the cottage, Jarrad leaned in and whispered, "Do you think they can hear us from here?"

"Not if you keep your voice down," Axel replied. "You know, I can't believe you got them to accept that balderdash."

"It was not balderdash! Every word of it was true!"

"Yes, but there's truth, and there's...."

"Uh, uh! Axel', Jarrad whispered, shaking his head. You must remember they see this work as the sole purpose of their lives. They are intelligent beings, and they have not had anything in their lives to distinguish one day from another—at least, not until now. Even with the power of a foretelling in play, there is no way to know how things will turn out today and, especially, after today, as the future remains uncertain and influenced by countless variables beyond their control.. We can only do our best."

Silence hung between them for a moment. Axel took a deep breath, letting it out slowly. "So, how are you going to start things with Clara?"

Jarrad shot him a sideways look. "What do you mean, 'How am I going to start'? There are two of us, remember?"

"Yeah, but you're the authority here. Who's going to trust the word of a sixteen-year-old?"

"You'll be seventeen in four Kivans," Jarrad retorted.

"Aren't you making my point for me? So, what are you planning to say?"

Before they could debate further, they found themselves at the cottage door.

Jarrad hesitated, then gave a wry smile. "I guess we'll find out together."

Jarrad knocked on the cottage door in a manner he hoped would sound like it just came from a neighbor dropping by to borrow a little flour... at a time when everyone was going to bed. The two men waited, for what felt like a good long time, before the door covering a small observation hole, set a little below the height of Jarrad's head, slid to one side.

A face appeared, encased in a shadow created by the light of a candle. "It is rather late," said a female voice through the door opening. "What do you want?"

"Madam Ramendi," Jarrad said, "I bring you greetings from Shaddra and Hukken."

The face in the eyehole could be seen to stiffen. Only after a moment did the woman speak. "Am I supposed to know whoever belongs to these two names?"

Jarrad visibly jumped at her response. He hesitated for an instant and said, "You could ask Eleth. We think she is the *Daughter...*" Here, he paused and slid slowly into his next words, "…of one of them."

"The woman's jaw dropped, and she stepped back from the door, slamming shut the sliding window cover as she did. Sounds of two distinct women's voices, though muffled, were heard through the door. A long moment later, the sliding cover moved again to reveal the woman's face. "It is possible we know those of whom you speak. Can you describe them to me? It will help jog our memories."

"Let me think. Shaddra is a very obnoxious messenger dragon, and Hukken is a pompous siris dragon. Does that help any?"

The woman stepped back again, leaving the viewing window open this time. Candlelight illuminated her face; her hand still pressed over her mouth in shock.

She slipped out of sight, and moments later, Jarrad heard the distinct sound of a bolt sliding free. The door creaked open, revealing a woman standing warily, gripping an iron fireplace poker—though she held it low, the tip tracing idle circles near her feet. Her posture suggested caution, not threat.

Jarrad had just realized she was close to his age when, behind her, he caught sight of a girl with fiery red hair. She couldn't have been older than Axel. Her hair was woven into long braids that cascaded to her waist, highlighting a feminine figure that could easily belong to someone a few years older. Jarrad suspected there was no coincidence in that. She held a candle steadily, her expression unwavering, her eyes shining with curiosity.

It was the girl who broke the silence first. "Why are you here? May we ask?"

Jarrad stepped forward, his voice earnest. "We're so sorry to disturb you at this hour, Miss Eleth and Madam Clara Ramendi. I apologize for not knowing your family name, Miss," he added, nodding to the younger girl. "But we've come on an important errand."

The older woman glanced past them, checking the shadows for others, then motioned them inside. Once they were all in the kitchen, she shut the door firmly and slid the bolt back into place. "You have us at a disadvantage," she said, her tone guarded but not unkind. "You seem to know who we are, yet you're complete strangers to us."

"My sincere apologies, Madam; let me make introductions. I am Jarrad Dismer. I would tell you where I am from, but to protect those who have *taken flight*, it should remain a secret for now."

Again, the woman's hand flew to her mouth, and as it dropped, she muttered in a hesitant whisper, "Are... they... still safe?"

"I assure you that not one of your children has been lost. You even have some grandchildren in the Colony. What is more, Shaddra and Hukken have come with us. They are not far from here."

"I knew it! I knew it!" the girl shouted and pounded her two fists together. "You brought dragons! I heard them! I did; I heard them! They were speaking in dragon speech!"

"Ahh, yes," Jarrad said with a broad smile, *"you, young lady, must also be the Daughter of Ceragon that we have heard about."*

May I introduce you to Axel... Daimon, who is the *son of Ceragon?* You two should become acquainted. I am certain you would have much to talk about."

At this point, both Clara and Eleth pulled chairs out from the table, sat down, and stared at their visitors. "This started out as a perfectly ordinary day," Clara said in a stunned voice, "but, in just five minutes' time, you have turned our world on its head."

Chapter Ten

FATE AND DRAGONS

For a moment or two, no one in the Ramendi home spoke. "I'm sorry," Clara said. "Where are my manners? Would you please sit? Unfortunately, all I have to offer are these chairs around my kitchen table."

While Jarrad and Axel pulled out chairs, Clara stood, saying, "I'll put on a pot of tea."

Jarrad began to speak. "Madam Ramendi..."

"Oh, please call me Clara. Everyone calls me Clara."

"As you wish... Clara. Please call me Jarrad. We know that we have dropped some particularly big news on both of you. I should start by saying that Axel and I are here at the dragon's request."

Eleth suddenly burst out. "*All* of them?"

Clara frowned at the girl. "Eleth, *please*, have some manners."

The girl noticeably frowned and looked down at her hands.

"Uh... yes, in fact. All one hundred and seventy-two dragons voted to ask the two of us to meet with you."

The woman nearly dropped the tea kettle she was setting on the stove. "One hundred seventy-two? Are there that many free dragons now? I have only seen ninety-seven take flight!"

Jarrad nodded his head. "Yes, I understand that includes the siris dragon, who has been with the Colony now for less than one Kivan. She was the one who told us about you, Eleth," he said, looking over at the red-headed girl.

Everyone could see her eyes drop, and a silent "Ohhh!" formed on her lips.

When she looked up, Jarrad tilted his head and, giving her a quick nod, continued, "A... number of those having *taken flight* are, now, proud parents, and a few of their offspring in turn are also soon to be parents. The dragons say they are expecting three eggs to hatch within the next Kivan."

"You have brought me so much positive news," Clara said. "But I fear the purpose for which you have come. Is it unwelcome news?"

"No, we have not come with bad news," Jarrad said. "But our purpose is extremely serious. We have come to make a request, and that request may place both you and Eleth in grave danger."

"Clara, still sitting at the table, looked intensely at the two men in front of her. "Ahh... yes," she said in a calm voice of understanding. "It is clear to me now. The dragons are seeking fulfillment of the foretelling."

"Both Jarrad and Axel dropped their jaws in astonishment at the revelation. Interestingly, Eleth joined them, displaying the same level of surprise.

"How did you know?" Jarrad asked.

"I work with dragons every day. They trust me and have shared their secrets with me. All the dragons know of the foretelling, and they know the signs that will precede its fulfillment." She looked over at Axel. "Ever since Eleth came to live with me about a year ago, I have known that there must be a *Son of Ceragon* out there somewhere, for the two are bound together in ways only the gods understand."

Both Axel and Eleth blinked in bewilderment and looked at each other. Eleth quickly looked away, but Axel found it hard to turn his eyes away from her. Her face, framed by hair the color of hackberry wine, was stunning.

Clara paused for a moment as if debating exactly what to say next. "But..." she said, with long spaces in front of each word, "before the *Son* and the *Daughter* can accomplish their work, there must be a *family* of free dragons, and there cannot be a family without all of the progeny of the Great Ceragon represented." She looked directly at Jarrad. "*The free dragons have requested you* to bring them draft dragons." The words were spoken as fact, not as a question.

"Jarrad slowly shook his head and blew air between his cheeks. "It seems today is a day of surprises for us all. I realize it may take some time to ponder this, but *do* you agree to help us do it?"

"It is intriguing that you use the word 'ponder.' For nearly thirty years, I have *pondered* the question of how to help a draft dragon *take flight.* I have never been able to produce a solution. Now, I assume you want to take *two* of them?"

There were nods from Jarrad and Axel.

"I have been able to plan how to get a draft dragon successfully from the coops to my house, but I have not been able to do anything more than that. I have no way to help them *take flight.*"

"We don't have a solution to that problem yet, either," Jarrad replied. "But we have resources, and if we combine efforts, I believe we can come up with a complete plan—together."

A boiling sound came from the kettle on the stove.

"Oh, your tea is ready," Clara said.

Jarrad smiled broadly and said, "Perhaps that can wait for now. We have two friends outside who will start tearing down the forest if we don't bring you out for a visit."

Even though the cottage was only dimly lit with candles, it was enough to limit the night vision of those humans not endowed with extraordinary gifts. Accordingly, Eleth took Clara by the hand, and Jarrad placed his hand on Axel's shoulder as they walked the short distance to where the two dragons impatiently waited for the person they held in esteem only slightly less than that of the Great Ceragon himself.

Eleth saw the dragons first and gasped audibly. It was the first time she had ever seen a dragon close and outside of the brooding pens.

Clara stepped forward and approached the dragons, who were bowing low, with foreheads nearly touching the ground. "Oh... my children...! Please do not bow to me! I am not worthy."

"Based on what I have been able to determine," Jarrad said, "there are ninety-seven dragons who think you are very much worthy."

The two dragons reluctantly raised their heads. Hukken stepped forward and spoke. "Uncle Jarrad is correct, fair Mother. No one, dragon or human, is worthier of our respect than you. This is the most important day in my life since the very day I first took flight. The dragons of the Free Colony have entrusted me with the responsibility of bowing before you on their behalf.

"*Uncle* Jarrad?"

"Um, yes... just as you freed us from slavery, Uncle Jarrad guided us to our new home and taught us how to live in the greater world." He is honored by us second only to you."

Clara smiled and looked back at her visitors. "It seems I am in very good company. You will have to tell me what you can of their new home."

Turning again toward Hukken, she walked up and touched his knee. "My, you have grown so big!" She turned to the other dragon and said, "You are Shaddra, my first. You were so small when I let you go. Such a little thing you were to send out into a big, dangerous world. I have worried about you most of all, and now, you have returned! You are here! Right beside me. I could die happy right now."

On the verge of tears, Shaddra said, "Please do not do so, dear Mother! You are still needed by us and all the dragons of the world."

"That's a lot of responsibility you place on me. Thank the gods, I have three others to share that burden!" Again, she turned back toward those behind her and smiled. Catching Eleth's eye, she beckoned with her arm. "Come here, Eleth, come and meet my children!"

"You are the *Daughter of Ceragon*!" Shaddra said to Eleth. "It is an honor to see you and the s*on of Ceragon* together."

"Eleth looked back at Axel with discerning eyes and pursed her lips. "We have only just met," she said. "There is much we must learn about each other. As for my part, I can say, We have no idea what will be expected of us."

Axel nodded in agreement. "I'll second that," he said.

For some reason, Eleth leaned over to say something to Shaddra. It must have been a question, because it appeared that Shaddra answered back. Axel had such excellent hearing that he could hear the flutter of butterfly wings if he as close enough and he listened. But he could not hear what was spoken between Shaddra and Eleth.

Hukken looked abruptly over to Jarrad. "Have you approached Mother Clara and the *Daughter* on the subject of draft dragons?"

"Jarrad smiled at Hukken and replied, "The subject has been brought up. There is much we have yet to discuss on that subject. Please give us some time."

"That's easy for you to say. Try standing out here for orais and see how you feel."

"It hasn't been orais."

"It sure feels that way," the dragon responded. "How long is this going to take anyway?"

"My... you are the impatient one. Why don't you go back to camp? You will find some food there. Settle down and get some sleep. Axel and I will join you as soon as we can. Oh, and watch out for either dragons or humans; we have no friends out there."

The dragons reluctantly took that advice, and the humans turned back towards Clara's cottage. As the group approached the dim sphere of light coming from the little house, Eleth let go of Clara's hand and dropped back to where Jarrad and Axel followed behind. Jarrad, taking the hint, moved forward to join Clara.

"Do you get the idea they already envision us as betrothed?" Eleth said in a frustrated voice. "It's like we have no choice in the matter!"

"What? Every word they've spoken about us could be crammed into a minute and a half.

"It's not how *much* was said; it's *what* was said in that minute and a half!"

Axel believed that Eleth was more than just pretty, which could certainly influence his judgment. Nevertheless, she had a point.

"Now, that you bring it up, I think that's exactly how they see us. What do we do about it?"

"Nothing for now. Let's see how things work out. Be sure to listen for little clues!"

For some reason, Axel felt some disappointment with this conversation.

They walked the remaining distance in silence.

***

Once back inside the cottage, everyone sat around the kitchen table as before. Not knowing what else to do, Clara stood up and went to the stove. "The tea is still hot," she said, "and hasn't steeped too much, I think. Eleth, would you please set out some cups?"

Eleth stood and went to the cupboard, retrieved some cups, placed them on the table, and promptly sat down. Clara poured the tea and set out containers of sugar and milk, whereupon she sat down.

Jarrad eased the group's tension by saying, "We know you two have work in the morning, so we won't make it harder. Still, there are some matters we need to discuss before Axel and I return home."

"You flew in on the dragons, did you not?" asked Eleth, "and now, you must go home on them. Is that not dangerous?"

"Oh, Eleth," Clara said with a tone of frustration in her voice, "They didn't face all that danger just so they could chat about their journey. There will be time to talk about those kinds of matters before they leave."

Jarrad laughed at this. "Clara, I've found it impossible to stand in the way of young people's curiosity. My experience with this young man, sitting next to me, is a perfect example of that."

Axel rolled his eyes.

"As for you, young lady, I will answer your questions by saying that we did face a certain amount of danger, for which we had to take special precautions. Nevertheless, it is not this journey that worries us most, but the future trip or trips in which we will be transporting draft dragons to the Free Colony. We are also worried about the danger you would be facing here during and after the procurement of those dragons.

"Speaking of which, Clara, you have somehow freed ninety-seven young dragons. Do you think you can do the same for two draft dragons?"

"Every dragon Eleth and I bring out of the coops increases the danger we face. But, yes, I believe we can get two draft dragons if we are allowed at least several Kivans to complete the actions and if you can provide transportation for them away from here at the right times.

"You, men and dragons," Clara said in the stern tone she used before, "must be aware that the king's guards do inspect my home on occasion. Fortunately, I nearly always get advance warning. But there is certainly the chance a warning won't come when it is needed most."

"Can you tell us how big a draft dragon hatchling might be at the time we come for it?"

"Let's see. Circumstances will determine whether we bring the hatchling here while still in the egg or as a new hatchling. An unhatched egg wouldn't likely be kept warm enough on a long journey, so it must be kept here and warm until hatching and for a time after that. The youngling itself wouldn't be able to withstand the rigors of a long journey until it is at least three Kivans in age. That means... it would probably be the size of a year-old ellam bull."

Axel said, "Oh!" while Jarrad got a faraway look in his eyes and explored the inside of his cheek with his tongue.

"I suppose we could rig some kind of sling to be carried in a larger dragon's claws or tied to its legs," he said.

"If you can do the escape part," Clara continued, "then the critical thing would be getting a message to you as to when the hatchling must be whisked away. The longer it stays here, the bigger it gets and the greater the chance for discovery."

"Clara," Jarrad said, "your task is to bring a draft dragon hatchling out of the coops and keep it safe and hidden until we can pick it up and whisk it away. Do you really think you can do that safely?"

"I have been working at my job for more than three decades. I am a fixture here. Everyone knows me, and I know them. I know their habits. I know what is strong and what is weak. I have been working to help dragons take flight for almost as long as I have been here. That has made me aware. It has made me cautious. I change my habits frequently, so no one can predict my ways, and everyone is used to it. That's just Clara, they say. I watch them, and it makes it hard for them to watch me. Now, I have Eleth, who has proven her intelligence, skill, and loyalty. We are a team. Together, we will get the dragons and do it right in front of everyone who works at the coop."

"What if the king's men pull a surprise inspection at the wrong time, or if all the guards are suddenly changed?"

"Then we will adapt."

Eleth put on a self-satisfied face and asked, "May *we* ask *you* if you two and the free dragons will be able to avoid all the dangers of carrying two dragons a distance of two hundred and fifty-odd tondrins through the heart of the King's Dragon Forces?"

Jarrad's eyes widened. "How did you know that...?"

Clara smiled knowingly and said, "We can think here, too. Eleth has been particularly helpful in figuring out where you come from. Eleth, how did you arrive at this conclusion?"

Eleth looked like she knew this subject was coming up and was anxious to show off her skills. Holding her mouth straight but failing to hide her pride in this task, she said, "I learned from Shaddra that you had been traveling by night over two days' time. I simply made some assumptions: first, that you avoided populated areas; second, that you live in a remote village or town near a large mountain range. The free dragons would need all that to stay hidden from the king's forces. Lastly, I estimated the dragon's speed at night and at low levels, which made it possible to calculate your flight distance at two hundred fifty tondrins, give or take twenty or so. Combining all that with a good memory of the geography of Sanara places you in the southwestern part of the kingdom, probably near or within the Kulu Mountains."

Jarrad repeated his habit of slowly shaking his head whenever he was surprised or astonished. "I hope there's no one like you working for the king... and what are you smiling at, Axel?"

"Me, what?"

"You heard me!" he said, turning to Clara and trying to keep his expression under control. "These children are getting completely out of... control." His laugh made the last word sound more like a cough.

He regained his composure and said, "Axel and I will work with the dragons too. We must, first, devise a way to carry a wriggling weight the size of an ellam bull to the Colony and then set up a system of communication so we can learn when we should arrive to pick up those ellam-sized beasts, coordinate other activities, and share warnings. Does that sound right?"

"Oh," Clara pleaded, "please do not call any dragon a beast. They are intelligent beings with an inner spirit. They are just like humans in every way but appearance. They have emotions like us..."

Here, Jarrad interrupted, "And they have personalities every bit the same as humans, for good or evil. I've closely observed dragons myself for nearly thirty years. Clara, I give you my apologies. I chose the wrong subject on which to make my jest."

Clara smiled deeply at Jarrad. "Apology accepted."

Eleth held up a hand to silence everyone and bring in their attention. "How long do you intend to stay here?" she asked, looking at both Axel and 'Jarrad.

"Every day we stay increases the danger substantially," Jarrad answered. To ensure your safety, we should leave tomorrow evening."

Eleth appeared extremely disappointed at this news. Looking out at the others from under deeply curled brows, she said, "But Mr. Daimon and I haven't discussed the things you said we should. You know some things about us, but you are total strangers to us. We want to know more about you: who you really are and what your stories are."

Axel noticed that Eleth's brows seemed to have lives of their own. They twisted, curled, and moved independently up and down and horizontally, totally at her will, always to provide the precise expression she consciously or unconsciously wanted to show. Then he looked at her amazing golden-brown eyes and noticed little green highlights around the edges of her pupils. Transfixed, he blinked, and suddenly the color of her eyes had changed to something more like hazel.

Jarrad wore a serious expression when he said, "Sharing information like that could get you killed, just as it could kill us."

Eleth put on a devious-looking face. "You are, of course, correct. Nevertheless, we are all conspirators working for a noble purpose, and, apart from the dragons, *we* are the core circle of this endeavor. How can we work together without knowing each other? How can the *son* and *Daughter of Ceragon* work together without knowing each other? And maybe there are some things that Axel still does not know about Jarrad and things I don't know about Clara that *we* should comprehend."

"Eleth, it's a good thing neither of your fathers is here today," Clara said with a frustrated smile. I think either one of them would have taken you behind the outbuilding for being uppity. Good thing I'm not one of them, don't you agree?"

"I don't remember my daddy, Boda Morkath. But I had Daddy, Tiimos Keiron, wrapped around my finger. I loved him and rarely used that power, though it did come in useful occasionally. Now... does anybody else have some good secrets? I love secrets, and I can keep them. I... uh... guess, except for what I just told you."

The other three in the room erupted in spontaneous chuckles at the remark.

"We won't get a lot of sleep tonight," Clara said, "but I think you have a point, Eleth. We should each talk about ourselves. Do the rest of you agree?"

Everyone at the table confirmed agreement with nods.

Axel took this moment to ask a question that had bothered him greatly. "Before we get into introductions, I really need to know something. I've heard the prophecy, but I'm confused. What's the difference between a son of Ceragon and any of Ceragon's other children, the dragons? Aren't all dragons children of Ceragon?"

"I see why you are confused," Clara responded. "The answer lies in the fact that dragons do not use the terms 'son,' 'daughter,' or 'child' to describe their offspring. A full-grown male is a drake, and a female is a dragoness, unless she is laying or taking care of a hatchling, at which time she is referred to as a 'hen.' Their children are called hatchlings, fledglings, or juveniles depending on age and regardless of gender. The comparable word for 'son' is 'dragonet,' and for a 'daughter' is 'dragonell.' "So, you see, a *son* of Ceragon is referring to a male offspring of Ceragon, who exists in human form; and the same idea holds for the words '*daughter*' and '*children*.'"

"I see," Axel responded with a vague look in his eyes.

"Now, if you are satisfied," Clara continued, "I will begin my story, as it is likely to be the shortest one."

Clara began her story by telling how she was apprenticed to the previous midwife of the Dragon Coops when she was twelve years old. Her family had been impoverished and simply could not afford to have their children stay at home after they reached a certain age. Clara was the oldest of five children. Only a year after her apprenticeship began, she received word that her entire family had succumbed to a dreadful plague of green fever.

Early in her apprenticeship, Clara came to realize that the dragons were not mere beasts but intelligent beings held in bondage. She was elevated to the job of head midwife at the age of nineteen, upon the death of her predecessor. There was always only one true midwife, because the dragons would only tolerate one at a time. What's more, if a midwife did not meet their approval, the breeders would refuse to mate until the right woman came along. Clara had no trouble with the dragons. They approved of her from the very beginning and began to share their secrets because they knew she would keep them.

Clara decided early in her apprenticeship that the dragons needed to be given their freedom. Shortly after becoming *the* midwife, she started working on a plan to do just that, one at a time. The remainder of her story was more of the same, except that her love for the dragons continued to grow, as did their trust in her. She successfully concealed her "taking flight" activities from the dragons until the previous year.

Jarrad told his story using the same words as he used to introduce himself to Axel. He described Axel's introduction to his family by saying that Shaddra came to him with a tale of a special young man who was orphaned in the destruction of his village. He left the remainder of that story to be told by Axel.

Axel was hesitant to tell his story. It was still too raw, too painful to even think about. Nevertheless, he did his best by saying, first, that he was about four Kivans shy of turning seventeen. He provided brief histories of his gran da and his da. As part of his narrative, he made it clear how and why the dragons came to call him *Son of Ceragon,* and he told his story up until the time he met Jarrad, and they decided to build his new business together.

Eleth and Clara were wiping tears from their eyes as Axel finished his story. "When Eleth came to me," Clara said, "I often pondered how poorly life had treated her because of her role. But you, young man, have suffered so very much that I wonder how you can bear it."

Axel responded with a weak smile and said, "I think of my family and my village every day and of what the king, along with his murderers, did to them. It inspires me to do something on their behalf. I can think of nothing that would hurt the King more than freeing his slaves. I also love dragons, which inspires me to do this work for the right reasons, not just revenge.

Eleth spoke last and started with the fact that she was adopted by Tiimos and Runa Keiron when she was just a baby and that she had recently celebrated her sixteenth birthday. She said that she was never content with doing the same things that other young girls did. Instead, she had always been eager for knowledge of any kind, just as long as it was truth. She learned how to be a doctor, as her father had told Clara when they were first introduced. But she never even told Clara that one night she happened to discover a thief in the Keiron's house, who had come to steal valuables that could be found in a rich doctor's home. But she did not scream, nor did she shout a warning to the house. Instead, she merely asked the astonished thief what he was doing and how he got into the house. The thief was, fortunately, not a violent sort who could have done her harm and simply answered her questions. She told him that, if he taught her how to pick locks and do other things that the thief was familiar with, she would not only keep from waking the house, but she would also reward him with some of the booty that lay about in her home. Over the next several Kivans, she met with the thief often, and he taught her how to case a house, avoid guards, pick locks, defend herself in a fight, and even how to use a knife, a cudgel, and a sling. They became fast friends, and he was always protective of her when around bad company. She remembered everything he taught her from the very first demonstration or explanation. Eleth was sorry that she was only able to leave him a brief note of explanation when the Kairon family was forced to flee.

She described herself as a voracious reader who quickly absorbed considerable knowledge of medicine, mathematics, history, science, and geography.

She also confessed that losing her adopted parents was the hardest blow she had ever experienced. She did not know if they had reached Kolodra safely and worried about them constantly.

Jarrad frowned and squinted his eyes. "I suppose you are like Axel. All he must do is see something once or have something explained once or read something once, and he remembers it and masters it, just like that."

Eleth looked at Jarrad in a thoughtful manner. "Okay... maybe not mastered it," he said.

This caused everyone to laugh, which they did heartily. It broke the tension that had built up during the telling of the stories.

Suddenly, both Axel and Eleth stood up from their chairs and turned toward the cottage door.

Eleth held up a hand to shush the others. "There is at least one dragon outside the door. She's talking in dragon language."

"Clara quickly stood up and scurried to the door, where she slid back the security window. "It's Shaddra!" she said in a hushed but urgent voice and opened the door.

Everyone scrambled outside in a rush to find out what would bring her here now.

Shaddra spoke in a soft but clearly audible voice, "There are about twenty soldiers on the road, heading this way on skellback. The skells are at a walk, but they will be here in no more than fifteen minutes."

Chapter Eleven

CHANGE IN PLANS

Jarrad took immediate charge as everyone piled back into the cottage. "Axel, pick up anything that we may have brought in with us. Eleth, put out the candles and dip them upside down into the water bucket to cool the tallow trails, then dry them off with a towel. The stove is just embers. It should be okay."

Clara picked up the teacups and gave them a quick rinse and dry before putting them back in the cupboard.

Jarrad pushed all the kitchen chairs back into place and headed for the door. "We'll go with Shaddra into the forest opposite from the road. Is that a safe place to hide?" he asked, looking at the women.

Eleth answered, saying, "There's nothing but trees over in that direction."

"Good, we're on our way."

The menfolk, joined by Shaddra, quickly made their way into the forest.

"If this was daytime," Axel commented en route, "I'd worry about Shaddra's tracks, but I think we're okay for now."

Barely five minutes later, a group of soldiers arrived in front of Clara's home. One of them, an officer by his uniform, dismounted and knocked firmly on Clara's door. The man waited a short time, then knocked again more solidly.

A woman's voice came from inside, saying, "Just a moment, let me put on a robe."

Five long breaths later, the sliding window opened, and a voice saying, "Oh, my," could be heard.

"Pardon me, Ma'am," the officer said. "I am Troop Commander Arnould, of His Majesty's Special Cavalry. May I speak with you?"

"Oh, most certainly," said the voice behind the door.

The door opened, and Clara stepped out, leaving it open behind her. She was wearing a nightgown covered by a white robe.

"Again, I am sorry for the intrusion at such a time. You are Mistress Clara Ramendi, Head Midwife at the Dragon Breeding Coops, are you not?"

"Why, yes, I am."

"Have you seen or heard anything unusual over the last day or anytime tonight?"

"I'm afraid that Eleth and I had a strenuous day over in the coops. When we came home, we had a light supper and went straight to bed. We saw nothing unusual during that time. Why do you ask?"

"There has been a report of dragons flying in the night sky in this area. We think they may be Kolodran spies, trying to discover the location of the Breeding Coops. Unfortunately, the report is a little old. It came from a farmer who claims he saw the dragons flying low sometime last night. The next morning, he walked to the local magister, which took several orais, and several more orais passed before the report reached us."

"All workers at the Coops are highly security-conscious," Clara said. "If either my ward, Eleth, or I had witnessed anything like that, we surely would have reported it ourselves and right away! But you are free to inspect my house if you think there is any chance of an enemy hiding here."

The officer accepted her offer and gave orders for three of his men to search the place. Clara and Eleth both stepped out of the door and stood aside as the soldiers entered. Within minutes, they heard the sound of soldiers opening and closing doors and cupboards. It was clear that the soldiers were looking for more than just people.

When the three soldiers returned, one of them spoke quietly with the troop commander. He nodded at the soldier and then approached Clara. "Why do you have so many blankets in the house?" he asked in a commanding voice—a voice that held a noticeable tone of suspicion. "There are far too many to be used by only two women."

"We are responsible for the care of newly hatched dragons, and young dragons are highly vulnerable to catching potentially fatal diseases. I frequently bring sick hatchlings here to watch them closely overnight. We use the blankets to make warm nests for them. I am proud to say that the hatchling mortality rate is now fifty percent lower than at any time since the breeding operation was brought to this location."

The troop commander tilted his head and looked at her sternly while he processed that information. "Thank you for your cooperation," he said abruptly and turned to his skell. But he stopped after a few steps and looked back at the women. "My soldiers will be stationed at strategic places around the area to look for signs of Kolodran dragons. If you see anything suspicious, you will report to us immediately."

With that, the officer climbed aboard his skell and ordered the troop out toward the road.

Both Axel and Shaddra clearly heard the entire conversation, and they kept Jarrad informed by using quiet whispers.

Jarrad looked up at Shaddra and said, "Maybe it would be a good idea for you to covertly follow those soldiers and see what they do."

"I thought along those same lines myself," she replied and disappeared shortly after the soldiers departed.

About fifteen minutes after that, Jarrad and Axel returned to the house.

"Shaddra is following the soldiers to see where they go," Jarrad told the women who were still in their nightclothes and robes. "I'm afraid that the danger here is too great, and we need to leave as soon as Shaddra returns. Axel and I will rejoin Hukken and wait for her there. Hopefully, we can use her report to guide us away from here."

Axel managed to get in a wave at Eleth as the two men marched into the forest near the road. As they walked, he looked up into the still dark sky and said, "There's a dark bank of clouds rolling in from the east."

Jarrad stared up into the sky and said, "I'm afraid I can't tell one color of black from another."

"Look on the eastern horizon. You should be able to tell there are no stars out that way. The clouds are coming in fast."

"Good, they may be able to help us get out of here without being seen."

When Jarrad and Axel arrived at the temporary dragon campsite, both Hukken and Shaddra were waiting for them.

Shaddra reported, "The soldiers traveled about two tondrins down the road and split into two groups. About a third turned south, down a small side road, while the remainder stayed on the main road, if that's what you want to call that wide path-like thing."

"Then, I guess we should head west," said Jarrad.

Upon lifting off from the ground, even Jarrad noticed that clouds were beginning to darken the stars to the east. It was not difficult to tell that a storm was on its way. But there was no telling when it would arrive. It certainly would not help them on their trip west as it would force them to fly at a lower altitude where they would be more visible from the ground..

The plan was for Shaddra and Axel to leave first, heading at moderate speed toward a small area of forest on the northwest side of a bridge crossing the Immaten River, a two-orai flight away. Hukken and Jarrad would follow at a distance, never losing sight of the lead dragon.

Shaddra used her stealth features on her underside and looked down for anything that may endanger the group, while Axel scanned skyward for signs of trouble. Shaddra retained enough visibility on top so that Hukken would not lose sight of her. Together, they would cover the more dangerous part of the journey with this coordinated vigilance.

Once the flight of two dragons reached the Immaten, the danger from the king's forces looking for mysterious dragons flying at night should have lessened considerably.

Axel looked down at the large river below. "It's time for Hukken to take the lead," he said, calling down to Shaddra. "I'm going to wave him forward."

"There is no danger forward, to the sides, or below that I can see," she replied.

"I agree." Axel turned and waved his arm at Hukken, first in a side-to-side gesture and then in a 'come on' sign.

Hukken closed in, then moved ahead to take the lead position. Axel waved at Jarrad as they passed.

With no warning, a crossbow bolt zipped past on Axel's left side and struck Jarrad in the lower back. Barely a second later, another bolt struck Axel's saddle. Two siris dragons, carrying grey-uniformed soldiers, followed close behind the quarrels and passed just underneath at high speed.

Axel quickly drew an arrow from his quiver, loaded it onto his bow, drew, and fired, all in one smooth motion, before the enemy dragons were more than a length ahead. The arrow struck the first speeding shooter in the back, passed all the way through his armor and body, bounced off the dragon's scaly neck armor, and then fell to the ground. Axel knew that his shot had killed the soldier instantly.

Axel not only knew how to shoot a bow accurately, but he was also excellent at anticipating where his target would be, whether a beast or a human. He read his target's intentions by observing its previous movements, its eyes, and the direction its head or eyes or ears turned. In this case, he also had to consider the movements of the dragon. He had no way of explaining this knack other than to bless the dragon and the woman, neither of whom he had ever met, but who died for his benefit.

The second enemy siris dragon flew ahead about twenty landrins and started making a turn for a head-on attack. Axel saw the rider pull out a backup crossbow.

Meanwhile, the dead dragonrider slid off his saddle and bounced as he reached the end of his tether line, while his siris dragon mount just kept flying straight on.

A brief look at Jarrad told Axel that his friend's wound was serious but not immediately life-threatening. He shouted out at Hukken, "Jarrad took a crossbow bolt! He's still alive but needs medical help as soon as you can get it for him! Take him out of the fight now! If I don't survive this next attack, get him back to Eleth as fast as you can. She's a trained doctor!"

Immediately, Hukken turned off to the left and passed out of view.

"Shaddra," Axel said, "it looks like we're going into a game of 'Coward's Out.' He's obviously coming straight at us. What's his plan?"

"He will be thinking a fight with a messenger dragon ought to be an easy kill, because I have neither his speed nor a flame-throwing capability," Shaddra said. "We are at a distinct disadvantage. What's more, we cannot try to escape. The siris dragon would outrun us in no time at all!"

"What's the effective range of a siris dragon firebolt in head-on flight?"

"No dragonrider would risk flying straight into the wake from his mount's fire strike. His weapon of choice in this instance will be the crossbow."

After quickly thinking through their narrow range of possibilities, Axel settled on a plan. It was a dangerous choice, but it was the only way to get them both through the duel unscathed. In his excitement, Axel almost shouted to his mount, "Remember, the dragonrider can't see very well in the dark, so I don't think he will use his crossbow until we are very close. Can you take this dragon head on in a visible color but change to a color that blends with the ground just before the critical range?"

"That I can do."

"At the point where you change color, we need to drop like a rock, straight down and fast."

"What? Such a move will be extremely hard on you."

"I guess I take what comes. Just by way of information, if he gets a shot off at close range, your dragon armor will not protect you from that quarrel."

"Is that supposed to be news?" Shaddra said. "Hold on!"

The king's dragon came just as Axel predicted. Its rider guided his mount straight at Shaddra and aimed his crossbow at Axel. At precisely the planned moment, the free dragon simply changed its body color to match the black sky behind, spread its wings full out as a brake, and dropped. The king's dragon rushed by overhead, its rider never firing his crossbow.

Strong forces induced by the sudden stop threw Axel heavily into the saddle. After that, he immediately felt his heart climb into his throat as the dragon dived, but he planned on this action and was prepared for it. Drawing his bow, Axel rotated in the saddle and loosed an arrow straight up and in the opposite direction from Shaddra's dive. Timed perfectly, his bodkin arrow struck the other dragon in the chest as it flew over. At such close range the projectile penetrated the dragon's armor to sink deeply into its vitals, and the siris dragon dropped straightway towards the ground.

Thank the gods for the practice I had with the young dragons, Axel thought, but he quickly realized that the gods must have played a more direct role than that; otherwise how could he have made such an impossible shot?

Shaddra performed another quick stop, again, crushing Axel into the saddle. But he never took his eyes off the falling enemy. He saw both dragon and rider strike the ground in a rather gruesome way. The rider would not be getting up.

"Axel! Axel!" Shaddra shouted, "There is a live dragon trying to return its dead master to the Dragon Group Headquarters, and it is getting away fast! It flies faster than I can, but we must not let the king get those jewels!"

"I've got to check on Jarrad first."

Axel looked around for Hukken and located him nearby, closely watching for a signal from Axel. Axel waved for Hukken to land in a small piece of open ground and asked Shaddra to join him there.

Immediately upon touching ground, Axel, virtually in a panic, rushed over to where Jarrad sat slumped in his saddle. Under his arm, Axel carried a roll of bandages taken from Shaddra's saddlebags. Cutting a slit in Jarrad's cloak and jerkin, he examined the wound. The quarrel just managed to penetrate the side of Jarrad's abdomen, so there were two wounds, both bleeding profusely. He did not dare to pull out the quarrel, lest it only make the wounds worse. Accordingly, he wrapped some bandages about his friend's middle and tied the protruding ends to the quarrel to secure pressure on the wounds themselves.

He pulled Jarrad's jerkin and cloak back down and made certain to keep the ends from flapping in the wind by wrapping the last bit of bandage about the man's middle.

"Okay, Hukken," he said, while stepping down from the dragon's saddle. "Please take Jarrad back to Eleth as quickly as possible. She's a doctor and will know what to do. Make certain to not bounce him around as you go."

Hukken nodded and leaped into the air but made a gradual ascent. In only a few minutes, he vanished from sight.

Axel ran over to Shaddra, asked for permission to mount, and together, the two were off in pursuit of the escaping Siris dragon.

"How do the king's dragons find their way home after their riders are killed?"

"From what I've heard, they are trained to follow any major river to the sea and then turn north."

"This is the Immaten River below, correct?"

"Yes."

"I recall from the maps Jarrad showed us that it follows a snakelike path to the sea. Is there any chance we can use this information to get ahead of the dragon and its cargo?"

"The king's dragon will follow the bends of the river, while we can fly straight. I believe there are some high hills along the river, but we can get over them easily."

"Go to it, then."

Shaddra altered her color to make it less noticeable to the siris dragon and increased her speed.

After a while, they saw that they would come up on the dragon as it made a left turn to follow a new bend in the river. The rider's body still dangled on a line below the dragon. Strong winds were buffeting both dragons, such that the dangling corpse was bouncing all over.

When the siris dragon made a turn at the river bend, the strange human pendulum swung far out to the side.

"You do recall, Axel," Shaddra pointed out, "that the dragon will try to kill anyone moving to take that body away from it."

"Got it. Come up on it from below and try to time your approach for when the body comes back to the center line of its arc. When I shoot, we need to drop again to catch the falling body."

"You're going to try to cut that tether line with an arrow, and in *this* wind?"

"Do you have a better solution?" Axel shouted. "Remember, we've got to get there when the body isn't swinging. As soon as I cut the line, we drop to catch it. Hopefully, we'll be able to come to a slow stop before reaching the ground. What's more, if we don't cut the jewel loose and get away from the body quick, the dragon will be on us in an instant."

"This is not going to be easy," Shaddra said. "The winds coming ahead of that storm are fierce, and they have some tremendous gusts. It is certain to affect your arrow's flight."

"Just do what you can in your approach."

Shaddra managed to come up under the siris dragon's tail just as the body swung into the invisible center line beneath the siris dragon. Axel drew and loosed a broadhead arrow, which... missed... the tether line. With the same smooth motion as before, Axel nocked another arrow he had been holding with his right hand and let it fly when the body returned its pendulum motion back to the center. This arrow cleanly cut the line, and the body dropped.

Tucking her wings in close to her body, Shaddra dove straight down. If he had not belted into the saddle, Axel would have been thrown off. While it only took a few seconds to reach the body, they seemed like long minutes. Despite the magnitude of the forces throwing him about, Axel managed to tie his bow to a specially made holder in the saddle.

Shaddra maneuvered so that Axel could reach out to catch hold of the falling corpse and pull it tight to his chest. He caught the body while the ground rose ever closer and pulled the red gem from the soldier's neck. Only then did Axel look up to see the enemy siris dragon, with a fierce expression on its face, chasing them in a dive, barely a hundred strides or so above them.

"I've got it; move out of here!" Axel shouted to Shaddra, releasing the body as he did.

When the messenger dragon leveled out, Axel fought the enormous force pulling his head down to see how the siris dragon reacted. He saw the dragon pick the body out of the air and level out to resume its flight to the sea at its highest speed.

"Quick, Shaddra, set us down where I can find some rocks!"

A moment later, Axel was already undoing his safety belt when the messenger dragon landed on the ground. He jumped off so fast that he twisted his ankle as he landed. He plainly heard and felt the ankle crack as it bent under him. The pain was overwhelming, but Axel fought it until he had successfully placed the Bechar on a rock and used another to smash it.

Only then did he allow himself a loud scream to express his pain, and he dropped to the ground, rolling in agony.

Shaddra looked down at Axel as he lurched around in the dirt. She heaved a sigh and said, "I know you are in great pain, but there is a dragon who will get away if we do not act quickly!"

Axel managed to get control of himself enough to choke out, "Shaddra... you... go! Go... without... me!"

"How am I supposed to do that?"

"You... you just go... find... the dragon and... bring him back!"

"I go? What do I say?"

"Hey, you're... the dragon!" Axel said in a shout.

"And that means what, exactly?"

"Just try to get close without it... killing you."

"And?"

"Etmar's fire! I don't know. Just say... 'Hi, my name's Shaddra. *May* I help you?' Just get out of here! He's getting away!"

Shaddra looked at him, shook her head three times, took a deep breath, and jumped into the air.

Staring in the direction she thought best to find a suddenly freed slave, Shaddra saw a black dot in the distant sky—at least it appeared to be a black dot out there against the billowing storm clouds to the east. Fortunately, the black dot seemed to be flying around in large circles, as if it really had nowhere to go. That's probably true, she thought. The change in the siris dragon's behavior made it possible for the messenger dragon to catch up rather quickly.

Once there, she readily noticed the other dragon was no longer carrying a dead dragonrider. She positioned herself about a landrin to the siris dragon's right side. He looked over at her with an obviously confused facial expression.

Then she started talking to him, not with human words, but in the dragon *High Language*—a language that communicated much information in fewer words and that communicated emotion as well as information.

"My name is Shaddra. May I be of assistance?

"Do you have orders?"

"Orders? Orders from whom?"

"Not from anyone. Just to.

"To whom?"

"Not to whom. To me! Just to me!"

"Oh. You mean 'Do *I* have any orders for *you?*' No. No, I do not. Is there any *other* way I may help you?"

"I do not understand. My orders have stopped coming. Who will tell me what to do?"

"I can tell you what to do."

"Then, tell me what to do!"

"You are to follow me. I will fly around a bit and stop occasionally, but do not lose me. Do you understand?"

"Yes, I will follow you."

As they flew, Shaddra said, "I told you who I am. Please tell me who you are.

"My name is Licor. I am a Strike Dragon assigned to the Second Branch, Northern Region, His Majesty's Special Assignments Regiment."

"Good enough. Do not get lost."

Shaddra returned to where she left Axel, with a second dragon following not far behind. The young man appeared to have recovered his self-control while she was gone.

"How are you fairing, Axel," she asked.

"I suppose I'm well enough to get out of here," he answered with a painful grimace. "But things need to be done before we can go check on Jarrad."

"By the way, Axel, this dragon with me is Licor."

"Nice to meet you, Licor," Axel said absentmindedly.

Licor did not reply.

Axel carefully climbed to his saddle, tied himself on, and said, "I see that you got your... dragon. You have done very well for yourself. I sure didn't want to be the one doing what you did."

"That was quite obvious." She gave him a flat-mouthed smile, but her twinkling eyes communicated everything she really wanted to say.

Axel and two dragons returned to the body of the dragon he killed. Axel hobbled over to the dead dragonrider, still attached to the dragon's body by a tether, rolled him over, and took the Bechar. He then got down on the ground and did a three-legged crawl over to where a rock, which might be a usable mallet, was lying. The ground here was soft and showed few stones of any kind. When he peered around for an anvil, the only thing that met this requirement was fifteen strides away.

Looking up at Shaddra, Axel said, "Sometimes a human's opposable thumb gets him into trouble and saves a certain dragon from doing her share of the work!"

Shaddra looked back at him with sad eyes and said, "Axel, I do not know what you mean."

Axel rolled his own eyes and lay down to painfully wriggle across the fifteen strides to the makeshift anvil stone.

Licor looked down at Axel and asked, "Is the human insane?"

"No, Licor, he is not insane," Shaddra said in answer.

Axel set the Bechar on a small stone outcrop and struck it with the mallet stone. As in every case before, the Bechar immediately turned into a glittering heap of white dust.

Licor stared at the dust and then at Shaddra. "Why did the crazy human do that?"

Shaddra just pointed at the jewel in the dead siris dragon's neck. What was once red now glowed sparkly white.

The siris dragon stared at the white jewel and said, "The insane man turned the jewel white. What does that mean?"

Axel threw the white dust out into the bushes, and then, using hand motions, suggested that Shaddra distract Licor's attention away from the dead dragon while Axel cut out its jewel. There was no need to let the king know about white jewels just yet.

***

On the flight back, the two dragons entered rolling banks of dark clouds that threw them violently about and pelted them with rain striking like needles. It forced them to fly lower than planned to see landmarks on the ground, but since both the dragons and Axel could see better than people on the ground, they were able to use the low, dense clouds for cover. Besides, no one down there wanted to be out in this rain either.

Though the flight lasted only about two orais, by the time they arrived at the same encampment as the night before, Axel was thoroughly soaked and numb from the cold. They carefully approached the campsite, where they found Hukken and exchanged greetings.

Hukken stared in total astonishment at the siris dragon, who landed next to Shaddra. Looking from one dragon to another, he said with a look of suspicion, "I see there is a new member of our party. Would you please introduce me?"

Shaddra grinned in an embarrassed way and said, "Hukken, please meet a new acquaintance by the name of Licor."

Licor glanced at him suspiciously and nodded but remained silent. Shaddra pointedly looked at Licor's neck and then back at Hukken. "He is a little confused right now and needs some help and guidance."

Hukken's jaw dropped in a very human-like gesture. "Bless the gods! Shaddra, how did you...?"

Shaddra interrupted him with a quick "We'll talk about that later, once we have a chance to get to know Licor better."

"Hey!" Axel called out from his position, still atop Shaddra's back. "We need to know... Hukken, is... is Jarrad still alive?"

"He was alive two orais ago," Hukken responded, "when I took him to the Daughter of..."

"Ahem!" Shaddra interjected, a warning edge in her tone. "So, you took him to Eleth. Good."

"Uh... yes." Hukken glanced at Licor, who still looked dazed. "When I brought Uncle Jarrad to Eleth, he was alive. The women carried him inside. No one has come out with any news since, so I assume he's still all right."

Axel patted Shaddra's neck and said, "I need to see Jarrad, and I won't make it walking. Would you take me over to the house?"

"I'll take you. It will be a good idea to provide them with a little warning that we are coming, given the situation, and that we are not dangerous. It is fortunate that I can send Eleth a signal."

She turned to Hukken. "Our new friend is not totally aware and may be unpredictable. Please watch him carefully and give him the *direct commands* he needs, as necessary. When I return, we'll have a delightful chat with him."

Licor listened to this conversation as if everyone were speaking a foreign language. He looked at Shaddra, intending to say something, but she cut him short, saying, "I order you to stay here and remain quiet until I return. At that time, you will receive important information regarding your future and about who we are. I will not be gone very long."

She glanced back at Axel but stopped to look Hukken warily in the eye, as if giving him a warning. "Ok, Axel. Let's go. Licor, I will return in five minutes."

Shaddra sent out a clear note of warning as she and her passenger flew over the cottage. By the time they touched ground, Eleth could be seen waiting just outside the door. She rushed over to give the dragon a hug and then climbed up to give Axel one, too, not even giving him a chance to undo his safety belt.

"We've been so worried about you! When Hukken brought Jarrad here, he had no idea as to what had happened to you two. Oh, wait!" Eleth said sharply. "You have blood on your clothes. Where are you hurt?"

Axel grinned lamely at her and said, "Fortunately, this is not my blood, but unfortunately, I am injured." He finished unbelting himself and carefully climbed down from the dragon. Eleth immediately saw his problem.

"Is it broken or just sprained?"

"It feels like it's broken, but I can put a small amount of weight on it. I felt a definite crack when it twisted, and the pain is intense."

"Then, it's not broken, but you may have a serious sprain or torn tendons. You couldn't walk on it at all if it was broken. Let me help you in, out of this rain."

"How is Jarrad?"

She looked him in the eyes and said, "The arrow struck him in the lower back and punctured his intestines. It was fortunate that the arrow was a bodkin, so the bleeding was not as bad as it could have been. It was also good that you placed tight bandages around him; otherwise he could have bled to death before reaching us. I had to operate to stop the bleeding and close his various wounds. He'll recover well enough from that. But impurities have entered his system and put him in grave danger, which could have led to severe complications if not addressed promptly. It will take a few days before we'll know how he'll respond to my medication."

"Your medication?"

"Let's get you inside, and I'll tell you all about it."

"Thank you, Shaddra," she called out to the dragon, "for bringing him safely back to us."

Axel added a quick, "Thank you, Shaddra, for a lot more than that!"

The dragon called back as she lifted into the air, "You are both very welcome. If you need either Hukken or me, you know where to find us."

Eleth and Clara helped Axel to hobble to one of the kitchen chairs.

When he sat down, Clara stood back and, placing her hands on her hips, said in a serious voice. "You realize we were not exactly expecting visitors today. Even if we were, we aren't equipped to handle even one sleepover guest, and *now* we have *two,* and *both* are apparently injured." She looked down and shook her head slowly. "... and one of them is seriously injured."

Axel marveled that Clara had developed ties to Jarrad and himself so quickly. "If it weren't raining like this," he said, "I would just sleep outside. I'm quite used to that. If Jarrad weren't hurt, he would do the same.... But may I ask, where are you keeping him?"

"He is sleeping in my workroom, which is the room connected by that door over there." She pointed to one of two doors leading to other parts of the house. "We don't have an extra bed, but we have plenty of blankets, many of which are thick and soft. We made a pile of about eight blankets for Jarrad to lie on. We could do the same for you."

"That's much better than what we've slept on for the last two nights... or... rather, days."

Eleth brought out a crutch for Axel to use. "We have another one of these somewhere, but I don't have time to look for it. You'll have to make do."

The person for whom the crutch was originally made was a little shorter than Axel, but he made do with it and hobbled into the next room, while the women shuttled back and forth bringing in the blankets, a pillow, and a lighted candle in a holder.

Eleth motioned for Axel to sit on a wooden chair that was placed against the wall. "The first thing we need to do," she said with authority, "is to get you out of those wet clothes. Unfortunately, we don't have any other clothes for you to wear, but we have plenty of blankets." She picked up a blanket from a nearby stack, handed it to Axel, and moved toward the door. "I'll be back in five minutes."

Changing his wet clothes proved to be somewhat harder than Axel figured. The material stuck to his skin, and getting his breeches over the sprained ankle was a form of torture. He just managed to get them off when Eleth came rushing into the room.

"Hey, I'm almost naked here!" he said as he reached for the blanket to cover his underwear and other private places.

"You have nothing I haven't already seen," she said, without showing any embarrassment. She smiled and said, "Of course, when I watched my father work on men, they were always asleep."

Axel rolled his eyes and said, "I'm not asleep, if you please!"

"Good, that will make it all the easier for you to remove your soaking underwear and hand it over."

Axel just looked at her in disbelief.

"I'm waiting," Eleth said firmly while tapping her foot. "I'll turn my back if that gets you moving." She turned and stood, tapping her foot.

Heaving a frustrated sigh, Axel struggled to remove his very clingy underwear beneath the blanket without exposing anything important. It took a while, but he succeeded. "I guess I'm supposed to spend the night naked."

"You're not naked. You have a blanket. These clothes should be dry by morning. By the way, I like the golden amulet you wear around your neck."

"Oh, this," Axel said, clasping his free hand around his sunstar talisman. "It's made from brass but looks like gold, doesn't it? It was my father's and belonged to my mother before him. It's all I managed to save from the fires in Frithden."

Eleth's face reddened. "Oh, I see. Um, your bed is over there." She pointed to a corner of the room where at least half a dozen folded blankets were stacked up upon each other. A pillow lay on the blankets.

Axel saw that his makeshift bed was in a corner opposite Jarrad's but at the same end of the room. Jarrad was on his back and sleeping soundly. When Axel recognized his friend, he took in a surprised gasp of breath.

Eleth noticed Axel's reaction and whispered quietly into his ear. I gave Uncle Jarrad a draft of papola extract for his pain and to help him sleep. I had to operate on him to close his internal, as well as external, wounds. Except for his loss of blood, he went through that surgery rather well. Fortunately, no major organs were damaged except for the intestines. Jarrad's white face is due to his lack of blood. His body will make more blood, and he will gradually regain his color.

"The real danger is from something we call a pestilence in the blood. It can happen anytime our skin is cut or punctured, but if the intestines are gashed or cut open in any way, as has happened with him, the pestilence is always sure and strong, and the patient nearly always dies. Without proper treatment, he would suffer a rather painful death within a few days."

Axel's face went almost as white as that of the man in the other bed. Does this prognosis mean he's going to die? If he doesn't get this treatment, that is?

"Until recently, there was nothing that would work. However, early last year, before I came to stay with Clara, I discovered that injured birds and animals would deliberately fly or climb into a landrin tree and rub themselves against the blossoms. They would come away almost covered with the yellow pollen from the blossoms. After that, I started sprinkling landrin pollen on patients with cuts and lacerations. Virtually none of those cases developed the pestilence. Now, I never go anywhere without a fresh supply of landrin pollen. This is the first opportunity I've had to try pollen on so serious a case, but I did it. I used a lot of it and sprinkled it around his insides before closing the wound. I'm thinking that I will mix some of it with water for Jarrad to drink. It might help."

She saw the shocked expression on Axel's face. "Don't look at me that way; I wouldn't give him anything I hadn't already tried myself."

"Okay, how long until we can tell if it's working?"

"We should know within a day or two. If it isn't working by then, he will die. If it is working, he still couldn't be moved for at least a sycle."

Axel started biting his lip when he heard this. Many people in Tarfal will be very worried about their absence for so long a time.

While Axel held the blanket closely about his body, Eleth helped him to lie down on his pile of blankets and began tightly wrapping his ankle with a long strip of cloth. "You need to stay off this foot for at least a few days, maybe more. In the meantime, I'm sorry; it's going to hurt a lot, especially if you put weight on it."

She smiled weakly. "I know you are hurting, and you may not easily get to sleep. I could get something for you."

"That won't be necessary. I've been awake for a full day and a night. I've also worked harder than usual. I'll sleep fine."

Clara came into the room carrying a bag made from a strange animal's skin. It was filled with something and tightly tied at the opening. "Here you are, Eleth, as requested."

"Thank you, Clara."

"This bag," Eleth explained, "contains crushed ice from our cool shed. Last winter, we cut out a bunch of ice from a pond and stored it in the cellar of the shed. We covered it with a lot of straw and sawdust, which we got from a sawmill down in Kelby, the nearest town, so that the ice now keeps for a long time into the summer. Clara was nice enough to break some small chunks off and tie them up in this bundle.

"My father taught me how to cut and store the ice. He also said that putting cold on a sprain or bruise can help reduce swelling and make the damaged parts heal sooner. I'm sorry, but the bag may leak a little and get you wet."

"That's all right. I've been wet almost all night."

"Just one more thing to do." She grabbed a couple more blankets and started placing them strategically under and around his leg and foot.

"What now?"

"We've found that raising a damaged limb helps in reducing swelling and pain."

"That is a bit uncomfortable."

"Do you want to be uncomfortable now or hurt more later?

"All right, you win. Raise my leg."

"Was there some sort of competition?"

Axel shook his head and said nothing.

Taking the candle with her, Eleth left the room but stopped in the kitchen. There she looked at the sopping bundle of clothes and smiled. It was amazing how this young man of sixteen years could be so muscular! She thought about the strength in those arms... but then stopped herself. There was no sense in developing feelings for a boy who lived two hundred and fifty tondrins away. Shaking her head, she set the chairs about the kitchen stove and draped the clothes across them to dry.

She went to bed to get whatever sleep she could, which she knew would not be much, since a glimmer of light through the window showed that the sunstar would rise very soon.

***

Axel awoke and was instantly alert. His eyes swept the room, found no danger, and then connected to his brain, at which point all kinds of ideas began to run through it. It's not dangerous, but what is this place? Ah, it's Clara's workshop! How long did I sleep? Is it morning or evening? Where's Jarrad? Is he okay?

He answered the last question by simply turning his head and seeing Jarrad still on his makeshift bed in the opposite corner. The rise and fall of his chest testified to his being alive.

"I've got to find Eleth," he said out loud, "and find out how he's doing." But he realized he was still naked under the blanket.

He was forced to satisfy himself by checking out his surroundings. The room was strangely furnished. In the two corners opposite the door were the visitor's makeshift beds. In the very center of the room stood a wood stove of curious design, and a comforting heat could be felt emanating from its iron sides. Its shape was not square or rectangular like virtually every other stove Axel had seen. This one was round! Its top was flat, and it stood on iron legs, but it had only an outside and an inside. There were no corners. There was a door on one side of the stove and vent holes placed strategically around the lower side. A metal chimney rose to and through the ceiling. Next to the stove lay a pile of wood and kindling.

Over against the far wall was the single armless chair he sat on last night—or possibly this morning—and yet another pile of wood. In the corner, just left of the door, was a neatly folded pile of blankets. Lastly, a stack of wicker baskets, perhaps numbering twenty or more, stood in the corner to the right of the door. Someone had, cleverly, made the baskets in such a way that the bottom of each one easily slid into the next as a way of saving space. Axel also noticed that the baskets were quite large and wondered what they could be used for.

Reaching for his crutch, he painfully used it to help get himself sitting up when suddenly the door opened and in walked Eleth. She was carrying another crutch and some clothes—his clothes.

"Are you always this much trouble?" she said sternly. "Your orders were to stay off that foot!"

"What can I say?" Axel said in his defense. "When a guy wakes up after a long sleep, he needs to take care of certain particulars. In this case they are rather urgent."

Eleth responded with a long, exasperated sigh. "Fortunately for you, I found the matching crutch in the supply shed. Here, take it and your clothes. You'll need both crutches to get to the outbuilding in back. Go through this door, turn right, and go through two more doors straight on. The last one will take you outside, where you'll see the outbuilding straight ahead.

"I'll leave the room while you get dressed, but I'll come back to check on Jarrad after you're gone."

When Axel returned, he saw that Jarrad was not only awake but also sitting up and sipping some tea from a cup.

Eleth turned to look at Axel with a bright smile on her face.

Oh, Axel thought, *I could stand here and look at that smile for orais.*

"I can't believe it," she said. "Jarrad should be burning with a fever by now and suffering increased pain, but he's not! His forehead is warm, but nothing like it should be under the circumstances. The landrin pollen works! It really works!"

"What?" Jarrad asked in a weak voice. "More landrins? Is that what's in this horrible-tasting tea you're giving me? There's got to be something strange about that tree—at least with you *children of Ceragon* around, there is."

Axel was suddenly almost in tears at finding Jarrad so well, but he merely grinned at his uncle and friend while slowly shaking his head.

"Hush, Uncle Jarrad," Eleth said. "You can talk later when you gain a little strength.

"I noticed that Clara isn't here," Axel said. "Has she gone somewhere?"

"Clara is at work today."

"Then, why aren't you also there with her?"

"We don't always go into the coops together. Sometimes Clara asks me to stay here. I don't know if she is trying to spare me from something awful, to keep me from learning secrets, or simply because there isn't enough work for two people to do. There are some days that neither of us goes in. It all depends on how the hens, eggs, and hatchlings are doing. If an emergency arises when we are out, then someone is sent to fetch us."

"Now, as for you, Mr. Daimon, would you please sit over in that chair so I can examine your ankle?"

"I will if you stop calling me 'Mr. Daimon.' It seems that *we* are the *children of the Great Ceragon* and blessed or doomed to be the center of some big future events. Don't you think we can be on a first-name basis?"

Eleth had to admit to herself that she was afraid of this handsome, young, yellow-blond-haired man. She was only sixteen years old, but already, in many ways, she thought like a mature woman. Maybe it had something to do with the dragon's blood. She hoped it had a similar effect on Axel.

Over the course of one day, her orderly life and planned future, devoid of boys, had unraveled. Now, she would be inseparably bound to him by some force, whether she liked it or not, and she still did not even know who he was. His story, while informative and sad, only told her what had happened to him, not what he was like inside. Every move to get closer to him involved danger and risk—to Clara, to the dragons she loved, and even to her parents... let alone to her heart. She only had to look at the two men's injuries to confirm.

"As you wish," she said. "You are Axel, and I am Eleth. Now, will you please get your ass over to the chair?"

Axel performed his best imitation of a salute and shuffled over to the chair.

Eleth unwrapped his bandage and examined the foot. "It looks like you aren't improving as quickly as Jarrad. It also appears you may have torn one or more ligaments, which take some time to heal. You'd better get used to those crutches, and you also need to get that leg up into the air and iced again."

Obediently, Axel hobbled over to the makeshift bed, lay down, and placed his injured leg onto the specially raised pile of blankets.

"I'll be back soon with the ice," she said and left the room right away.

She returned on schedule to set the ice bag loosely around Axel's ankle. She also brought a cup of what appeared to be tea.

"Don't tell me that's the same stuff you were feeding Jarrad."

"All right, I won't tell you, but drink it anyway. I want to see if, somehow, it will reduce your swelling. This time, I've tried sweetening it with sap from a loma tree."

"You know there are people who go around selling magic cure-all potions."

"Look, I don't know if this will help. But it won't hurt, and you need all the help you can get."

Axel just raised himself up on one arm, took the cup, and gulped it all down while taking only one breath.

"How on Tamerel did you ever do that?" Jarrad called from the corner of the room. It's been a half orai and I still haven't finished my cup."

"I just figured it would be best to get it out of the way as fast as possible."

"Axel," Jarrad said, "you never cease to amaze me."

Eleth stood wide-eyed above Axel and said, "I've tasted that tea myself and must admit you surprise me, too."

At this moment, the sound of the front door opening and closing was clearly audible from the adjacent room. An instant later, Clara came through the door to the workshop. She smiled when she saw everyone there and especially when she saw Jarrad finishing the last of his tea.

With a questioning look on her face, she moved her eyes over to Eleth.

Eleth just smiled and tilted her head back towards Jarrad.

Suddenly inspired, Clara spun on her heel and fetched a chair from the kitchen, carrying it into the workshop. "Well," she declared, setting the chair down with a decisive thump, "since moving to the kitchen has been vetoed, I suggest we ladies at least sit down instead of loitering about."

"What is it you want to discuss?" Eleth asked, perching herself on the seat offered.

Clara folded her arms. "I want to know what happened in the early hours this morning! How is it that I find two strong men in my workshop, who both happen to be physically damaged?"

"Don't look at me!" Jarrad protested, raising his hands in surrender. "All I recall is getting shot in the back with an arrow—and then waking up here."

All eyes swung to Axel, who did his best to look innocent. "Who, me?" he said, wide-eyed.

He hesitated. "We were ambushed by two of the king's siris dragons. One of the riders shot Jarrad with a crossbow bolt. I managed to take him down."

"What?" Eleth exclaimed, her eyes widening. "You killed the same rider who shot Uncle Jarrad?"

"That's what I said, isn't it?" Axel replied, a little defensive. "The second rider fired at me but only hit my saddle. He swooped past and circled back for a head-on charge. I had Shaddra halt mid-air and drop—right as the dragon streaked overhead. I fired as we fell, hitting the dragon square in the chest. It died instantly, and the rider went down with it."

Jarrad gaped. "You fired an arrow while falling and managed to hit a charging dragon going the opposite direction?"

Axel shrugged, almost sheepish. "Yeah, somehow. I'm as surprised as anyone that it worked."

"So, you took out two riders and a dragon," Eleth said slowly. "But what happened to the second dragon?"

Axel's expression sobered. "I'm not proud of killing them. The dragon, too. I only did what I had to. I still see every face, every time. They never leave me."

Jarrad nodded, his voice gentler. "Believe it or not, that's a good thing. I killed a bandit thirty years ago—the memory still haunts me. Those images fade, but they'll keep you honest. They'll remind you not to take a life unless you must."

Eleth pressed on, anxious. "But the second dragon? Did you just let it go?"

"No. Shaddra and I gave chase and caught up to it over the Immaten River."

Clara frowned, puzzled. "How did a messenger dragon catch up with a siris dragon?"

Axel explained, "It wasn't trying to get away. It followed the river's bends while we cut straight across. When we caught up, it was still carrying its rider, who was dead and dangling from a tether."

Clara's eyebrows shot up. "I've always heard that dragons will fight until death to bring their dead riders home. Did you kill it too?"

"No," Eleth interjected, frustration edging her tone. "He said he only killed one dragon. So, what did you do, Axel?"

"Shaddra managed to sneak up on the dragon from the rear and underneath its belly. I was able to cut the tether line with a bowshot, and Shaddra dove so I could catch the falling body. When I caught him, I broke the chain holding his Bechar, and then we got out of there fast. That's where the blood on my cloak came from."

Jarrad let out a low whistle. "I knew you could shoot, but that's incredible!"

"The siris dragon didn't come after you?" Eleth asked.

"No, it followed the rider's body, not the jewel."

Eleth leaned forward. "Why risk so much for the Bechar?"

Axel drew a shaky breath. "Once we had it, Shaddra dove for the ground. I jumped off and smashed the jewel between two rocks. That's how I twisted my ankle."

Jarrad stared at him. "By the gods—did it work? Did you set the dragon free?"

"I think so. We brought him back with us. His name is Licor. He was dazed, but Shaddra is working with him. She'll be able to tell us more soon."

Clara clasped her hands to her face, awe in her voice. "You freed a full-grown dragon by destroying its Bechar?"

Axel nodded. "I think so. But we'll have to wait for Shaddra's word to be sure."

***

That evening, Clara and Eleth prepared a simple meal of ellam stew. The ice in the cellar of the shed made it possible for the women to keep a large piece of ellam meat fresh for a long time. Clara had no skell, and walking to the local village butcher took a long time. Other kinds of food were kept there, too. The cellar saved them a lot of wear and tear on their feet and time that could be used more productively.

Jarrad had to be satisfied with a thinned-down version of the stew, with fewer and smaller pieces of meat and vegetables. If he handled this well, he might get a better meal tomorrow.

Clara and Eleth were picking up the dishes from the meal for cleaning when Eleth suddenly looked toward the front door. From the next room, Axel yelled out, "We've got a dragon visitor!"

Eleth opened the door to find, as expected, Shaddra standing there. She had a bit of a worried look on her face.

"What's wrong, Shaddra?" Eleth asked. "Can we help with something?"

"Yes, *you* can," Shaddra responded, "you and Axel. Can you both come with me to the dragon campsite? Hukken and I are having trouble with Licor."

Axel appeared, hobbling out on his crutches. "What can the *two of us* do to help Licor?" he asked.

"Can you get around on those artificial legs long enough to reach the camp? Both you and Eleth are needed; I can explain the situation on the way over."

Eleth looked hard at Axel, as if giving him a definitive, silent 'no,' but he only responded by shrugging his shoulders.

Out of sheer habit, Axel grabbed his bow, awkwardly strung it, and buckled on his waist quiver. "All right," he said, "if you need us, we'll go. But *please* walk slowly."

Shaddra started talking almost as soon as the cottage disappeared from their sight. "Hukken and I are trying to see if Licor can be trusted to live among the free dragons and join us now that he is free from the jewels' power. So far, it is not going very well. He has come out of the daze you saw him in, but Licor is now fixated on getting revenge against humans for all that they have forced him to do."

"Okay, but how are two humans, especially younglings like us, going to make any difference there?" Axel asked.

"You will make a difference because you are more than just humans; you are special beings with unique abilities."

"Yes, I get it; we are the *son* and *Daughter of Ceragon*. I can see where that might lead, but I know something about the desire for revenge, and it's going to take a lot more than the two of us to change that."

"Actually, you just mentioned the real reason why we need *you*."

"You mean *me*, as in Axel 'Daimon?"

"No, I mean *you* as in Axel Fletcher."

"I don't understand."

"Let me give you some more of Licor's background," Shaddra said, with a heavy sigh. "It will help you understand."

"Licor was assigned as a strike dragon in His Majesty's Special Assignments Group. The king has long entrusted this group with the responsibility of serving as the special missions strike force. They were given assignments of exceptional sensitivity, most requiring stealth, secrecy, and often assassination. For several years now, the humans of this force have been tasked with dressing up in enemy uniforms and attacking small, isolated villages along the Sanara border to make it appear that Kolodra, or Mandara, was responsible. On one occasion, there was a secondary or perhaps even a primary assignment to kill a particular person accused of a serious crime and to kill all he knew and all who knew him."

Axel stopped so suddenly he almost tripped over his crutches. "Frithden!" He said with a gasp. "Oh, gods above, Licor helped to destroy Frithden and... my family!"

The news caused Eleth to stop just as quickly. She stared at Axel's stricken face, and, in so doing, tears started streaming down her cheeks and dripping from her chin. She said nothing. But her heart ached for her newfound friend.

"There is more," Shaddra said. "Maybe you'd better sit down for this; perhaps over on that rock."

Bowing his head and breathing in gasps, Axel said, between his heavy breaths, "I think... I know... what you are going to tell me."

He made his way over to the rock and sat down, bent over with his forehead resting on an open palm. Eleth, kneeling beside him, placed her arm around his shoulders in silent support.

Shaddra found it difficult to even look at Axel but soon found her courage and said, "Licor was the siris dragon who shot the firebolt that killed your father," she said quietly.

At the news, Axel's head fell to one side, and it seemed that he might fall. But he caught himself and sat up on the rock for some time, with his eyes closed, breathing heavily. After a moment, he regained some control over his breathing but did not lift his head.

"When you came to get us, Shaddra, you didn't mention it was so you could give *me* some news. You said we were needed to help Licor. Why did you do that?"

"That *is* the reason why I came. However, there was no way you could possibly help him without knowing exactly who he was, and I emphasize the word 'was.' Now, he needs to learn exactly who he *is*.

"What kind of person are *you,* Axel?" she said with a firm but compassionate expression on her face.

"Shaddra!" Eleth exclaimed. "You mustn't ask a person a question like that! Especially not now! It's heartless and cruel!"

"No!" said Axel in a loud voice, still not raising his head. "It's a question that needs asking! Even if we had not brought Licor here, it needed to be asked... and... it required answering."

He lifted his head now and looked up at Shaddra. Hot tears gushed down his face and dribbled off his chin. "You are a wise dragon, and there is no question why the other dragons of the Colony call you 'Mother.' It is an honored term that reflects your contributions, your protection, your love, your caring for others, and your wisdom. Now, I see it also refers to your caring for humans as well as dragons. I see so much of Clara in you, Shaddra. Even though I have known her for only a day, I see you have always been kindred spirits."

"What exactly do you mean?" asked Eleth in a gentle way.

Turning his head to look straight into Eleth's eyes, Axel said, "I mean that Shaddra knew I still harbored a strong desire for revenge in my heart—a desire for revenge against both the dragons and the soldiers who attacked and destroyed my village. But the dragons, at least, were slaves—mere puppets dangling from strings controlled by the king and others of similar mind. I don't know about the dragonriders. Maybe they were slaves, in a way, too."

"Licor tells us," Shaddra said, "that the human 'flying officers,' meaning the dragonriders, of his group are murderers at heart, who enjoy their work of death and destruction. The King uses the men and women of this special unit because he knows they are people who love killing and can be relied upon to do dirty work.

That is not, necessarily, true of the regular flying groups in the Dragon Corps, he says."

"That means the two men I killed yesterday were some of those who raided my village," Axel said while staring straight ahead, as if voicing his thoughts. "It doesn't really change how I feel about having to kill them. What I did tears at my gut, even now."

He looked again up at Shaddra and wiped the tears from his face with a sleeve. "It appears those two men received proper justice for their actions. I can't shake off a sense of guilt for being the one called upon to kill them, but by the gods, I would kill them again and everyone else who set a vile hand to the destruction of my village! Still, not everyone involved was guilty of a crime."

Shaddra smiled down at the young man and stared into his eyes. "There remains a distance to travel in your journey to understand your life, Axel, but you have come a long way in a short time. Now that you've answered the important question, we must move along and have a chat with a certain siris dragon. It's time he finds out what kind of a dragon *he* is."

Chapter Twelve

LIVE FRIEND OR DEAD ENEMY

When Shaddra and the two young humans arrived at the dragon camp, the first thing they noticed was... was a trail, specifically a big, fresh one. It was ten strides wide and long enough to reach out into the forest, where its end disappeared. The answer to how it was created came into sight not long after their arrival. Coming out of the trees toward them was Licor, and he was, indeed, following the trail.

Shaddra clenched her jaw and stepped directly in front of the siris dragon, which towered over her. "Let me guess," said Shaddra. "You have been pacing back and forth along this trail since I left?"

Licor paused, his eyes narrowing as he glared down at her. He grumbled curtly, "Is there anything else to do around here?" he growled, his malevolent tone apparent.

He noticed the two humans beside Shaddra. "What did you bring them for?" he asked with a malevolent snarl curled across his lips. "Are they the first to die for their crimes?"

Shaddra maintained her composure, her eyes locked on Licor's. "Licor, I will have you know this youngling has the power to kill you long before you could even send off a fireball."

Licor glared at Axel and Eleth and growled, "No human can do that!"

In half the time of a sharp breath, Axel dropped his crutches, removed the bow from his shoulder, took an arrow from his waist quiver, set it on the bow, drew, and fired.

Licor heard a thunk close to his right ear and turned his head only slightly to see half an arrow sticking out of a handspan-thick branch, barely a stride from his head. The arrow protruded through to the other side of the branch by a span.

"Just so you know, Licor," Axel said with a half-smile, half-smirk on his face, "at this range I don't need to worry about striking a vulnerable place in your armor. But, just in case you are not convinced, that arrow is embedded in a knot on that branch, which is just about the same size as your eye."

Still looking at the arrow, Licor moved his eyes barely enough to confirm the shaft was lodged dead center in a knothole, which matched the youngling's description.

Licor turned to look closely at the youngling. "Who are you? I've never seen any human who could do what you just did."

Shaddra coughed and said, "Licor, I would like to introduce you to Axel, the *son of the Great Ceragon*, and to Eleth, who is the *Daughter of the Great Ceragon*."

"Hah!" Licor bellowed. "Do you really expect me to believe that?"

Suddenly, Eleth made a quick turning movement that seemed to be nothing but a blur. Licor again heard a thunk from the branch next to his head. This time, when he looked, he saw a knife, about a handspan in length, buried halfway into the same branch, not a thumb's distance from the arrow.

"Oh, my! Licor," Shaddra said. "It seems I was wrong. I should have said either of these younglings could kill you before you had a chance to kill them."

Licor glared at the two younglings and said, "You've shown how they're dangerous, but that doesn't mean they're the foretold ones."

"Do you trust your nose, Licor? Tell me, what is it that you *do not* smell right now?"

"What do you mean? I smell the woods; I smell you and Hukken, and I smell... I smell... nothing. else. I..." Suddenly Licor's head jerked back, and his eyes opened wide in amazement. "I do not smell humans!"

"But they are standing right before you. Is something wrong with your nose?"

Taking on an expression of wonderment, Licor said, "I do not smell them because they smell just like you and Hukken. I... I... cannot believe it. They *are* the *Children of Ceragon*!"

Licor lowered his head as if to bow when Axel suddenly said forcefully, "No! No dragon bows to us! We should bow to you and to every dragon who has been enslaved or mistreated by humans. I do not know how we're going to do it, but our purpose here is to change the world so that no dragon is ever so mistreated!"

Licor took a whole step back in amazement. Shaddra looked down at Axel as if seeing him for the first time. Eleth walked over to Axel's side, slipped her hand into his, and looked up at Licor expectantly.

"Who are you, young humans?" Licor said. "Why have you come to me?"

"Axel," Shaddra said matter-of-factly, "is the human who set you free from the power of the jewel in your neck. He is the one who killed the dragonrider who was your master. He is the one who cut away the dangling body of your master as you flew homeward, and he is the one who turned your jewel white."

"My jewel is white?" Licor asked incredulously. "Like the one I saw yesterday?"

"Actually," Axel said, "it's more like clear glass, which sparkles with many colors when the sunstar has a chance to shine on it."

He stepped forward and held out his hand. It held a jewel, which appeared white in the shaded light available in the little meadow. "This is the jewel you saw in your comrade who died after attacking Shaddra and me. It looks exactly like the jewel in your neck. But *you* are still alive, and *you* are free."

"So, answer my question!" the dragon said again. "Who are you, and why have you come to me?"

"Axel took a deep breath and blew it out slowly. "Licor," he said. "You and I are bound together in a way you would never imagine. Just less than one year has passed since you and your 'Special Assignments Corps attacked a small village by the name of Frithden. Do you remember it?"

"Yes, we have destroyed other villages like it, but that one was different because we were also sent to kill a specific human, a bowman."

"You were the one who killed that bowman, weren't you? You killed him with a fireball."

"Yes, that is true. How could you know that?"

"I know because I was on a nearby hillside, where I could watch you. You see, Frithden was my home village; the people killed there were my friends and family, and the bowman you killed with that fireball was my father. I saw it all."

Licor bowed his head slightly and looked at the ground. Silence hung between them for a moment before he looked up, meeting Axel's eyes. "Why am I still alive?" he asked, his voice rough with confusion and pain. "Why have you not killed me? When I first saw you, I would have killed you, just like I would kill every human I could for what they have done to me! Why am I not dead?"

"I haven't killed you because I would rather have a live friend than a dead enemy."

"But your family? Your father? You... you do not want revenge?"

"My Da taught me the difference between right and wrong, and he also taught, by example, what the differences are between wanting revenge and wanting *justice* for those *responsible* for a crime.

"Tell me, would you have killed my father if the jewel had not forced you to?"

"In my time, I have killed many humans, but never once because I wanted to."

"Then, why should I blame you for my father's death? It was a crime, yes, but one for which *others* are responsible! They will, eventually, be punished." Axel said the last sentence with a slight quiver in his voice, but his facial expression was resolute and his eyes piercing in intensity. "How can *I* seek revenge against slaves, who were forced to do something that was just as revolting to *them* as it was to *me*?"

Licor stood shocked, not able to speak. Shaddra stared at Axel with warm, knowing eyes. Hukken simply smiled, while Eleth looked down at her hand, which still grasped Axel's hand, and then up at his face.

Licor sat back on his haunches as if his body strength had given out after much exertion. He looked around at his surroundings and at the others with him. "This glen is a holy place," he said after a moment. "In this place, I have come to know two dragons, who carry no jewels, and two humans who, by some miracle, are the *son* and *Daughter of Ceragon* from the *Great Foretelling*. I have learned of my emancipation from slavery, and I think I have found four friends—the first real friends I have ever had. You have done so much for me. How may I, in turn, be of service to you?"

Hukken broke his silence by saying, "Would you like to start by making one hundred and seventy-two other new friends?"

Licor jumped to his feet and stared incredulously at Hukken. "One hundred and seventy-two? There are one hundred and seventy-two more dragons like you?"

"Some are pretty young, but I guess they still count."

"But one hundred and seventy-two!"

"Yes, I think that was the number I used."

"And none of them have jewels in their necks?

Hukken smiled broadly. "Since you are the first and only dragon to ever have been freed from the power of his jewel, the only kind of dragon we have in the Free Colony are those without jewels; I suppose that will change once *you* arrive."

Licor suddenly looked thoughtful, even apprehensive. "I'm not like them. Will they accept me?"

"If you agree to accept them, abide by the rules of the Colony, and defend them from all potential harm, they will accept you. If you learn to love them, they will learn to love you."

Over the next orai, many questions were asked and answered on both sides. In the end, it was clearly decided that Licor would join the Free Family of Dragons and that both Hukken and Shaddra would escort Licor to his new home. Everyone knew there would be many more questions to be answered once they reached home.

Shaddra announced she would return in a sycle or so to determine how much Jarrad had recovered. She might or might not have another dragon accompany her when she did.

“Oh, Licor,” Axel said, almost as if in an afterthought, “how did you and the others with you happen to find Shaddra and Hukken when we were flying home last night? Do the king’s dragons normally fly at night?”

“We only flew at night when there was sufficient light from Kivan. Last night it was too dark, so our masters ordered us to land and rest for the night. Several orais into the night, one of our flight officers caught sight of a shadow moving in the sky and shouted out that he saw a dragon flying overhead. Since our flight was the only team of king’s dragons ordered to search this area, he declared the dragon he saw up there to be an enemy, and we rose to attack. However, we did not catch up to the enemy until we were above the Immaten River. We did not realize there were two dragons until we managed to climb above them and to their rear. My master then ordered me to run a high-speed attack on the siris dragon’s rider from directly behind.”

“Thank you, Licor; that answers some important questions. I know you and the others have a long flight ahead of you. It would be best if you got started sooner and use as much of this night as possible for protection.”

There was not that much to pack up, but Axel helped remove the saddles from Shaddra’s and Hukken’s backs. The knife and parts of the arrow were retrieved from the branch. When everyone saw that there was nothing more to say, they just exchanged farewells, and the dragons set off, out to the west.

***

For Eleth and Axel, the walk back to the cottage, as expected, required a lot of time. Unexpectedly, it turned out to be a ‘get to know you’ session for two strangers, who, now, could no longer remain that way.

“Eleth, I’ve never seen anyone who could have made the knife throw you did.”

“Have you even seen that many knife-throwing contests?”

"I have. My Da...," Axel's voice hesitated for an instant at the thought of his father, but then continued, "would take me to all the big market fairs in the towns and larger villages around us. I saw the best throwers in all of Northern Sanara. Not one of them could match your throw, even at half the distance."

"Thank you, but your skill with a bow was unbelievable. I'll bet you took the prize at all the shooting contests.

"Actually, not."

"No? How could anyone beat you?"

"My Da wouldn't let me compete in any of the contests. He always said they were 'dangerous.' I don't think I understood what he meant until now."

"Axel, honestly speaking, I have to say that you aren't the person I envisioned for you. I considered you to be all brawn and no brain. But the way you handled that tense situation with Licor was indescribably well done!"

"I guess I've always had the gift of gab. My Da told me, more than once, I could talk my way past fifty daewols and call them friends afterwards. He faced that many once. Had the scars to prove it. Based on what he said about them, though, I'm pretty sure his compliment was exaggerated."

"That's certainly not like me," Eleth said, shaking her head. "If people aren't seeing things that are true as I know they are, I'll tell them all about it and keep telling them until they run away screaming or accept it. But, just to talk about things, about feelings, about impressions—I don't do that well, even with other girls my age."

"Eleth, I must tell you that *you* are more than the person I envisioned you to be. You are smart, creative, and, from what I've witnessed, an excellent physician. Who knows what other skills you have, besides that knife? You are also beautiful. Every time I look at your face, especially when the light is set just right to turn your hair ablaze, I can see nothing else. As for not being able to express your feelings, I say, how do you express them when you're so different from everyone else? Others simply don't understand."

This time, Eleth stopped suddenly and looked at Axel. She just stood there staring at him until she said, "Flattery will get you somewhere, but my limits are very conservative."

"I didn't say that to get anything from you," Axel replied. "Honest. I said it because it was true. Up until now, the last thing I wanted in my life was any kind of girl thing. I make bows and arrows, and I'm proficient at it. I got involved with dragons, not because I wanted to—who in their right mind would want to—but because they saved my life, because one went out of her way to help me bury three hundred half-charred remains of my people, and because they have made me one of their own. I've become close friends with many of them and am open to making more. There has simply been no room for girls."

"Now, somehow," Eleth said, with a knowing look, "room has been made. You had no choice in that, just as I have had no choice but to bring a boy into my life. Face it; we're stuck with each other."

They started walking again.

"When I first learned about you, I didn't want to come here. I told Jarrad you were probably ugly."

Eleth put her hand to her mouth to hide her smile and stifle her laugh. She recovered after a few seconds and said, "Your words prove that you are poor at foretelling."

"Guilty as charged and never gladder of it."

"Now that we are, in some sense, together, what does that mean? What do we do?"

Axel was quiet for several hobbles on his crutches. He stopped to look directly at her and said, "For now, we do exactly as has been planned. We work on getting some draft dragons to the Free Colony, though things have been somewhat delayed. We will have to wait until Jarrad is able to travel, and we'll begin making some kind of sling or carrying basket once we get back to Tarfal. You and Clara will have to get two draft dragons out of the caves without anyone else knowing, and heaven knows where you're going to keep them in that small cottage. Your task will be much harder than ours."

He was silent again for a while. "You know, Eleth, sooner or later, it's going to get too dangerous for you two to stay here."

"Clara would never leave her dragons. I would have a very tough time doing the same."

"Hmm. That means we must find a way to free all the dragons in the Breeding Coops."

"You have got to be kidding! None of them have had the opportunity to fly since they were fledged. There are always eggs and hatchlings that would never survive a two-day flight, especially at night. How would you overcome those obstacles?"

Axel thought for a moment. "It would be worse than that. Whether we succeeded or not, it would be tantamount to declaring war on the king. If we aren't prepared, the whole colony could be at risk."

The slow trip to the cottage ended much sooner than either Axel or Eleth anticipated.

"Let's get you inside," Eleth said. "I want to take another look at your ankle. I shudder to think what it may look like after this little excursion. But you haven't complained about it."

"I haven't even thought about it, except as a hindrance to travel."

"Strange. Let's get in there and look at it."

Inside the cottage, Eleth directed Axel to sit on a chair standing near the wall in the workroom. Clara was currently occupying the other chair. She followed the two young people with her eyes as they entered.

Kneeling, Eleth slowly and carefully unwrapped the bandage around Axel's ankle. Once the bandage was off, Eleth pressed her fingers around the ankle in strategic places. Eventually, she sat back.

"Strange, the swelling appears to have gone down and not increased, as should have happened after standing up and walking as you did, even on crutches. Hmm, let me try doing something." She twisted the ankle in several directions and asked whether each move caused him pain.

"Yes, there is pain, but it is quite bearable." He repeated the phrase with most of the moves.

"Axel," she said, "those ankle twists should have caused great pain. This evidence leads me to two possible conclusions. Either your dragon powers include a blessing of rapid healing, or the landrin tea I gave you is serving as a marvelous painkiller."

"It could be both," Axel said.

"The only way to tell is to test it on others and see if a difference occurs."

"Does that mean you're going to come poking around me?" came a voice from the far corner of the room.

Eleth smiled in Jarrad's direction and said, "You know that's exactly what it means."

"I'll have you know, I have serious issues, which include a very long row of stitches across my abdomen. I would prefer to not be manhandled just to satisfy your curiosity."

"Like it or not, it is my job to, as you say, 'manhandle' you. You can take some comfort in the fact that you are going to get 'girl handled' rather than 'manhandled.'"

"There is no sense of privacy here at all," Jarrad muttered.

Eleth helped Axel hop over to his bed, where she again propped up the afflicted leg. She turned to get up, only to find Clara standing there holding a fresh bag of ice.

Handing over the bag, she said, "Thought you might be able to use this." Clara then walked over to the chair and sat down.

Eleth looked down at Axel, and she felt a bright flash cross through her brain. "Um, Clara," she said, turning back to look at her adopted aunt. "I could sure use your help. I need to know quickly if Jarrad's condition suddenly changes, which it could. Would you mind moving your chair closer to Jarrad, where you can see clearly what is happening to him? We will need to know if he has a sudden high temperature, nausea, vomiting, or difficulty breathing; acts incoherently; or shows any other extreme difference from what you see now. I'm particularly worried about shock. The sooner you can alert me to any problems, the better it will be for everyone."

"Hey, you folks are acting like I'm going to die or something."

"I've seen patients die with lesser injuries than you have. I'll be over to inspect you in a moment."

Clara stood and started moving her chair, but she looked over at Eleth as she did. Eleth winked at her in a way that Jarrad couldn't see. Clara just smiled, gave a silent chuckle, and finished moving her chair next to Jarrad.

A bit later, Eleth moved to check on Jarrad. She unbuttoned his torn jerkin and pulled his breeches down enough to give her a view of the entire suture.

"Hey, what did I say about privacy?"

"You didn't complain when I cut you open."

"I wasn't exactly conscious then."

"It just so happens that I saw a lot more of you then, both inside and outside, than I am seeing of you now. I'm afraid I've seen this kind of thing many times before."

"And no one protested."

"Some men really liked it. Can't imagine why."

"Ah, my girl, you may be a wonderful physician, but you have a lot to learn about men."

Eleth turned back to look at Axel. "Perhaps I will have to find myself a teacher."

Jarrad rolled his eyes. "I'm not sure that young men provide the best answers to these questions."

"I guess I'll have to make do with what I've got," she said with a bright smile and a chuckle, "since the only other male I know is encumbered for now."

"Now as for you, Sir. You are recovering remarkably fast. Faster than I have ever seen." She poked him and said, "Does that hurt?"

"Yes, but it's bearable."

"How about here?" She poked him again, quite hard.

"Ouch, you did that on purpose. Yes, it hurt."

"Okay, now I'm going to roll you over and look at the entry wound." She helped him turn over to his stomach and looked at the wound. There was still some redness about the wound to suggest the presence of putrefaction. She replaced the dressing and helped him roll back.

"I'm going to change the dressings on your other wound, after which you are going to get a large dose of the landrin tea."

"I wouldn't feed that stuff to a hirvior," he said.

"You can say that, but I think the tea and other uses of landrin pollen I've applied are what have saved your life. Anyone else in your situation would be in a great deal of pain right now, and that pain would last until you died within the next three days."

Jarrad just looked at her strangely.

Eleth left for a while but soon returned with two steaming mugs of landrin tea. Jarrad and Axel looked at each other with distasteful grimaces on their faces.

"I saw those looks," Eleth said. "Medicine is supposed to taste bad. That's how you know it's working."

"Axel," Jarrad said, "can you see the flaw in that logic?"

"All I know," Axel answered, "is that I am currently in the hands of a doctor, who is running the show. She could make our lives very unpleasant if she so chose."

Smiling wickedly, Eleth handed the cups over and told Clara to see that the men drank it all. Axel just looked at his cup and grimaced. Taking a big breath, he let it out and sipped a small amount of the hot brew. "Etmar's fire," he said, "that stuff is really bad."

"Clara spoke up from the other side of the room, "I don't care if you are the *son of Ceragon*; you will please watch your language in my home! Now, tell me what happened with the three dragons out in the forest."

"Hey," Jarrad said, his tone indicating that he felt excluded from something important. "Tell us all!"

"Okay, but since I am now encumbered over here," Axel said, "I think Eleth needs to take the lead."

Eleth stared daggers at Axel but weakly agreed.

"Oh, but I get to tell the part about the knife!" Axel said with a broad grin.

Rolling her eyes, Eleth said. "Yes, sure, you can tell that part. I'm anxious to hear what you have to say."

***

The next day, Axel was able to put some weight on his foot, so he stopped using both crutches and relied on just one to ensure he didn't put too much weight on his injured ankle.

Again, Clara went to work without Eleth that day. Jarrad was sleeping heavily, which Eleth was glad to see.

She came up to Axel and asked, "Is your foot up to a little exercise?"

"I think so, unless you're planning a hike up the nearest mountain."

"No. No mountains, but it will be high."

'It will be high, but not a mountain. How did you work that out?"

"Come and see. It's one of my favorite places. The trail can get a little rough; take both crutches."

For Axel's sake, their progress was slow and cautious. A narrow trail wound ahead, leading almost due east for quite some distance. After half an orai, Axel estimated they had covered only a fraction of a tondrin. He couldn't help but wonder how much farther they still had to go. Then, quite suddenly, the trees ahead vanished. A few more careful steps brought him to the edge, where the ground fell away almost vertically, plunging down to the sea far below.

Axel gave a long, slow whistle. He had never seen the sea before, and viewing it from this vantage point was nothing like what he could ever imagine. Carefully looking over the cliff's edge, he estimated the drop at more than two hundred strides.

My word, he thought, *that's five landrins! And it's almost straight down!*

"These are the Dremlin Cliffs. Only a few people know about them. Come sit here beside me," Eleth said from behind him.

He turned to see her sitting on a wide, flat rock that made a perfect seat for two. He did as requested and found he very much liked the warm feeling at his side.

"I've explored nearly all the area within two tondrins of the cottage. Clara has given me a lot of free time, often saying that she didn't need me at the coops that day and that I should go out and do something constructive with myself."

She gave a short half-chuckle, half-laugh, and said, "As if there were anything around here to permit a person to do something constructive. I thought of vegetable gardening, but we readily get all the food we could want here. I thought of flower gardening. However, the sheer number and variety of wildflowers in this area would easily overwhelm my modest efforts. One day, I thought of searching for moonstools—not as a way of doing anything constructive. I simply thought that Clara would like them.

"That day, I saw three kota, a little camouflaged terana in the bushes, and smelled the essence of a drugol. Of course, it was from a long distance away. I don't know if you have some knowledge of drugols, but any creature foolish enough to get sprayed by one would likely commit suicide as soon as possible."

"We have drugols where I come from," Axel said. "Animals getting hit by drugol spray will usually run off a cliff or drown themselves in a river if it's close enough. It's a good thing that the drugols' dull white color makes them very visible. Everything runs from them. I suppose they live rather lonely lives."

"My father taught me a way to treat victims of drugol spray. We apply large amounts of alcohol *externally*. That usually makes the smell tolerable within a few orais, though it would be a very miserable few orais for both the patient and doctor. Unfortunately, animals do not have access to that resource."

"What else happened on this excursion? Did you find any moonstools?"

"The intriguing thing about that walk into the woods happened when I found a brook, flowing down a ravine, which opened onto flat ground. I recall only the rustling of my skirt against the bushes and the tumbling water. I kneeled by the brook and cupped my hands into the water to drink. I remember it was bracingly cold. But, when I stood, my movement must have scared a rock sondril. It took off from some bushes only a few strides away with feathers flying. Almost immediately, I saw a short-winged forest siris leap from a landrin tree at the bottom of the hillside and charge after the sondril. I remember how beautiful the siris was as it jigged and jagged after its quarry with talons bared. It nearly caught the sondril twice before it flew around to the far side of a kitki tree that was less than fifty strides away from me, and then it turned back in my direction. As soon as the sondril passed the right side of the tree, its wings stopped, as if it had been turned to stone in midair, and it fell straightway to the ground. The same thing happened to the siris when it passed the tree. Its wings simply stopped, just as if it were suddenly a part of a giant painting, and it, too, fell to the ground.

"I remember swearing by the Goddess at the sight, but I didn't move. Right away, as I stood there, I heard a tremendous, high-pitched buzzing sound coming from the area around the tree. I tried focusing my eyes and ears on the source of the sound until I saw something that was both fascinating and shocking at the same time. I saw hundreds of thumb-sized insects come flying out of hidden nooks on the tree, heading straight for the bodies of the two birds. In only a few seconds the birds were completely covered with the insects.

"I was horrified, but I continued to watch with my dragon vision as the insects grabbed hold of the obviously dead birds with tiny hooks on the end of their legs. They repeatedly jabbed with their stingers into the bodies of the birds. The poison they injected seemed to turn almost instantly whatever it touched into some kind of liquid, which was then being sucked up by strange-looking mouths on the front ends of other insects.

"I just stood transfixed until the little creatures started to fly off, one by one. In a few minutes, it was all over. There was nothing left of the two birds but skeletons, beaks, and tiny talons.

"I kept on watching until the insects left and saw them settle into woven holes in a giant web in the tree—yes, it was like a gossamer-thin spider's web. I looked even closer and saw that the web started twelve strides up the side of the kitki tree and stretched straight and level over to another kitki tree on the other side of the stream, perhaps forty strides away. That part of the web also started about twelve strides up and extended to the top of the other tree. There could have been thousands of insects hiding in little web cavities between those trees.

"After the insects left, I looked around and saw dozens of tiny skeletons of birds, bats, and a few tree-climbing animals scattered around the bases of both trees and on either side of the stream."

"Did any of the insects bother you?" Axel asked.

"No, not one of them did. At first, I thought it might be because of my dragon blood. But I then realized that the insects only attack creatures that disturb the web. There were no big animal bones, and all the bones were close to the web. There was acid on the strands of the web; I could see and smell it from where I was if I concentrated, and I think that acid could kill a bird all by itself. The acid would certainly mark the victim, making it easier for those insects to find and consume it afterward." She shivered, even though the day was still warm.

"The insects you saw were veps," said Axel. "One of the popular ways for animals to commit suicide when attacked by a drugol is to run or fly into a veps' nest. It's a very fast way to commit suicide.

"Interestingly," he said, "you just reminded me of a memory I would as soon forget. I happened to see a chuda, which is about as dangerous and tough a killer beast as you can find, when it accidentally brushed a nest like the one you described. Immediately, it was attacked by thousands of veps, which soon blinded it. It ran about screaming in a guttural voice and bumping into everything—trees, rocks—until at last, it ran into a small bog, where it became stuck fast in the mud. I watched the veps kill it within five or ten minutes and spend the day consuming it, right down to the mudline. I know this because I stayed to watch. In the end, the only things left were its bones, still sticking out of the mud. The veps even consumed its tough hide and mane."

"That must have been an awful experience!" said Eleth.

"Uh," Axel said, "to change the subject, how did you discover these cliffs?"

"I knew about the cliffs because there is a place over on the north end where we dump dragon eggs, which have died. Dead eggs turn highly acidic after about two sycles, and if one breaks open, it smells almost as bad as a drugol attack and burns anything it touches. That would cause all kinds of trouble. So, we bring all the dead eggs out to the cliffs over there, where they can fall to the water without even striking the cliff on the way down."

She sighed heavily, "No, I didn't find any moonstools that day, but I found this place. It came complete with a comfortable throne and was perfect for both enjoying a wonderful view and thinking—thinking about constructive things. It was here that I came, long before I met you, and deeply pondered the idea that I was a *Daughter of Ceragon* and the sacrifices that had been made to give me that name. What did I really know about it? Nothing. Nevertheless, I realized that I was working almost every day with some of the most wonderful dragons in the world: female dragons who had so much more wisdom than I, even though I have studied much in my life.

"The dragons won't talk to any humans except Clara and me. They started out respecting me and confiding in me because I was the *Daughter* and, somehow, they knew I would keep their trust.

"I have come here many times, sometimes to see the first red-gold of the morning and the waves crashing against the rocks, and sometimes in the evening to see the shadows creeping across the water until everything turns black, except for the glow of a dragon moon that gives a baaria-red tint to everything when it is up in the sky.

"When the dragon's eye was in the center of Kivan, I knew that it was watching me and saying, 'You're special; you know that.' But it also asked, 'What have you done with the gifts that the gods have given you?'

"Until you came, I couldn't answer that question."

She stopped talking, and Axel began asking *himself* the same questions she had been asking.

"You and I," she said, "have received our gifts because of the blood that our mothers drank seventeen years ago. But why them? Were they somehow chosen simply because our fathers were capable of getting the blood for them? Or had each of our parents already passed on to us certain traits that only needed the blood to trigger their powers?

"Why is it," Axel asked, "that death has played such a significant role in our lives and in the lives of our parents? How many more will die because of us? Are we ever going to get answers to these questions?"

"Unless Retha chooses to drop by to enlighten us," Eleth responded, "then those questions will remain unanswered for a time. It's clear, however, we have been charged by the gods to do something important. We must concern ourselves with learning what is expected of us and fulfilling what was foretold. Otherwise, there is no purpose to all the deaths and no purpose to our lives."

Axel looked thoughtful and took a long time to respond to her words. At last he said, "You and I have been tasked with the most difficult job on the planet. No matter what gifts the gods have bestowed upon us, two people alone cannot accomplish this task. We can, however, start with relatively small things, like sending two draft dragons to the Free Colony."

"You're saying that will be a small task?"

Showing a weak grin, Axel responded, "Only in a relative sense. But we'll face much bigger challenges in the future, and we won't be able to do those things with the tools and friends we now have."

"I'm afraid you're right."

"What, then, do we do?"

"We do whatever the gods inspire us to do."

A sudden brisk breeze started blowing up the cliff from the waves below. The breeze was cold, so Axel took off his cloak and wrapped it around the front of the two young people to serve as a windbreak. He put his left hand flat on the rock between them and was pleasantly surprised when Eleth searched it out and rested her right hand on his.

"I must admit that, while I thoroughly enjoy working with Clara and I love the dragons deeply, it gets lonely around here. When Clara is out, like now, I have no one to talk to. Of course, I've always been a bit of a loner, but before, I had Tiimos and Runa. We used to talk a lot about work and anything that seemed important at the time. I've never had anyone my age as a friend."

"I'm, probably, in a very different situation," Axel said. "I knew everyone in Frithden and had many friends. My favorite was Jemmy Sandor. We used to explore everywhere together. We'd hunt, fish, and..."

At that instant, they both heard the noises made by someone, no, two someones, striding through the brush some distance behind them. There was no running away, so they sat and waited.

Eleth spoke in a quiet voice and said, "You're my cousin, Tirro Vesta, up from Kelby. A lot of Vestas live there, and you're not likely to know many of them. You walked six tondrins to see me. You are apprenticed to a carpenter named Hacon Dowsby. He specializes in fine wooden furniture."

Three minutes later, two men in uniforms of the King's Service approached them.

"Why, Officer Molton," Eleth said, "I always see you at work. What brings you out here? It's a great view; why don't you join us? Oh, and who's your friend?"

"This is Officer Wilster. Sorry, we can't join you. We're on assignment. We've received a few reports of dragons flying in the area."

"I see dragons flying here all the time. What's the problem?"

"These dragons were flying at night."

"Can they do that?"

"If the reports are true, the dragons can fly at night; otherwise, they may just be a product of someone's imagination."

"Why are you looking here in the daylight?"

"A few higher-ups think the dragons may have been Kolodran. For some reason, they are interested in the area, possibly due to those recent sightings or the unusual activity that could indicate Kolodran's presence. Anyway, the higher-ups are worried that Kolodran spies may be landing by sea somewhere along the coast."

"This location is a rough area for a boat landing. Look at those cliffs! And I'm told the shoals are highly dangerous."

"We've just been assigned to the area; ours is not to question the bosses. Who's your friend? Haven't seen him around here before."

"Officer Molton, please meet my cousin Tirro Vesta, my only living relative. He walked all the way up from Kelby to see me."

"Axel raised his right hand to shake greetings with the men."

"That's a pretty hefty walk—about six tondrins."

"My master gave me three days off while we waited for specialty supplies for a big project we have coming up."

Eleth squeezed Axel's hand once underneath the cloak.

"Who is your master?"

"Hacon Dowsby."

Again, Eleth squeezed Axel's hand once.

"I know Hacon, some. Tell me, how is his sister doing now? Heard she was in a pretty bad way."

Eleth squeezed Axel's hand twice.

"I'm afraid Mr. Dowsby doesn't take to discussing his personal life with me. I'm just his apprentice. He's all business in the shop."

"All right, so what's it like working in a furniture shop?"

"Most of the work is repetitive. Mr. Dowsby manages all the fine fitting and carving. I spend most of my time sizing and cutting the wood according to plans. I really like working on the lathe, though. I'm good at it, and Mr. Dowsby has given almost all that work to me."

Eleth squeezed Axel's hand once.

"I see you have a crutch and a bandaged foot."

"Yes," Eleth answered, "he walked all the way here just fine but twisted his ankle stepping off our back porch while going to the outbuilding in the dark."

"That's too bad. How are you getting back home, son?"

"Clara and I think we'll arrange for him to travel with whichever cooper makes the grocery run into Kelby," Eleth answered.

"That should work. Sorry we bothered you. We'll be on our way."

The two men shuffled off along the edge of the cliff and disappeared. When the sound of their movements finally faded out, Axel said, "You're a pretty good liar."

"Is that supposed to be a compliment?"

"I guess it all depends on how you take it."

They both laughed at this.

"Let's head for home," Eleth said with a smile.

Axel thought, again, how he could watch that smile for orais.

***

Most of Axel's days in the cottage were spent learning how to walk on his rapidly healing ankle and talking about all kinds of things with Jarrad, who was also healing amazingly fast. Within only another five days, Jarrad could walk about the cottage using the crutches, which were also too short for him, and his wounds mended rapidly, becoming little more than red scars on his abdomen and back. His pain similarly receded.

Once, when both Clara and Eleth were away working in the coops, Jarrad happened to look across the room from his bed to see Axel seemingly staring into space. He was sitting on his own makeshift bed, legs pulled up to his chest, and with his mind, to all appearances, a million tondrins away. When Jarrad called his name, Axel did not respond.

"Axel," Jarrad said again. This time Jarrad called out quite loudly, "Where are you?"

"Hmm?" Axel said, still in a bit of a daze.

"What have you been pondering so deeply over there?"

"Me? Oh, nothing much."

"To the contrary, I think you have been contemplating something of consequence."

"Jarrad, sometimes your perception can be quite annoying."

"It's one of my faults. Now, what has got your head drifting about in the clouds?"

"It's this place, Clara and Eleth, and the dragons. It's playing with my mind."

"Oh, in what way?"

"When I first came to Tarfal, I wanted only two things: to get revenge for Frithden and to become the best bowyer and fletcher that I could."

"Has something changed those wishes?"

"Remember how Clara said her world was turned upside down?"

When Jarrad nodded, Axel said, "My world has been turned upside down in the same way."

"I'm listening."

"Well, first, because of Shaddra and Licor, I no longer feel the need for revenge."

"Yes, you told me that story."

"But it's much more than that."

When Jarrad merely raised his eyebrows in a curious manner, Axel continued, "It's this whole *Son of Ceragon* thing. Up until this trip, those were just words. Now, it has meaning. My parents gave their lives so that I could become what I am. Eleth's parents did the same. There's so much death and destruction associated with the *Foretelling,* and I'm right in the middle of it!"

"You didn't cause any of it."

"No, I'm the result of it. It all happened to make me the way I am and Eleth, too."

"So, what has changed?"

"I can't stop thinking about things I've never really thought about before."

"Such as?"

Axel shook his head and pursed his lips in a strange expression. "The *Foretelling* states that Eleth and I are supposed to bring justice and freedom to a world where neither exists. What's more, we're supposed to bring those things to both humans and dragons! Etmar's fire, I just wanted to be a bowyer, and now look at me!"

"You poor thing. What are you going to do about it?"

Axel rolled his eyes. "You're so sympathetic. Hey, I don't know what to do. I don't even know how to start."

"You gave freedom to Licor, didn't you?"

"Yes, that's one dragon out of thousands."

"So, you've made the first step. With a few more like that, you'll be well on your way. Have you ever climbed a mountain?"

"Yes, more than one, and I know the old saying about what it takes to climb a mountain."

"Isn't the answer to your question rather obvious, then?"

"Freeing Licor wasn't easy, and I was so afraid that I was going to lose you! If that was just the first step, what are the next ones going to be like?"

"Did I say it was going to be easy? If it was going to be easy, why would the gods need to prepare a *son of the Great Ceragon* for Tamerel?"

"You're saying Eleth and I have been given our special abilities because they will be needed in fulfilling the words of the *Foretelling.* I suppose I should have understood that from the time I first heard the words. And don't you say "Better late than never!"

"But it's not late. I think you are learning what's important right on time."

"Now, you're saying this visit was meant to get me started doing what I must do."

"That's one way of looking at it."

"I must admit that, over the last few days, I've changed the way I think about many things. I guess, if nothing else, events here have made me want to be more sober in my thoughts and more aware of the needs of others."

"Sounds like a good thing to me."

"I just realized that would make me a lot like you!"

"Oh, that would be a disaster, wouldn't it?"

Axel blew air from his cheeks while shaking his head, only for him to realize he was copying one of Jarrad's idiosyncrasies.

"I can't believe you two have healed so quickly," exclaimed Eleth when she walked through the door an orai later.

"The only differences from the normal treatment you've received are the applications of landrin pollen to Jarrad's wounds and the daily doses of landrin tea. It must be a powerful medicine, and who knows what else it can do?"

"Perhaps you should show us how you used it and how you made the tea," Jarrad said. "I'm certain we would find many uses for it back home."

"It's easy. I'll gather some fresh blossoms, and we'll make some tea together for tomorrow's dose."

"Uh, how long do we have to keep taking that stuff?" asked Axel.

"Apart from a few patients my father treated before my coming here, all we have is a sample of two. Axel can probably stop after tomorrow's dose, but Jarrad had better continue for another sycle."

"Oh, wonderful," Jarrad said with a smirk on his face.

Eleth grinned widely at Jarrad and said, "If you discover any negative effects, like nausea, rashes, high temperatures, and so on, you may discontinue at once."

Chapter Thirteen

LIVING A NEW LIFE

Late one evening, Axel and Eleth heard a dragon's call from outside the house. They both ran to the door, but there were no dragons outside.

Axel pointed out the obvious. "I think the dragon or dragons want to meet us out at the campsite."

Clara and Axel both looked at Jarrad. Then their eyes moved to Eleth.

"All right, Uncle Jarrad can go." She was getting used to calling him that. In fact, she was starting to notice that he and Clara were spending a lot of time together. Why not simply start calling them "Aunt" and "Uncle"?

"Just take the crutches and use them," she said to her uncle. Not that he needed them in the house, but this was rougher countryside.

As all had expected, Shaddra waited for them at the dragon campsite. She was not alone, but her companion was not Hukken.

"Greetings, my friends," Shaddra said. Let me introduce you to another from the Colony. This is Langa, a female messenger dragon, who has accompanied me on this trip. The Dragon Council decided that with the king's men at high alert, we needed to be stealthier and find ways to make our journeying back and forth safer. Licor helps with this, too. Langa, as you know, these are Clara, Jarrad, Eleth, and Axel."

Langa bowed deeply and said, "I know Mother Clara, the one who helped me to take flight nearly twenty years ago. Forever in my heart, I will honor you."

Clara stepped forward and placed a hand on Langa's bowed head. "You do not need to bow to me, young one. You have become a strong adult dragon now. I do remember you. You were, of all my dragons, the one least anxious to take flight."

The dragon lifted her head, saying, "That is because I loved you and wanted to stay with you!"

"But aren't you glad that you did boldly take the flight into the unknown?"

"Indeed I am. I now have a mate and a dragonell, who are my greatest joys. They have come into my life only because of you."

Langa looked at the others. "You are Jarrad; I met you once in the Colony. All the dragons recognize you as a friend."

She turned her attention to Axel and Eleth. "I know that you two are the *son and the Daughter of the Great Ceragon.* You have come to change the world. I hope my family and I will be able to serve you in so doing and live to see that glorious day."

Jarrad spoke next to ask what news they brought from the south.

Shaddra laughed and said, "Always, always, Uncle Jarrad, you are the one who needs to jump right into business."

"I'm afraid I've had more than a sycle with nothing to do but sit around here and worry about my friends in the Colony. How is Licor adapting to his new home?"

"We are finding that Licor, at heart, is a wise and caring dragon. He has already been in intense discussions with the Council of Elders regarding the defense of the Colony. He has offered his expertise in training all the dragons who wish to learn how to organize a defense force, how to set up a system of sentries for early warning of attack, and how to fight in dragon-on-dragon battles. He knows that such battles are inevitable, and we cannot hope to escape them just by hiding."

"He's done all that in just one sycle?" Jarrad asked in complete amazement.

"He knows what we are up against and how the enemy fights. He will be a good military leader."

"How can you trust him with such high responsibilities so soon after meeting him for the first time?" he asked.

Shaddra and Langa looked at each other before turning back to Jarrad. Shaddra responded by saying, "When dragons communicate in high speech, it is not the same as when you speak in human speech. We communicate emotions and truth that cannot be hidden. Falsehoods are not possible. Just as among humans, with us, there are basically good dragons at heart and basically bad. The difference is that we can readily tell the bad from the good, and we separate ourselves from each other."

Langa took a turn expressing her feelings. "Mother Clara could discern these differences and made certain to send us only those who were good at heart. Is the case not so, Mother?"

Clara looked embarrassed but slowly nodded her head. "To one who is in tune, as I have been, the heart of a dragon can be read almost from the time they break from the shell, even without the ability to speak or understand the High Language. I never, ever helped a dragon with a bad spirit to take flight. If only people could so easily be categorized."

"Now let *me* get to business," Shaddra said in great earnestness. "You and Axel are needed back home. Both people and dragons are beginning to ask about you and to worry about you. Your projects, including the plan to bring us draft dragons, are beginning to fail due to lack of leadership."

"You haven't spoken with people directly about my projects, have you?" Axel asked.

"Of course not. We dragons rarely speak with humans. But I can get remarkably close without them knowing. As you humans say, "I keep my ear to the ground."

"Jarrad and Axel, you look healthy enough now. Are you able to travel?" she asked.

Axel looked at Eleth while Jarrad looked at Clara.

"Axel is well enough now," Eleth reluctantly answered, "to do just about anything he wants. The pain in his ankle will keep him from doing anything out of line. He will continue to limp for a few sycles. Jarrad is still recovering but is probably in good enough health to travel if he is careful. He's going to limp for a while, too."

"Then it is settled; we must take Jarrad and Axel back home," Shaddra said.

Eleth showed a very worried look and said, "But Kivan is now quite visible in the sky at night. You will be seen."

"That is why I came along on this trip," Langa explained. "Both Shaddra and I can make ourselves invisible. From the air, our riders are barely visible, but they are completely invisible from the ground."

Shaddra said, "We will start sending messenger dragons to visit you and Clara at least every Kivan and, perhaps, more often than that if it appears necessary. For now, it is fortunate that Clara helped a high proportion of messenger dragons take flight. You can keep us updated on your progress with the draft dragons, and we can keep you updated on Colony events. We can also offer our help if it will prove of value to you."

"This trip has proven to be a fun vacation," said Jarrad. "But I guess it's time to get back to work."

"Does it take an arrow in the back to make you go on vacation?" Axel asked.

"It does provide a certain amount of incentive. All right, give us an orai or so to collect our things and say goodbye, Shaddra. When we return, we'll load on the saddles and be off."

***

The trip home for two messenger dragons and their passengers was uneventful. What proved difficult was explaining to everyone why the two men had suddenly disappeared for ten days, without much explanation. Axel and Jarrad had originally said they would be out hunting and exploring for a few days but never described where they would be going. After five days of absence, their employees in both the mill and the workshop began to worry, and they told others in the village. Search parties had been sent out, of course, with no result.

Now, trying to stick to reality as much as possible, they planned to say that Axel had seriously twisted his ankle while they were high in the mountains and that made getting home very difficult. The townspeople raised questions such as "Why didn't you build a big fire so we could find you?" And why didn't Jarrad just walk out to get help?

Jarrad responded by saying, "We did build a fire, but it was located behind the north ridge of the upper Mysura Canyon, which meant you couldn't see it. Additionally, I could have left Axel alone to seek help, but that would have put both of us at risk from the killer beasts. Besides, I also fell and seriously bruised my hip. Neither of us was going anywhere until we felt better."

Their answers did not exactly satisfy everyone's curiosity. Eventually, they both just kept repeating, "They had to wait until Axel's ankle healed enough to permit them to climb down the ridge and go home." A lie repeated often enough did become believable. Both Jarrad and Axel's visible limps from their real accidents also helped convince the doubters.

***

Fala Prudo and Bardin Shotley, Axel's two dedicated apprentices, stood proudly in the workshop, prepared to contribute their skills and enhance the community. Their enthusiasm for their work was evident in the way they meticulously prepared themselves for the day ahead. As Axel took his place among them, he couldn't help but feel a sense of pride in these young apprentices who would help him elevate bow production to new levels.

Axel began by introducing the two to the Knights of the Circle as apprentices and obtaining their oaths. Both apprentices came from families of carpenters and were already equipped with basic knowledge and skills that would serve them well in this trade. Axel started by explaining why he had carefully selected specific landrin logs from the forest and why the sawmill operators had cut them into particular sizes and shapes. Together, they examined each blank with utmost care, ensuring that the grain ran straight through to the tip without any breaks or deviations. Any mistakes at this stage could lead to disastrous consequences—broken bows and potentially broken arms. With this crucial step completed, Axel moved on to introduce his apprentices to the power bow-making process.

Alton set both his apprentices to sort out yolka and kota horns, instructing them on how to cut them into precise strips of suitable thickness and trim them down to perfection for the first round of inspection. The workshop hummed with activity as both apprentices worked diligently under Axel's watchful eye.

As they progressed in their training, Axel gradually entrusted them with more responsibilities and specialized tasks, giving them a chance to hone their skills in specific areas before switching roles. The process continued seamlessly as they worked together with precision and dedication to produce top-quality power bows for their community.

Axel demonstrated to the apprentices the method of creating a strong and flexible glue using landrin tree blossoms. He had only discovered this technique a few Kivans before arriving in the Mysura Valley. Locals, both adults and children, were hired to gather thousands of landrin blossoms. After boiling them in large amounts of water, a sticky resin was released. The mixture was then strained and boiled again until it became a thin gel. This versatile glue was used to bind shaped landrin wood blanks and thin cuts of other woods to create finished bow stocks, whereupon they were placed in special vices to apply intense pressure evenly across the lengths of the stocks over a period of two Kivans while the glue dried.

The apprentices assisted Axel in constructing a small building that housed a stove and water barrels, with pans sitting on top to collect dripping water at a steady rate. A rack of semi-finished bows filled the remaining space in the building. Over several days, the steam made the wood pliable when under pressure.

Custom torsion frames were built to mold the cooling bowstocks into their unique recurve shape—causing the ends of the bow to bend away from the shooter when unstrung but returning to their traditional shape when strung. At this point, shaped pieces of horn, a handspan in length, with the thickness of half a thumbnail, were glued to the ends of the two limbs for the purpose of stiffening them. The stiffened ends induced the bow to store more energy in the limbs when the bow was bent rather than in the ends and gave greater power to the arrow when loosed.

Bardin took on the role of managing the process of molding bows into their distinctive shape, surprising Axel with his quick learning abilities.

Fala soon excelled in the task of cutting and shaping the pieces of horn for application on the ends of the bow. She became skilled at finalizing the bows and making their strings sing with a satisfying but quiet twang.

She also discovered a way to add color to the traditionally plain bows produced in Axel's shop. By mixing pigments with the thinned landrin blossom glue, she turned it into a thin, glossy paint that could take on a variety of lustrous shades.

The final steps involved Axel measuring and marking the draw weight of each bow, followed by a test on the range. He carefully performed his measurements and marked the draw weight and length on each bow. His ultimate goal was to build a diverse collection of bows in varying lengths, draw weights, and, thanks to Fala, an array of colors, to get the whole valley interested in archery.

Axel oversaw the entire operation. He constantly watched his apprentices to make certain that no shortcuts were taken, that pieces were always fitted snugly, and that the bows always felt balanced. Any bow failing to meet his strict requirements was tossed on the fire. However, these instances were infrequent, as the three of them collaborated seamlessly. Sometime in the future, Axel planned to gradually introduce his apprentices to the methodology used in the making of steelbows. But, for now, he retained that secret to himself.

Another process Axel retained for now was the production of arrows. Arrows were produced by using the lathe and a contouring device, known as a jig, to cut and strip arrow blanks made of landrin wood. Carved horn nocks and fletching made from shaped sorset and kiplan feathers, each a handspan long, were meticulously glued and bound with waxed ellam thread to ensure that feathers provided the correct spin to keep arrows on their targeted course.

Wickedly sharp steel broadheads or bladeless bodkins were attached to the fronts of the arrows. Broadheads were used in hunting to make a beast bleed out quickly. It was a humane way to keep beasts from suffering. Bodkins were made to penetrate armor and hardened targets.

***

A strange thing happened when, once, Axel decided that a completed bow did not feel right. He decided to burn it and tossed it into the fire. An orai later, he returned to see that the bow was still lying in the fire, entirely unscathed. Even the bowstring, which he had not thought to remove, was not burned. The string was made with fur from ellam manes, spun together by housewives in the village. That, at least, should have easily burned, but it was not even hot. He called Fala over and asked her what might be different about this bow and its string.

"I tried painting the bowstrings on three bows with landrin glue as an experiment, alongside the last batch of bows. I tested them out on the range, and I think it gave them extra strength and may make them last longer without fraying. It also looks like it will eliminate the need for waxing. Other than that, nothing is different. I was going to show the three bows to you in the morning."

"Interesting. Both landrin wood and ellam horns are easily destroyed by fire," Axel noted. "Let's do some tests and make certain it's the glue, or should I say paint, that made this fireproof."

The team painted several different kinds of scrap wood with the landrin paint and, after letting them dry, threw them on a large fire. Only non-painted wood burned. The test pieces did burn in places that were deliberately left unpainted.

"I assume the paint must reflect heat," Axel concluded.

"My, my," Fala said with a grin on her face. "If we painted an entire person with that glue, they might be able to withstand a dragon attack."

Axel rubbed his cheek. "Oh, yes, I can see that happening. In the meantime, we'd better test the bows before painting them, or the discards will pile up to the roof."

"By the way," Bardin quipped, "I haven't heard any complaints from the leatherworkers in Tarfal for some time. What's happening there?"

"Oh, that," Axel responded with a big smile. "You know how they were so disappointed with the low sales prices I demanded regarding their vending of the waist quivers they produced."

"Yes, they made their complaints rather clear."

"It seems they changed their minds when they found the quivers were selling as rapidly as they could be finished."

"There's nothing like happy customers and happy suppliers," Bardin concluded with a grin as big as Axel's.

Axel commenced teaching his first training classes in handling the bow, by coincidence, on his seventeenth birthday. He began by teaching three classes, each meeting twice a week. The classes lasted from one to two orais each, but students were required to practice for at least one additional orai each day, every day of the week. Without fail. Students needed to develop unused muscles, learn to draw and aim the bow properly out of sheer habit, and become as comfortable with their bows as they would be with an old friend.

He taught his students how to load and fire quickly and with accuracy, using the techniques he himself had invented. Some villagers developed their skills faster than others, so Axel hired a few of them as part-time instructors to expand the reach of the training program. Many villagers also practiced for much more than the required one orai per day and developed their bow skills much faster than others.

As a reward to the advanced learners, Axel showed them how to make an arrow curve in flight, making it possible to strike a target that was hiding behind an object or barrier. Although this feat had definite limitations, it was achievable with proper patience and practice.

Throughout each class, Axel emphasized that while shooting arrows for practice and competition may be enjoyable and helpful in improving accuracy, the true purpose of an arrow is as a weapon. Its design and intent are to kill, plain and simple. Both hunters and soldiers understand the deadly potential of an arrow to take the lives of animals and humans alike. The bow and arrow should never be taken lightly.

"It's not a toy," Axel would say. "Not for children, not for adults. Always identify your target clearly. Many hunters have been killed by an arrow mistakenly released by a friend, thinking their target was an animal. Never even draw back on a bow unless you intend to shoot, and don't hesitate to hold off if there is any risk of harming innocent beings. Furthermore, never kill for amusement or pleasure. Even dangerous beasts should only be killed if they pose a threat. The world already has enough suffering; why add to it? And always remember, a wounded beast can be three times as dangerous and won't likely show mercy.

"The king employs a large number of crossbowmen who shoot their arrows in a coordinated manner at a designated area target. You do not have that luxury. You must be able to aim and take down your intended target with precision, no matter how far it may be, preferably with just one shot. In the midst of battle, you may find yourself needing to fire your second shot before the first one even reaches its target. Your enemies will likely outnumber you, making this skill crucial.

I will teach you how to release a second shot swiftly in the time it takes to catch your breath, followed by a third shot and a fourth if necessary."

Life in the isolated communities of Tarfal and Mikell was uneventful, and people had very little to do in their free time. But suddenly, hidden archery ranges began popping up all over both towns, carefully concealed from the prying eyes of the king's representatives. The king had a strong dislike for archers and made it clear that anyone caught with a bow, even an ordinary legal bow, could face severe punishment. More and more citizens, male and female, young and old, wanted to learn, so more classes were scheduled. Children started using bows as early as six years old. Archery became the most popular form of diversion, and weekly contests were held to determine champions in various groupings. The Upper Mysura Valley, literally, became crazy for bow shooting.

Axel's shop was hard-pressed keeping up with demand, even though by then it was finishing a score of bows and accompanying arrows each sycle, and with that production number rising every Kivan. One practical effect was that, for the first time in memory and after only six Kivans of training, a whole Kivan passed with no one from the valley being killed by a killer beast.

***

Jarrad was having much more difficulty with his task. He bought a year-old Ellam bull without horns and began formulating plans to construct a carrier that a firedrake could lift. Tell the truth, he was not even sure a firedrake could lift that much weight.

He started by making a simple balance scale and determining how much a yearling bull weighed. First, he set out a pile of logs to match that weight, tied them up into a tight bundle, and called in Shaddra to get the help of a strong firedrake from the Colony. He soon found that the dragon could lift the bundle of logs to a reasonable height but tired after a few orais of flight.

The news was not encouraging. It meant that even if a suitable carryall, basket, or pouch could be made to hold the draft dragon, there would still need to be a large flight of very visible dragons working in rotation to carry the heavy burden. How could they be disguised? How could they be protected? A fast enemy siris dragon would be able to follow them all the way home. How could they prevent the king from discovering the Colony?

Once, when Jarrad complained to Axel about the difficulties he was having with this task, Axel responded, "My GranDa talked all the time about how important having information about what your enemy was doing is one of the most important factors in war."

"How does that apply here?" Jarrad asked.

"Wouldn't the king's forces have a need to move large and heavy items quickly by air? How have they solved the problem?"

Jarrad slammed his palm against his forehead and brought it down to wipe across his face. With an element of disgust in his voice, he said, "It looks like I need to have a talk with Shaddra."

"Why Shaddra?" Axel asked with genuine curiosity.

"Because if Shaddra doesn't already possess a specific piece of information, she can usually obtain it quickly."

***

Over the first three Kivans since his arrival at the Free Colony, Licor observed progress in military training among the dragons, which developed rapidly. Every dragon over fifteen years of age was enlisted in a "flight." A flight consisted of ten dragons. Two "squadrons" were organized, each consisting of two firedrake flights and one flight of siris dragons.

Licor served as a drill sergeant and took no guff from anyone. The Free Dragons learned more dragon and human swear words than they ever thought possible. At first, firedrakes trained with other firedrakes, and siris dragons trained with other siris dragons. Later, Licor developed things he called "tactics," which involved more complex combinations of firedrakes and siris dragons. Leaders of each grouping were switched around frequently until Licor learned the strengths and weaknesses of each dragon in his charge and, finally, settled them into a leadership structure that could get all the dragons comfortably working with one another.

The dragons were put through maneuvers designed to train them to automatically respond to any kind of threat but also to take on an active attack if necessary in a way that might minimize their losses.

In an air war, there was never time to think. Every scenario had to be practiced, memorized, and embedded into the brain so precisely that the proper reactions took place as quickly as a human pulling a hand away from a just-touched hot stove. Fortunately, that worked well with the very essence of dragon behavior.

A practical advantage held by the free dragons was that they could instantly communicate with one another over relatively long distances using the dragon's high speech. It made rapid adjustments to in-air maneuvers possible and more effective. Yes, the enemy dragons could hear these communications, but their human controllers would never let them respond.

There could easily have been some kind of rebellion over the stressful exercises Licor put his troops through. But with so much arrayed against them and after years of inactivity and boredom, the idea of fighting and winning was more than challenging for the free dragons. It was thrilling.

The idea of having to kill others of their kind, however, was harder to accept. However, Licor made it abundantly clear that humans controlled the king's dragons, and they would not hesitate to kill free dragons. They killed dragons all the time in battles against the armies of Kolodra and Mandara. He also emphasized that their own primary targets were to be human dragonriders and their jewels, rather than the dragons themselves. The Free Colony needed dragon recruits much more than the destruction of enemy dragons.

Licor knew that the king's dragons were all at the command of humans, and humans were slow—slow to understand what was happening, slow to make decisions, slow to communicate commands, and slow to react to commands. He also knew every standard maneuver used by the King's Dragon Forces and how to defeat it with a smaller force. His squadrons were tiny compared to the forces arrayed against them. But the free dragons would soon be able to fight independently or as groups and strike quickly, like veps; insects no bigger than a human thumb but perfectly capable of bringing down a full-sized dragon when motivated.

***

Dragon eggs frequently died and turned rotten in a short time. The breeding coop guards knew that as bad eggs grew older, the shells thinned out and the risk of a break grew rapidly. Anything could cause a rotten egg to crack, unleashing an abominable stink that would persist for days.

Until now, Clara never had difficulty getting viable eggs past the king's guards who were posted as gate security. She merely mingled a good egg with a bad one being taken out for disposal. The guards knew Clara and Eleth so well that a simple nod was the only requirement to get them through the gate, even when they were sporting the large-sized wheelbarrow required to carry many of the eggs. Some guards claimed to be able to identify a rotten egg at a glance, though no one ever seriously tried to prove it. If an egg were truly bad, all it would take to crush the shell would be a slight touch. Clara and Eleth were the acknowledged specialists when it came to managing the eggs and spotting problems. Their skills were unquestioned.

Standard procedure was to carefully carry dead eggs out to the Dremlin Cliffs in a wheelbarrow for disposal. They were cushioned with blankets to reduce the likelihood of a crack developing in one of their shells or, gods forbid, an actual break.

On this day of all days, Clara and Eleth were carrying two viable draft dragon eggs along with one very rotten firedrake egg. The firedrake egg was nearly two measuring stones in weight, while the draft dragon eggs were closer to three stones each—a weight that Clara was hard-pressed to lift by herself.

On this trip, they chanced upon some guards not far from the coops. The two soldiers were not working the gate but presented themselves out on the trail, some eighty strides from the coops.

"What are you doing with eggs outside of the coops?" one said accusingly.

"Oh, hello, Officer Wilster!" Eleth said. "I'm sorry; you gave me a bit of a start."

"Clara and I are trundling these rotten dragon eggs over to the Dremlin Cliffs. That's the only place they can be dumped without forcing evacuation of the coops."

"I don't understand," said Officer Wilster.

"These particular eggs could break open at any time. If one of them breaks too close to the coops, the stench would make a wide area unlivable. It could be so unbearable that we might have to evacuate some of the coops. That would put other eggs at risk."

"You know," Eleth said, "these eggs are awfully heavy. We could use some help with the wheelbarrow if you're interested."

"Just let them go do their job," the other officer said plaintively to Wilster. "That's just it," said Officer Wilster. "What if one or more of these eggs is, in truth, viable? They could keep the good eggs instead of throwing them down the cliff and sell them. Anyone could have bribed these women to get an egg out to Kolodra. How do *we* know the eggs are dead and rotten?"

"You find out for yourself, Wilster," the second guard said. "I don't need this. I'll see you at the guard shack. Goodbye!"

Officer Wilster stood his ground and turned to the women. "You need to prove to me that these eggs are bad, or I'll take you to my captain and you can explain it to him."

"What if we just gave the eggs over to the nice officer and made them his problem?" Clara said to Eleth.

Wilster stepped back and pulled out his sword. Pointing it at Clara, he said, "You aren't moving from this spot until you can prove to me that these are bad eggs! If one breaks, I'll arrest *you* for causing the disturbance!"

Eleth shook her head and said, "This is more trouble than it's worth, but I'll give you the proof you want. But remember, you're the one who wanted proof."

"What do you mean?"

"As dead eggs get older, the acid inside grows stronger and begins to seep through the shells in small quantities. If you want to tell whether an egg is bad, all you must do is touch the shell with your finger, and you'll know."

"That's all?" said the soldier as he looked down at the eggs.

Clara took the opportunity to give Eleth a very quizzical glance, unseen by Wilster.

"All I have to do is touch one? Any one?" the officer asked.

"Any one you wish, but you may regret doing so."

"Why?"

"I told you there's acid seeping out in small quantities. You'll know what I mean if you touch just one."

The soldier bent over the wheelbarrow with an outstretched hand and finger.

"Do not touch it so hard that you break the shell!" Eleth warned.

Intrigued by the discovery, Wilster lightly brushed one of the bottom eggs with a finger and, immediately, started screaming in pain and jumping about, holding one hand with the other.

"Don't say I didn't warn you, Officer Wilster!" Eleth said loudly. "I suggest you go wash that acid off as quickly as possible before a blister starts to form."

Immediately, the soldier disappeared down the path until even Eleth could not hear his crashing steps through the underbrush.

Clara looked down the trail where the fleeing officer disappeared and said, "I don't understand. There's no seepage on even a bad egg for two or three weeks, and he touched a good egg!"

Eleth chuckled to herself and said, "It was sap from the *sitalida* plant."

"What?"

"My father loved plants and spent many orais researching various plants for the potential to use them in medicine. Sitalida is a parasitic plant that grows high up in trees and uses its sap to digest plant material from its host. It's harmless to humans; however, if you get the sap on your skin, it feels like it's burning hotter than a coal from your stove. Once washed off, the pain gradually goes away. Unfortunately, Tiimos never did find any beneficial use for it. But, maybe, I have."

"And how did you...?"

"I merely painted all the eggs with sitalida sap before we left the coops."

"And how are we going to...?"

Eleth smiled broadly again and reached under the blankets. She pulled out a pair of thick leather gloves. "Once we get home, we'll wash the sap off the eggs, and everything will be perfectly fine."

Clara looked at her protégé with new respect and said, "It certainly pays to plan ahead for emergencies, does it not?"

Chapter Fourteen

FIRE

One day a visitor came to the bow shop. A full year and a half had passed since Axel came to live with his Uncle Jarrad. It was the beginning of the Season of Harvest. The changing season brought bright colors to the mountains bordering the valley.

"Ah, to what great privilege do we attribute your esteemed presence in our humble shop today, dear Uncle?" Axel asked, a hint of mischief in his voice.

Jarrad turned to Fala, one of Axel's apprentices, and asked, "Did you understand what he just said?"

"Absolutely, sir," Fala replied, with a broad grin. "Axel asked you, 'Why are you here bothering us?'"

Jarrad chuckled, his eyes twinkling with amusement. "Ah, thank you, Fala! You see, Axel, I'm just passing through, stirring up a bit of trouble and mayhem, as is my habit." Today I have come with a special request. I require assistance for a project that may hold special significance for you.

Axel glanced around at his apprentices and the four new hires brought on to keep up with the growing demand for bows, with orders now arriving from as far away as Bushey, in the distant north of Sanara. They had all stood to recognize Jarrad as he entered. Bardin met Axel's eyes with a quizzical half-smile and a nod, while Fala simply lifted her hands in a gesture that seemed to say, "Whatever Jarrad wants, he gets."

"If it is important, you know that we would be happy to help," Axel responded.

"Yes, it does happen to be important to you as well as me, but it's going to entail some work."

"What do you mean?"

"Come with me and I'll show you."

Jarrad led the way out of the shop and over to where the wooden waterwheel that powered their little sawmill and the machines in Axel's shop was turning. It seemed to be turning much more slowly than usual.

When they reached the sluice that supplied water to the wheel, the reason for it turning so slowly became readily apparent. The water level in the sluice channel was down to a fraction of its normal flow.

"Okay," said Axel, "what do we do about this?"

"There's still plenty of water over in the stream itself," Jarrad said, "but the lack of rainfall over the last few Kivans has resulted in a severe drop in stream levels. We'll need to divert more of the river into this channel and, maybe, build a head gate so that when water levels return to normal, the resulting flood doesn't tear our waterwheel apart. I've already enlisted the help of the sawmill staff, and they are rounding up materials to build the gate. I'm afraid, however, that the job of making a better channel to get more water coming down to the wheel will fall for now on us."

"Are you saying that we need to start moving rocks and whatever to divert all or part of the stream?"

"Alternatively, we sit around and wait for the next hard rain, which may not even come until the middle or end of the Season of Sleep. Everything in our shops that depends on water power will likely stop working within a sycle or two. Still, it's your choice."

"Fala, Bardin," Axel asked with a big grin on his face, "how would you and the others like to go play in the water?"

Both apprentices and employees groaned at the prospect but shrugged their shoulders.

They followed Jarrad to where part of the stream was diverted into the sluice and toward the waterwheel. There, he showed them what needed to be done and handed out shovels. Mostly, the work involved wading out into the open end of the sluice channel and deepening it by picking up rocks from the bottom and placing them in the water off to the left side of the sluice canal—making a V-shaped entrance to funnel more water into the canal.

Jarrad had conveniently also brought a pry bar to help loosen the rocks. "Please don't injure your backs," he told them. "All the bigger rocks should be rolled and have at least two people working on them."

The eight of them worked diligently for two orais before some more men arrived, carrying picks, shovels, wooden planks, and other supplies to work on the headgate. It soon became apparent that picking up and moving rocks was the easier of the tasks being performed here. The men dug holes to hold heavy vertical beams on each side of the channel. Much of the time, they were digging through layers of firmly packed stream rocks.

Finally, well after high sunstar, Axel, Jarrad, and the others had an appreciable increase in water flowing down the channel, enough to make the water wheel turn satisfactorily. But the men working on the sluice gate had barely been able to get the beams into place. They would certainly be back tomorrow to finish the job.

Axel sent his staff home with hearty thanks for work well done, while he and Jarrad headed back to the house. They collapsed down into the chairs on a shaded wooden porch and just tried to catch their breaths.

"My muscles aren't going to let me forget this day's work for a sycle," said Jarrad.

"Just walking back to the house was almost too much for my legs," Axel commented by way of response.

The two had been silent for a few minutes when there came a ringing from the bell over on the large shed.

"Oh, no!" Axel said in a plaintive voice. "Can we just ignore it this time?"

Jarrad forced his way out of his chair and said, "Can we ever, really, ignore it?"

"Guess not," Axel said and painfully rose from his chair.

Suddenly, two dragons appeared in the yard right in front of them.

"Please don't do that, Shaddra!" Jarrad said in annoyance. "You just scared the insides right out of me!"

"My humble apologies, Uncle Jarrad. Langa and I have come on urgent business."

"What kind of urgent business?"

"I bring both good and bad news."

"All right," he said, "you choose which to tell us first."

"The good news is that a messenger has met with Clara and Eleth. They have successfully brought two draft dragon eggs out of the breeding caves. The eggs have hatched, and they now have two healthy young hatchlings."

"That is such wonderful news, Shaddra!" Jarrad said, smiling broadly. "But that doesn't sound urgent. What is the real problem we need to address?"

"You will need to accompany us to understand the situation."

Axel looked quizzically at the two messenger dragons. "This sounds pretty ominous."

"I am afraid that is exactly what it may be," Shaddra replied.

Axel retrieved the two dragon saddles from the shed. He knew his muscles would have trouble with this trip, and he could only imagine how hard it could be on a fifty-something-year-old man, especially after working a day as they had. The two men would have to belt themselves in, for sure.

Twenty minutes later, the two dragons took off into the sky with Axel on Shaddra's back and Langa carrying Jarrad. The wind whipped past them as they flew.

"Where are we heading?" Jarrad shouted loud enough to be heard over the sound of their beating wings.

Shaddra's response was grim. "To the eastern end of the valley. Something important has happened there."

"What kind of important?" Jarrad pressed, obvious concern creeping into his voice.

"Licor has ordered a constant watch on all sides of the Colony. Langa spotted something concerning while she was patrolling the east side."

Axel leaned in towards her, concern etched on his face. "Langa, what did you see? Are the king's forces attacking?"

The dragon's answer was terrifying. "No, but it may be even worse news for your human companions."

Jarrad's eyes widened in shock. "Worse than an imminent attack from the king? What could possibly…"

"Look ahead," Langa interrupted, cutting him off. "Tell me what you see."

Jarrad squinted through the rushing wind and saw a dark storm brewing on the horizon. "I see... clouds. Many grey clouds," he reported uncertainly.

Langa nodded grimly. "Correct. We'll fly low beneath those clouds so you can get a better look at what lies ahead."

As they descended closer to the ground, Jarrad's eyes widened in horror. "Oh, gods above," he exclaimed. "It's a forest fire! It's spreading quickly, just this side of the rim!"

Axel had already noticed the blaze and was worriedly scanning the area below them. "It's being fueled by the winds, and it's only getting bigger!" He shouted, concern etched on his face. Suddenly, he remembered something, and his gaze turned back towards Tarfal.

"Jarrad!" He called out urgently. "We have to do something! There's nothing to stop that fire from reaching Tarfal and Mikell!"

Jarrad followed Axel's frantic gaze; his heart sank at the sight below them. "Oh no!" he said in a gasp. "Both towns are made entirely of wood... if that fire reaches them, they'll be completely destroyed."

But Axel's reply was even more grim. "It's not a matter of 'if'; it's a matter of 'when.'"

Jarrad used a finger and a thumb to rub his short graying beard for a moment and shouted, "We need to land and talk the matter over."

The dragons found a bare, rocky flat to settle down onto. There, both Axel and Jarrad climbed down from their saddles, not once even thinking about their overused muscles.

They knelt down together on a patch of dirt, whereupon Axel asked, "What do we do? Get word to Tarfal and Mikell so everyone can evacuate?"

Shaddra interrupted the conversation to say, "There is only one place where they can go to save themselves. It's an island in the river, upstream from Tarfal. The river is wide there."

"Then why did you bring us down here and show us the fire?" Axel asked.

"We came because sometimes you must witness the danger to truly accept what must be done. You must leave before the fire destroys the towns and your workshops."

"Shaddra," Jarrad said, "leave for where?"

"The dragons will take you to the next valley, where there is no danger from the fire."

Axel and Jarrad looked intensely at each other. As if reading each other's minds, they both glared over at the dragon. "Shaddra," they said in unison, "the towns are unprotected! Everyone will die!"

"But if you stay, *you* will die. If you are not burned, you will starve from the loss of all your shelter and provisions. You must leave. The dragons will help you build a new home in the next valley."

"Surely the lives of these other humans are less important than the S*on of Ceragon* and Uncle Jarrad," Langa said innocently.

"Shaddra and Langa," Axel cried out, trying to hold back his emotion, "only a little more than a year has passed since I watched my village burn right in front of my eyes. I won't let that happen again!"

Jarrad patiently tried to explain. "Shaddra, I have lived with these people for nearly thirty years. They are my friends—even in a way, my family. I cannot just leave them. If the king's dragons were to threaten the Free Colony, Langa, would you run away to save your own life?"

"Of course not; I'd stay to fight as long as I could."

Jarrad held out his hands in a pleading gesture, and slowly shaking his head, he said, "That is exactly what we will do to save our friends."

"Can they not evacuate...?" Shaddra muttered.

"Evacuate to where?" Jarrad asked, collapsing his face into one hand. "You said the nearest place safe from the fire would be on that island in the Mysura River, which is two tondrins up the valley. Most could get there, but they would have no shelter and would soon starve because they had to leave their supplies to burn. It's close to harvest time now, so all the crops would be destroyed, too. The distance to the nearest human settlements is so great that sufficient amounts of food and supplies wouldn't reach the two towns in time to prevent hundreds of deaths, maybe a lot more."

"It's true," Jarrad continued, "that, with the dragon's help, we could get the word out fairly quickly to other communities. But it would require at least three sycles to load any measurable amount of food into wagons and get it here, and that's assuming there's that much food just lying around somewhere.

"The fact is, with nights starting to get colder, no shelter, and little food, we are looking at an unbearable loss of life here."

"That isn't acceptable," Axel ranted. "We can't let that happen! We can't!"

"*We* may have no choice," Jarrad said plaintively.

"There is *always* something that can be done!" Axel insisted. "We have some time. The village can make some kind of firebreak to stop the fire!"

"The fire will reach town in two or three days," Jarrad said. "How big of a firebreak could we make in that time? An average lumberman can cut down a tree in about one-fifth of an orai, but there are thousands of trees that would not only need to be cut down but also moved out of harm's way. What's more, there's the undergrowth, which is dry as paper. A fire can travel along the ground just as easily as from tree to tree."

"Actually," said Shaddra, "I have seen fire travel from one place to another by means of sparks and burning material carried by the wind. They can carry a fire as far as one tondrin."

Axel leaned on one arm and closed his eyes to hold back the tears.

Suddenly jerking up to his knees, he said firmly, "I don't give up that easily! Let's get back on those dragons and fly up the valley. Maybe, while there's still a little light, we can find someplace that we can use to stop that cursed fire!"

Jarrad nodded in resigned agreement, and the two mounted up again.

The dragons flew circles above the forest, gradually working their way up the valley. The forest looked endlessly the same, and their task seemed only the more impossible to the men as they flew.

Just less than halfway back to Tarfal, Axel rubbed his eyes as if to clear his vision. His eyesight, which was substantially better than Jarrad's, had noticed a subtle change in the ground. He shouted over to Jarrad, "What is this place? The forest is different here for some reason. It looks thinner, much less dense."

Jarrad looked down, trying to figure out what Axel was referring to. After a moment, he spotted some familiar landmarks. "Oh, this is Bokin's Bottom."

"Bokin's what?"

"Bokin's Bottom. Let's land, and you'll better understand what it's all about."

The dragons settled into a patch of open ground.

Still atop their mounts, Axel and Jarrad looked at their surroundings.

"This terrain is not the same as what we've been seeing everywhere else," said Axel. "The trees are much more scattered and rather sickly looking."

"That's because this place is normally a bog. In wetter years, a small stream from the northern mountains fills this area up and forms a shallow bog, with water anywhere from one to two strides in depth. I don't know what keeps all the trees from drowning, but a fair number have been able to survive. When the bog dries out, it leaves behind this thick, tinder-dry grass and undergrowth. A fire would pass through here even faster than through the forest."

"In a wet year, what keeps the water from just flowing through?"

"Do you really think that's important?" Jarrad asked.

"For some reason, I really do."

"Okay, as you wish. Langa, would you and Shaddra please take us over to the river, straight south from here?"

"Gladly, if you think it will help," she said.

They landed near the banks of the Mysura River, roughly sixty landrins from their previous stop. The Mysura was a medium-large river with a swift current, deep and wide in this stretch. Downstream from where they stood, the river plunged into a rocky canyon.

"What's that over there?" Axel asked, pointing toward a line of low hills stretching across much of the valley, about a thousand strides to the east.

"Oh, those are the Midvalley Knolls," came the reply. As you can see, they're heavily forested and won't stop any fire. And down there, where the river disappears, is the start of the Bourem Narrows. That's where the Mysura squeezes through a narrow gorge for nearly the length of a tondrin."

"Okay, Jarrad, what did you want to show me here?"

"Notice this ridge of rock on my right."

Axel looked down at the ground and saw, just over on his left, a line of strange-looking red-black rock paralleling the river like a thick wall. The rough little ridge rose, perhaps, one stride above the ground on the northern bank and two strides above the level of the river. It stretched for two hundred strides, from one large rocky hill to another, and appeared to continue from there on down to the narrows. It had a general width of, perhaps, five strides. "Okay. Yes," he said, "I see the ridge of rock."

"That ridge is called the dike. In wet years, it serves as a dam to block a small creek and floods all of the ground to the north of us. The ground is very flat, so the water backs up a long way."

"Shouldn't there be at least a tiny pond here, even in a dry year?" Axel asked.

"No. That crack on the west side of the dike allows a small amount of water to drain through. In a dry year, all the water flows out. In a wet year, the water flows down from the canyon to the north at a rate that is more than a hundred times the amount flowing out through the crack. So, the water backs up and forms the bottoms."

"How far does it back up, then?"

"How far...? Um... In a particularly wet year, the water backs up all the way to the road located on the north side of the valley."

"Interesting."

"Interesting?"

"Yes, it is, and how wide is the bottom... er... what did you call it?"

"Bokin's Bottoms. I have no idea how it got that name, but it gets pretty wide. It averages more than two tondrins in width. People around here hate it because it completely blocks off all travel through the forest. The shortest crossing spot is right here at the little dam. But the ground in this place is almost solid rock and very rugged."

Axel looked around again. He looked at the ground lying about them. He looked upstream, and he looked downstream. He took a long time looking downstream.

"Can we go up and look at the narrows from the air? After that, we can go home."

"What in the world do you have going on in that strange mind of yours, Axel?" Jarrad asked.

"Now, I know you are dying of curiosity, but I have to work on this idea in my mind for a bit. I'll tell you all about it when we get home."

"You're not going to leave us out of this conversation, I hope," said Shaddra.

"No, Shaddra, I won't leave you out. In fact, you may just end up being an integral part of it. More even than you wish to be."

Shaddra gave a questioning look at Langa and then shot the same look at Jarrad. He just shrugged his shoulders.

When they made the landing in front of Jarrad's cottage, Axel and Jarrad stepped down and immediately removed the saddles from the dragons.

Axel led the entire group over to a place of soft dirt that was still receiving light from the slowly setting sunstar. He knelt in the dirt, used one hand to smooth away some debris, and, grabbing a nearby stick to serve as a pen, started drawing. First, he drew two wavy diagonal lines.

"This sketch," he began, "shows the upper Mysura River Valley. The wide eastern end is on the right, and the narrower western end is on the left. The top line generally marks the base of the northern escarpment; the bottom line traces the course of the Mysura River itself. Up here"—he indicated the upper right corner of his map—"is where the road climbs from the eastern lowlands, zigzagging with switchbacks as it enters the valley."

He traced the road with his finger. "Inside the valley, the road follows the lower edge of the escarpment for nearly the valley's entire length. Then it turns south, here, toward Tarfal and Mikell." He pointed to the left side of the map, scratching in a few crossed lines to represent the streets of the two towns.

Axel smiled. "This area running across the center of the valley is known as Bokin's Bottoms. He drew a series of rough, back-and-forth marks in the middle of his rustic map, starting near the road, curving sharply east, and ending at the river. That's where we stopped earlier and saw how a bog looks when the water is drained away. The dike runs between the Bottoms and the river.

Axel's Map

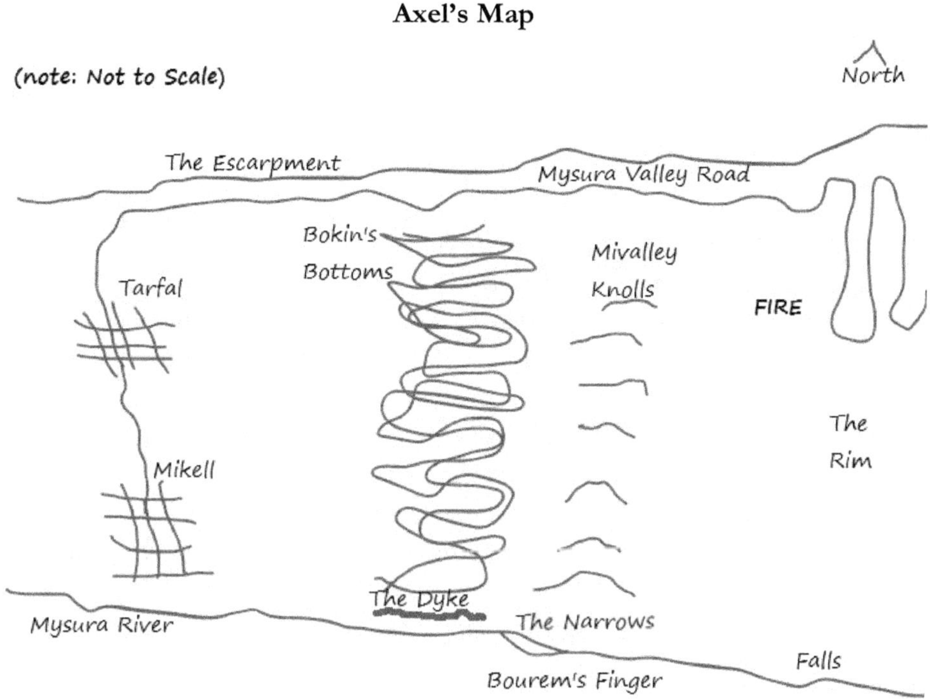

"Just to the east of the Bottoms is a line of hills you called the Midvalley Knolls." He glanced up at Jarrad for confirmation. "The Mysura River flows west to east along the entire southern edge of the valley, and here"—he pointed to a spot just beneath the Knolls—"is where it cuts through what you called the Bourem Narrows."

He paused, looking thoughtful. "At the Narrows, the river quickens and becomes a series of cataracts. I found it fascinating, during our overflight, that the river splits around a small island near the beginning of the Narrows—an island crowned by a towering rock. What do you call that feature?"

"We call it Bourem's Finger," Jarrad replied.

"Interesting. One day I'd like to learn who this Bourem was—or is. After the narrows, the river widens again and flows for about ten tondrins before tumbling over the valley rim in a large waterfall at the far right.

"Lastly, there's a fire burning near the rim—right here." He pointed to the right side of the map, just south of the road and west of the escarpment. "If left unchecked, the fire will sweep from the eastern end of the valley all the way west. That's a problem for us."

He looked up at the group. "Does everyone agree with the map as I've laid it out so far?"

Everyone's eyes, including those of the dragons, were intensely studying the map.

"I'll take your silence for agreement, at least for now. All right, the problem at hand is, 'How can we prevent the fire from destroying Tarfal and Mikell?' First, do any of you have potential solutions in mind?"

"None that are realistic," Jarrad said with a weak laugh.

"Let's suppose, Uncle Jarrad, that the gods are with you, and they will fulfill, on your behalf, any wish that is at least plausible. Would something come to mind?"

"I would ask the gods to build a massive firebreak between us and the fire."

"Is there any way to build a firebreak without the intervention of the gods?"

"We could never hope to do that; it wouldn't be possible even if we used every person in the Valley. It would require cutting down and hauling away hundreds of thousands of trees and trampling down or removing undergrowth covering a thousand times the area of Tarfal and Mikell combined."

"What if you had the Dragons of the Free Colony to help? Could you do it then?"

Everyone stared at Axel in complete shock.

"Don't look at me that way!" Axel said. "This is just hypothetical. Jarrad, answer me, if you had the help of the free dragons, could you build a workable firebreak?"

It took a moment for Jarrad just to get his mind off the very thought of using the dragons. Finally, getting control over that mindset, he answered, "No... I still could *not* build the firebreak."

"Why not? The dragons could offer more than sixty pairs of super powerful arms with accompanying bodies to knock down trees and push them out of the way. Wouldn't that be enough?"

"No, it would not."

"Why not?"

"Because they, nonetheless, would not be able to get rid of the flammable material in the area of the break. In the first place, sixty dragons wouldn't be enough to do all the work, especially in clearing out everything that can burn from the firebreak; second, there would still be the problem of undergrowth. Grass and dry shrubs would literally have to be removed or covered, and third, we could never build a break wide enough to prevent sparks from flying over and starting new fires."

"Jarrad, you do have me convinced. There is no way we could build a meaningful firebreak, even with the help of the dragons."

Jarrad grimaced at Axel and let his face drop into a stern-looking frown. "What does all this folderol have to do with saving the town?"

"A great deal, I think," Axel said, reaching out a hand and grabbing Jarrad firmly by the shoulder. "I have an idea, and I'll use this same map to help illustrate my points.

"As I said, this middle section represents a place known as Bokin's Bottoms. It is normally a bog, filled with something like a two-stride depth of water, give or take a little. Let me ask you now, how likely is it that a fire would cross a bog?"

"But there is no bog," said a very frustrated Jarrad. "You may recall that the stream it gets its water from has dried up!"

"Oh, so you are saying, Uncle Jarrad, that the only way a bog can get water is from the top?"

Understanding hit Jarrad like a thunderclap, and he gasped deeply. "You're going to take water from the river?" His eyes grew unfocused as he turned his mind inwards and started reviewing new possibilities. The dragons looked more puzzled.

"When I was young—" Axel began, then caught himself, glancing at Jarrad with a wry smile. "Well, younger, anyway. I loved playing in ditches, puddles, streams—anything wet, really. I was always fascinated by how I could coax the water to do what I wanted, though it usually had a mind of its own. Still, I managed to learn a few interesting tricks along the way.

"For instance, if I wanted to make water from a stream flow uphill into a new bed at a higher level, there were ways to do it. I discovered that, if I started digging a trench some distance upstream, at a point higher than my intended destination, I could divert the water into the new channel and cause it to flow where I wanted.

"But with the Mysura River, that won't work. The banks there are nothing but solid rock, with no way for us to dig a trench. So, scratch that idea."

Axel paused, then continued, "But there was something else. If the elevation difference wasn't too much, I could build a dam downstream from where I wanted the water to go. The water would back up, rise, and eventually spill over into the new channel."

Jarrad stared at him, incredulously. “You want to dam the Mysura.” It was a simple statement. Then, in a near shout, he said, “You crazy half-dragon! You really do!”

Axel grinned. “What, have you got something against dams?”

“Only that there’s no way in Etmar’s Realm you’re going to slap a dam across a river as deep and as fast as the Mysura in one or two days!”

“Would I have made the suggestion if I couldn’t do it, or... I mean... if we couldn’t do it?”

Langa leaned next to Shaddra and said in the High Language, “I think by ‘we’ he means dragons.

“Langa, of course I do!”

“Langa was shocked at Axel’s understanding of her words and looked at him strangely.

“No, Langa, I didn’t understand what you said, but I guessed.”

“The obvious question,” Axel continued, “is, 'How can I build a dam here on the Mysura in two days without using dragons?'" The obvious answer is I can’t. But I think the opposite is true. I *can* build a dam here... and a big, wet firebreak to go with it... *if* I have the help of both the Free Dragons *and* the people of the Valley.

“You act as if that is so easy to do,” Jarrad said.

Axel looked up at the dragons and said straight out, “The humans have no choice. When they see their options, they’ll accept help from any source available. The real question is, can we get the Free Dragons to reveal their existence to the people of the Valley and help them to build a temporary dam?”

The two dragons stepped back in utter shock. They looked at each other and conversed in their language for a moment.

Then Shaddra said to the group, “The Free Dragons have lived for nearly thirty years in peace and freedom from fear because we have maintained our secrecy. The king does not know about us, so he does not send his forces to kill or capture us. Once the people of the Valley know who we are and what we are, then any one of them could pass on the secret to the king’s people. He would offer a fortune to anyone carrying that news. We would never know the same kind of peace again. Clara and Eleth would be in danger, too.”

“What you have described is known as an *ethical dilemma.* “Axel said. “You want to do something that is good, but in so doing, you may bring down something terrible on yourselves and others you love.

"My Da taught me about ethical dilemmas. He believed it was wrong to kill humans, and it was wrong to kill dragons. But if he hadn't done both, I would never have been born. Perhaps that seems like a rather small, personal thing unless there is some truth to the foretelling about a *Son of Ceragon.* If so, it suddenly becomes a significant thing. I think it is interesting that Eleth's father had to live through the very same ethical dilemma as my Da, and because he chose correctly, there is now a *Daughter of Ceragon,* who is helping to care for two young draft dragons. That is a story that does not yet have an ending.

"But now, let's consider for a moment *your* ethical dilemma as you just related it."

"Wait, Axel," Shaddra said. "It is not Langa and I that you have to convince. If you want to suggest that the Free Dragons reveal themselves for an important cause, you must convince *them*! They are the ones who must decide to take upon themselves such a dangerous course of action."

Jarrad said he agreed with Shaddra. "It would be best if you go back with Shaddra and Langa to speak with the Free Dragons. Whether or not they agree to help, I will have to inform the town council and prepare the town for whatever may happen."

"Before you go, however, tell us how you would suggest building this dam," he said.

Axel glanced around at the three pairs of attentive eyes fixed on him. "I'm not suggesting we build a traditional dam," he began. "We just need to slow the water down and raise the level by five or six strides at a specific spot. We could do that by creating a massive logjam at the narrows. If dragons and humans work together to push large trees into the Mysura upstream, they'll float down and become trapped where the river narrows. I noticed during our flyover that there are already some logs caught there, which proves it's possible."

Jarrad frowned. "But won't the water just flow around the logs?"

"If we only had a loose pile, yes," Axel replied. "But imagine starting with long, branchless logs as a foundation, then sending down trees with all their leafy branches intact. Those would fill the gaps and trap more water."

He paused, thinking. "Does the town have any black powder?"

Jarrad looked surprised but nodded. "The mine keeps a supply. Why do you ask?"

"I'd use it like the miners do, to blast rock from the hillsides near the narrows. The fallen rocks would land on top of the logs, forcing everything down and plugging leaks. Then we'd add more logs and trees; even just bundles of leafy branches would help."

"It wouldn't be a permanent dam, of course," Axel continued. "But we only need it to hold for a few days, a sycle at most. That should be enough to back the water into the Bottoms and form the firebreak we need."

Jarrad considered this. "Are you sure the logs will jam up the narrows? What if they just wash over into the cataracts?"

"Some might at first," Axel admitted. "But with enough logs, any that hit the narrows at an angle will jam, and the ones behind will pile up as well."

"One more concern," said Jarrad. "When the water rises, it'll put tremendous pressure on the logjam. What stops it from just collapsing and tumbling down the cataracts?"

Axel nodded. "That's a fair point. Luckily, there's an island at the top of the cataracts. It splits the flow, narrowing both channels and giving the logs something solid to brace against. The greatest pressure will be in the middle—but there, we've got a solid island of stone."

Jarrad gave a short nod. "All right. I'll call the townspeople to the market square before sunrise. That gives you until then to get the dragons on board. If they don't come, we'll have to evacuate and save what we can."

Langa, who had been silent, finally spoke up. "How do you think the townsfolk will react to the sudden arrival of sixty dragons?"

Axel grinned and stood, reaching for a saddle. "That's your problem, Jarrad."

Chapter Fifteen

ETHICAL DILEMMAS

Axel had never been to the Free Colony. Riding on Shaddra's back, he had a clear view of the mountain valley about him, so he kept a sharp eye open, hoping to see what it looked like from the air. His keen dragon eyesight missed very little as he scanned the cliffs and ridges, the smaller side valleys, and the tree-covered slopes. There was nothing that looked the least bit habitable.

"Feel privileged, Axel," Shaddra said. "You will be only the second human to see the Free Colony."

"As I recall," Axel said, speaking into a swift wind blowing into his face, "the first human to see it was the one who found it."

"I really do have to remember you are half-dragon. You never forget anything you see or hear."

"I don't think Jarrad would let me forget if I could. I'm the only person he can talk to about such things."

With Langa flying just behind, Axel still had no idea where Shaddra was leading him. She weaved in and about hanging mountain valleys and rocky crags. Waterfalls in countless numbers made the canyons look like decorative features of a home for gods.

Shaddra seemed to be heading straight for a solid cliff face halfway up a steep, rocky mountainside. Her speed was not diminishing, and the mountainside was approaching very fast.

"Uh, Shaddra, that's solid rock we're aiming for."

"Is it? What do you think I should do?"

"I don't know about you, but I'm going to close my eyes!"

A few seconds later, Axel felt the air about him change temperature. The wind slowed, and Shaddra's back end suddenly dipped down, while her front came up. All sounds, even for ears as sensitive as Axel's, ceased, and the air about them went still. He opened his eyes to see Shaddra's wings still beating slowly and silently as she allowed her front end to meet the ground, or whatever they were on.

He was in a huge chamber within the mountain. The opening could not have been very large, but this chamber was so large that Axel could not see its dimensions, even with the aid of his dragon eyes. He slipped off of Shaddra's back and noticed there were other dragons here. They were actually on something like a wide road running into the mountain. On one side, there were dragons of all kinds, standing in line. The lead dragon would open its wings and run out into the void, and the next dragon would move up to take its place. On the other side, the roadway was open, but every few minutes or so, a dragon would suddenly appear with its wings spread. The dragon would lower its back side, while its front side would rise, enabling it to effortlessly land on its four legs. That dragon would immediately turn off the road and either scurry down one of the many side openings or move over to a waiting area out of the path of incoming dragons. The place was a busy area with comings and goings happening every few minutes. Frequent high-language communications reached Axel's ears, clearly coordinating the landing and takeoff of dragons.

"What do you think of our flight center, Axel?"

"I am totally dumbfounded."

"I'll tell you more about the Colony when I have the chance. For now, just know that we occupy many chambers like this, with several even larger. It is as if the gods built this mountain especially for us."

"Shaddra, what would you say if I told you I think that is exactly what happened?"

"It's not normal for gods to interfere with what happens on Tamerel," Shaddra said, "so that concept is a challenge to believe. On the other hand, no other force could possibly have done this. I think I'll keep my mind open."

Shaddra led Axel through a passage that seemed to be very long. Langa followed along close behind. They passed almost no other dragons, and the ones they did paid little attention to Axel. At last, they came across a larger opening, which, in turn, branched off into several other passages. Axel knew that they were walking in near-pitch darkness, but he could clearly see everything in the dim light.

What was this place called? He had never been in rooms so large, so indescribably vast. He decided to call them halls, like the room the Mysura Community Council regularly met in. The side areas he called enclosures or rooms, depending on size and if they seemed to be a destination, and passages if their purpose was more to lead to a destination.

Shaddra, eventually, stopped in front of the opening to an enclosure. Here, Axel removed the saddle he had ridden on and placed it in a nearby alcove. Shaddra, meanwhile, spoke some sounds using dragon language that Axel, in part, understood. Not the words, if that's what they were, but the emotion and a feeling that sent a message saying, in a way, "I'm sorry to intrude, but I'm standing outside your home. Will you see me?"

After a very brief moment, Axel heard a second communication, also soft in nature, coming from inside the room. He discerned the message's meaning as, "I recognize you and appreciate that you have come to my place. Please come in." Axel also clearly recognized, not the voice, but the feeling that the sender was Hukken.

Not knowing anything about dragon etiquette, he followed Shaddra into the room, thinking *Just do what the others do. If I mess up, they'll forgive a first-timer.*

Inside, Shaddra and Langa stood side by side across from Hukken. Axel tried lining up along with them. The three dragons bowed their heads slightly, and he heard a jumble of *high speech* communications, which seemed to last several minutes. Finally, Hukken looked down at Axel. "Welcome to my home, *Son of the Great Ceragon*. Shaddra and Langa have described the state of affairs. It is an intriguing situation we find ourselves in, one fraught with danger and potential for reward."

Axel was amazed that Hukken took this news so calmly. But there was something in Hukken's eyes as he spoke, something that said a lot was happening inside his head.

Hukken looked up at Shaddra and Langa and spoke as if he were addressing Axel specifically. "We must order an immediate assembly of the Free Colony. Send messengers to call in all scouts to participate for its duration. It will begin in one orai. Be certain everyone understands who will be speaking to us."

Axel's eyes widened, "You're bringing in every one of the one hundred and seventy-two dragons for this meeting?"

"Actually, we'll have one hundred and seventy-five. While the three recently born firedrakes are just hatchlings, they will still be with us in the assembly. We could only have it more complete if Uncle Jarrad had been able to be here. No one would miss this event. The decisions made under this full dragon moon will tell us exactly who we are and are not."

When he said, 'Uncle Jarrad,' Axel thought, "They really think of him as family. *For thirty years, that's exactly what he has been. I'll bet he'd have an equal vote in every decision that is made here.*"

"In the meantime, we understand that you have been awake and working hard all day. Please take this orai to rest, to organize your thoughts, or just to meditate."

Hukken led Axel to a small room that was surprisingly comfortably furnished.

"This is where Jarrad stays when he visits with us. I'm certain that he would not be offended if you considered it your home while you are here. I'll return to take you to the Place of Assembly in one orai."

The room was furnished with two comfortable-looking stuffed chairs, a table with two matching wooden chairs set up to it, a bed, and a bedstand, upon which stood a large candle and a tinder kit. Axel headed straight for one of the chairs, sat, and started going over the events of the day in his mind. The task before him seemed overwhelming. If he failed, then the two towns in the Upper Mysura Valley will be turned into ash just as surely as if they had been attacked by dragons. Only, this time the people wouldn't all die suddenly but gradually from starvation and exposure. Somehow, his mind never even grasped the thought that he, too, might die.

The stuffed chairs had tall, contoured backs, which made them even more comfortable than they appeared. Gradually, the fears in his mind began to fade away.... The last thing he remembered was... the words, "Why two chairs?"

***

A voice came through the darkness. "Axel," it said.

It struck Axel as odd that he still had to close his eyes to sleep, even in complete darkness. When he opened them, he could see almost as clearly as he could on an overcast day. But the moment he shut them, everything vanished into blackness. He reasoned there must be some kind of light invisible to humans but that dragons could use to see in the dark.

"Axel!" This time, it came much more loudly.

"Yes, Shaddra. Sorry, it's just that I'm very comfortable right now. I suppose it is time."

"You suppose correctly. I hope you know what to say because this is the most attentive audience you will ever have."

Axel rose from his chair and followed the sound of Shaddra's voice to a main passageway where he found her standing. "Where are we going to have this meeting?" he asked.

"We are going to what is officially known as the 'Assembly Hall of the Free Dragons.' Yes, I know it's a long name. When you see it, you'll understand why it has such a name. But we generally call it, simply, the 'Place of Assembly.'"

Axel trotted to keep up with Shaddra as she walked through the halls; she probably knew better than Axel had known the dirty streets of Frithden. "When we go into the Hall, you will see a path leading to your right and a high, flat stone. That is where you will stand. Everyone in the Assembly Hall will be able to see you there and hear what you say."

***

Axel neared the Hall, looking down at Shaddra's feet, making certain he did not get lost. But as the walls started to widen out, he heard a cacophony of high-pitched sounds, which told him the dragons there were talking excitedly among themselves. When they approached the path that apparently led to the speaker's platform, everything hushed. He looked up and around to see the most amazing sight he had ever beheld in his short life. The Place of Assembly was cavernous beyond belief.

He stopped short of the platform and looked about him. The hall was a huge hollowed-out bowl shaped in the rock, probably two hundred strides wide and two hundred deep. The lower sides were sloped and carved into terraces, just perfect for the dragon audience to sit comfortably and see the podium platform from any place in the expansive room. The speaker's podium was a high flat rock rising up from a low place on one edge, but it was big enough to hold the largest dragon.

The walls of the room towered above him and curved in toward the middle, forming a kind of roof over the areas where a seemingly endless supply of dragons now sat. Nevertheless, the hall was so large it could have held double or even triple the number of dragons as it did now. Perhaps even more. As for the ceiling... it was an open circle through which Axel saw a dark starlit sky and a red Dragon Moon. It formed an eye that would stare down on the events of this night.

Hukken stood on the speaker's platform. "Tonight," he said, "we are privileged to hear for the very first time from Axel, who you already know is the *son of the Great Ceragon*. His visit here is of special consequence to the human community in the Upper Mysura Valley. As you also know, he will ask us to make a decision this night—a decision that will have grave consequences, whichever way the vote may go. Let me, therefore, ask Axel to come up here and tell us what is in his heart."

Axel looked at the crowd around him and found his legs to be very weak, weaker than after a day of hauling large rocks in the stream bed. Somehow or another, his legs moved. They moved as if there were a jewel commanding them to walk, and he soon found himself standing in the middle of the speaker's platform, staring out into a forest of dragon faces.

Dragon hands are not shaped for clapping. They have three thick fingers, a mostly opposable thumb, like humans, and retractable claws. However, the claws just do not feel right when clapping. Therefore, dragon applause is different from humans and certainly more intimidating. The hall was now filled with the thunderous sounds of nearly two hundred dragons slapping their tails on the smooth, rocky floor of the Assembly Hall. The ground, literally, shook from their applause, and the noise was deafening, but the sound gradually withered away, and the room became deathly silent.

Axel found his lips to be very dry, and he tried to moisten them with the tip of his tongue, but his tongue was just as dry as his lips. At that moment, he thought he would rather be facing fifty daewols.

He focused and found he could force words from his heart to his mouth.

"Greetings to my dragon family," he said in a moderately loud voice and quickly realized that he did not have to speak loudly to be heard here. Sound carried so well through this vast meeting hall that Axel was certain he could have a simple personal conversation with anyone sitting on the terrace farthest from him.

"You are already very much aware of why I am here," he said, letting the words flow from his heart with only a modicum of forethought. "Perhaps you have already made up your minds about the question I am presenting. That is perfectly all right with me because I know that, as we learn more about what is true, we all change our minds as necessary.

"Since you already know the question, you also realize there are two possible ways of answering it at this particular time. If I may use a human analogy, on the one hand, you may say, 'No, we will not, or cannot, help the humans of the Valley.' On the other hand, you may say, 'Yes, we will assist this community of humans who are so much in need of our help.' In order for a fair and wise decision to be made, both the advantages and the disadvantages of the dragons helping the people of the Valley must be presented. May I ask if there is anyone here who is knowledgeable and willing to come up and stand beside me to present the arguments against this this course of action?

Hundreds of surprised facial expressions appeared on every tier in the room, but it quickly became obvious that no one was willing to go up and debate against the *Son of the Great Ceragon.*

When no one volunteered, Axel looked over to the side he had entered from and said, "Shaddra, you are fully knowledgeable of everything that is happening. Are you not?"

Shaddra seemed to be every bit as reluctant to speak as the others. But she replied softly, "That I am."

Axel looked out at the crowd and asked, "Would you be willing to accept Shaddra as a fair speaker *against* my proposal?"

There were cries of "Yes" and "Mother Shaddra can speak for me!"

Axel looked over his shoulder and held out his arm. "Shaddra, my friend, you have already voiced arguments to me as to why helping the people of the Valley would be harmful to the Free Colony. Would you repeat those arguments now and add any you have thought of since?"

Shaddra approached the speaker's platform every bit as slowly as had Axel. Clearly, she had mixed emotions about what she was about to do. But nothing could stop her from telling the truth as she saw it, Axel was sure.

Every eye in the hall was staring at her with an air of expectancy. She looked out at the audience and said, "I told the *Son of Ceragon* earlier today that the Free Dragons have lived in these caverns for nearly thirty years in peace and freedom from fear. The caverns provide a measure of safety and protection. But it is the fact that the king does not know we exist, which truly protects us. If he knew there were dragons in Sanara that he did not control, he would declare war upon us—a war that we could not hope to win. Once the people of the Valley know who we are and what we are, any one of them could pass the secret of our existence to the king. True, the king would not know *where* we were, but he would set his army of two thousand dragonriders with the task of finding us. We would never again have the freedom of the skies that we now have.

"What's more, if the king knows there are dragons in Sanara who do not wear jewels, he is going to ask where they came from, and that will lead inevitably back to Mother Clara and the Daughter of Ceragon.

"Even if the humans of the Valley are grateful for the assistance we provide and swear to keep the secret of our existence, there will always be someone who knows that the king would offer a fortune for information regarding this colony. It may not happen right away, but sooner or later our secret will become open knowledge. We would be forced to fight for our very survival against overwhelming odds."

Shaddra bowed to the audience and to Axel. "Thank you," Axle said to Shaddra and the audience in general. "You have presented the situation exactly the way you see it, and I wanted nothing less."

Shaddra descended from the platform, looking over her shoulder at Axel as she did.

Axel stepped forward at this time and took a deep breath. "I have spent the last orai in a room here in the Colony, which is normally occupied by 'Uncle Jarrad' when he visits. In both your use of the word 'uncle' and mine, it is an honorific, meaning that we esteem Jarrad so highly that we consider him close family, only one step away from that level of closeness we would give to a father or a brother. Since few of us here even have a living father or brother, the term 'uncle' bears even greater significance."

At this point, Axel slowed down his words. "I have my own reasons for calling him '*Uncle.*' *What* are yours?"

There was silence in the hall as the dragons thought over the question.

"Is it because, when you or your parents found yourselves suddenly facing the world alone, he appeared and wrapped his arms around you and cared for you and loved you, even when that caring could have cost him his life? Indeed, that very caring is what cost Jarrad's father his life. All his father really wanted was that the king stop treating his people as slaves, and he was killed for that.

"I'll admit that, at first, Jarrad did what he did because a goddess said he should. However, the goddess also said, 'You make your choice, and you will live with the consequences of that choice.' Is that really why Jarrad did what he did? Because he was afraid of the consequences of a wrong choice?

"Maybe that very first time, when he knew nothing about dragons and nothing about the beautiful spirits you are. Yes, it's possible, but I don't think so. Even back then, Jarrad Dismer lived, as he still lives, a life based on the answer to one question, a question he always asks himself before making any decisions. That question is simply, 'What is right?'

"The reason why he obeyed the Goddess, the reason why he risked his life, and why he worked so hard on your behalf all came down to the fact that it was the right thing to do.

"Yes, the reality that he loves you more than his own breath might have had some influence later on. But you get my point.

"Let me ask you, where is Jarrad right now? Is he here, within these rock walls, safe with you? No. He is in Tarfal, trying to find a way to save members of another race that he also happens to love. He is there, not because he loves you any less; he is there because it is the right thing to do. The lives of nearly four thousand people are threatened, and he will do everything possible to save them. I will be joining him there soon for the same reason. Whatever happens to the humans of the Valley will also happen to us."

Axel paused to look around at his audience in a wide sweep. "Unfortunately, the timing of this fire is awful. It may mean that the gods will have to find another *son of Ceragon*, and you probably know what that entails. Action on the foretelling will have to be postponed for a while.

"Clara and Eleth, right now, have two very young draft dragons living in Clara's cottage. If Jarrad and I happen to die in Tarfal, Clara will be faced with a very difficult decision. What will she do with them? They will soon be too big to keep in her home. If Jarrad and I aren't around to bring the dragons out, what will happen? Will the draft dragons have to be sacrificed?"

A murmur of high speech rose up from the dragons upon hearing these words.

Axel let the sound carry on for a few minutes and then continued his speech. "That might sound a bit like blackmail or even a little black-hearted. If you feel this is so, I am sorry. I'm only trying to present what would likely happen if Tarfal and Mikell were destroyed. There will be more than just humans affected there.

"The fact is, the gods often require sacrifice, which is a nice way of saying *death*, with no immediate hope of reward. I've told some of you about my parents and what it cost them so that I might be. Both of my parents gave their lives for me. What did they receive for the lives they surrendered? Not much. But *I* am here to speak to you because of them and their sacrifices.

"You know who my father was. But do you know who Eleth's father was? His name was Boda Morkath, and her mother was named Careen. They both offered their lives within a Kivan of Eleth's birth so that *she* could live and so that *she* could become the *Daughter of Ceragon*. What reward did they get for their sacrifices? They got nothing. They didn't even get to see their daughter grow beyond her first Kivan. But *we* got Eleth, and you will discover that the *Daughter of Ceragon* is a treasure and a delight.

"One day soon you will meet the *Daughter* and see that she has Clara's heart. You will see how wonderful a person she has become. You will see how she has come to love you as much or more than I. Eleth's parents gave everything for her, and my parents sacrificed everything for me, but according to foretellings, *if* you are worthy, *you* will be given the world because of *them*."

Axel paused again before continuing with his message. "Now, Shaddra has mentioned the danger that Clara and Eleth may find themselves in should you go to the aid of the Valley. It is clear that Clara and Eleth *are* in *ever-increasing* danger the longer they stay in the Breeding Coops. It is only logical, therefore, that the next step in the fulfillment of the *Great Foretelling* will be the rescue of *all* dragons in the Breeding Coops and the bringing of Clara and Eleth home to their children. Do we know how that will happen or what it might cost? No. Not right now. But it will happen *if* the Free Colony starts believing that *now* is the time to set the process in motion. What's more, it will only happen if the Free Dragons can become partners with humans, who have also been slaves, and build a future together.

"You may ask, how is it that humans have been slaves? Do they wear jewels on their necks? No, they do not wear jewels. But let's consider the case of Clara. Do you think that she *willingly* places that jewel in the neck of each newborn hatchling that is bred in the coops? No! She does it because she is forced to do it. Is that not slavery? Still, she fights against her masters at every opportunity, and that is why you can sit before me in this assembly—because she was the one who *gave you flight*!"

Axel's speech was suddenly interrupted with the noise of tails thumping the ground and high speech from all around the gallery. After a few minutes, he held up his hands to quiet the crowd, and they obediently complied.

"My grandfather was a king's flying officer, taken away from his parents when he was about my age, and forced to fight and kill and risk his life until the day he found a way to escape his bondage. He was the first to make me understand about the slavery of dragons and his hatred of it. He was also one of those I buried after the massacre at Frithden. What's more, that was *not* the first time the king killed large numbers of his own people for his own good pleasure! Other villages and small towns have also been destroyed at the king's whim.

"Twenty-five years ago, this part of Badares was a peace-loving kingdom known as Locarno. But King Deroth sent his armies to steal that country away and kill anyone who might oppose him in the future. Many of those who managed to escape the destruction wreaked by Deroth found their way to the Mysura Valley to start new lives. But they remember the crimes of Deroth, and he hates the thought that such people even exist.

"Just like everyone else all across the kingdom, the people of the Valley are forced to pay exorbitant taxes just so the King can buy more of his little red playthings, which control the dragons, and he has demanded a large number of the Mysura Valley's sons and daughters be taken from their homes and trained to fight in the King's forces. I also know that in just the last year, more than forty such sons and daughters have returned to Tarfal and Mikell... in boxes. In summary, let me say that the King has turned Sanara into a kingdom of slaves. Even so, the time is soon at hand when the dragons and humans of Sanara will join hands to eliminate slavery here in all its forms. Think on that, but remember it will only happen if dragons and humans can learn to help each other in many ways and soon. The Mysuran people must not be destroyed, for they will be the first humans to join you in the enormous task ahead.

"I ask you to think over all that I have said. Yes, many of you will be able to find logical holes in my arguments. But there is a question that you cannot avoid answering today, *just now*." Again, he paused before continuing, "That question is, '*Are you going to do the right thing*?'

"If you make the correct answer to this question and act upon it, I promise you, this moment shall be the beginning of a great movement that will end only when the *Foretelling of Ceragon* is fulfilled.

"I must leave shortly for Tarfal. I hope to have your answer before then."

Axel turned toward the exit to leave but found Shaddra and Hukken blocking his way. They were smiling. Only then did he hear the thunderous noise bouncing off the round, rocky walls of the Assembly Hall to crash upon his ears.

Chapter Sixteen

FIRE AND WATER

Jarrad stood alone on a speaker's platform in front of slightly less than four thousand men, women, and children gathered together in the community's Open Market Square. He was breathing rapidly and looking into the early morning sky on the western horizon.

"All right, Jarrad," came a voice from the crowd. "It's dawn, so what's the big reason why you had Head Councilman Bassen blow the rally call this morning? What's so important?"

"Yeah," came another voice, "you've got everyone, including all of us from the mine and the lumber mill here. We're already going to be losin' a half day's work because of this. It had better be somethin' big."

Jarrad shouted to make himself heard over the cacophony of voices in the crowd. "I'm afraid that what I have to say *is* very important. It's important enough that it may mean life or death for everyone here! But we still have a few minutes before the first real light of the sunstar rises over the mountains. We must make certain everyone is here for this announcement. It *is* that important!"

"What could possibly be that important?" came as another shout.

It was at that moment Jarrad saw what he was looking for.

"The reason I have asked..."

"You mean 'ordered,'" someone interrupted. "I wouldn't be here if I didn't *have* to be."

"The reason you are here this morning," Jarrad shouted even louder, "is because the village is in danger of being destroyed by fire!"

The crowd went quiet, but low murmurs were passing from person to person. A lone voice spoke out from the front. "What fire are you talking about?"

"A lightning-caused fire has broken out in the forest, south of the road, just this side of the Rim. Everything is tinder dry, and there is absolutely nothing between us and that fire to prevent it from burning the forest all the way here and then burning our town!"

The crowd suddenly became absolutely silent.

After a moment, a female voice shouted from the middle of the crowd, "But that's twenty-five tondrins away! How can you possibly know about a fire that's so far away?"

"I saw the fire myself."

"But the Midvalley Knolls would keep you from seeing anything that far away. Are you certain you just didn't see a thunderstorm on the horizon?"

"It was no thunderstorm. I was close enough to the fire to see the flames and smell the smoke."

"You were actually near the Rim, then?"

"I was."

"And when did you see this fire?"

"Late yesterday, just before the setting of the Sunstar."

"Impossible! How could you be at the Rim last night and here this morning? There's not enough time, even if you rode the fastest skell."

"But I didn't ride a skell, my friends! I rode one of those!" Jarrad pointed to the sky over the heads of the crowd as he spoke his last sentence.

The crowd all turned their heads as one to look up into the sky, where Jarrad had pointed. Numerous black bird-like objects were flying directly toward the village.

"Those are dragons!" someone shouted. "The King sent his dragons! They'll burn down our village!" All of a sudden, hundreds of screams and shouts rose up from the crowd as people verged on sheer panic.

B O N G! An ear-piercing noise stopped everyone in their tracks and brought their attention back to Jarrad. He had just used a sledgehammer to strike a large piece of brass sheet metal that he had the local blacksmiths hang behind the speaker's platform.

"Those aren't the king's dragons," he bellowed, "and they will do you no harm! Those dragons are here to help us save the town from the fire!"

The townspeople fell silent for a brief moment before resuming their murmurs, with some shouting to make their voices heard. The crowd erupted in a restless rumble, but some voices stood out more than others.

A man in miner's clothes shouted, "Dragons only destroy!"

A woman carrying a baby screamed. "Dragons don't help people! They probably started the fire!"

Multiple voices were proclaiming variants of "We should run and get out of here!"

B O N G! Again, the non-ignorable sound brought everyone's attention back to Jarrad. This time, almost as if from out of nowhere, a small dragon dropped down out of the sky and sailed to an effortless stop just behind Jarrad. On the dragon's back was a figure everyone readily recognized as Axel Daimon.

Axel unbelted himself from the saddle, stepped down, and hopped up onto the speaker's platform to join Jarrad. "People of Tarfal and Mikell!" Axel shouted, "I have just inspected the fire that is burning over by the Rim. At its current speed, I estimate that it will reach the two towns in less than three days! As it stands, there is nothing to stop it.

"I was able to clearly see the fire while flying on the back of this messenger dragon. She is my friend and an excellent go-between we can use to gain the help of the Free Dragons that you see circling above our heads. They are willing to help us stop the fire well before it reaches the towns."

A rumble of voices again spread across the crowd in the square.

"Again, listen to me!" Axel shouted. "The dragons that you see aren't the king's dragons! They are the Free Dragons of Sanara. They answer to no king, but they are perfectly willing to help their friends, and they count *us* as among their friends!"

Councilman Bassen strode up to the speaker's platform to converse with Axel and Jarrad. "Is this statement true?" he asked. "How can there be dragons that aren't controlled by the king?"

Jarrad put his arm on Bassen's shoulder and said, loudly enough for most of the crowd to hear, "For many, many years there have been dragons in the mountains who have not answered to the king. Axel and I were able to make friends with these dragons and convince them that the people of the Valley are their friends and will treat them as such. On that condition, the dragons have agreed to help."

"But you and Axel are the only apparent witnesses to this fire. The people need more than that to believe a claim so important to their lives and, I must add, to believe that the dragons will help."

"Hmm," said Jarrad. "I see your point."

"People of the Valley," he suddenly shouted to the crowd. "The head councilman has told us you need greater evidence of this fire before you can commit the effort required to stop it. I think he is right. Accordingly, the head councilman has agreed to witness for himself whether the fire is where we have claimed."

"I... uh... what?" said the councilman.

"We have two dragon saddles, and the councilman will use one. Do I have a volunteer to use the other saddle?"

Immediately, two hands were raised.

"I want to go," Bardin Shotley called out.

"No, ladies first!" shouted Fala Prudo.

"But I volunteered first," shouted Bardin.

"You're not going without me, Bardin Shotley!"

"Enough already!" Jarrad loudly ordered above their voices. "A saddle isn't absolutely necessary to ride a dragon. It just makes it more comfortable, and Hukken would never let anyone fall."

"Yaahah!" shouted Fala. "Then, I get to ride Hukken! I can ride any skell bareback, and now, I'll be able to ride a dragon too!"

Axel knew that Bardin was also more than an adequate skeller, and he'd give Fala a challenging run for the best in the valley. Either one could definitely ride a dragon without falling off.

"Since I see no other volunteers, your job is to go witness and report on the fire. We should see you back here in about an orai. Oh, and I hope you haven't eaten any breakfast yet."

"In the meantime, Axel and I will present our plan for stopping the fire to the town."

Hukken and Langa settled in behind Jarrad and stayed while their new riders assumed their proper positions. At a silent signal from Shaddra, the three took off in an easy glide, all for the benefit of their new riders.

Jarrad, who was still standing on the platform, called out to his audience, "I suggest that you sit. Find yourselves a comfortable piece of dirt and listen well. Your very lives will depend on what you do.

"I invite Axel to speak with you. I do so for two important reasons. The first is that the plan, which we are about to present, has been the child of his mind. It is to him that we may owe our lives before only a few days have passed. I also commend this young man to you, because it has been his hard labor, keen mind, and warm heart that have brought the dragons here to offer help in doing things we could never do for ourselves."

Jarrad stepped down from the speaker's platform, and Axel took his place. As the two exchanged places, Jarrad rested a hand on Axel's shoulder for an instant, and the crowd became totally silent.

Axel stepped onto the speaker's platform and looked out at the crowd. He chewed on his lip for a moment, took a breath, and said in a loud voice. "My friends and neighbors here in Tarfal and Mikell: A few minutes ago, I told you of a big fire near the Rim that, if left as is, will burn through all of the forest in this valley and consume our communities, our livestock, our planted fields, and everything that survivors of the fire, should there be any, could possibly use to sustain their lives. There is no question that this fire will destroy everything we value, including our very lives, unless we can find a way to stop it.

"With the dragon's help, I have discovered a way to stop the fire. But actually stopping it will require every bit of work we Mysurans can put into the task, and it will require the help of our friends the Free Dragons.

"Many of you are aware of the place known as Bokin's Bottoms, on this side of the Mid-Valley Knolls."

"But the Bottoms are dry," an older man called out from the crowd. "The fire will burn right through it."

"You are absolutely right," Axel answered. "The fire will burn right through it unless something happens to make the bottoms wet again."

"How are you going to do that?" came the same voice.

"Oh, I'm not going to do it," Axel said loudly. "You are! You and the dragons are going to work together to fill the Bottoms with water!

"There are two parts to this plan. The first is that the dragons will lead in creating a temporary dam on the Mysura River at the narrows. They will do their part by pushing over trees into the river upstream. These trees will float downstream in the river until they catch at the narrows. The mass of trees, most still bearing their leaves, will slow the flow of the river and cause it to back up."

"Okay," someone said, "that's the dragon's job. What's ours?"

"We will need the miners to set up explosives on the sides of the narrows to bring down whatever rock they can get into the narrows. It must end up narrow enough and shallow enough to stop the trees and dam up the water as much as possible.

"In addition to that, there is a rock and earth ridge known as the 'dike' along the edge of the Mysura, where it passes the Bottoms. It's nearly two strides above the river, five strides thick, and two hundred strides long. The rock it's made from is hard and has a dark-brown color with an endless supply of black and white spots or speckles in it. Because it dams up a side stream, it is the usual reason why the Bottoms fill up with water every year. Unless we can lower that ridge or get rid of it entirely, it will act as a reverse dam and keep water from flowing from the river into the bottoms. If we can lower it by at least one stride and get water to flow into the bottoms from the river, it will make the best firebreak possible! It will flood everything from the road to the river and extend it to two tondrins wide or more.

"Since the river is low right now, it will be more work, but there's still plenty of water in the middle. It does not wash up on the banks as it used to. I suggest you fetch shovels, picks, ropes, axes, saws, and skells to help the dragons get the logs from the high banks into the water. The dragons will help anyone needing to cross over to the south side of the river, whether to bring down more trees or to get over to the narrows to set the explosives. Remember, the fire will pass the Bottoms in about two days. That means we have *less* than two days to build the dam and get water flowing into that dry bog."

"How are we supposed to ask the dragons for help with a job?" someone yelled from way back.

"Oh, yes," Axel said with a laugh. "I forgot to tell you that the dragons talk. If you need help from them, just ask. I'd ask politely, though, if I were you. But just ask. Oh, and don't lie to them either. Dragons are honorable creatures who don't tolerate deceit. If they find out you've been lying, they may get angry.

"I know most of you have children who need care and attention. Please organize yourselves to manage that responsibility first. Every able-bodied person, man or woman, is needed, in one way or another, except for those who are taking care of children,.

"Okay, miners meet over on the north side of the market square. Lumbermen meet on the south side. All other workers should go to the west side. Go!

"I expect that Councilman Bassen and my apprentices will return in a half orai. Let's be prepared to start work as soon as they are here. Get yourselves organized and prepared now. We don't have much time!"

A half orai later, right on schedule, two messenger dragons and a siris dragon sailed into the center of the market square. Their three passengers set themselves onto the ground and immediately began making rounds among the three groups, telling everyone what they had seen. The news seemed to touch a spark to everyone's backsides, and people were moving much faster than before. Small groups of people bustled off in different directions with a definite purpose in their strides.

Axel managed to catch Fala as she was heading for the city paddocks. "How was the ride, Fala?" he asked.

"It was okay, I suppose."

"Why only 'okay'?"

"No matter which way I told Hukken to go, he just went his own way. No skell would do that!"

"I'm so sorry, Fala," Axel said, trying to hold his smile. "You need to remember that every dragon is as intelligent as you are, so riding one is always a bit of a negotiation. After the unbearable torture that you have been through, I think you should make up for it by grabbing a skell and heading over to the river, just to spite Hukken."

She gave him a knowing look and smiled grimly. She shook her head and, with her fists clenched, strode off in the direction of the paddocks.

As the populace started returning, carrying supplies of all sorts, Axel and Jarrad worked as traffic managers, connecting people assigned to certain tasks with the dragons whom Hukken had designated to work for the same purposes. Dragons began to land, gathering people with terrified expressions on their faces and departing for their designated tasks.

Other people drove through town on wagons pulled by teams of skells. Jarrad stood by the road to direct these folks to their assignments.

A number of women started collecting water jugs, blankets, cooking utensils, and any other necessities the people on the river might need.

Once all the workers, including the many women and older children who had joined them, departed town, Langa and Shaddra dropped down to pick up Jarrad and Axel. They first flew down to the narrows to see what was happening on its rocky slopes. There, they found miners already at work with sledgehammers and long steel bars, double-jacking holes into the rock. Once deep enough, they would fill the holes with black powder and fuses to blast rock into the river below.

After this, the two messenger dragons flew up to where the Bokin's Bottoms dike paralleled the river. Here people were concentrating on opening a place in the wall that appeared weakest. They were pounding on the rocks with sledgehammers and using pry bars to break out pieces of the dike. They seemed to be progressing, though it would be difficult to tell if they could be ready in time.

Flying further upstream, Axel and Jarrad soon saw the first of the logs floating down the middle of the stream. Given that these logs lacked leaves, Axel assumed they were likely the easiest targets. These were the logs that were already sitting on the banks and only needed a shove. Others soon followed, and many of these had leaves and extensive root systems that stuck up out of the water.

When they entered the mid-valley hills region, the river narrowed, the water deepened, and there were more trees right on the edge of the river. Here they found six dragons working to push trees into the river. Three dragons were working on the south bank, and three were on the north. Many trees were growing right on the banks so that when pushed over, they would fall directly into deep, swift water. For those working in the area, the large number of trees growing so close to the water was all too tempting. But footing on neither of the banks was very conducive for this kind of work. There was a lot of loose shale, and a misstep could send either a dragon or a human skidding into the water.

A coniferous tree keeled over and crashed into the water just as the two messenger dragons passed over. Axel instantly recognized the dragon responsible as Licor, and Axel yelled down at the top of his voice to get his attention and commend him for his work. Licor looked up, but just as he did, the shale rock under his feet gave way and sent him sliding into water up to his shoulders in depth. He quickly found some shallow water and scrambled up the hill and out of the river. He looked up again at Axel with a not-too-pleased expression on his face. At that instant, Axel heard some High Language communications going on.

"Shaddra, I don't think I want to know what he just said."

"Actually, what he just said is not translatable into human," Shaddra answered, "and that is probably a good thing."

Further up the river, the riverbed widened out, but the river itself was very shallow on the edge here. Axel saw a tree that had been pushed over into the water but was not moving downstream at all. On one end, a team of six skells, standing in water up to their bellies, was hooked to the tree with ropes, while on the other end, a siris dragon and a firedrake were ready to push near its roots. A group of humans wielding a two-handled saw were diligently cutting through one of the thick roots, which seemed firmly entrenched in the sandy river bottom. As Axel watched, the root gave way, and the tree trunk slid handily over twenty strides toward the swift water. Two more townspeople were chopping away with axes at a sturdy branch that was keeping the top from moving in a similar way. It appeared that with so many people and dragons working together, the tree would be heading down the river very soon.

Two more trees floated past them in the current while Axel and Jarrad observed the combined efforts of the humans and dragons below.

Upstream, Axel and Jarrad saw more combined groups of people and dragons working together on other trees. Axel shouted over to Jarrad that he was glad to see the humans and the dragons working so well together. Jarrad shouted back that he wondered whether that might be due to the humans' fear of being eaten if they stepped out of line or the dragon's fear that they would have to face Axel if things did not go right. Axel laughed at the suggestion and said, "It's more likely they're afraid of having to face Shaddra than me."

Shaddra looked back at Axel and said, "You know, Axel, you may be slow, but you are definitely learning."

They continued up the river for a few orais, looking for any problems in dragon-human cooperation and finding none. On the way back down the river, they counted no fewer than fifty trees and logs floating along in the center of the current. Some had hung themselves up in shallow water, and there were dragons already working to get these freed up.

When they reached the bottoms, two men and a woman were quick to rush up and report on their progress toward breaching the dike. They already had an opening about two strides in width broken open across the lowest part of the dike and had removed rock down a full stride from the original top. They were working to further cut away rock from the hole and to widen the opening.

Hopefully, Axel thought, *the miners will have enough black powder left over to help us make this hole bigger.*

As if on cue, the group heard the first of four distinct blasts, about two minutes apart, coming from further downstream. Axel and Jarrad looked at each other and gave similar nodding signals. It was time to look at progress on the dam—the most important part of the whole effort.

Even from forty landrins upstream, Axel and Jarrad saw, through all the dust that choked the air, one major difference from their last visit. The top three-quarters of Bourem's Finger was missing. A light wind streaming from the east and through Bourem's narrows was blowing the dust away so that gradually they began to see a complete picture. The finger had mostly fallen to the north, and huge slabs of rock were now crushing a dozen or more large trees in the northern gap. Water that would normally pass through the north gap was now almost entirely blocked.

On the south side, a piece of the high, rocky canyon side was missing. Here, too, giant slabs of rock had fallen into the river. But, on this side, the river was only partially blocked. Now, all the water that was once flowing through the canyon was rushing through an opening only one-third as wide as before. Roughly a dozen fallen trees lay semi-submerged in the opening, but water seemed to flow around them fairly easily. The water that had flowed through the canyon on the north side of the finger was now backing up and joining the water that flowed on the south. The southern opening was presently about forty strides wide, seven strides deep, and flowing as fast as a skell could run at full speed. While the three trees looked precariously on the verge of being swept down the gorge and onto the cataracts, water was actually backing up into the wider canyon upstream.

Jarrad signaled he was going to head upstream, and Axel had Shaddra follow right behind. When they reached the Bottoms, they landed close to the team working on the dike. One of the people jogged over to give a report.

"We've probably done about as much good as we can here in this location," he said. "We have a gap thirty strides in width, and we've lowered its height by almost two strides in places. What we need now is for the river to rise. The river must rise by at least a stride in this location, or we will have wasted our efforts.

Axel rubbed his jaw and looked over at Langa. "You know, Shaddra and Langa, you have been so much help already that it's difficult to thank you enough for what you have done. Can you keep on going for a while?"

Langa pointed over at Shaddra and said, "You can count on me, Axel, for twice as long as that old one over there."

"Old one?" Shaddra said with a harrumph. "I'll have you know I'm in the prime of my life, and I can still best you any time you want a competition!"

"Ladies, ladies," Jarrad said in a calming voice. "Or dragonesses, or whatever the appropriate term is for a female dragon. We feel privileged to have two fine, healthy dragons with us today, and the truth is we couldn't do what needs to be done today without either one of you. Therefore, if you don't mind...."

At just that instant, a firedrake and a siris dragon came barreling down the valley at high speed and only a hundred strides above the water. When their riders saw Jarrad and Axel on the riverside, they brought their mounts up sharply and made a quick turn, which brought them over to where they could land next to the dike.

"Whoa," shouted Jarrad, "Whatever lit a fire under your dragon's tails?"

"I'll have you know there is no fire under my tail," said Licor in his usual gruff voice.

"Uh, sorry, Licor," Jarrad said. "It's a human figure of speech."

Then Axel noticed that the riders were Bardin and Fala. "Okay, you two," he said, "what are you all excited about?"

"Bardin swallowed and blurted out, "We may have a problem."

"A big one," said Fala.

"Fala and I were roping kitki trees up by the mid-valley hills," Bardin said in between panting gasps for air. "We'd rope them, then Licor and Goran would grab the ropes and pull the trees over into the water, 'cause their roots are so short. Once a tree was in the water, we'd cut the ropes close to the tree and start all over."

"Yes, but the last time we did it, we chose the wrong trees," Fala said.

Axel tried to wrap his mind around the idea of choosing the wrong trees. "What do you mean by…?"

Bardin interrupted Axel's question, "We threw ropes around two trees that were rather close together and on a steep slope. When the dragons pulled them out, their roots caught on a buried tree trunk and lifted it out of the ground. There was nothing holding it in place but some sand, which gave way, and it fell into the water."

And that, Fala said, "caused the buried log to roll over and into the river."

"What's the big deal?" asked Jarrad. "It seems we got three trees for the price of two."

"The big deal," Bardin said in a plaintive tone, "is that the buried log was twice as big as any other tree in the Valley! It's more than a hundred strides long, almost three strides thick, and it is now barreling down the river lengthwise like a huge battering ram, roots end first! It's moving faster than anything else in the river, and whenever something like a big tree gets in its way, the ram just pushes it aside and keeps on coming! I don't know what the state of the dam is right now, but if this thing hits anything that isn't rock solid, it's going to plow right on through and take everything else with it."

Axel and Jarrad each looked at the other and said, "Uh, oh!"

Axel's face turned white, and he muttered, "It has to be stopped."

"Stopped," Fala said with a laugh. "That log couldn't be stopped with a dozen dragons."

"If I have to, I'll get a dozen dragons."

"Hey, I just said the log can't be stopped. Maybe it could be turned or somehow brought to shore, but I don't know how we could even do that."

"What is making this log float root-end first?" asked Jarrad.

Bardin answered the question, saying, "The roots are acting like a sail. Water pushes against the roots more than any other part of the log. That keeps it going straight down the river."

"Does that mean if we can turn the roots, the whole log will turn?"

"That won't be easy to do," said Fala.

"Hey," Bardin said with a light in his eyes. "We were using ropes to grab the tops of trees and pull them down into the river. What if we were to loop a rope around one of the thick roots on the log's front end?"

Fala shook her head. "Then what? It would drag whatever we tie the rope to into the river or just snap the rope."

Axel thought about this for a moment and said, "I know you two are some of the best skellers in the valley. You're used to throwing ropes to loop around the necks of fast-moving skells. Could you throw a rope and loop this tree's roots from shore?"

"Only if the river is very narrow," said Fala.

The only place where the river is like that is in the narrows, just before the dam," Axel said.

"It's also where the current is fastest and strongest," noted Jarrad. "It means we'll only have one chance, and we'll have to be prepared with backup in case the first throw fails."

"If we can catch the head and turn it in the current, the stress will still be great, but not as great as if we were to try to stop it."

"What if we had three or even four ropes ready to throw?" Fala said. "We could have the other ends already tied off and just concentrate on the throws."

"That means," Axel summarized, "we could have four attempts to throw ropes and catch the log, four possibilities of rope breakage, but with each catch, the stress will be shared by multiple ropes. If we let the current drag the front over to one side and secure it there, it will add to our dam and help us to better stop trees coming later."

"And, if we fail," said Jarrad, "the log will tear out what's left of our dam. The increased current will rapidly eat away at the dirt and rock on the sides of the river and undo all the labor contributed by the miners on that side. It will never be any narrower or shallower."

"All the more reason why we need to make it work the first time," Axel said firmly. "I see you have some rope with you. Is it enough for what we need to do?"

"Not likely," said Bardin.

"I recall the miners down at the dam site were using ropes to scale the sides of the canyons. We should be able to get some more rope there. Where is this log now?"

Bardin and Fala looked at each other. "It has been moving very fast," said Fala, "and I think it will pass this point on the river within the next half orai."

"I agree with Fala's assessment," said Bardin.

"Bardin," Axel said, "would you ask Licor to take you down to the dam site, find the miners, and get as much of the strongest rope as you can? No miner is going to give Licor any guff."

"We're off."

"The rest of us, let's get down to the narrows and find a place where we can pull this off."

***

Three dragons—a firedrake, a siris dragon, and Shaddra—landed on the rocky landslide, which resulted from explosions set off earlier that day on the south side of the river. Axel descended from Shaddra and looked closely at the hillside caused by the blasts. The man-made avalanche had brought a significant portion of the steep rocky slope down into the river. The result was, in fact, a ninety-stride-wide avalanche that closed off two-thirds of the river. The upstream side of the avalanche slanted rather rapidly north and east, away from the old riverbank, until it reached the fastest-running part of the river; there it turned straight downstream to the east until it reached the first of the rough dams formed by trapped tree trunks at the top of the cataracts. The far downstream side of the hill fell steeply to the river, but the actual end seemed to disappear over the edge of the rim into the cataracts. The end result was a relatively short, straight stretch of bank running along the narrowest part of the river. There were a number of very large boulders, scattered about near the shore, which could be used as tie-downs for ropes.

Axel waved a hand out toward Fala in a 'come here' gesture, inviting her over for a conference. Jarrad readily joined in. As always, the dragons placed themselves within easy listening distance.

"Based on how you've seen the track of the log until now," Axel asked, "how do you think it will approach these narrows?"

Fala walked apart from the group, looked around, and climbed some distance further up the hill caused by the blasts, where she turned towards the river and examined it for what seemed a long amount of time. At last, she said, "It will come straight down the middle of the river above and begin a slow turn where it meets the backflow from the avalanche. When I say 'slow,' I only mean it in relation to its normal travel speed. Once the roots fully catch the midstream currents again, the tree will pick up speed at a very fast rate. The backflow from the tree trunks in the river won't be enough to reduce that speed in any significant way. The log will crash at high speed into whatever you're calling a dam over there."

"Okay, okay," Axel said in a loud voice. "We know what will happen if the log comes through as *it* wants. What can we do to make it come through the way *we* want?"

"The narrowest section," Fala pointed out, "is the only place where we could be at all hopeful of throwing a loop of a rope around a tree root." But she also said it would be the fastest place, and the log would have the most power to pull us in or snap the rope.

At this point, a fourth dragon landed on the slope, which was beginning to get a little crowded. It was Licor carrying Bardin, and a large amount of rope was tied behind the rider.

"Archos' bloody excrement," Licor bellowed upon landing. "Can we get that rope off my back now? I think you found the absolutely worst way of tying that stuff on that could be imagined."

"I'm sorry, Licor," Bardin said as he jumped down, "it's very difficult to tie a heavy burden to a dragon who isn't wearing a saddle, and we were in a hurry. But, at least, we brought a lot of good rope, and that makes you a hero."

"I will never tell my children that I became a hero by carrying rope."

"In my list of memories," Axel said, "it will qualify you as a genuine hero, especially if we can get this gods-cursed log turned in time."

"Are we in time?" the dragon asked.

"Yes, Licor. It should be coming directly at us within the half orai."

"Bardin, Fala told us that the log will hit the backflow from the landslide right about there." He pointed to the spot Fala had identified. "Then it will make a turn toward the middle of the river and pick up speed rapidly from there. Do you agree?"

Bardin looked at the river, both upstream and downstream. "She got it right. The only places we'll be able to place ropes are right here, where the current meets the curve in the slide and heads out midstream. Any further upstream and the toss will be too far; any further downstream and the current will break the rope if we can make the toss at all in that swift water."

He continued, saying, "There are plenty of large boulders along the shore we can use to tie down the back end of the ropes before they're tossed, but once we catch it, we're going to need every hand pulling on it to bring the front end to shore. The stress on the ropes will be immense, and it might slip out of our hands until only the anchor rock is holding it. In that case, the rope might snap and come whipping back at us. It could come back fast enough to tear off an arm... or a leg... or even a head."

Fala came over and said something into Bardin's ear. He looked back into her eyes and nodded.

"One other intriguing point, just brought to my attention, is that if the log is captured correctly and makes a large-angle connection with the shore, the trees and other debris striking it will just drive the root end more solidly into the bank, and the dam will become more secure. But if the root end goes too far into the channel, then because the length of the log is longer than the channel's width, the angle with the bank will be sharper. That would cause the debris caught by the log to exert pressure away from the bank as much or more than into it. Unless such a connection with the bank is reinforced with ropes or rocks or anything solid, that pressure might cause the southern side to give way and take the whole dam with it."

Axel thought about all that had been said for a few minutes and then climbed up to talk to the firedrake. The dragon considered Axel's words, nodded his head, and took off straight into the air.

Axel stumbled back down the steep rocky slope over to the group and said, "I think we all know what needs to be done; let's get to work. Fala, you choose the rock to use as anchors and estimate the length of rope to set out below each one. Bardin, you break out the rope and divide it among the four places selected by Fala. Make certain there's enough rope in each place to make the throw. Fala, you put the proper loops on the throwing end of each rope, while Jarrad and I will start tying the ropes to the chosen anchor rocks."

"Oh, yes, Shaddra, would you and Licor please go up and find how much time we have until this big log pays us a visit?"

The two dragons went up and returned within just a few minutes.

Axel finished tying the knot he was working on and ran over to the dragons. "That was fast," he said.

"You'll see why soon enough. If you take a breath and hold it, you'll see the log rounding that bend up there before you have to expel that breath."

"Oh, bother," Axel muttered and yelled to the others. "We've got less than five minutes. Is everything in place?"

Everyone nodded their heads and looked expectantly at Axel.

"Okay," he said. "Fala and Barden, you will be prepared to throw the ropes in turn. There will be no second tries on any one rope. Once the rope is missed, you go to the next rope. If the rope catches, cinch it down tight, hand it to the others, and prepare to throw your second rope. If we can get more than one rope on the log, that's wonderful. But we still need to be ready to throw the next rope in sequence. If a rope is stretched out really tight, then, by all means, take cover; it will likely be on the verge of breaking. Please stay as safe as you can!"

"I see it!" shouted Bardin.

Axel had only seen the sea once, but he imagined the gnarled roots and the massive trunk that were speeding in his direction to be the head and body of a gigantic sea monster. Perhaps, in a way, that's exactly what it was.

The four assumed positions in front of the rocks. Fala and Bardin held ropes leading over to the first two selected rocks and were slowly swinging their loops about their shoulders and over their heads. Jarrad and Axel stood behind Fala, far enough to let the rope twirl freely but close enough to make a quick grab for a clotheslined rope if she succeeded or Bardin's if she failed.

The dragons stood by the rocks, ready to barge in at any point where their help could somehow be required. Hukken positioned himself in front of the others.

A collective intake of breaths was loudly audible when the log approached the corner and Fala let her swinging rope fly out over the river. Everyone exhaled loudly as the loop on the rope's end sailed birdlike until it wrapped around a thick chunk of root.

Instantly, Axel, Jarrad, and Bardin reached for the heavily vibrating rope and started pulling toward the shore. Hukken came up and stepped on the rope.

Nevertheless, not a second passed before the rope was torn from their arms and even out from under Hukken's foot, as if it were a bowstring being loosed. All of a sudden there was a loud CRACK, and a frayed rope end snapped through the air dangerously. All the humans, except for Bardin, who stood out of lethal range, found themselves lying on the ground with Hukken's tail lying across them.

"OUCH!" he yelled, "along with some High Language expletives that Axel did not understand, but the dragons did. All of the dragons, including Shaddra, were shocked.

"Hukken," she said. "I've never heard you use such language! In fact, I never thought you even knew such language!"

I do not know about his language, said Jarrad, "but I do know that if he hadn't taken that whiplash for us, you'd have three human corpses lying in front of you! Thank the gods for dragon armor!"

"Help!" came a shout from the right, next to them all.

Fala was the first to recognize Bardin's issue and jumped to help pull on the second rope, now held only by the young man. The others quickly reacted by adding more hands to the rope that Bardin was holding. It all happened quickly enough that Fala was able to duck under and pick up the third rope in succession. She opened the loop, twirled it only twice over her head, and let it fly. This one, too, caught hold of a root, whereupon Bardin let go of the second rope and headed straight to the third to join Fala. Fala followed suit, letting go and moving to pick up the last rope. She soon had the final loop sailing out toward the log.

All kinds of things then happened simultaneously. Hukken stepped on the back end of the second rope, from which Axel and Jarrad dropped off to join Bardin on the third, who let go of the third to join Fala on the fourth, while the firedrake stepped on the back end of the third rope.

The second rope slipped out from under Hukken's foot with a loud twang and stretched out so tight that everyone there was sure it would break. Acting on instinct, they all ducked lower but kept pulling hard on whatever line they had in their hands, all the while keeping a keen watch on the second rope.

Nothing happened for several long seconds until Fala noticed that the scraggly root ball was starting to move toward their bank.

"It's moving! It's moving!" she screamed, and it only took another long second for the others to see it too. For two more seconds, it moved closer into shore. Now, if only...."

SNAP. The second line broke with a noise that had become all too familiar. This time, no one was close enough to be hurt by the whiplash. Nevertheless, the log continued to strain on the ropes, which were still attached.

Everyone pulled hard on the ropes they had committed to. Both the siris dragon and the firedrake moved in closer to help protect if any more lines broke.

The front end of the log seemed to stand still, but ever so slowly the back end was dragged by the current toward the far shore. The front end, with its head of straggly roots, now started to move like a slow-motion arrow toward the near bank. It struck and stayed, even as the other end crashed into the opposite bank.

Wasting no time, Fala tied her rope tightly to a nearby rock, soon to be followed by Bardin and Axel, who tied their ropes to other rocks. Jarrad fetched what was left of the first rope and handed it to Fala for turning into a fourth anchor line.

"I see a problem in this," said Jarrad.

"Yes, I know," said Axel in response. "All the ropes are tied to roots on top of the log. If something strikes it right, the log could roll, making us lose grip on the roots or even snapping ropes."

"We need to do something about it then!" Jarrad said sternly.

"We are doing something," Axel said. "I do suggest, however, that we move some distance away from the log."

"Sorry, but I don't in any way understand what you're saying," Jarrad said, with a frustrated voice. Nevertheless, knowing Axel as he did, he led the group away from the water.

At that moment, Axel waved his arms widely and said, "Watch!"

A heavy stone struck the ground on the bank of the river and bounced twice before plunging into the water. Other rocks followed; some dropped straight into the river, while others hit the ground, either staying there or bouncing before rolling into the water. All were striking very near their target, which, from appearances, was the root end of the log. Most landed just downstream from the log. One hit the log, and everyone cringed, but the log stayed steadfast. After each rock was dropped, a firedrake could be seen lifting upward from near the river.

Jarrad counted twenty-five firedrakes, who had dropped rocks and then flown up to the ridges above and out of sight. Within five minutes they returned, each carrying a boulder-sized stone in their forepaws. These, too, were dropped on the target, and ten minutes after that, another flight of dragons dropped stones, and after that still another flight dropped stones.

As the dragons left, Axel stepped forward and waved his arms as before. "Okay," he said, "let's check to see how successful our air attack proved to be."

The dragons were very accurate with their attacks indeed. Though some big gaps remained, a new jetty of rock had been 'thrown' up, making the typical depth of the water from the bank out to twenty strides and down from the log for twenty strides next to nothing. This end of the log was basically, and tightly, landlocked. The current thrust the other end solidly against the far bank. The log would not be going anywhere for some time.

Even as they watched the results of their work, a large leafy tree floated into view upstream. Within a few minutes, it ran into the giant log and wedged itself firmly between it and the bottom of the river. Other trees were coming into view. Some were sharp-needled kitkis and soft-needled kitkas, while some were broad-leafed trees. When they reached the big log, many slipped underneath, only to get caught by the tree dam further downstream. Within an orai there were dozens of trees attaching themselves to one or the other of the two dams. Within three orais the lower dam had extended itself all the way to the upper dam.

Water pressure against leaves, branches, and thickly needled trees had pushed many of them down to the very bottom of the river and all the way across. A fair amount of water was still leaking through, but water was also backing up steadily.

As the water rose, trees were pushed up and over the log and onto the top of the lower dam. The weight of the trees pushed everything down more tightly and caused the dam to build up vertically. Ever less water managed to filter through to the other side.

By evening, the water level behind the dams had risen close to three strides above its original level and was still rising.

While Jarrad and Langa stayed to watch the dam and made certain nothing gave way or provided the possibility for a negative incident, Axel and the others flew upstream. Axel and Shaddra stopped at the dike, while Bardin, Fala, and the larger dragons kept on going to a place where they could add more trees to the river.

Axel saw that the water level had risen to the dike's base but was still below the level needed to spill into the Bottoms. Nevertheless, the water was steadily rising.

Night fell, but the bright dragon moon provided enough light for those who were not too exhausted to continue working. Some found places to put in a few orais' sleep before heading back out to work some more.

The waiting part was frustrating. If the water did not spill over into the Bottoms and keep spilling until it became its natural state of a muddy, watery bog, and before the fire crossed over the mid-valley knolls, all their work would be in vain, and hundreds would pay for that failure with their lives.

Hoping to learn how much time they still had, Axel and Shaddra flew up to see the fire. It was now a firestorm. They could not approach the fire itself because of fierce winds that seemed to race directly into it from all directions. Huge spiraling columns of fire climbed into the sky to altitudes higher than Axel could have imagined if he were not on the back of a dragon. The winds were blowing from the east, and massive billows of smoke from the fire drifted rapidly all the way up the valley. By now, anyone in the towns still doubting the fire's existence must have come to their senses.

The rocky border of the Rim stopped the fire on the east side. On the north, the road and escarpment were containing the fire. Hopefully, the river and the roaring falls tumbling over the Rim would limit the fire's spread any further to the south. There were no bounds on the west, meaning if there was no bog in the Bottoms within the next few orais, the western part of the fire would continue up the valley into the mountains and destroy everything in between.

Axel and Shaddra flew back west and south to the river. There, they saw numerous groups of humans and dragons working together to get more trees into the water. They could see more than a hundred trees of all kinds floating down the Mysura. Axel would soon have to put the word out for the groups to stop their work and take a much-needed rest. The trees transported by the river up to that time will determine whether the dam functions or not.

They flew back to the dike, and this time they were rewarded with the sight of water pouring through a fifteen-stride-wide opening in the rock, which had already flooded an area the size of Tarfal. Not satisfied with the opening they had, about thirty people still worked on widening and deepening it. This group included miners who appeared to be setting up another round of explosives.

Axel asked Shaddra to fly down to the narrows and readily saw that it had become one huge logjam, with nothing of the original two dams on the south fork showing. More trees could be seen floating in to add to the logjam. On the north fork, the fallen dirt and rocks were holding, but the level of water backing up behind it could be seen meandering its way toward the top on the east end. The northern dam would have to be watched for a few days to make sure it did not give way and turn into a flood that would destroy all their hopes.

Axel requested that Shaddra fly down to meet Jarrad and Langa. They all met with big hugs.

"With all the trees that I imagine are coming down the river right now," Jarrad said, "I think we can pass word on up the river to cease work on felling more trees. Our effort will either succeed or fail with whatever trees are now coming. But I think it will stand long enough for our needs, and I think it will stop a sufficient amount of water to get to the level we require. Does it appear that way at the dike?"

"Yes, I think so," Axel said. "Water is passing over and through the dike in amounts I couldn't have believed before. I think we can spread the word to gather in the market square. But we should keep spotters, including both dragons and riders, at the dike and the road where it bypasses the Bottoms. Someone also needs to monitor the north fork at the location formerly known as Bourem's Finger. Can you get out a call to identify the first spotters and those who will relieve them, say, after four orais? We need rotating shifts to last at least two days."

"I'll make the call for watchers as soon as I can get to Tarfal," said Jarrad.

"Sounds fair. We'll meet you at the market square at High Sunstar. We can keep everyone informed of the fire's status at that place."

***

The water level in the makeshift dam rose at a sluggardly pace, while the fire seemed to advance like a racing skell, and smoke filled the valley. Fortunately, water was now pouring into the Bottoms in a torrent, which spread out into the dry bog and ever narrowed the gate by which the fire could break through to the upper valley. When night fell, those watching from the road could no longer tell what was happening in the Bottoms, but they could readily see how close the fire was coming. Even the dragons had difficulty seeing from the road whether the bog was wet or dry without slugging their way into it. Fortunately, the wind shifted to come from the west as the night cooled the land and started blowing the smoke to the east. With the blinding smoke moving out of the way, dragons and their riders flying over the Bottoms could tell where the water lay by looking for Kivan's reflection coming from what would have to be wet bogland.

In the early morning orais, word finally came to the market square: water in the bog had reached the road and was spreading out laterally from there. Nevertheless, the fire was dangerously close, and the watchers feared sparks and flaming debris they had witnessed in the air might cross the bog.

Someone woke Axel, who had been sleeping on the ground in the square, to give him a message. Rubbing his eyes, he walked over to the speaker's place to call out to the crowd before him. Most women and children had gone home, but nearly all the men and dragons who had worked hard all day were sleeping in the market square.

"I am sorry to wake you, but please listen to what I have to say. Your efforts this day have been successful; the bog has now nearly been filled, and the fire is right upon it. The main body of the fire has been stopped. You may congratulate yourselves for that." Axel stopped to allow for a loud cheer, which certainly could have been heard all over both towns. After a moment, he held up his hands for quiet. The crowd obediently became quiet almost instantly. "The danger is not over. There are numerous sparks and fiery particles drifting in the air, which could ignite new fires on the western side of the bog. Fortunately, the cool night breeze is taking most of the particles to the east and back into the ground already burned. Still, as the light returns and the valley below warms up, the wind will change direction again, and those tiny fire starters will be coming back at us. We must be prepared for whatever might happen. I think we should pair up, one human and one dragon, to find and put out new fires while they can still be smothered with a shovel and some dirt. Hukken and Councilman Bassen, would you be kind enough to make appropriate assignments so that we give every dragon a chance to get to know and work with someone from the town? Also make certain that shifts are organized to give everyone, dragon and human, a chance to rest and get something to eat before the wind shifts again."

When the morning light made the situation clear, Axel and Jarrad were able to see for themselves that the fire had burned right up to the eastern edge of the reformed bog. There it consumed all of the combustible material possible, and, by the time the wind shifted in midday, there was little to cause the formation of sparks or any burning material that could cross the bog. A small watch was still kept for insurance, but Axel sent out a call for everyone else to meet again at the market square at High Sunstar.

The square soon filled up with humans in the middle and dragons along the outside edges. People and dragons filled the entire square and the ends of most side streets. Axel formally announced to the crowd from the speaker's platform that they had finally defeated the danger from the fire.

"Before we all return to our homes with thankfulness to the gods for having spared us, or at least for giving us the strength and wisdom to defeat this demon fire, I would ask each and every human here if we would fall to one knee for a moment to honor those without whose help the fire could never have been stopped... the dragons of the Free Colony." At this, Axel dropped to one knee and bowed his head. Every other human present instantly followed his example.

He stood and said, "Before we break up this afternoon to get some well-earned rest, I have one last thing to ask you. That is, I don't wish to disrespect our king in any way." At this point, there were some laughs around the crowd. "But I must say that the dragons have taken a significant risk over these last few days to help us. They have lived peacefully and freely for many years because the king does not know about them. We owe our very lives to the Free Dragons, so we must help them by ensuring that no information about their assistance in stopping the fires leaves this valley. We need our own common version of what happened, without the involvement of dragons, and that must become our history. I would ask the high council to create that story and see that everyone in the valley learns it well. We must also create our individual stories to describe what we ourselves did, but we must stay in line with the common story. That is the history we must believe in so strongly that even a hard night at a pub would not cause us to say anything differently. May I rely on you for that?"

A tremendous cheer rose up from the crowd, and a small group off on one side started chanting, "Stand for the dragons!" over and over again, until Axel raised his hands for silence. "Good. If I ever hear of anyone saying anything about the dragon's presence, anywhere, I can make the person involved intensely regret his or her words, and I am even more serious about that."

Then, he said his own 'Thank you' to the crowd and sat down on the ground.

At this point, Jarrad stood and shouted, "There is one more who should be thanked, and I think you already know who I'm talking about. I won't propose that we take a knee for him; else I would fear the wrath of his all-too-accurate bow. But let us remember in our hearts that Axel devised the plan to stop the fire and brought together men and dragons to accomplish this monumental purpose, personally leading us through the enormous effort that saved our town and our lives.

"A great shout arose from both the people and the dragons, and it continued for several minutes without dying down. Axel, for his part, smiled weakly and said "thank you" several times repeatedly to those around him. As the crowd finally broke up, he received hearty slaps on the back from just about everyone who could reach him.

When most everyone was gone, Hukken came over to Axel with Shaddra in visible form, close behind. "Dear and honored Axel," he said, "it is obvious that your age serves only to distract from the fact that you are, inside, a grown man. I am prone to believe that your dragon blood had a profound influence on your strength, your ability, and your wisdom. I must also believe that the gods chose you for the traits you inherited from your human parents, who sacrificed everything to bring you to us, as these traits complement your dragon blood and contribute to your unique identity and potential. Without a doubt, you are indeed the *son of the Great Ceragon* with a magnificent destiny ahead of you, but a destiny that will also be filled with trouble and pain. I hope we dragons will never be the cause of that last part. In any event, I can say you may count on my support in any action you may propose to make the Great Foretelling come true."

Axel gazed back at Hukken with a vaguely surprised expression on his face.

Shaddra stepped forward and said, "You know, for Hukken, that was in fact a very short and sweet statement. As for me, I'll just say I am grateful for the first day I met you, and every day since, and every day yet to come." She bowed her head once and took off straight into the air.

"Those are pretty heavy burdens to bear," Axel said to no one in particular and heaved a sigh.

Chapter Seventeen

EXTRACTION OF THE DRAFT DRAGONS

Even though the weather was getting colder, Eleth still frequently took walks out into the forest in her spare time. She enjoyed exploring further away from the cottage and seeing new things. Her walks also gave her time to contemplate what she was learning in the coops and, especially, what she learned about the dragons themselves. On this particular trip, she thought a lot about how the dragons in the coops seemed to be nervous about something. They admitted to not knowing what was happening. But something was definitely happening outside in the world. The male dragons coming into the coops to breed were continually passing messages and gossip about what events were occurring among the outside dragons. At that moment, even the male dragons felt nervous and were unable to explain the reason for their anxiety. All they knew was that the humans were having them go through unusual training and exercises. The most intriguing part seemed to be that the training concentrated on protecting something big, rather than the normal attack and defense exercises.

She tried imagining what kind of big thing might possibly need to be protected. The male dragons had been keen to point out that whatever it was, it would be moving. It might be moving in a manner similar to a convoy. If so, she wondered what kind of enemy would attack a convoy.

It certainly would not be the Free Dragons, who barely had anything more than a hit-and-run capability as of yet, and even that, hopefully, remained unknown to the king's forces.

The two draft dragons were now just about big enough to sustain the rigors of travel. That meant they would soon be whisked out of here, if 'whisked' was the proper word to use in regard to draft dragons.

Keeping the two dragons in the cottage had proved to be rather difficult. Training for the elimination of body waste was easy because the dragons could understand human speech. They simply needed to be told where to do their business, and that's where they would go. They would even politely ask to be let out of the cottage so they could go out, dig a hole, and bury their waste when they were through.

The most difficult training was tail training. Draft dragons have long, strong, and flexible tails. When fully grown, they would have two wicked spikes growing from the end of their tails, one from each side, which they could adroitly use in self-defense. Young draft dragons had no spikes, but their tails moved about freely and with considerable force. While in the cottage, their tails frequently caused damage, both to things and to human body parts. Never on purpose, but what's a little dragon to do? No matter how much training the dragons received, there were still frequent accidents. Bruises healed themselves over time, but the potential damage to breakable objects forced Clara to pack away all of her treasured mementos collected over the years. She only felt safe enough to return them to their original homes once the dragons were moved permanently out to the new paddock.

The two dragons had long since outgrown the cottage. Now they were housed in a paddock that Eleth built, with some help from Clara. The paddock consisted of an irregularly shaped confinement fence set up within the forest. It was big enough to give the young dragons room for exercise but still kept them in a concealed area. Of course, the draft dragons could easily tear the paddock down, though they were asked not to, so they obediently stayed within the bounds set for them. The whole thing was hidden in densely forested land, covered with kitkas and lomas, just four landrins away from the cottage. The paddock was invisible from the cottage, the road, and especially from the air. However, if the dragons were not moved soon, they might starve.

Draft dragons were the only dragons that did not eat meat. They *could* eat just about any kind of plant matter, apart from thicker branches of wood, and they ate lots of it, but they did not particularly care for the taste of evergreens. Eleth kept herself very busy, just cutting low-hanging leafy branches from the lomas and other broad-leafed trees in the nearby forest to keep the two satisfied. But, with the change of season, the leaves were beginning to fall, and the dragon's primary source of food was disappearing. Eleth expected to receive information soon about the plan to rescue the two draft dragons. Those details had better come soon.

What Eleth worried about most was how to save Clara if things went wrong. One reason Eleth spent so much time exploring the forest around the cottage was to find potential hiding places and escape routes if they ever became necessary. She even went so far as to hide some extra clothes, knives, dried food, and anything else she could think of that would be useful if they needed to make a run. She had no idea where they would go from the hiding place, but one thing at a time. She'd work it out.

Early one night, Eleth heard an unmistakable call in the dragon High Language and was thrilled to find Shaddra waiting for her over at Axel's original campsite. It had now become a well-established spot for meetings with Shaddra. The dragon's message tonight was a welcome one. A flight of six dragons would be coming to pick up the draft dragons in two sycles from that very night. Since the flight would consist of four firedrakes, besides Langa and Shaddra, they would not be able to conceal themselves. Therefore, they planned the operation to coincide with Kivan's darkest phase.

The problems about how to carry the two dragons on their trip to their new home had been solved. Shaddra had, on one of her frequent spy runs into the king's dragon camps, discovered that heavy burdens were frequently needed to be carried by the firedrakes in the flying corps. Draft dragons could not fly, so for cases where a large load needed to be carried through the air, the flying corps had developed an extra-large basket, made from woven salma reed stalks, to fit a firedrake. The basket could contain a young draft dragon very well and keep it comfortable. Four of the baskets, left outside and unattended during the night, proved easy to steal. Now, the biggest requirement was a very dark night.

While waiting for the targeted time to move the two dragons, Eleth continued to work alongside Clara in the coops. Again, they heard the rumors, but this time they came with more detail. The Breeding Coops were unmistakably in the process of relocation. Reports of unidentified dragons spotted near the area after dark had grown too frequent to dismiss. Some powerful individual had apparently decided to move the coops to a new, concealed location. Even now, an advanced site was being meticulously carved out of solid rock at a secret, heavily guarded location—far from prying eyes and intruders. No one had heard when the move might take place, but most coopers and midwives believed it would likely occur within a few Kivans.

.

On the evening of the day before the extraction team's planned arrival, Eleth was preparing for bed when she noticed large flakes of snow glancing off of her bedroom window. In only a few minutes, snow covered the ground outside with a thin layer of white.

After a night of very difficult sleep, she rose in the early morning orais to find mostly clear skies and nearly a span of fresh snow out on the ground. Eleth sat back on her bed with her hand over her mouth.

She hurried to Clara's room only to find the woman already out in the kitchen preparing an early breakfast, a big one. Catching Clara's eyes, Eleth asked in a low voice, "What does this snow mean?"

"It means, if the sky is clear tonight, starlight will reflect off the snow and make any flying dragons more visible. Unless we are blessed with the same storm clouds that brought the snow, it will increase the danger of moving the draft dragons."

"Can we change the date of the move?"

"You know that the flight of dragons coming to carry away our two younglings departed two days ago and should arrive any time now. Since they are coming from the south, it's possible they wouldn't even know about this early snow until they were nearly here."

"Can we delay their departure from here until the snow has melted?"

"The extraction team will face enormous danger both coming here and returning home. They cannot stay. The only question is whether they return with the draft dragons or without them. If the younglings go with the company, they will also be subject to the danger of being seen and attacked.

"Unfortunately, the presence of the snow will also make it much more dangerous for the younglings if they stay. Leaves on the trees will fall more quickly now, making it difficult to feed the draft dragons and to keep them hidden."

Eleth shook her head and muttered, "Then, I guess the decision is already made."

***

Less than an orai later, when Shaddra's call was heard in the house, Eleth wound a scarf around her neck and reached for her cloak. After resting a hand for an instant on Clara's shoulder, she ran out the door, wrapping her cloak around her as she sped up the trail to the meeting place. Surprisingly, there were eight dragons spread out under the trees: not six. There were four firedrakes, two siris dragons, and two messenger dragons. Riders accompanied all but the messenger dragons. Each of the firedrakes wore oddly shaped baskets on their underbellies.

Eleth found herself staring at the sight of more dragons in one place outside than she had ever seen before. She had seen this many, and more, at one time, but they were resting in nesting boxes. She recognized Shaddra, Hukken, Langa, and even Licor, whom she had met only once. But not the four firedrakes. She ran up to Shaddra and gave her the best hug she could manage and did the same with the three others she knew. Licor seemed very embarrassed by the hug.

"I do not feel very worthy to be embraced by the *Daughter of the Great Ceragon*," he said.

"Oh, please don't worry about that," Eleth said. "From what I have heard about you, you could stand unashamed anywhere. All of the Free Dragons are indebted to you. Would you please introduce me to the other members of your company?"

"I would gladly do so, Honored One," Licor said, "for these have proven themselves most capable in our Free Dragon Corp. We are yet to be battle-tested, but I would stand by these four in the worst of conflicts. We have Torkar, who is an eminent member of the High Council over the Free Dragons; then Arnal, Nabor, and Sental."

Eleth spread out her arms and said, "I just want you all to know that you are welcome here, at least by Clara and me. Clara says she will come out soon to meet with her children as soon as I can go take her place in getting things ready for the four, or rather the six, who will stay in the cottage."

Suddenly, Axel came from nowhere to stand in front of her. He reached down, picked up her hand, and wrapped it in both of his. She looked down at it, stunned.

"Sorry about being so bold, but we need your help right away. It's Jarrad … again. He's sick. Very sick."

Eleth needed a moment to shift her focus from her hand to the reality that Jarrad was sick.

"Tell me what has happened," she asked.

"He was riding Hukken. Everything seemed fine until we made our stopover by the Ibisen River yesterday morning. Not long after we stopped, he started coughing, and as the day progressed, he coughed more and more. When it was time for us to depart, he was in no condition to remain atop a dragon. He also vomited for the first time. That's when we decided he should fly the rest of the way in one of the baskets. He vomited twice after that. Fortunately, we cut a hole in his basket big enough for him to vomit into the air to ensure he didn't have to sit in it. But he's in a bad way now."

"Has he coughed near anyone's face," Eleth asked, "or has anyone touched his vomit?"

"I don't know for sure, but it's possible."

"All right," Eleth said. "Let's assume everyone is exposed. I want you to take care of the dragons and whatever in the camp needs doing. None of the riders can stay here. Everyone is to come down to the cottage, where I can look you over and get you places to sleep. Bring your spare clothes and personal effects. Jarrad is to stay here with two people until I can go get materials to make a litter. In the meantime, keep your faces away from his, especially when he is coughing. Oh, and everyone is to avoid touching your eyes or your mouths until I can get you all into the house and cleaned up."

"Whoa!" someone next to Axel said. "What's that all about?"

"Never you mind, Bardin," Axel said. "She's the doctor, and you do what she says."

Pretty soon there were three men and a young woman marching down to the house right behind Eleth. She opened the door for them and called out, "Don't touch anything." She disappeared for a few minutes and came right back carrying some blankets.

"Clara, I'm sorry to keep you from your children, but would you please help those who stay here to get washed and changed into clean clothes? They should put their dirty clothes in that corner until we can get them laundered."

"You!" She pointed at someone hardly older than her own age. "What's your name?"

"Bardin, ma'am."

"Don't worry about calling me 'ma'am,'" she said. "Wash your hands and come with me, and we'll get some poles from the shed out back to use for a litter and carrying food for the dragons."

The man and young woman, who remained after Eleth and Bardin left, stared at Clara. "Who's that girl?" asked Fala.

"Hasn't Axel told you about Eleth?" Clara asked.

"No. He just said we were going to get some dragons."

"Do you know who Axel is?"

"Of course, we do," Fala answered. "He's someone special. He saved our town and everyone in it."

"Then, you may consider Eleth to be a female Axel. Obey her, even as you would obey Axel. Now, help me get some tubs of water heating on the stove."

Eleth led Bardin back to the shed, and together they built a litter using the blankets.

"Pardon me, ma'am, or... what is your name?"

"Oh, sorry. My name is Eleth, and what is yours?"

"I'm Bardin. I'm apprenticed to Axel in the bow shop."

"That tells me a lot about you. Axel would never let just anyone touch his bows and equipment. Now, follow me and help me carry out some of these packages."

"Bardin's face turned bright red, but he hastened to follow her directions precisely."

She opened the door to one of the buildings, entered, lit a candle, and, after covering it with a glass chimney, descended down some stairs. Bardin followed close behind. The room below was cold; colder than it had been outside in the snow.

After reaching a lower level, Eleth grabbed some paper-wrapped packages and handed them to Bardin. Once he had a pretty decent load, she picked up a fairly large load of packages for herself and led Bardin back out of the cellar. Outside, they placed their packages onto the litter, after which Eleth ordered them back into the cellar for a second load. Once everything was secured on the litter, they each took one end and began marching out toward the dragons. Bardin struggled with the heavy litter to keep going through the snow. He noticed, however, that Eleth seemed to take the load with relative ease.

How can she do that? He thought when they neared the meeting site. He was sweating in this cold, and she didn't even look tired, let alone sweaty.

Axel heard them approaching and came out to meet them. "What have you there?" he asked.

"We knew you would be coming tonight, so I went shopping for some meat for the dragons."

"Shopping? Wouldn't buying that much meat be a little obvious as well as expensive."

"All right. So, I went hunting. What's the difference?"

"Interesting. What did you come up with?"

"Let me think. I brought in four or five teranas, six or seven kota, and a yolka."

"You downed a yolka with only a knife?

"I could have used a sling, but the knife was sufficient."

"And you dragged it home by yourself?"

"Of course. I didn't need any help."

Bardin, who had been nearby listening in, stared in amazement, and his mouth dropped open as far as his cheeks would let it.

Axel plastered a big grin on his face and nodded in an approving way. "Jarrad is in that basket over there. If you look at him, Bardin and I will take breakfast over to the dragons. We'll meet you there in a few minutes and haul Jarrad down to the house for you."

As they carried the litter over to the dragons, Bardin was thinking, *She brought down a yolka with only a knife and dragged it home by herself! Who is she?*

Eleth lit three candles, casting a warm glow in the workroom, where she tried to make Jarrad comfortable. Sweat beaded on his forehead as he lay in his makeshift bed of piled blankets, his head throbbing with pain. Eleth took notice of his discomfort and placed a gentle hand on his forehead.

Half an orai later, Eleth again placed a hand on Jarrad's head and asked, "Now that we have you in the house and in a bed—well, at least sort of in a bed," she asked, "do you still feel the same? How is the headache?"

Jarrad winced and replied, 'It hurts so much that my eyes are crossing. Which one of you should I be answering the questions to?"

"If you can crack a joke, you can't be as sick as you think." Eleth said with a hint of amusement.

"Oh, I can think I'm a lot sicker than you can think I am."

"I've got news for you. You *are* as sick as you think you are. Your head is burning; you have been coughing and vomiting. There is no question you have a kirous fever," Eleth stated firmly. "There are many kinds of kirous fevers. Any one of them can mean your death if you move from that bed. You are definitely *not* going on any adventures tonight or tomorrow night or maybe even after that."

Jarrad let out a groan of frustration, while Axel interjected, "But we've got to have six riders."

"Then you'll have six riders; however, one of them won't be Jarrad."

Axel turned to her with a puzzled expression and asked, "And how *do* you plan to find our sixth rider, Eleth?"

Wrinkling her brow, she asked, "Why don't you start by telling me the reason why you need six riders?"

"All right, I guess I'd better start back at the beginning."

"Yes, why don't you, since it sounds like your answer will be rather complex?" Eleth replied.

Axel took a deep breath and began his explanation. "A few sycles ago, when we first got the baskets and tested them using weights equal to a year-old ellam bull, we realized that the original two firedrakes would only be able to bear the young draft dragons for about six orais. After that, they would have to rest. They could keep on flying alongside, but they couldn't carry any dragon passengers for several orais.

"That's when we knew two extra firedrakes would be needed to share the load." Axel continued. "We first hoped that those not on shifts could serve extra duty as security guards, but after carrying all that weight for so long, we saw that the original two could hardly be counted on in any battle. Then we decided to bring two siris dragons as security escorts. Any attacking force would target them first. The off-duty firedrakes would serve to directly protect the dragons carrying the cargo, while the siris dragons would go after the attacking force. Shaddra and Langa decided on their own to come along and provide reconnaissance ahead of the group to help us avoid potential fights."

"So again, why do you need so many riders?" Eleth questioned.

"It's very simple," Axel replied. "Since every king's dragon has a rider, any dragon seen flying without a rider would be deemed suspicious and either attacked or approached for identification. Shaddra and Langa would be invisible; therefore, they would not need riders. We have six other dragons, so they need six riders."

"But you aren't wearing uniforms. If the king's forces see riders not wearing their uniforms, wouldn't they attack anyway?" Eleth pointed out.

"Unfortunately, you are correct," Axel conceded. "Shaddra and Langa have been able to steal more saddles for our mounts, but not uniforms for us to wear. It's challenging for even an invisible dragon to get inside a military barracks. We've had to settle for wearing clothes that are close to the king's military uniforms in color."

"Thank you," Eleth said, understanding their predicament now. I also see that you still haven't introduced me to the remainder of your team."

"I guess you have me there. Everyone!" Axel shouted out across the room. "Come over here and let me introduce you to someone important. Unfortunately, Clara is still off visiting with her children. I will introduce you to her later. Clara is the one who first helped the Free Dragons to *take flight*. She considers them her children, and they worship her only slightly less than the 'Great Ceragon,' the first dragon on Tamerel. Clara is smart, brave, and loving, and I can vouch for that through my own personal experience.

"Standing here beside me is Eleth Kairon, who has had the misfortune of becoming the *Daughter of Ceragon*, even as I have become the *Son of Ceragon*. There is much about those names that I couldn't even begin to tell you about. But, for now, please note that you must never underestimate her. She will always surprise you. Oh, and she is a fully trained doctor, as Jarrad will witness. This is not the first time he has lain in that blanket bed with something that could potentially kill him."

A weak voice came from over where Jarrad lay: "Sometimes, however, you would rather die than take the medicines she gives you."

Eleth reached down for a pillow and threw it dead center at Jarrad. "You lived through it last time," she said, "and you'll live through it this time, though you came closer to death than you think. Am I so attractive that you risk death just to spend time in our makeshift beds?"

"If I were thirty years younger, that might just be true."

Eleth's face actually reddened at that remark.

"Uh, Eleth, let me introduce you," Axel said, "first, to my two apprentices, Fala Prudo and Bardin Shotley. Don't let their ages fool you. Both Fala and Bardin are brilliant and talented, or else I wouldn't have chosen them as my apprentices."

"If you're going to talk about age," Bardin said, "don't forget to count yourself."

Axel grinned at the young man and said, "You'll find that Bardin is usually the first to come up with distracting comments."

"These other two fine gentlemen are Ketter Harbert and Rook Dermin." He motioned toward two men who appeared to be in their mid-twenties. "They are two of the finest archers in the Valley, which means two of the finest in the kingdom. Ketter is a first-class potter and sculptor, while Rook is a builder. If he lived in one of the major cities, I think he would very soon be called a master builder.

"I have gotten to know these admirable people so completely over the last year; they may as well have been my brothers and sister. That's why I invited them to become a part of this adventure."

"It's wonderful to meet all of you," Eleth said. "Please remember that I would rather not have any more of you joining Jarrad as a patient in what is actually our workshop and not a hospital. Tell me, how is the snow going to affect your mission?"

A kind of shadow passed over the faces of the people gathered around Eleth.

Axel answered this question by saying, "There isn't so much of a problem if the enemy is looking from the ground up. We tested it out, and even with the additional light reflecting from the snow, our dragons are hardly visible up there at night."

"What about from above?"

"There, we have a double problem. If the enemy is above, our dragons appear as silhouettes against the snow and are highly visible. But that same enemy isn't very visible to us, and that will reduce our reaction time. What's more, we aren't certain how high we can safely fly while carrying two young draft dragons."

The conversation died down quickly with that thought.

At that moment, Clara returned from her visit with the dragons. When she closed the workroom door, the glow in her face showed how overjoyed she was at the reunion with more of her children. However, when she gave a quick glance at the assembled group, everyone could tell she was also excellent at reading faces.

"Okay," she said. "Why don't we start with introductions; after that, we can summarize the problems we are facing."

Twenty minutes later, after introductions and general discussion of the issues were completed, Clara said, "To help the discussion from this point, may I suggest we start with listing the things that we cannot change?"

There seemed to be general agreement with that idea.

"May I be the one to start?" Clara asked. Looks were exchanged among the group members, followed by shirks and expressions of "Why not?"

"Okay, first, we have one member of the company who is too sick to continue. He will have to stay here until he is, again, well enough to travel. Since it is highly unlikely that this company will be able to stay long enough to take him home, he will have to remain until a dragon can be sent for him at a later time.

"Second, that leaves the company one person short. The fact that you will have a dragon with no rider may be serious if you are seen since every dragon in the king's forces always flies with a rider.

"Third, you will be flying at night, when the king's dragons don't normally fly. But suspicion of Kolodran spy activity in this area will likely mean that the king's dragons will be in the air and that ground forces will also be on alert.

"Fourth, we have fresh snow on the ground, which will likely make your company more visible, especially by high-altitude flights, but also perhaps by dragon units on the ground.

"Fifth, the two young draft dragons cannot stay here much longer. Given the recent snowfall, it is likely that they will be discovered soon.

"Lastly, you have no choice but to return home. Whether you carry the two draft dragons with you or not, you cannot stay here for long.

"You may have other issues to bring up. However, I suggest delaying addressing those issues for now. Your company is composed of both humans and dragons, and all members of the company should have a voice in deciding what to do next.

"The sunstar will be rising within the next orai. Let me propose that I go to the Coops to tell them that Eleth is very sick with, with kirous fever and that I must return home to take care of her. That will free the two of us to play whatever role may be appropriate for us in today's activities. I suggest you all meet to discuss the issues while I'm away.

"That puts all our fish into one bucket," Axel said. "Any objections?"

There were none.

***

When the sunstar peeked out from behind the trees in the east, everyone gathered at the meeting place. Everyone, that is, except Clara, who was in the house caring for Jarrad. The group formed a kind of circle in an opening in the forest that barely contained them all. Axel stood alone in the center; humans formed the next layer, and the outer layer consisted of dragons, with their heads towering over the shoulders of the humans. That was quite fitting since dragons both see and hear better than humans do.

"May I be the first to speak?" Axel asked. Almost immediately, everyone turned their heads to the center of the circle, and no one spoke.

"Jarrad and I have been the nominal leaders of this company since the dragons first reported their strong desire to help two draft dragons take flight. I think that makes me the one to get the questions asked and answered and the lot of us leaving for home. We must depart this place as soon as possible, for this size of group will attract attention.

"The first and second questions are essentially two sides of the same issue. That is, we made it halfway here with a riderless dragon; can we make it back home that way without attracting notice? The second is, if we need that additional rider, what do we do about it?"

Bardin raised a hand and responded, when called upon, "I believe that the chances of being discovered due to the lack of an extra rider are low. But the costs of being wrong are extremely high. If we are discovered because of the missing rider, it is very likely that some or all of us will be killed. The low chance of discovery won't mean a thing then."

"Any other thoughts?" Axel looked around at members of the group. No one responded to the question. "Uh, huh. I can tell from your looks that you have chosen to try finding a rider. Who should it be?"

Bardin half-raised his hand again, and, when Axel nodded his way, he said, "There's no question as to who it should be. Everyone's been thinking it should be Eleth from the time we first met her."

Upon hearing this, Axel reached out into the group surrounding him, took Eleth's wrist, and guided her to the center of the circle. When she came beside him, looking rather embarrassed, he leaned over and whispered into her ear, "You're going to be the center of attention a lot. Get used to it."

"Before you can even consider accompanying us on this trip," he said, "you must consider Jarrad's medical needs. Can you be separated from him without jeopardizing his life or health?"

Eleth looked out into the group and said, "Jarrad has a very serious disease, but now that he has received medical care and we have additional medicine to provide as needed, his chances are excellent. I, personally, don't need to be nearby to see to his care, but someone does."

Axel stepped forward but looked back at Eleth. "Clara is, right now, seeking leave from work so she can take care of a very sick person. If that person ends up being Jarrad, could you and would you join our company?"

"I suppose I could, but I've never ridden on a dragon before."

"We could have you ride Hukken," Axel suggested. "No dragon provides a safer and gentler ride than he does. Isn't that true, Hukken?"

"It would be my privilege and honor to have the Daughter of Ceragon be my passenger, and I would protect her from any harm."

"We would need Clara's permission," Axel said. "She is still, after all, the one responsible for your care. We'd also have to arrange to get you back here from the south and take Jarrad home. That could be worked out, too."

Axel rubbed his chin and looked out at the others on the team. "The remaining questions have to do with our safely transporting the draft dragons to the Free Colony. Correct me if you think I'm wrong, but there is no question as to our leaving here early tonight with the draft dragons. We cannot remove the dangers, but we can be more prepared. Licor, you are the one most familiar with the tactics used by the king's dragons. What special precautions should we make that we have not already addressed?"

"When I was one of the king's dragons, we never operated at night. We must assume that the policy regarding night operations has changed since then. However, a large organization such as the King's Flying Corps finds it challenging to adapt to change. I think they will continue to use the same tactics as they did during the day. If they have a large force, they will attack from two or more directions, but a large force is more easily seen and is often difficult to control.

"I would assume the King's officers would prefer to have many smaller units out there to cover more territory. If one of these units is certain about the identification of its enemy, it will strike with speed and aim for the part of the enemy's forces that would be the biggest threat to them."

"In our case," Axel said, "I think they would most likely aim for the siris dragons first. Any other thoughts on that?"

There was silent agreement from the group.

"That means we must concentrate on two things. The first is early warning, and the second is quick response.

"The third," said Eleth, "is the protection of our passengers."

Axel looked at her and thought about that for a moment. "Well said." He turned to the group as a whole. "How should *we*, then, be most prepared?"

Hukken said, "Much will depend on what altitude we can fly at. Licor has taught us that the enemy forces are very fond of surprise attacks from high altitude. In the dark that would make them virtually invisible, possibly even to our reconnaissance team. If we are attacked by a small group, I would recommend the same actions on our part, whether we have advanced warning or not. We, siris dragons, will likely be the first targets. Our job must be to split the attacking forces and take them away from the firedrakes. We have surprises available to us to defeat whatever the forces are that follow us, including strategic traps and ambush tactics that can catch them off guard. The resting firedrakes will have the responsibility for protecting the passengers like a fortress wall. If either siris dragon can shed himself from the forces targeting him, then he should circle back. His new objective will be to provide help wherever the need is greatest. Lastly, remember the tactics we've been working on for so long."

"Does that summary meet your approval, Licor?"

"I could not have done a better job myself."

"That's enough for now," Axel said with a wave of his hand. "Let's all go try to get some rest, and we'll talk one more time before taking off tonight."

***

That evening, just at the setting of the Sunstar, the team met before lifting off. As expected, Clara was not thrilled about having Eleth take part in the extraction of the draft dragons. She could think of no human life more precious to her at this time. What's more, Eleth must live to accomplish so much more than the tasks of this night. But she also knew that Eleth was born to take risks for the dragons. She just wished that Eleth did not have to start taking on those risks this early in her life.

"I have so many children and loved ones who are risking their lives tonight," she told the group. "I couldn't bear losing even one of you. As for those who I have first met today, I want nothing more than to see you again after all the drama is over. Please take care of yourselves and each other."

Of course, Clara did agree to let Eleth participate. If she didn't, many lives would be at stake. One compensating benefit was that she would have several days to get better acquainted with Jarrad. In her whole life, Clara had never been close to another person of her age and, especially, not one of the opposite gender. As a midwife, it was forbidden for her to have a husband or even a close male friend. Under the circumstances, she no longer felt compelled to live by that rule. But what would be the result of this? What could result? She did not know, but she knew she wanted to become better acquainted with Jarrad Dismer.

When the night was as dark as it was going to get, Axel gave out the last few instructions before the team took off. "By now, our dragon friends are so well trained," he said with a nod toward Licor, "that you will respond to an attack without even thinking about it. We humans are a bit more than a step behind them in that area. All I can say is we humans need to hang on tight, use our heads, and support each other. Even though Langa and Shaddra are keeping watch over the heavens, the heavens are very large, and we must all be alert for the unexpected, especially since there are many clouds in the sky tonight that can hide an enemy. Keep your formation tight, as would be the dragons of the king. After all, that is who we must make them think we are. We will talk again at the Ibisen!"

At that, the humans climbed aboard their designated mounts and belted themselves into their saddles, and the flight of ten dragons and six humans rose into the air.

Chapter Eighteen

TRIAL BY COMBAT

A mere twenty minutes after lifting off from the dragon camp, both Axel and Eleth heard high-pitched sounds. Even though they did not understand the exact words being communicated or where they came from, the sounds carried an unmistakable message: 'WARNING! DRAGONS! WE ARE UNDER ATTACK!

Hukken and Licor instantly peeled off in opposite directions, following a tactic that had been drilled time after time. As Hukken dived to his right, a scorching fireball shot past, singeing Eleth's eyelashes as she looked at it.

Eleth, struggling to move against the strange forces that were pressing against her, yelled to Hukken, "What's happening?"

Hukken yelled back, "You heard the message. We are under attack. I know nothing more. Look back and tell me what you see!"

Eleth twisted back and searched the skies as directed. "It looks like Axel and Licor have turned away in the opposite direction from us, and there are two siris dragons following them. And there are two other dragons—siris dragons—chasing us! I see nothing going after the firedrakes."

"It's just as Licor said it would be. They will try to destroy us first and only then go back for the firedrakes."

"The two dragons behind us are closing in fast!" Hukken cried out. "I think they're using the momentum from their dive. Hold on, we need to maneuver now!"

At that, Hukken made a second sharp turn. Since he was going slower than his attackers, he was able to make a sharp turn to the left that the attackers could not match. They flew right on by and struggled to correct their course. For the second time, Eleth felt like she was being crushed into her saddle.

"If there was only one attacker, I could probably handle him easily," Hukken shouted, "but two will eventually be able to wear me out and hit me from the side. I'm afraid we are in grave trouble."

"I have an idea," Eleth shouted. "It's dangerous but could get rid of one or both of our attackers. Can you turn north?"

"Back to where we started? Is that a good idea?"

"If this attack was not coincidental, then we would have had more than four enemies to worry about. If the encounter is just a coincidental meeting with a standard enemy patrol, they have an assigned area, which they left to attack us. There should be no more enemies up north to join the fight."

"All right. North it is. I'll be doing some zigs and zags, but we'll go that way."

"Go about one tondrin past Clara's place and look for a narrow ravine coming out of the hills."

A moment later, he said, "Yes, I see it ahead. But I must perform some maneuvers to slow the reaction times of these pests behind us."

"If you can, get your chasers to follow you at low altitude into and up that ravine. There are two isolated kitki trees, one on each side of the stream and about forty strides apart. We have to glide between those trees at the lowest level you can go, without touching the ground. If you flap your wings, we will die!"

"What are you saying, Daughter?" What lies between those trees?

"I'm leading our pursuers into a veps' nest!"

Hukken turned his head to look at Eleth in shock but then quickly looked forward again.

"We are coming upon the ravine you spoke of. Are those the trees?" Hukken asked, pointing with his three-fingered hand.

"Yes."

"How low must I go?"

"If any part of us goes higher than ten strides, we die! And don't flap your wings once we start to glide. The veps will attack anything that touches the web."

"Here we go, then. If this fails, the enemy dragons will strike at us from above."

"I guess we must be ready for that."

Hukken collapsed his wings and dove straight for the ground like a falling arrow, bringing his two attackers with him. With only a gasping breath before striking the ground, he flared his wings wide, made a quick left turn, and stretched his wings out straight to glide, virtually at ground level, between the two kitki trees.

Hukken's flight path was so low that his hind legs tore through some scrub bushes on the ground. As they passed between the trees, they saw, only for the blink of an eye, a gossamer veil passing above them.

The maneuver would have stopped their breathing if both had not already been holding their breaths out of fear. One of the attackers followed Hukken directly between the trees but at a slightly higher altitude that brought him straight into the web; the second came in higher than the first, and only part of a wing touched the web.

Hukken quickly ascended, flapping his wings with all the strength in him, to get away from the rising ground of the ravine and the attackers, but neither of the king's dragons pursued them.

Upon rising over the rims of the ravine, Eleth and Hukken turned to see the fates of their attackers. The acid in the web had apparently blinded the first dragon and destroyed its wings. It dropped abruptly to the ground and started rolling and gyrating around, bellowing screams of agony as the veps attacked its eyes, mouth, and nose. The sounds echoed about in the ravine, but they ended abruptly, as if the dragon had died of a heart attack, and it now lay still. Its rider, crushed in short order by the writhing creature, was still attached to the dragon's saddle.

The second dragon was able to keep flying for a landrin or two. Even as Eleth and Hukken looked down, they saw its left wing crumple. The dragon struck the ground hard and cartwheeled twice before crashing again and coming, literally, to a dead stop. Its rider, who was somehow still alive, struggled to release himself from the saddle and run away. It did no good. He, too, must have touched part of the web and managed to get only a few steps from his mount before he was enveloped by veps. Both enemy dragons and their riders were now blanketed with thousands of dreadfully buzzing veps.

Above the madness, Hukken and Eleth circled slowly, each feeling a mixture of relief, regret, and a gripping sorrow for the wreckage they had caused.

"They won't bother us anymore," Eleth said solemnly.

"May their spirits be blessed by the Great Ceragon," Hukken added.

Unable to look at what was happening below any longer, Eleth said, "Let's go see if we can help Axel." Her tone expressed a worry that Hukken readily shared.

Axel held on tightly at the first word of warning, knowing exactly what Licor was about to do. The two fireballs shot at them missed widely as Licor dropped down speedily to his left.

Looking upward and back, Axel quickly assessed the situation. "Licor, we have two siris dragons behind us. Hukken turned to the left as planned. Try to get me a chance for a bow shot as you evade."

The enemy riders carried crossbows and were maneuvering their dragons to get shots at Axel. Their dragons crossed back and forth, staying as close to directly behind Licor as possible. This gave Axel the most difficult choice of shots with his bow and favored the crossbows greatly.

Licor abruptly turned to his left and gave Axel an instant to loose his arrow, but it missed the human rider by a finger and glanced off the dragon's scaly armor.

One of the enemy riders shot his crossbow, and that bolt, missing by some distance, flew off into the air.

"Let's try the climb and inside turn move we practiced," Axel shouted.

Licor waited for the proper moment to undertake the maneuver. When it came, he turned up and, rolling to his left, dove straight down. The move gave Axel the opportunity to take a shot straight up, from his perspective, but one that was perfectly level relative to the ground below. It was much the same as a move he had tried before to stop an enemy. The arrow went true and struck the front dragon's rider in the chest. Only at that instant did Axel realize, based on the shape of her uniform, that the rider was a woman. She clung to her mount for a moment as the dragon performed the last command of its rider and jinked to its right. It would have been a good command if the rider were not already dead. In this instance, as the dragon turned away, the rider slid silently off the saddle and became like the tip of a cracking bullwhip. Her tether line snapped in two, and she went soaring as if she were a dragon herself.

Straightaway, the second rider seized an opportunity and cut Licor off at the very bottom of the dive. His dragon raked Licor across the hind leg with its extended claws and grazed one of his pectoral flying muscles. The wounds were not mortal, but Licor was disabled and bleeding profusely. The wound also hindered his flying ability, putting him at a distinct disadvantage in the next stage of this fight.

Now, the king's dragonrider saw his opportunity. He could set his dragon for a quick head-on strike or dance around and wait for the perfect opportunity to strike close in while Axel and Licor were severely limited in how they could move. Axel and Licor could only react.

The two foes squared off as if for a joust. "Licor, my friend," Axel said, "it's all or nothing. I'll shoot for the best target available. Please protect yourself."

"Whatever happens, *Son of Ceragon*, it has been my pleasure knowing and working with you."

The enemy dragon began its charge. Licor moved forward, but without the grace of the oncoming foe. The enemy came toward them at twice the speed Licor could muster.

A green flash appeared suddenly from the right and collided with the enemy dragon while it was still some distance away. The rider fired his crossbow but was torn completely away from his mount and fell with a scream that ended only when he hit the rocky ground below.

Axel quickly realized that a new dragon had come crashing in from the enemy dragon's left rear. The two dragons were now tangled in a deadly embrace, fluttering slowly down to the ground, teeth and claws tearing at each other as they descended.

"Quick, Licor," Axel shouted, "get down to the rider that just fell!"

Licor obediently dived for the ground as commanded, and, in a matter of seconds, Axel jumped off Licor's back and raced to the rider's body, where he located the jewel in an instant. Finding rocks was a more difficult task. He had to brush a finger's depth of snow away from the ground with his hands and feet before he found suitable rocks and could smash the jewel. He was fortunate that the body had landed close to the banks of a swiftly flowing river, or it may have taken much longer to find the rocks he needed.

Licor had already turned to the other dragons. They both lay stunned right next to the bank of the river, about thirty strides away, and both had nearly ended up landing in the river itself. Licor hobbled over to them and found Eleth there, too, unmoving. He wondered if she was dead but noticed slight rising and falling movements in her chest.

"Eleth," he called softly, his hand resting gently on her shoulder. "Please, say something."

She shifted slightly and let out a faint groan.

Licor's heart soared with relief, and he nearly shouted with joy, "You're alive! Praise the Great Ceragon!" But instead, he called out, "Axel, over here!"

Axel ran over to join them and, bending over Eleth, reached for her hand.

The first of the others to regain consciousness was the enemy siris dragon. He appeared largely unhurt but dazed. Licor took his hand and, with a long backward glance, led him over to the side where the new dragon's condition could be better determined.

"I don't understand," the dragon said. "Who are you?"

"I am a friend," Licor said. "Your orders are, for now, to rest and let me see if you are injured."

The dragon nodded his head and followed his orders.

Meanwhile, Axel checked Eleth's body for wounds and, finding none, looked for broken bones or any other kind of damage. He could see nothing but was still greatly concerned. Suddenly, her eyes fluttered and opened.

"It's you!" she said. "Are you okay?"

"Better than you, I think," he said with a smile and a slight touch of his hand against her cheek. "Be careful. There's no telling what kind of internal damage you may have received."

Eleth slowly turned her head back and forth. Then, she moved it forward and backward. She felt the top of her head and said aloud, "Ouch!" when she touched a sensitive spot. "I'm going to have a good bump there and a possible minor concussion."

She carefully checked her back in step-by-step detail as best as she could under the circumstances, after which she asked Axel to gently press in certain places with his fingers. Finally, she unbuckled her belt and gingerly stood up. "How is Hukken?"

At the words, all eyes looked over at the prone figure, who was now raising his head, exposing his chest. Everyone, including Hukken, readily saw the feathers of a crossbow bolt sticking out, just under his ribs. Dark, purple blood flowed steadily from the hole created by the bolt and dripped in a small but steady stream onto the snowy ground. His natural armor had protected him from other harm, but the wound from the crossbow bolt looked deadly.

"Oh, Hukken!" Eleth shrieked and, running to his side, started probing around with her fingers.

While Eleth worked on Hukken, Axel grabbed bandages packed with his gear and started tightly wrapping up the gashes on Licor's legs and wing. With quick side-long glances, he also kept track of what was happening with Hukken.

"This bleeding is too much for a simple arrow puncture," Eleth said. Something important has been pierced. If I pull the arrow out, it may only worsen it."

Licor looked over at the wound and said, "That is the place where a dragon's liver is found. I've seen wounds in that location before." After a pause, Licor continued, "Hukken, my friend...."

Hukken raised his arm and interrupted him. "You don't have to say it, Licor," Hukken announced. "I am sorry, but the only way I could stop the siris dragon's attack was by rushing in for a collision. I can see my wound is fatal. The bleeding cannot be stopped."

"No!" Eleth shouted. "I won't let it! I have my surgical gear; I'll sew up your wound inside."

"Out here?" Hukken protested. "What are you going to put me out with? I know you do not have enough of your pain medicine to do surgery on a large dragon. If you can cut into me at all because of my armor, I will only be in that much more pain and bleed to death that much faster."

"I'm sorry, *Daughter,*" Licor said. "I've seen this wound many times before. It only occurs in close-up fights, where a crossbow has enough power to penetrate dragon armor. This type of injury always results in the dragon slowly bleeding to death."

"But I can't let Hukken lie here in the middle of nowhere, just to bleed to death!"

At that moment, Shaddra landed not far away and immediately deduced what was happening. She walked over to Hukken and said, "Apart from Clara and Jarrad, you are the oldest and best of my friends. What can I do for you at this time?"

"Since my end will be the same, no matter what, tell us what has become of the other enemy dragon."

"Axel killed its rider, and he fell into a thick forest. The dragon has been wandering the skies in that area, searching through the trees for its master. Langa is keeping watch from a distance to see whether its search is successful."

"And how fares the four who are taking the draft dragons home?"

"I have met with them and apprised them of the situation as best I knew it at the time. As a group, it was decided to continue flying toward home in the hopes that we would be able to catch up at the first camping site."

"In that case, I have decided what should be my fate," said Hukken. "I wish to say goodbye to you here and now. I am still able to fly, though not swiftly. I do not want any of the king's soldiers to find my body and learn about the Colony, which they certainly would do if I died here.

"I have decided that I shall return to where Eleth and I left two dead dragons less than an orai ago, and I shall suffer the same fate as they."

"Hukken! What are you saying?" cried Eleth. "Those were horrible deaths!"

"Yes, horrible to those who watched; but their deaths, while extremely painful for a short time, were quick. If I stay here, it will be orais of pain before I die, perhaps even a day, and I *am* in intense pain.

"I ask only that Shaddra accompany me and bear witness to the location where my bones may be found. At some time, hopefully soon, you may be able to come and prepare a fitting burial for my remains. That is my wish."

Everyone, but the bewildered, yet now free, siris dragon, was in tears. Eleth reached for Axel's hand and buried her head in his shoulder. He put his free arm around her back.

"Hukken," Axel said, "Licor and I yet live because you and Eleth chose to sacrifice yourselves. I could never have imagined this when I first met you. But my children and their children, too, shall know your name and ever hold it in a place of honor. I just wish we could have had that talk about promises."

"I trust that you will be faithful to the *spirit* of the promises you made."

"You are wise, my friend, and *I* am now wiser because of the things you have taught me. I will be faithful to the spirit of my promises. I have learned that those who seek revenge rather than justice are doomed to find nothing but sorrow." Letting go of Eleth's hand, Axel carefully removed the saddle from Hukken's back.

Standing up on trembling legs, Hukken flexed his wings. "Again, I think I have one more flight in me," he said. "Shaddra, best of friends, will you accompany me?"

"It will be the saddest journey of my life. I saw the carnage you left behind there. How can one fly when one's heart is breaking?"

"For me, please do your best."

"I will, and I will see that the free dragons also hold you in memory as our first martyr. I fear you won't be the last."

"May your spirit be blessed by the Great Ceragon!" Eleth cried out.

At that, Hukken nodded to Eleth and each of his friends, one after the other. He winced as he turned away.

Axel took the opportunity to whisper quietly to Shaddra, "It's wet here, but the temperature is reasonable. Someone will wait in this area for your return," he said. He pointed to a forested area about a hundred strides away. "Those trees will provide some cover for those who wait."

Taking a deep breath, Hukken took off, using slow and gentle flaps of his wings as he worked to gain some altitude. Everyone watched his departure with tears still freely flowing. Shaddra followed a little distance behind Hukken. Within a few minutes, both dragons disappeared behind a forested hill.

***

Axel watched until he could see Hukken no more and then turned to the others. "I've patched up Licor as best I can, but we need to find Langa. Eleth, can you stay in this area with our new friend until Shaddra returns and until, hopefully, Langa, Licor, and I return with the other rider's jewel? Find some cover over in those woods. Maybe you can learn this dragon's name and help him understand who we are. I don't think he will be a problem.

Speaking quietly back to him, she said. "If he does become a problem, he will wear a new decoration in his eye."

Axel turned to Licor. "Can you carry me for a short distance to find Langa? She won't be far from here."

"I am not at my best right now," Licor answered, "but as long as we are not attacked again, I can do better than that."

Axel and Licor flew off into a cold wind. In the distance, beyond them, a bank of clouds covered the horizon while Eleth looked over at the siris dragon beside her and said, "Well, my new friend, it appears we have another storm approaching. Let's move over into those trees."

The dragon looked over at her and asked, "Are we friends?"

"Of course, we are. Would I have gone through so much trouble to free you from slavery if I were not your friend? My name is Eleth. We could be much better friends if I knew your name."

The dragon tilted its head to one side and looked down. "I am Konnor." He paused for a moment before saying, "Licor spoke to me in the High Language before he left. I... once knew Licor before he disappeared. I don't understand why he is here with you."

Eleth picked up Hukken's saddle with one arm and, raising her other upward to the dragon, motioned for him to follow her. "I heard him speak to you," she said as she walked, "just before he and Axel departed, but I don't speak the High Language, so I didn't understand what he said."

"It was most strange. He said, 'You are the *Daughter of Ceragon,* and the *Great Foretelling* is about to come true."

"Licor spoke the truth to you. I am the Daughter *of Ceragon.* I didn't ask for the job, but my parents sacrificed their lives to give me that gift. The young man you just saw leave with Licor is the *Son of Ceragon.* The reason Licor is our friend is that we freed him from his master, even as we have freed you, so that the two of you may help bring on the Great Foretelling."

Konnor, who had been following behind Eleth, paused again to think a moment. He looked at Eleth in amazement. "Never could I have believed that I might have any role to play in bringing about the Great Foretelling!"

"You shall not be alone. In addition to Licor, there are more than a hundred dragons who have never worn a jewel. We all work together for a purpose beyond all worth."

Konnor caught up with Eleth, who had not slowed down. "It is difficult to believe there are a hundred free dragons. Who was the one my rider shot? I heard some of what was said but did not understand much."

"He was Hukken, one of the noblest dragons to have ever lived. He was born free. He hoped only to see the *Foretelling* fulfilled but became its first martyr instead."

"I feel guilty for my part in his death."

"A slave should never feel guilty for what he is forced to do. But now you are free to do whatever you wish. The difference is that you *will* be accountable for your actions from this time forward, whether they are for good or for ill."

***

Axel pulled his cloak tighter and secured the strings, trying to keep the wind from tearing it loose. The air had grown colder; the storm front was unmistakably closer now.

"Do you see Langa?" Licor called up from below.

"No, she might be camouflaged," Axel replied, scanning the horizon. "But I do see the siris dragon—just to the right of our course. I think he's spotted us, too. Where did the rider fall?"

"See that small hill left of the tilled field?"

"Yes, I see it," Axel said. "Looks like whatever was growing there has been harvested."

"The rider fell into the dense grove on the southern side of that hill. Kulek isn't close enough to find the body, but he's too near for us to get any closer."

"Who's Kulek?" Axel asked.

"The enemy siris dragon," Licor explained. "I knew him from my days in the Special Corps."

"Was he with the group that attacked Frithden?"

"No. He wasn't involved in that raid—nor was Konnor, the dragon we just left with Eleth," Licor pointed out. "But they and their riders were part of the king's Special Mission Force, as was I. Their riders were responsible for many deaths, and they used their dragons as weapons. Kulek may be getting tired now, but he is still very dangerous."

A voice came as if from the air beside them. "I'm glad to see you here."

Axel yelled back, "I'd say the same to you, Langa, if I could see you. But it is nice to hear your voice. What do you think? Is there any chance of getting in close enough to find the rider?"

"Not if he is anywhere in front of you. Perhaps you want to wait until the siris dragon is exhausted."

"If we did that, the snowstorm would be upon us, and we'd never be able to find a body that is covered with snow."

"How long do you think we have until the storm hits?" asked Licor.

"I think we have maybe three or four orais. No more."

Langa's eerie voice again spoke out of the air beside them. "The siris dragon will stay in this area until it finds the body or is weakened to the point it cannot go on. We must come up with a plan or give up on this endeavor."

"I would hate to lose either the jewel or Kulek," Licor said. "I suggest we return to Eleth and wait for Shaddra. Together, we may be able to devise a plan."

"Let's do as you suggest, Licor," said Axel. "If nothing else, we can decide to go on to join our firedrake friends."

As the first to appear back at the bank of the river, Shaddra had no trouble following the tracks of a young woman and a dragon over to the nearby woods. There she found the two deep in conversation. The subject left her speechless.

"But if we're going to free the nesting mothers," Konnor was saying, "there is no reason why we can't try to free the dragons in the king's Cadet Dragon Reserve. We should also attack the king's Reserve for Young Dragons, too. They are all very close together and think of the blow against the king!"

"That's easy for you to say," Eleth responded, "but we don't know where the Bechars for all the younglings in the last two reserves are located. Without that, we would never have enough resources to carry out those raids."

"When you undertake these raids, why don't you attack the king's castle, too?" Shaddra's voice came out of the nearby air. She was still in her invisible mode and caught the two totally unaware.

"Oh, Shaddra," Eleth said with a sarcastic grin, "you certainly know how to scare an innocent young woman to death!"

"Somehow, Eleth, I think you lost your innocence today... when you killed two dragons and two dragonriders."

"But that wasn't all me. Hukken and I conspired together…. Okay…, it was mostly me. But tell me, please, how was Hukken's end?"

"After all that you had already fed to those veps," Shaddra said, "I could not believe how many more there were to go after Hukken. Instead of starting at the bottom of the ravine, Hukken chose to come down from the top. He flew directly through the remaining tatters of the web, which were still substantial in size, even after it had been mostly torn apart by your pursuers earlier. Maybe the veps were able to make considerable repairs in a short time. Anyway, the web immediately paralyzed Hukken, or at least he became stone-still. He sailed a ways before falling directly to the ground and died within a few minutes from the follow-on attack by hundreds or even thousands of veps. I watched closely to see how much he suffered. It was difficult for me to watch, but he never made a sound, died quickly, and did not suffer for long. His bones will be found some distance away from the others and will be readily identifiable when we come for him. The veps in that nest will be very well-fed after today."

"I'm glad it was not I who watched," Eleth said. "It was hard enough to bend over his wound and be unable to do anything for it. You two have been close friends for most of your lives. How could you bear it?"

"I considered it my duty and a last honor to a great dragon."

"Look," Eleth cried out, excitedly pointing up into the air. "Axel and Licor are flying in from the east. They aren't accompanied by a second visible dragon, so I fear they have failed to destroy the jewel."

"The odds were never in their favor," Shaddra said.

Licor sailed in gradually and landed a short distance from the wood. Axel hopped off and went immediately to check on Licor's leg. After a moment, he reached into one of the bags at the side of the saddle, retrieved more bandages, and again tended to the leg.

"I must start thinking bigger regarding medical supplies," Axel said to Licor. "You're using up every bandage I've got, you big warrior, you."

"What can I say?" was the response. "Big dragon, big wounds."

Shaddra walked over beside the siris dragon and gave his side a gentle bump with her shoulder. "At least you're still safe, the both of you."

"Maybe safe," Axel said, "but very frustrated."

"Um, Axel..." came an uncertain voice from Eleth. She pointed at the charcoal grey dragon at her side and said, "Konnor and I figured you would have a difficult time with Kulek, so we have been working on a plan."

"This is Konnor next to you?" Axel asked.

"Yes, he appears to be, but who is Kulek?" asked Shaddra.

"Oh, I haven't introduced you, have I? Shaddra, Licor, and Axel, this is my new friend, Konnor. I simply adore the white mottling in his charcoal skin, don't you? Anyway, the name of the red dragon, who is out there protecting his rider, is Kulek."

"That's very nice to know," said another voice. A second messenger dragon appeared beside the group and said, "My name is Langa. Looks like we are all getting chummy here. Now, what's this about a plan?"

"Yes, I know about Kulek," Axel said. "So, you two have just gotten to know each other, but already you have a plan to grab the jewel from the downed rider?"

"Oh, they have gone way beyond that," said Shaddra with a sarcastic grin.

"Huh? What's that supposed to mean?" Axel asked.

"We'll tell you about that part," said Eleth, "after we get the jewel. Yes, Konnor is a very intelligent dragon, and we spent some time discussing the problem you were facing with Kulek."

"Whatever you plan to do, better have it happen before that snowstorm hits," quipped Axel.

"Yes, Axel. We even made the snowstorm a part of our plan. Essentially, we think that you and Licor should distract Kulek to the west and away from the area where the rider fell. Since messenger dragon arms are too weak to carry a human body, we propose that Konnor and I hide in the low clouds of the coming storm as you lure Kulek away. Meanwhile, Konnor will drop down out of the clouds and carry me in his arms toward the south, such that Kulek sees and pursues us, thinking that Konnor is stealing the body. Finally, you, Langa, and Shaddra can double back and find the jewel."

"Wait, wait, wait!" exclaimed Axel. "That all went past me pretty fast. First, I wonder how appropriate it would be to use a newly freed dragon on such a dangerous mission."

"Do you think I cannot already see how I have been blessed by the sacrifices each of you has made to set me free?" said the charcoal-colored dragon. "Yes, it has only been a few orais since my master died and my Bechar was destroyed. But it does not take long to understand what it means to be free from someone else dictating what my body will do. Kulek is a friend of mine who is enslaved. Now that I know what freedom is like, I will do anything to free him. As for Eleth, she risked her life, and Hukken gave his to save me. I would die rather than let her be harmed."

"That's enough about dying. We've had too much of that already," said Eleth.

She walked up to Axel and reached for his hand. "Kulek is tired now. Even with Konnor carrying me in his arms, we should be able to outrun him. The big question is how quickly you can find the body and the jewel. Kulek may discover our ploy and come back for you. You'll have to decide what to do if that happens. Konnor and I will have to be ready for a fight if Kulek catches up with us before you find the jewel. Face it, Axel, is there any alternative plan to try?"

"The rider was a woman," said Axel, "but she wore a uniform. Kulek won't follow you just because you're a woman."

"That's why I have these." She turned and walked back to where a bundle of clothing and armor lay on a fallen log, from which the snow had been brushed away."

All the latecomers first cast their glances at Eleth, then shifted their attention to the spot where Konnor's former rider lay. The body was draped in only the undergarments usually worn beneath a uniform.

"I had to get his uniform off before rigor mortis set in or the body froze," said Eleth. "The blood in the uniform has frozen, but that will warm up and actually make it more realistic."

Axel scratched his head. "Do I have any say in this plan?"

"Of course, you do. You can say, 'Yes, it sounds great.'"

***

It took some time for Eleth to get changed into the unfamiliar flying officer garments and armor. While she undertook that task, Axel approached the charcoal dragon and asked, "Konnor, how did your flight manage to find the Free Dragons on their route home?"

"Flight Command," the siris answered, "specifically instructed our flight to scour the area around the Breeding Coops for signs of enemy dragons and to destroy any other dragons we encountered, for none would be friendly. My master, who served as our flight commander, had us flying at high altitude and using the clouds as cover to prevent our discovery by potential enemies. He saw your flight down below as shadows against the snow and ordered a standard swift attack."

"Does that mean no other flight of the king's dragons should threaten us tonight?"

"I believe you are correct. We were the only flight assigned to this sector."

"Thank you, Konnor. That eases my mind considerably."

More time was required for everyone to assume their starting positions. Fortunately, that coincided with the first clouds rolling in with the storm front. The clouds were not fluffy ground-hugging hideaways but rather a steep wall reaching from horizon to horizon and climbing higher than the dragons could fly. Still, they worked to hide Eleth and Konnor until Axel and Licor could draw Kulek several tondrins to the west.

Konnor landed softly enough for Eleth to climb into his arms.

"I expect this experience is as new for you as it is for me," Eleth said. "But I've seen many a dragon mother cradle her nestling in her arms. My heart has broken a little every time I've seen those mothers separated from their children. That's what we are working to stop."

"My memories of my mother are faint," Konnor said. "But I would do anything to see her once again."

"This is a start; let's get it done!"

Konnor took off gently then and, after a moment, climbed steeply until they popped out of the clouds. The sky was still dark, but the white of the ground was clearly visible.

They left the cloud bank sooner than would be best for fooling Kulek, but they needed to give Axel as much time as possible to look for the rider before the storm clouds obscured everything. Fortunately, Kulek was some distance away chasing after Axel and Licor.

Ten minutes later, Kulek looked back and appeared to conclude that he was chasing the wrong dragon. Immediately, he turned around and flew directly toward the newcomers.

"Uh, Konnor," Eleth said, "I don't recommend waiting for him to catch up. Let's get out of here."

Konnor promptly turned southwest and flew as fast as his wings would carry them. Unfortunately, Kulek had an angle advantage that steadily ate at Konnor's starting distance advantage.

"At this rate, Kulek will catch up to us in about twenty minutes," Konnor said. "I cannot fight him or outrace him with you in my arms."

"Then I need to move to your back," Eleth responded.

"But how? If I land, he will be on us before I can take off again."

"Then we'd better not land."

Konnor looked down at her in curiosity."

"Start a slow climb; roll halfway to your right, so that you are on your back. That's when you need to drop me."

"What?"

"First, let me turn so I am facing you. If you drop me when you are upside down, I will land on the bottom of your saddle and will catch hold. After that, on my signal, you continue your slow roll until you are right side up. As you roll, I will climb around the saddle until I am on top."

"Are all humans this crazy?"

"No, just me, as far as I know."

"We will lose much altitude in this maneuver."

"But we'll gain significant speed for our recovery."

"This will be a story worth telling my children's children. Should I live to have any."

"Should *we* live to have any?" said Eleth.

"Let me turn in your arms first."

"Don't let me scratch you with my claws. I don't wish to mar your beauty."

"Oh, Konnor, you are a fast mover."

"I'm a what?"

"Never mind, I'm rolling over now."

"Okay, do you have me tight?"

"Any tighter and I will crush you."

"Let's go. Start your roll."

When Konnor started his roll, Eleth experienced a wave of nausea coming over her, but she forced it down as best she could, knowing she had to be alert and at her best in this little maneuver.

"Okay, I'm looking at the ground. Be ready to dive for me if I miss the saddle. Let me go. NOW!"

Eleth suddenly found herself on Konnor's chest, just behind the saddle. She had managed to grab only a stirrup, which should have fallen over to Konnor's back but instead lay loose on his chest. Without thinking, she carefully pulled on the stirrup until she was able to grab what Axel called the billet strap and climbed to her knees.

"All right," she yelled, "finish your roll."

The sound of the wind whistling through her helmet picked up as Eleth walked gingerly on her knees, up the side of the saddle that was slowly turning toward her. By the time Konnor completed his roll and leveled out, she had grabbed the now very short tether line and used it to drag herself into the saddle.

Quickly she looked back and saw that Kulek had dived with them and was only two hundred strides behind. But, as she looked, she saw Kulek suddenly spread his wings to pull out of the dive. He'd seen she was alive and knew this situation was a ruse. He was turning back.

"Level out, Konnor," she yelled, "Kulek is turning back!"

The command came none too late, as she could clearly see the birds in the trees below even in the darkness that surrounded them.

Konnor turned his head to look back at Eleth. She could see the stress that he had been under. "Daughter," he said, "I must admit you severely tested the limits of my free will on that move."

"Konnor, I only first met you today, but I think I love you already. If you have any strength left in you, maybe we'd better turn around, too, and see if we can go help Licor."

When they came close to the area where the first attack took place, both Eleth and Konnor strained their eyes to find any sign of a dragon, but none could be seen in the air in any direction.

"Let us start a circle pattern here," suggested Konnor, "and expand it out slowly. They must be on the ground. Perhaps there was a battle."

"I truly hope that wasn't the case. There's no winning for us in any kind of battle."

Konnor slowly expanded the radius of his flight. In this manner, they flew for close to half an orai, until a multi-colored messenger dragon suddenly appeared in front of them and to their right.

"I think that's Langa," Eleth said. "Since they can change color, I never know which one I'm looking at for sure until I'm up close or can hear her voice."

"Follow me!" the messenger called and started descending toward a low hill. It was, definitely, Langa.

Upon reaching the far side of the hill, Eleth clearly saw three dragons below. Since they did not appear to be in a fight, she had to assume the Bechar had been found and smashed. However, there was no way to tell, as of yet, if anyone sustained injuries in the process.

Konnor landed a short distance away from the redwood-colored dragon he called Kulek, who stood statue-like with eyes not concentrating on anything in particular. Approaching delicately, Konnor spoke to Kulek in the High Language, causing the red dragon to turn his head slowly to gaze at him. Eleth, still on Konnor's back, listened intently, but only discerned a feeling of friendliness and assurance. After a few minutes, the two changed to speaking in something she understood.

"Konnor," Kulek said softly, almost in a daze, "what have they done to me?"

"Don't worry, my friend. You are safe."

"But, Dura, my rider? She was killed."

"I am afraid so, Kulek. She was honorably killed in battle."

"Dura was good to me. I'm sorry that she died. What do I do now?"

"Kulek, you may do anything you want to do. There is no one to give you orders anymore."

"But I have no idea what to do. I've always followed orders."

"I'm in no position to give you orders, but may I offer a suggestion? These dragons are friends, as are the humans. You know of the *Great Foretelling.* The woman on my back is the *Daughter of Ceragon,* and the man before you is the *Son of Ceragon.* They would like to take us back to their home. If you come with us, you will have time to think and decide what you want to do."

Axel came around to stand beside Konnor and offered a hand to assist Eleth down from her saddle. "That was very close," he said. "The rider's body was completely buried in snow and seemed to take forever to find. Once we found her, we couldn't find any rocks under this snow. Langa warned us that she saw the red dragon approaching and we'd better hurry. I finally had to place the jewel on a stump and smash it with a heavy log. The siris dragon was right above us and preparing to shoot a fireball at me. Licor nearly attacked him, even with his weak leg. It might be a good idea to carry some tools in the future for handling tasks like this.

"After the jewel was smashed, the red dragon relaxed and followed Licor down. It just stood there in a daze until you arrived."

"Is everyone okay?" Eleth queried the group. After receiving multiple nods, she asked, "Where is the rider's body now?"

"She is over in that copse of trees, about eighty strides up the hill. Why do you ask?"

Eleth did not answer the question but instead went over to Kulek and bowed slightly in front of him. "We are sorry that your rider was killed in battle. It is obvious that you cared for her. She deserves to be treated honorably. Would you think it appropriate if we take care of her remains in the human fashion?"

Kulek looked down at Eleth in a kind of wonderment. "I have never seen a dead enemy soldier taken care of in that fashion. They are always left on the battlefield or carelessly dumped into holes."

"We humans do bury our dead, but the task should be undertaken with dignity, respect, and care. If we prepare a grave for her, would you like to say some words of tribute in her memory?"

"I would not know what to say, but if that is the fashion of humans, I feel she deserves that respect."

"That is an appropriate choice. Konnor, may I ask that you dig a hole about two strides deep over there in that level ground? You should be able to estimate how long and how wide.

"Axel, you and I can go fetch the body."

Axel looked at her with a "What are you doing?" kind of expression but went along with the game.

When they reached the body and out of hearing range from the dragons, he said anxiously, "We are wasting time and need to get out of here before we're discovered by more enemy dragons!"

"I know that, Axel. But Kulek has been through a very distressing experience. We must respect him and attend to his needs if we hope to win him over to our side. There are many ways that things can go wrong when a dragon is suddenly thrown into an entirely new and frightening world. Each dragon will be different. This one was obviously attached to his rider. We can best win him over by respecting that relationship he had."

"All right, I'll go along with this, but please hurry!"

By the time Eleth and Axel reached the grave site with the body, everything was ready. Eleth expressed silent thanks that dragons had the strength and tools necessary to dig an appropriate hole quickly. Eleth and Axel lowered the body as carefully as they could and stood back.

The two humans and all of the dragons, except Shaddra, who was on watch, stood by in respect as Kulek approached the grave and said simply, "This is the place that Dura will remain until we all come together again in the *Sight of the Great Ceragon*. Dura was good to me."

With that, he stood back and looked at Konnor. On that signal, the charcoal dragon gradually pushed dirt into the grave and over the body. Finally, Axel picked up the now-clear shards of the smashed Bechar and laid them on top of the grave.

Eleth waited a moment before walking up to the side of Kulek's head, which was bowed. "We are about to depart for our home," she said gently. "It is a long journey, but we wish to have you come with us. There, you will get to meet many other dragons, who are like you."

"I know not what your destination is," said the red dragon, "nor what fate awaits because of my decision. Nevertheless, I choose to go with Konnor and with you. May Ceragon bless this choice."

Smiling broadly, Eleth answered, "I assure you; the Great Ceragon is watching over you."

"Listen, everyone!" Axel said, intensely enough to catch everyone's attention. "We'll never catch up to the others tonight. But there are still several orais of dark. Let's use them to get as far away from this place as we can."

The party was gone only ten minutes when Shaddra reappeared. She toppled a young balibi tree and used it to scratch out, as best she could, all signs of the grave and scatter a layer of snow over its top. At the last, she placed the tree directly across the surface of the grave as a final attempt to make it invisible from above. Only after all this did she jump into the air and attempt to catch up with the group of dragons flying before her.

Chapter Nineteen

BIGGER GAME

Three siris dragons, two messenger dragons, and two humans spent the day camping in a broad-leafed, outer forest dell next to a tiny stream. The storm moved further to the north, the skies turned clear, and warming temperatures rapidly melted the ground snow during the day, so much so that the white blanket was totally gone by nightfall. That made accidental discovery of the party at night much less likely and travel much safer. Accordingly, Axel had the group up and moving as soon as darkness provided enough cover.

Two orais into the flight, a crease of red light appeared on the eastern horizon. There was not, however, enough light from Kivan to cause much concern for the travelers.

As they approached the stopover camp from their northward journey, Axel decided to send Langa ahead to see if the group of firedrakes and their draft dragon cargo had left any messages behind. Langa returned swiftly with unexpected news: the entire group of firedrakes was still at the camp. They had chosen to stay an extra day, giving the others a chance to catch up. This led to the reunion of the entire party, which now included two new members.

Fortunately, the draft dragon team was fully prepared to take flight at any time. Accordingly, after sharing assurances that everything was in good shape and a few quick stories about what had caused the delays, the now united group departed for home.

Getting all the way back to the Colony while it was still dark involved fewer rest stops and swifter flight, but the exhausted troop finally arrived at the Colony just as first light was creeping over the mountains on the second day. Cheering crowds of dragons of all types greeted them. Both the two little draft dragons and the two new siris dragons found the greeting overwhelming. It required some time, but they eventually managed to become accustomed to the new situation.

The Colony dragons were thrilled to have Eleth among them and treated her with special reverence and care. They did not miss the fact that both the *Son* and the *Daughter of Ceragon* were in their midst. Neither Axel nor Eleth missed the tone of the high-language messaging that flowed about them, like the quiet but penetrating sound of a brook.

While the dragons of the Colony clustered around Eleth, Axel, along with the four recently added human members of their community—Fala, Bardin, Ketter, and Rook—began removing the baskets from the four firedrakes.

Another one overwhelmed by the welcome and the vast cavern system of the Colony was Eleth. To her, it made the caverns of the Breeding Coops seem insignificant. Langa went immediately to rejoin her family, but Shaddra, who did not have a mate, took some time to show Eleth and Axel around the Colony. When they came to the assembly hall, Eleth first walked out into the center and twirled around in a circle, arms spread out, while looking up and around. Tall and lithe, she was. A gleeful smile brightened her face, and her dark-treeberry red hair was thrown out behind her as she turned. Axel stood on the edge of the hall, looking at nothing but her.

When she stopped spinning, she noticed the speaker's platform and made her way to the top. From there, she looked around the hall, trying to picture it brimming with dragons. Turning back to Axel, she said, "This is where you asked the dragons to help with the fire." It was not a question. "I could never have done that."

It's not a good idea to use the word 'never,'" Axel replied. "You don't know your future. Of all people, you should know that."

She lowered her eyes, lost in thought. After a moment of silence, she lifted her head and asked, softly but with conviction, "Why us? Why were we the ones chosen for this impossible task from the moment we were born?"

"I have some thoughts on that," said Shaddra, for whatever they are worth. "We are taught that our lives do not come from nothing. Out there, perhaps away from Tamerel, perhaps not, are spirits. Each dragon and each human is born with one of those spirits inside, and that spirit is the essential part of our nature. Even as dragons are different from each other and humans are all different, so are the spirits. The gods choose who receives what spirit based on the spirits own desires The spirits, in turn, bring with them particular talents, but that is just the start of explaining who we are, as our bodies also reflect the unique qualities and experiences inherited from our parents and ancestors, including cultural traditions, values, and life lessons that shape our identities. That is the reason you were born to the special people who procreated you. In your cases, the gods also granted you something unusual, allowing you to have both human parents and dragon parents. Remember, Eleth, that your dragon mother, and Axel, your dragon father, also sacrificed their lives for you. The fact is, inside, you are so very much like dragons; I would not be surprised to learn that your blood is purple."

"I... I have never seen my blood," Eleth said.

"Neither have I," said Axel. "That, in itself, is unusual. We should have had the common cuts and injuries that any child gets, but I haven't and, based on what Eleth said, neither has she. I don't know if I want to find out."

"Same here," Eleth said in a barely audible whisper, yet her voice still carried across the hall. "I think we'd better go get some sleep now."

***

Eleth wanted to see the house and the place where Axel and Jarrad lived before she returned home. Accordingly, after resting through the day, Axel arranged for some of the dragons to give him, Eleth, Fala, Bardin, Ketter, and Rook rides down to Jarrad's house. Everyone but Axel and Eleth headed back to their homes after touching down and removing the saddles from their rides that night, while Axel arranged for Eleth to sleep in Jarrad's bed. When the sunstar rose, the two had an early breakfast and rode skells into Tarfal.

From the moment they entered the town limits, an unmistakable sense of unease settled over them. People carried on with their daily activities, yet their expressions frequently displayed grief or simmering anger. They were greeted by the many people Axel knew with smiles and glad handshakes. But the smiles faded quickly and were replaced by looks of concern or resignation.

Axel was about to approach a small group of people who had gathered in front of the grocer's store and ask what had happened during their absence when Fala and Bardin came running up.

"We heard you two were in town," Fala said.

"Axel nodded at their friends and asked what had changed while he had been away.

The two looked at each other as if afraid to talk. "You'd better sit down over there," said Fala."

"Axel followed Fala's point and saw some empty chairs the grocer had set out in the shade of his storefront for people to use in the hot afternoons."

"All right, if you wish," Axel replied.

They dismounted and joined Axel's apprentices in occupying the chairs.

"Okay, lay it out straight. What's up?"

"You see..." Fala said in a hesitating way. The first thing is that we discovered the fire was set on purpose."

"What in Etmar's Inferno are you saying? And I'm not trying to be funny."

"Councilman Stefan was riding on the Valley Road out by the rim three days ago to visit his brother in the lower valley. When he passed the approximate location where the Valley Fire got started, he happened to notice a line of wagon tracks heading off into the burned-out forest but not returning to the road. Their tracks were visible because the vegetation had been burned away and the easterly wind had prevented ash from filling them. That made him really curious, so he followed the track about half a tondrin until he found the remains of an incinerated wagon sitting right next to the blackened stump remains of a once thick grove of conifers. From the tracks, it was obvious that the wagon had been pushed and pulled several times back and forth to get it right under the trees. The tracks showed that the driver then released the two skells. The wagon ended up in an entirely unnatural place to park any such vehicle."

Unable to contain himself, Bardin jumped in to replace Fala. "That wagon was carrying several kegs of pitch. It was easy to tell because the metal hoops left behind were the same kind used to carry pitch for leak-proofing boats, buckets, and other such things. There were boot prints all around from at least two men, and skell prints led away in line, not side by side. It's quite clear that someone brought in a wagonload of pitch, spread it around, set it afire, and skedaddled."

Axel looked up at Eleth and said, I'll be a..."

"But that's only the first thing. The skell shoes, which made the prints, were, undoubtedly, military issue. The blacksmith went out to the site and confirmed that. He also said that the remains left by the fire showed that the wagon was a military wagon without question. He had worked on many military wagons when he lived in the lower valley.

Eleth laid a hand on Axel's shoulder and said, "I can't believe the king would order his men to destroy nearly four thousand of his people?"

"Why not?" Axel replied. "He ordered his dragons to destroy four hundred people in Frithden."

Eleth put her hand to her mouth in shock. "Oh, Axel, I'm so sorry I forgot about Frithden."

"No problem, Eleth. You kind of have to be from there to remember Frithden anymore."

We need to tell you about something else that happened while you were away," interrupted Fala.

A woman from a small group that had gathered to listen approached the group of four young people and asked, "May I tell you about this part, Axel?" I was there." Axel recognized her as the wife of Councilman Kiel Bessen.

"Axel jumped to his feet and removed his hat. "Yes, please do."

Yesterday, a troop of the king's soldiers entered our town, bringing with them coffins bearing some of their fallen. Twelve in total—Tarfal's and Mikell's bravest sons and daughters: ten young men and two young women, none older than their early twenties. Alongside these, eleven more of our children were returned, wounded from the same great battle that claimed the lives of the twelve. We fear for their survival, as their injuries are severe. Over the past three years, the king's command has conscripted thirty-five of our youth to fight in his wars—and many more before that. The twenty-three who returned yesterday were among those recently conscripted.

"Where are the wounded now?" Axel asked.

"They're at Doc Netton's house," came the reply, "but the doctor himself is away in Helmand. The midwife is doing her best to care for them."

Axel glanced at Eleth, who nodded silently. Turning to Fala and Bardin, he said, "Please take Eleth to Doctor Netton's place. I'll come as soon as I can."

"I'll need my medical supplies," Eleth called back to Axel as she hurried off to join Fala. The doc's office was just on the next street.

Axel pointed at Bardin. "You know where those supplies are?"

"Sure do."

"Okay, ride Eleth's skell and get them over to the Doc's place.

Bardin jumped on the skell and left without waiting for further instruction.

Axel turned back to the woman on the street. "Where are the King's soldiers now?"

"They must have been afraid of what we would do. An officer gave a quick, cold speech about how thankful the king was for the sacrifices of the people of Tarfal, turned his soldiers around, and left town without having them dismount from their skells. They didn't even bother taking the bodies from Mikell over to where they had been born and raised."

"It was fortunate that the soldiers left as fast as they did," said an older man from the little crowd of people who had gathered nearby. "Town folks were reaching for their bows and pouring out into the streets. But the soldiers were already gone."

"People are angry," said another person. "We're frustrated and even furious now that we know who set the fire. The wagons carrying the bodies and the wounded were even the same kind as the one that started the fire. The thing is we don't know what to do about it."

Still another voice shouted out, "The king has gone too far this time. We've got to take some action!"

"What is the council doing?" Axel asked the group.

"What can they do?" said Mrs. Bassen. "Nothing."

Axel picked up his reins, mounted, and turned his skell toward the council building. "Nevertheless, I'm going to pay your husband a visit."

Axel found the council building besieged by dozens of angry people. But as he dismounted and the crowd saw who he was, they parted and let him approach the doors. Four guards stood outside the locked door of the building to keep people away, but they, too, moved aside at Axel's approach.

One of the guards spoke, "It's good to see you here, Mister Daimon, sir," and he opened the door for Axel.

"Axel found Bassen inside with a half dozen other council members. They were arguing loudly in a manner that made it difficult to hear any one voice. Bassen saw Axel first and raised both arms to get the others' attention. Following the head councilman's eyes, they all turned to see Axel approach the group with a grim look set across his face, and they immediately fell silent.

"I've heard about what has happened," Axel said. "Now, you find yourselves with a town full of people who want blood, and, if they can't do anything to hurt the king, they may very well turn against you. Don't you agree with me?"

When a chorus of boisterous agreement besieged him, Axel shouted to be heard. "Unfortunately, Jarrad cannot be here with me, but I have a proposal to make, and I think he would agree that it be presented to the town. Let me give you some of the basics, and if you're satisfied with them, I would ask that you call for a community meeting this evening to discuss the idea with the people of Tarfal and Mikell."

An orai later, an announcement was placed on the noticeboard outside of the council building. Within an orai after that, every person in the two towns knew of the planned meeting and who would be the primary speaker.

Axel, meanwhile, rode back to Jarrad's house. He had a fire of his own to build.

Within an orai, a small dragon suddenly appeared in the dragon meadow.

Axel, who had been waiting anxiously in the shade of a nearby tree, greeted her. "Thank you for responding to my message in the daytime, Shaddra," he said. "I need to ask you to arrange an urgent meeting with the Free Colony Council as soon as possible."

"As you wish," Shaddra responded. "I will also send someone to carry the both of you, Honored Ones, up to the Colony." She disappeared, and Axel assumed she was already on her way.

Two orais later, Eleth joined Axel just outside the house. She was accompanied by Fala and Bardin, who had served as guides to make certain she found her way.

"I see you've signaled to the dragons for a meeting," she said, looking at the smoke rising from the remains of Axel's signal fire. "You told me about your method of communication."

"Yes, Shaddra responded and should return any time now. How are the eleven wounded?"

It took some convincing for the midwife to let me treat the soldiers. Fala had to threaten she'd personally bring Axel to throw the midwife out. The medical bag that Bardin brought seemed to be the final convincer.

The eleven are all gravely injured and near death from their wounds or blood corruption. It will take time to see how they respond to my treatment, but some will never be whole. At least three are fighting for their lives as we speak."

"Did you use the Landrin pollen?"

"Yes, I used it all on their wounds and gave the ones who were awake some tea. It required every bit of the pollen I had on hand, so I gave several of the victim's relatives a task to gather some more. I also improved many of the repairs made by whoever served as the clumsy battlefield surgeon, ensuring that the wounds were properly closed and reducing the risk of corruption. Now, we must mostly wait and watch. There is one more thing, however."

"Like what?"

All the soldiers had been beaten, probably with stiff reeds or thin wooden rods, but not all at once. I didn't ask them if that was just a standard punishment for even menial crimes or if soldiers from the Valley had been set apart especially for the punishment."

She sighed and looked back in the direction of the town. "Such a welcome I find in your town."

"Wait until tonight to decide on that question. I've arranged with the Community High Council to have a town meeting in the market square this evening. I need to speak with you and the dragons about some of your ideas before we go to that meeting."

"My ideas?"

"Yes. Do you think I shut my ears when you and Konnor spoke together?"

"I also have ears to hear," said a voice out of the air beside them as two dragons appeared not four strides away. Bardin and Fala, who were still not used to the comings and goings of messenger dragons, nearly fell off their skells.

Placing a hand on Eleth's shoulder, Axel said, "I hope you're ready for a short visit to the Colony."

"What for?" she responded with a frown. "I need to get back to my patients soon."

"It's something very important, and your presence is required. Don't worry, we'll only be gone for about two orais."

Axel patted one of the nearby skells and looked up at Fala and Bardin. "Will you two go back to the Council Building to make certain everything is going well concerning the town meeting this evening? You have my authority to make certain it does."

"What authority is that?" asked Fala.

Axel's face reddened, and he answered in a hesitating voice, "Uh, you see, the High Council declared me to be, uh, provisional mayor and will put that motion to a vote at the meeting."

"Yes, sir, your Lordship," said Bardin, shaking his head with an extended laugh. "We'll make certain the meeting starts at the setting of the Sunstar, just as they have always done."

"Sorry, we don't have saddles," Langa said, "but the journey is short. Some of the Dragon High Council members have expressed great surprise at this sudden call for a meeting," Shaddra pointed out. "They wished you had given some indication of what you wanted to discuss."

"Unfortunately, that would only have confused them," said Axel. "Let's be on our way. There is much to discuss, and we must return by the setting of the Sunstar."

***

When Shaddra and Langa landed in the Colony flight center with their passengers, they found Torkar waiting for them. The firedrake, with a hide the color of anyu bark, seemed a little concerned as he approached the two humans.

"Is there a problem?" asked Axel, noticing Torkar's apprehension.

"I know you, uh, asked for a meeting of the High Council, but... uh... you see, word has gotten around the Colony what the possible subject of your request regards, and... uh... I'm afraid nobody wants to be left out. Accordingly, the location of the meeting has been changed from the Council Room to the Assembly Hall of the Free Colony."

Torkar said the last sentence quickly as if to sneak it past Axel's attention.

"The... Assembly... Hall," Axel said with a sigh. "I suppose everyone is already there waiting for us."

"Oh, of course. I'll take you right there."

Axel rolled his eyes and gave a deep sigh, but obediently followed Torkar.

"Why are you so upset about this?" Eleth asked as she rushed to keep up.

"Oh, I was just hoping to speak with the council first. Now, it looks like we get to speak to everyone. I hope you are prepared."

"Prepared for what?"

"To present your idea about capturing the King's Reserve for Dragon Breeding."

Eleth stopped dead in surprise. "You want me to talk about the Free Dragons taking over the Breeding Reserve?"

"It's your idea, isn't it?"

"I... yes, but it was just an idea. I have only a limited plan."

"Then, maybe you shouldn't have talked about it so much. Come on, they're expecting us."

"But I don't know what to say."

"That's easy; tell them what you've already told the dragons on the flight from Clara's place."

After several minutes of passing from one passage to another, the hallway widened out, and commotion filled the entire space. There was noise in the form of common speech and in the High Language. The tumult all carried with it a sense of excitement and concern.

Suddenly, they found themselves once more entering the largest room that Eleth had ever seen. It seemed even more impressive this time. Even in the Breeding Reserve, no room was so large, and this room was filled with dragons of every type and color. Eleth even saw, in a specially reserved place, the two young draft dragons, which had barely arrived early the day before.

Shaddra stood on the high podium. When she saw Torkar enter the side entrance, followed by Axel and Eleth, she started to speak. "May I have your attention?" she called out.

When the noise only increased, she whistled a shrill, high-pitched note that caused everyone in the room to jump in shock. Only then did the dragons quiet down and listen.

"Thank you, everyone. Today we have two very special guests to speak to us. One is Axel, the *Son of Ceragon*, whom you know already and have worked with before. The other is a very special guest. She is Eleth, the *Daughter of Ceragon*. I do not need to remind you what it means to have both the *Son* and the *Daughter* with us here today. I am aware of what the Son and Daughter will reveal to us today, and it is a serious matter. Already, we have suffered the loss of one of our best, a good friend whom I miss terribly. There are sure to be other martyrs who will fall, perhaps many, before the fulfillment of the *Great Foretelling*. Everyone must understand that without making decisions, taking risks, and working hard, we can never gain anything.

"Now, I present to you first, the *Son of Ceragon*."

The room shook again with the excited thumping of tails that had been so intense when Axel first stood on this podium. They did this knowing the seriousness of Axel's message, yet they continued to cheer.

Eleth was tempted to put her hands over her ears but knew the effort would improve nothing. Would she really have to get up there and speak?

Axel felt his throat suddenly go paper dry. Funny, he thought, this should get easier the second time around. But it was not. He literally dragged himself to the high podium. *At least,* he thought, *I shouldn't have to be up here alone.* "First, please let me introduce to you," he said, "Eleth Morkath Keiron, who, as you have been told, is the *Daughter of Ceragon*."

Eleth involuntarily stepped back at this introduction, startled by the tremendous applause from the dragons that vibrated the very walls of the hall. But she found herself backing into Torkar, who gave her a little shove.

Realizing there was nothing else to do, she started forward in short steps and stopped when she reached Axel's side. The tail-thumping only increased as she did.

When she arrived at the podium, Axel stepped aside and let the dragons give her the appreciation she truly deserved. This time, the crowd was slapping their tails in an even greater frenzy for the Daughter, if that was possible.

There seemed to be no stopping the approbation until Axel raised his hands for silence. He paused a moment for the hall to quiet down and then said, "Only a year ago, Eleth and I were strangers to each other. But necessity has caused us to find one another, and we have learned that we work well together. What's more, we have discovered that, though many of our talents are similar, a great many others are complementary. It means we can do so much more together than we can by ourselves."

We have invited you here today to present some important ideas for your consideration. Now, ideas, by their very nature, are dangerous things. Yes, ideas can cause wonderful things to happen. But they can also lead to death, disaster, and, worst of all, dashed hopes. Today, you will have to decide whether you are willing to take the risks and bear the consequences of your choices.

Not too long ago, I stood in this exact location and urged you to embrace significant risks. So far, there have been no negative consequences from the decisions you made that day. Your decision to assist your neighbors resulted in the saving of hundreds or even thousands of lives, and your neighbors became your friends.

"Tonight, based on what you decide here, I will be meeting with your human friends and asking them to become something even greater than friends. I will be asking them to become your allies and partners. I will ask them to take the same risks you did when you attacked the river and put out the fire. Yes, I will be asking them to risk their lives, as you did, but more than that, I will be asking you to risk your lives again, all in a common cause. That cause is mutual protection and the bringing of freedom to both dragons and humans in the Upper Mysura Valley and potentially much more than that."

The room again filled with applause that thundered in Axel's ears. He raised his hands to calm the crowd so he could continue with his thoughts.

"As you probably know, the Daughter of Ceragon has been taught by the best: Mother Clara herself, and she works every day in the King's Reserve for Dragon Breeding. Because of that, she has become even closer to the dragons in that reserve than I have to you. I cannot help but envy her for that."

The room again started to fill with reverberating noise, but Axel quieted it down quickly.

"Today, Eleth has some news. This news started out as a rumor, but your scouts can now confirm it. Along with her news, Eleth has a proposal. Please listen closely to what she has to say." Axel stepped back to give her sole access to the high podium. As he stepped back, he raised his hands as before so she could concentrate on what needed to be said.

Eleth stared out into nearly two hundred dragon faces, all of which looked right back at her expectantly. The weight of their attention pressed against her chest, smothering any words that tried to rise. Why am I here again? Oh—right. The breeding caves. Something about...

She cleared her throat, forcing herself to speak. "Good dragons of the Free Colony," she managed to say. I… I talk to dragons every day, but never have I seen so many at once, and... it is very daunting to stand up here and speak to all of you together. At any one time, there are about one hundred fifty dragons in the Breeding Reserve. But I rarely see any more than thirty or so at one time. Among the dragons found in the reserve are breeding mothers, newborn hatchlings, drakes brought in for their role in the breeding process, and mounts for about twenty guards. The king constantly worries about the safety of the reserve because it is the primary source of new dragons for his military forces.

"The Reserve is also the place where Mother Clara has worked for nearly thirty years and where most of you spent the first few days of your lives.

Her voice grew somber. "Now, persistent rumors in the Reserve are saying that the king is preparing a major move that would shift all dragon breeding to a new location. He is apparently worried that the current location is too remote and vulnerable to attacks or kidnappings undertaken by Sanara's enemies. If the rumors are true, Clara and I are worried that the new location will be positioned close to multiple military reservations, and we will no longer have the privacy necessary to help any new dragons 'take flight.' Since we must look at the king's dragon forces as our enemy, this means that his forces will continue to grow, while ours will either grow at a slower rate or decline in numbers. It may also mean that Clara and I could become permanently separated from the Colony."

Shouts of "No!" were loudly repeated throughout the hall for a moment or two, until Shaddra walked up to join Eleth on the podium.

"I can report to you," Shaddra announced to the audience, "our spies have confirmed the king intends to move the breeding reserve sometime within the next year. We have already confirmed the location of the new site, and it will, indeed, be situated within a cluster of multiple Dragon Force bases. Huge caverns are being hollowed out of hills in that area to serve as extra protection.

Shaddra turned to look at the young woman beside her. "With that in mind, Honored Daughter, what did you wish to propose?"

Eleth chewed on her lip for a moment and said, "The obvious thing to propose is that the Free Dragons and their human friends raid the Breeding Reserve before the move and, upon freeing the dragons there, bring every possible one back here."

She paused while low mumbles from all across the audience spread out before her.

"You are, of course, aware of the risks that such an action would require us to take, Honored One," said Shaddra. "We could never enter the Breeding Reserve without human help, and we are not at this time prepared to transport either the breeding mothers or their hatchlings."

Walking back out onto the podium, Axel called out, "Excuse me, please, may I have a word or two at this point?"

Both Eleth and Shaddra gladly backed off from the podium, leaving it to Axel.

Axel stepped out to the edge of the podium, then lowered his head as if in deep thought. Slowly lifting his head, he gazed out over the crowd and down into the faces of those closest to him. "The people of the Upper Mysura Valley," he said, "have never had a great love for the king. I told you once before that more than forty of their sons and daughters who fought for the Crown have been carried home in boxes, just over the last year.

"I was told that the last time a group of their children was brought home in this manner, the townspeople actually attacked the accompanying soldiers with rocks and clubs, driving them abruptly from their town. The king's magister for the valley was present at this event and became so frightened of the people that he fled to the safety of the coast along with his entire retinue of constables and has not returned since.

"Now, just two days ago, the king's forces unceremoniously returned twelve more bodies in caskets to Tarfal. Along with the twelve bodies, eleven severely wounded soldiers from the community were returned because they were not expected to live. The *Daughter of Ceragon's* special medical skills may yet save some of those injured soldiers and restore their health. Others may live, but with severe, permanent disabilities. Chances for three of the soldiers remain very low, yet there is still some hope.

He drew a breath as the crowd of dragons shifted. The crowd murmured in anger and shared grief for the people of the valley.

"Again, the people of the Valley reacted with anger, but the king's troops, who accompanied the bodies, wisely departed the area quickly and, as I said, without any ceremony. By now, they would have reported their reception to the king's agents.

"But there is more. In the past few days, we have uncovered evidence that leaves little doubt. The king's own soldiers set the fire that you and the Mysuran community helped extinguish."

A cacophony erupted at this news: shouts, curses of all kinds, and much more.

"King Deroth bears little affection for the Mysura Valley. He knows how poorly the people there think of him, and, in turn, he wishes only to remove the troublesome sore it has become. He will never again find Tarfal or Mikell willing to sacrifice their children for his wars. But, if left unattended, the valley's hatred for the crown may spread, and he can't have that either. It is almost certain that he will try to silence the people there once and for all—and when he does, he will cast blame elsewhere, most likely on his hated enemies to the south, the Mandarans."

"The main reason I have come to the Colony today," Axel announced, "is not related to the intended move of the Breeding Reserve; however, it may have significant implications. The people of the Valley are at risk of being attacked and destroyed by dragon fire, even as the people..." He found himself choking up at this memory, but he forced himself to continue. "…the people of my home village were murdered not so very long ago.

"I fear the king has already attempted to destroy Tarfal and Mikell, given the signs we discovered regarding the origin of the forest fire and the soldiers' actions related to the most recent sacrifices endured by the children of Tarfal and Mikell. At the least, he is certainly aware of their animosity to his reign. He is also aware of the Valley's isolation and its vulnerability. I have no doubt the valley is high on any list he's made of internal enemies, and it may soon find itself attacked by the king's dragons, even as Frithden was."

He looked around, letting the silence build.

"The people of the Valley are extremely thankful to the Free Dragons for the help provided in saving the town from the great fire. This gratitude is evidenced by the fact that no one has, so far, ventured to seek gain by passing information about the Free Colony's existence to the king's forces. But though the people of the Valley remain true, we cannot expect the king to remain ignorant forever. The secret will eventually be discovered, and we must be prepared."

Axel's voice grew steady and strong. "Here, we have the intersection of two peoples. One is the community of Free Dragons. The other is the human population of the Valley. Each has its needs. Each has its strengths. It is obvious that the time has come for these two peoples to unite and support each other in these dangerous times, even as the Son and Daughter of Ceragon have united for a common purpose.

He stepped forward, urgency in his tone. "Today, I wish to ask of you good dragons a favor, even as I will ask a favor of the people of the Valley in a few orais' time. I will ask that you and they become allies and not just friends. Even as you will need human help in freeing the dragons of the Breeding Caves, they will need help in defeating the king's assassins who wait only for the command to attack. Unfortunately, it is almost certain that each of these endeavors will result in casualties, both on your part and on the part of the humans occupying a valley not far from this place. While the dangers are great, the potential return is well worth the effort. In this, we remember the words of the Great Ceragon: 'A life lived for itself is not worth the life that was sacrificed.'

"I suppose it isn't fair to bring in the memory of the dead for one's own purposes. However, I can testify that I exist to deliver you this message today only because a great dragon willingly sacrificed himself for my benefit. I live only because Hukken died. That being said, our purpose must never be to die for our cause but to live for it, in full understanding of the risks involved."

"Eleth and I must now leave you to meet with the people of the Valley. You will have ample opportunity to discuss our proposals after we have left. Thank you and goodbye for now."

***

Just as the sunstar first touched the line of peaks that bordered the Mysura Valley on the west, Councilman Bassen stepped up on the speaker's platform in the Community Market Square on the south edge of Tarfal. He solemnly raised his hands for attention, and the crowd immediately silenced their many individual conversations.

"The towns of Tarfal and Mikell," he proclaimed, his voice ringing clearly across the bustling square, "have endured tragedy and nearly faced disaster. Yet, we persist—thanks to the strength and resilience of our people and the aid of good friends. But now, it has become evident that we may soon confront the greatest challenge we have ever faced."

"The very king, to whom we should look for friendship and protection, may now have become our worst enemy. Because our king cares more for his armies and for his power than for his people, he may have actually declared *us* to be his enemy. We have little proof of this, but a wise man always keeps his eyes open for signs of a storm, and the signs are there.

"As things now stand, we have nothing to use in defense against so great a power as that wielded by the king. Unless we can find a way to change that, we may find ourselves destroyed by dragon fire, even as happened to Frithden and at least four other villages that we know of since Deroth ascended to the throne.

"You are all familiar with Axel Daimon and what he has done for this village. He is a young man of wisdom and understanding. He also has good counsel from others, who know much of what is happening beyond the confines of this valley, which allows him to make informed decisions that benefit our community.

For these reasons and because of the dangerous times we find ourselves in, the Community High Council has voted to proclaim Axel Daimon Provisional Mayor of Tarfal and Mikell. This vote is subject to confirmation by a general vote of the citizens. As temporary mayor, Axel would have limited powers; to call for assemblies of the people and provide direction for them, to direct the creation of a self-defense force, and to negotiate with others for the benefit of the townships. He would also be subject to recall at any time, by vote of the people.

"Accordingly, I wish to call for a vote to sustain this decision. First, I ask that Axel be blindfolded so that he cannot see who should vote for or against him." One of the councilmen dutifully applied the blindfold and turned Axel so that his back faced the audience.

"Now," the high councilman continued, "would everyone please sit down?" He carefully looked about the square to ensure obedience to his request. "At this point, I ask that anyone who wishes to vote *against,* I repeat, *against* this calling of Axel to be provisional mayor, please stand to be counted."

The councilman waited and looked closely about the square. "Since I see no one is standing, I must assume that there will be unanimous approval for the appointment of Axel Daimon as temporary mayor, but would you please now stand and confirm if such is your personal decision?"

Together, virtually all the people in the square rose to express their votes.

"It appears," said the councilman, "that the vote is unanimous. Axel, you may remove your blindfold, and would everyone please sit down?"

As the crowd again found their seats, the high councilman said, "I wish to have Axel come to the speaker's platform to deliver a message he has prepared for us."

Axel thought speaking to two hundred dragons was difficult; now, here he was, again, looking out over a crowd of more than twenty-five-hundred people. *This should be getting easier,* he thought, *not harder.*

Taking a deep breath, he stepped forward and said, "Many of you know I make my living as a fletcher and a bowyer. I also happen to have six of your fine young people working for me in my shop. These six people are intelligent and inventive. Recently, they began using a type of glue that we typically use in bow making for a different purpose. They began applying it to our completed bows as a protectant and, because it could be colored in different ways, as a decoration. Only by accident did we later discover that this new paint was fireproof. No wood product, protected by this paint, could be burned in a fire.

"Out of curiosity, I got one of my dragon friends to test the paint against dragon fire. I don't know what quality in the paint gives it such resistance to heat, but the wooden chair that we tested wasn't even warm after being struck repeatedly by dragon fire.

"The good news is that this paint is made from common landrin tree blossoms, which are found all around us. Using natural pigments, it can easily be produced in about a dozen different colors and in large quantities. If used on glass, the untinted glue will remain transparent yet serve to prevent that glass from being melted or shattered by the heat of dragon fire. Remember, however, the product is also strong glue and should not be applied to anything that you don't wish to have stuck fast in whatever position it originally may have lain."

At this point a general laugh arose among the audience.

Axel continued, "Why should this paint be so important to us at this time? As the good councilman clearly explained there is ample evidence that the king's dragons will soon attack Tarfal and Mikell. The new paint is one weapon we can use in our self-defense, but the king's dragons are also capable of fighting on the ground, using their great strength and their terrible claws and teeth to spread death and destruction.

"Before any attack by the king's armies occurs, we must take every possible precaution to protect and defend ourselves. We must have a thoughtful plan for addressing our problem as a whole, with smaller plans for addressing every contingency, and these plans must be carried out.

"The first step in our basic plan is to paint every building in Tarfal with the new product. You can choose the color or colors for your home or business, but you must do it.

"If only this was all we needed to do to ensure our safety, but you know that is not the case. The second part of our plan is that we must increase our skills with the bow and other weapons. This means we should plan ways to best use our weapons in defense of the town, especially against dragons, but also against infantry, mounted troops, and draft dragons. This should include the construction of protected firing platforms on the roofs of strategically placed buildings and hidden strong points at strategic places along the roads. For example, we should make strategic defense positions on the switchbacks leading up to the rim and, perhaps, where the Valley Road passes Bokin's Bottoms. We must also identify ways to plant hidden black powder bombs where the enemy may tread and to plan and build ambushes to strike enemy troops when they are unwary.

"The third part is especially important. The time has come for us to become more than just friends with the Free Fragons. We must now ally ourselves with them. This means we help them with their challenges, and they help us with ours. But, be warned, even as our problem may involve the sacrifice of lives, so may theirs. I am told that this concept has already been voted on and accepted by the Free Colony. Their vote means they would be able to help provide us with both early warning and active defense against attacking dragons and ground forces.

"Lastly, we must provide active assistance to the Free Fragons in their attempts to remove the chains of slavery from as many of their brethren as possible. This tactic is a way to personally attack the king, for he loves his pet slaves. Each new free dragon would strengthen our dragon allies and become another friend to help us in our defenses against the king.

"I will need to leave for a time to escort Eleth back to her home. During my absence, I ask Councilman Bassen and the High Council to begin organizing efforts to raise defenses for the townships."

Axel turned back to where the Councilman stood. "Please, sir, create whatever subcommittees you deem necessary to lead specific efforts in the general defense, even as far out as the Rim and the switchbacks below. Bardin Shotley and Fala Prudo can direct you on how to make the special paint. Rook Dermin and Ketter Herbert should oversee weapons training and provide assistance to those tasked with designing and constructing defenses. The council will create other roles as they see fit. There are many people with skills that can be applied in this effort.

"We don't have time to debate every cost and sacrifice that this alliance may require. But you should know that these decisions are not made lightly. We still have much to discuss and to decide. Thank you for listening. Please direct your questions and suggestions to the Valley Council."

When Axel turned and stepped away from the speaker's terrace, the entire crowd in the square jumped to their feet, applauding and shouting. Axel stopped to wave briefly at the people around him, then turned again and departed.

***

After the assembly, Axel walked with Eleth over to Doc Netton's office, where the eleven wounded soldiers were being treated.

"When would you like to be taken home?" he asked, hoping it wouldn't be tonight.

"I would have asked you to take me tonight," Eleth responded, "but Doctor Netton is not due back until sometime tomorrow. All the patients will need close watching during that time and by someone with more skill than the midwife. I've already arranged to spend the night here, which is probably a good thing for other reasons."

"Other reasons?"

"Yes, I'm talking about your reputation and mine."

"What do you mean? You're in no danger from me, and you know it!"

"Yes, I know it, but do the people of the Valley know it?"

"It's not their business!"

"Funny how people tend to decide for themselves just what their business is."

"I guess the truth is you are my business."

"Oh, I am? How is that?"

"Lots of ways, I guess. You're the closest thing to family that I have. You are in so many ways like me, yet different enough to keep me genuinely interested. We have, for the most part, the same purposes in life and many of the same friends. We are both orphans. You nearly died to save my life, and there is always the big reason."

"The big reason? What is that?"

"It's... um... that I really like you."

She stopped and turned to look at him, but not noticing, he kept on walking, staring at the ground. "You do?" she asked.

Only upon hearing this did he turn back to her. "Yes, I do," he said, staring into her eyes. "What's more, you'll never have cause to be afraid of me. I'll never lie to you, and I will protect you, even with my life, if that's what is called for. However, I believe you are capable of taking good care of yourself in most situations. I don't ever want to get on your bad side."

Eleth responded with, "Thank you, that's a lovely compliment," and punched him in the shoulder hard.

"Ouch. So much for honesty."

"There's such a thing as too much honesty."

"I'll try to keep that in mind."

Eleth looked away for an instant and then back again, pursing her lips. "Okay, speaking of honesty," she said, "I don't know how, but I already knew all of what you just said; I mean, I knew before you said it. It was nice to have my hopes confirmed."

"Hopes?"

"That's what I said, isn't it?"

"Yes, you did. That *is* nice to know," he said.

They approached Doc Netton's place, and Axel knocked on the door. It was opened by the midwife, who ushered them inside.

"Has there been any change? Eleth asked the midwife as they entered the large room designated for patient care. It was cluttered with cots set up to manage the unusually large number of patients.

"All their fevers have come down at least some from the time you left. Three patients are awake and talking even now. Four more have been awake for variable amounts of time but are now asleep. Two patients haven't awakened, but life signs are good. The last two are still worse off. I hope you have some ideas for them."

"I'll take another look and see what I can do."

Eleth turned to Axel and said, "With luck, we'll be able to leave for home tomorrow night. It will probably depend on the patients who are the worst off. Why don't you check with me tomorrow morning?"

***

A bright light from the rising sunstar flooded into Axel's room, causing him to throw his arm over his eyes in a vain attempt to hold onto the dark for a few more minutes. The night had been one of the most restful he'd had in two sycles. It was also filled with good dreams that he wanted to hang onto. But the dreams were, now gone and there was much to do on this day.

He rose, dressed, and hurried through breakfast. There was much to think about today, but everything in his brain was pushed aside to make way for an image of Eleth. He'd lost his dreams but retained an image of Eleth, with that curly, dark red hair and a smile to get lost in.

He checked first in his shops and found everyone already at work.

"Look who finally decided to come to work," Bardin called out. "If I didn't know better, I'd think you owned the place."

"We've got to remember, Bardin," Fala added, "He's got something much more attractive than a bunch of bows and arrows to grab his attention."

Axel grinned and shook his head. Assuming a full posture, he coughed and said, "Yes, just you remember who is boss around here, and everything better be spotless and as organized as a tinker's workbench."

"I think any tinker would grade this shop as a finely tuned operation," said Bardin. "Wouldn't you agree, Fala?"

"Yes," agreed Fala, "finely tuned it is."

"Since everything is so finely tuned here, I'm going to leave you two in charge today. As you say, I, uh, have other things demanding my attention."

Axel strode to the door. But he stopped and turned back to face his apprentices. "What about the landrin paint? What's happening with that?"

"We have a meeting scheduled with the paint committee at high sunstar," Bardin replied. "We'll show them how to make the paint and add color. They will have the responsibility to spread the knowledge to the various neighborhood groups."

"Sounds good to me. I'll see you in a while."

"Say hi to Eleth for us," Fala shouted as Axel turned to the door. She was grinning from ear to ear.

"Yes, Fala, I will do that," he said over his shoulder and was gone.

Axel rode first to Doc Netton's place, where he found one of the beds empty and Eleth asleep in a chair. She woke at the sound of his boots on the floor, even though he had been trying to be quiet. He knelt beside her and looked into her face. She was not smiling, but her face did seem to brighten some when she saw him.

"Hi, there," was all that Axel could think to say.

"Hello, yourself." She looked wistfully over at the empty bed and said, "We lost Alasha last night. Her family was here with her when she died. She never recovered consciousness. I didn't even know her, and it broke my heart. They took away her body early, before the rise of the sunstar."

"And the others?" Axel asked, looking over at the ten other beds.

"Their families have been in to see them, too. That kind of detracted from my sleep. Four are recovering well, considering the damage they suffered. They'll have to stay here for a sycle at least, but they will live. Although Flin will never be able to walk again, he will still be able to control his bowels. He almost lost that. Fortis has lost the lower part of his left arm and has some internal injuries that will take some time to heal. Lyssa has chest injuries but is improving. All, but three patients, have been awake and alert, off and on."

"Two of those three are doing better but are still in very serious condition."

"Lyssa was my mother's name." Axel said, with a faraway look on his face.

"But you never knew her, right?"

"Yes, but my da talked about her all the time. So, I became familiar with her indirectly. I can't help thinking she was given to my da by the gods, and my da to her."

"Based on the limited information I gathered from the Keirons, I believe the same is true for my parents."

Axel sighed, then said, "When is Doc Netton due back?"

The doctor arrived in town late last night and dropped in to check things out. He seemed satisfied with the care that has been given and was highly curious about the landrin pollen medicine. He went home to rest from his travels and is due back here within the orai,"

"Did you get any sleep?"

"Some. There is a bed in the other room. But I ended up waking every two orais or so to check on the patients. Alasha had family members with her for the entire night. When I noticed that her last minutes were near, they called in the entire extended family. We had fifteen of them here for her last orai, but she went peacefully. An orai after that, the family took her body home to prepare her for burial. Practically the whole town will come out for her funeral early this evening."

A voice called out softly from one of the beds. "Are you Axel?"

"That's Flin," Eleth whispered softly.

"Yes, Flin, I'm Axel. What can I do for you?"

"I think you've done plenty already. My father visited me last night and told me all about what you said in the town assembly and how you saved the Valley from the fire. I know you're doing the right thing to protect the town, and I want to contribute."

"Don't you think you should concentrate on getting well first?"

"Not if I can make a difference now. Look, I know I'll never walk again, but thanks to Eleth, I'm alive, and that means something."

"We don't want you doing anything that will keep you from getting well."

"This won't keep me from getting well. In fact, it will give me a reason to live. The Valley is going to need defensive redoubts, and I know how to build them."

"What do you mean?" Axel asked.

"I was a skilled mason before being pressed into the king's forces and I was a good one. That's why I was assigned to the King's Construction Corps. I learned all the necessary techniques for building defensive structures according to the king's methods. Unfortunately, when I started making suggestions regarding how the structures could be improved, my supervisor told me the king's way was tried and true. He had me reassigned to the infantry for being a 'disturbing influence' in his organization. That's how I got this wound.

"I may not be able to do much actual construction, but I possess the knowledge to design the strongest defensive redoubts that can be created in a short time. I also know how to hide them. That was the suggestion that really got me in trouble."

"Very interesting," Axel said, nodding his head. "But the construction of redoubts can wait for a sycle or two. Look, I must go on a trip for a few days. If you just concentrate on getting better over that time, I will find you when I return so that we can discuss your ideas further. Does that sound good enough?"

"I hate to say it, but I guess you're right. I'll be very much looking forward to seeing you again."

"Axel placed a hand on Flin's shoulder. "So will I."

"Oh, did you really invent a way to make wood resistant to dragon fire?"

"Yes, I did, but with a lot of help from my apprentices."

"Wonderful, I'll have to integrate that into my plans."

Axel just gave a quiet chuckle at this remark.

The next item on Axel's agenda was the council hall. There, he found the entire council noisily debating how to address the many problems at hand. He stood outside the door and listened for a while before stepping inside. The room went deathly silent. "My, that is a big change from what I heard outside. Councilman Bessen, would you give me a summary of your discussions?"

The councilman rubbed his hands together and looked at the floor. "Axel, you need to understand that up until now, the community council has been responsible for little more than solving problems between individuals and groups within the citizenry. We have established laws and tried to enforce them fairly. But what we have before us now is totally beyond our understanding. We can't seem to agree on anything, and we certainly don't know where to start."

"I see. Most of you are businessmen, aren't you?"

"Yes, I suppose so. We've got owners of the mines and lumber companies here, plus prominent farmers and shopkeepers in the town."

"Okay, tell me, how do you solve problems in your work? Councilman Bessen, you're a mine owner. How many problems do you face there?"

"I face all kinds of problems every day. How to get the supplies we need over long distances, how to get excess water out of the mine, how to keep equipment in repair, how to determine who's doing the job right and who wrong, and many others."

"Do you personally solve each one of those problems?"

"Some I do, but usually only after getting recommendations from my lead men. Others I assign out to the most experienced people, and they choose how to solve them."

"Isn't that pretty much what the rest of you do in your businesses? Even those of you who run a business almost entirely on your own seek advice from others, don't you?"

There were nods and expressions of agreement all around the room."

"Why don't you do that here? In my business, I begin each day by listing all the problems that I know I will have to face that day. After that, I prioritize them. Finally, I decide which ones I have to do myself, which ones I can give to my apprentices, and which ones should only be done if everything ahead on the list works out better than expected or, maybe, I can even put them off until tomorrow.

"I would suggest that we start by finding some slate boards and listing all the challenges that we face and jobs that must be done. We should also list all the important questions that need to be answered. We can assign a symbol or a number designation for how difficult each task or question will likely be to answer or perform. After things are prioritized, assign the most capable people available to find the answers. Your job isn't to solve the problems but to find and organize those who can and will. Remember that.

"Do you keep slate boards in your home, Axel?" asked Councilman Stefan. "How do you manage all that you have hanging over your head?"

"I do it just as I just showed you and even as we have discussed. The difference is that I do it in my head. The gods have both blessed and cursed me with a perfect memory."

The councilman's mouth slowly opened, and his eyes widened in unfeigned amazement. Axel simply held up his palms to his chest with thumbs out and returned a "that's the way it is" grin.

"Lastly, everyone," Axel said in a loud voice as he turned to the group, "you need to realize that you aren't in this alone. You need to work with the dragon high council to mutually solve each other's problems."

One councilman raised his hand and said, "But the dragons will have their priorities and we will have ours!"

"Of course, isn't that wonderful? Just as two businessmen come together to build something big that neither could do on his own, you will have an opportunity to try some give and take, find where you have common interests, and work out differences. You are partners now with the dragons! You will live or die together! What's more, you will make beautiful friends in the process. All I ask is that you be polite, which I doubt will be a problem when you are working with someone twenty times your size.

"Notice also I said *someone*. I don't know how many of you got to work closely with a dragon during the fire. If you did, great. If not, you will quickly discover that dragons aren't beasts. They are every bit as intelligent as we are and, in many cases, more so. They will readily know if you are being deceitful or hiding something. But, in return, they will be totally honest with you.

"Some of the dragons are flying down to Jarrad's place at high Sunstar. Why don't you come out and meet them?"

That evening, Axel and Eleth attended Alasha's funeral. Most citizens of Tarfal and many from Mikell were there, along with some members of the Dragon High Council. Afterward, a good number of the townsfolk stayed to meet the dragon representatives; some out of curiosity, a good many out of a desire to know them better, and some to renew acquaintances with friends made during the fire.

Afterward, Eleth and Axel went back to Jarrad's to get ready for the flight north.

***

The two men, standing before the desk of King's High Commander Liard Beorg, commanded the Special Missions Force, the most vicious killers in the powerful Kingdom of Sanara, but their bodies shook in deadly fear of the man behind that desk.

High Commander Beorg slammed his fist on his desk, and even the floor trembled. "How can you tell me that six of our finest flying officers and dragons have been defeated in battle, right in the middle of the kingdom?" He shouted the last part of that sentence so loud, no one in the building could have missed it.

"The fact that these battles occurred in the middle of the kingdom, goes against the concept that this is a foul plan of either Kolodra or Mandara. But they are the only ones capable of assembling the resources to accomplish this kind of attack. All six of our dragons were on simple missions to check out sightings of a few dragons flying at night in that area.

"Our dragons don't lose battles! To have six dragons fail to return from their missions and only two of their bodies be found is unimaginable unless they were ambushed! That's what we must assume. They were ambushed, probably to gain control over their rider's Bechars, and apparently successfully.

"There is mischief here. Your failures have attracted the attention of Adjutant Brasa. He wants answers, and you better find them by the time I next see you, or he'll have all of us broken and mucking out dragon stables for the rest of our lives!"

The two regional commanders normally detested each other, but their joint heads were on the block, so they cooperated. They divided the country near the Ibisen River into squares and sent their dragons out in search patterns. Within three days they had something to report to their superior.

"So, what are your conclusions?" the High Commander said with a straight face.

"While there is much room for conjecture, we have concluded that, based on the locations of the deceased dragons and the numbers of missing dragons, this enemy has, somehow mastered the ability to see, and thereby fly, at night. Their purpose appears to be striking any of our dragons venturing forth at night, using the element of surprise. They are obviously sending massive numbers to attack straight at our flying officers from the cover of darkness and with the purpose of dismounting them. Since they can see in the dark, the officer's Bechars are retrieved from their bodies, and those dragons not killed are stolen. There has also been speculation that this enemy force is seeking to locate the position of the King's Breeding Reserve."

High Commander Beorg nodded his head. "The evidence does seem to support your conclusions. Do you have any recommendations?"

"Our night flights," said the spokesman of the two, "are limited to when we can use the light from Kivan to our advantage. Obviously, extreme care should be exercised while flying at night, including limiting flights to essential purposes. We might want to consider enlarging the size of our night flights and increasing night surveillance searches for the enemy, especially around sensitive sites, such as the dragon reserves. Finally, we should put more effort into figuring out how their night flights are made possible."

"Your conclusions are sound," said the High Commander, "at least, based on the limited information we have at hand. I can't help but think there is some key element of information that we are missing, which could put this whole problem into perspective for us. For now, let's act on what you have, but be alert for something more.

"I have been given strict orders that nothing like this will happen again, or Brasa will put us all on the block."

High Commander Beorg turned to the commander of the Southern Special Action Force and asked, "What was the result of your agents' activity in the Upper Mysura Valley?"

"I'm afraid, sir, the attempt failed."

"Failed? What do you mean failed?"

"I mean that our agents were able to start the fire near the rim as planned. The fire burned its way half the distance up the Valley, destroying everything in its path, and then it stopped."

"Indeed? Our surveys said that a fire there would turn everything in the valley into black dust! What kept it from wiping out that miserable pair of settlements?"

"The flying officer, who performed the post-action survey, reported there is a barely visible bog just beyond the center of the valley that stretches all the way from the river on the south to the Atabu Escarpment on the north. Before the fire, it probably couldn't have been seen at all from the angle of our observation dragons. The bog acted as a fire break and stopped the fire dead."

"Archos' bloody excrement! Shouted the High Commander. Both Brasa and Deroth are going to be livid when they hear the news."

"Pardon me, sir," said the Northern Group Commander. "I am not as familiar with the Southern part of the realm as I am with the north. Why is the king so angry with this particular group of people?"

"They are mostly refugees from the old kingdom of Locarno and their descendants. Locarno was the southern kingdom we conquered twenty-six years ago. As such, those people are a center of anti-imperial sentiment. The king is also angry because they have become too expert at avoiding payment of their taxes and because they attacked a small troop of his cavalry with rocks and clubs when the soldiers were only performing their duty. What's more, they drove away the king's magister for the valley, along with his detachment of ten men. Now, His Highness wants to make an example of the valley!"

"What happens next?" asked the Southern Group Commander, with his eyes raised.

"I assume the king will eventually finish off what the gods have failed to accomplish."

Chapter Twenty

A CHANGE OF SCENERY

Shortly after dark, two dragons took off from the Dragon Meadow behind Jarrad's cottage. Since the dragons were invisible, all that could be seen, from the air or ground, were two small, dark, ragged bundles soaring across a dark night. The first Kivans of winter were upon them, but Axel and Eleth were dressed to take the cold air that streamed into their faces. They both wore multiple layers, covered by heavy, hooded cloaks and scarves, which they drew high across their faces, such that only their eyes could be seen. Their hands were protected by woolen gloves covered with large leather mittens. Fortunately, the tough hide of the dragons needed no extra protection.

The little flight of dragons made two rest stops before finally reaching the previously used stopover location near the Ibisen River. There, the dragons searched for the softest ground in the area to settle in, while the two young people rolled out blankets and tried to get as much sleep as they could during the day, which proved to be clear and warm once the morning had passed.

Once the skies darkened, the flight was off again, stopping twice for rests before descending in the final dark of the night to get a thorough look all around Clara's cottage. They readily noticed a new addition to Clara's property. There was some kind of large wooden awning or extended roof attached to the bigger outbuilding in the back, and a skell was grazing in a new paddock next to the awning. Shaddra and Langa also made a circular check around the cottage to make certain that no king's men were hiding in the now, mostly leafless forest, looking for visitors. No warning call in the dragon language was made since there would be no one in the cottage to hear it.

When everything seemed to appear safe, the dragons glided into the campsite. Eleth and Axel dismounted and sneaked, more than walked, down to Clara's cottage. Forty strides from the door, Axel dropped behind some bracken and waited where he could keep an eye on Eleth, his bow at the ready.

Eleth, meanwhile, slowly approached the door, opened it carefully, and looked inside. She disappeared for a moment but came back out within a minute and waved to Axel.

"Looks like nobody's at home," she said, "and there is no indication as to where they may have gone. I'm worried. It's too early for Clara to have gone anywhere."

Axel looked around at his surroundings, running his tongue behind his lower lip as he did. "I don't think we have any choice but to wait for them," he said, looking over at Eleth. Why don't you see if you can scratch up some breakfast and I'll go see to the dragons?"

"Keep your eyes open, Axel. There's something strange about this."

Axel went around behind the house and stepped down into the cold storage room. Some packages of meat still remained and were reasonably fresh. He trundled two of the larger packages under his arms and marched off to the campsite. The dragons were waiting, eager for news, and were very disappointed to learn that Clara was not at home. They were, however, eager for breakfast.

"Let me take off your saddles," Axel said, "and when you are through with breakfast, perhaps you can look around; maybe see if there's anything important out there. There is a chance I will have some news for you when you get back."

To keep the saddles out of the weather, Axel carried them back to the cottage and stored them in the outbuilding in back. In so doing, he checked over the new awning. Large and well-constructed of wood and overlapping shingles, it extended out along the entire fifteen-stride length of the outbuilding. The awning's roof stood five strides high at its peak and slanted to permit water to run off and keep whatever was to be stored there protected from the weather. Created to cover the entire western side of the outbuilding, extending out roughly ten strides from the building wall, it had open sides that could be covered with canvas curtains hung from strong steel hooks. A wooden table and half a dozen stacking chairs were also set up against the wall to shield them from the elements. Axel wondered what the purpose for this strange addition could be but came up with no solution. When he went inside and told Eleth about it, she was just as surprised as he and had no idea as to how it might be used.

An orai later, the front door opened, and in walked Clara and Jarrad. They were holding hands.

"Hey, we were worried about you two," exclaimed Axel, with a frown. "Where have you been?"

Eleth looked down at their hands and said, with a big smile on her face, "I think our friends have been busy."

"Oh, I was showing Jarrad the Dremlin cliffs," Clara said with a smile, even bigger than the one worn by Eleth. "We went to see the sunrise over the ocean. But that led to other things." She paused for a moment and said, "Jarrad just asked me to marry him, and I accepted."

Eleth gave a delighted gasp. "That is absolutely wonderful!"

Axel was stunned, though he managed to mutter, "Yes, wonderful, but... you live two hundred fifty tondrins away from each other."

"That," said Jarrad, "is something we need to discuss."

"What do you mean by that?"

Jarrad motioned toward the chairs in the kitchen. "Maybe we all better sit down at the table."

"First, have you eaten?" asked Eleth, who was carrying some plates.

"Jarrad and I ate early this morning," answered Clara.

"Okay," said Eleth. "You talk; we will eat."

Clara licked her lips and said, "We got word in the coops the other day that the big move will take place in the mid-season of growth. It's still just a rumor, but everyone seems to think this is really it. The mothers in the coops are very worried, and they are begging me to do something to set them free before that happens."

"The only way that will take place," Jarrad said, "is if the Free Fragons stage a massive raid on the coops. Do you think that we can get them to do that? Maybe some of the people in the Valley would be willing to help?"

Axel put his fork down on the plate and looked over at Jarrad. He tightened his lips and lowered his head without losing eye contact. "I'm... afraid... that..." Axel said, pronouncing his words very slowly and maintaining a very serious look on his face, "we are way ahead of you!" He ended his sentence loudly and with a big grin plastered across his face.

"What! Okay, okay! Something has been going on back home that I don't know about. What have you got up your sleeve?"

"First, let me tell you what's been happening in the Valley. After that, I'll tell you about the Colony." Axel proceeded to summarize of events over the last few days and how they had resulted in the humans of the Valley becoming allies with the dragons of the Colony.

"I've long known about the friction between the Valley and the king's government. But now, you mean to say that the Valley is in danger of attack like Frithden?" asked Jarrad in all seriousness.

"I'm afraid that's the consensus, both on the part of the Community Council and the dragons of the Colony. It's what led to their alliance. The dragons will help in the defense of the towns and the towns will help in the raid against the Breeding Coops. We just need some plans to start working on."

"That's a lot of planning to do."

Here, Eleth interrupted, asking, "Just when and where do you plan on having this wedding?"

Jarrad smiled at Clara and clasped her hand over the table. "It all depends on when the Breeding Coops raid is to take place and how successful it is."

"It looks like the raid on the coops has to be successful," said Eleth, "or we are all going to be in grave trouble."

"Yes," said Axel, "it means I'm going to have to build my own house."

Everyone laughed at his remark.

"Now," Axel continued, "you need to tell us about this new awning out in the back. Does it have something to do with dragons?"

"Oh, yes, the awning." Jarrad looked over at Clara. "It seems that Clara and I got to talking about the fact that we don't have a place where we can get together with any of the dragons to make plans. Eleth's medicine made me better quickly. Consequently, I thought I would put myself to good use. I hiked down to Kelby to buy some materials, a wagon, and a skell."

Eleth looked shocked. "You hiked where?"

"Honestly, Eleth, I was feeling so good, and we didn't want to provoke the curiosity of the Coopers, so I decided to walk down to Kelby. Anyway, I bought a small wagon and a skell, plus some construction materials, and I hired a few people to come up here to build the extended roof. I even made some of your new glue and put a thick coat all over to prevent leaking. Now, we have a place where the four of us can meet with Shaddra and Langa and any other dragons, of reasonable size, that happen to pay us a visit. The best part is that, from the air, the awning looks like it was put there only to protect the wagon and the skell."

"By reasonable size, you mean messenger dragons, I gather," Axel said.

"We have room in the yard for two or three larger dragons to stand outside of the shelter with their heads inside and still be hidden from the road by a thick strand of trees. I do have to admit we should only meet at night if there are larger dragons present. We wouldn't want to have them seen by enemy dragonriders flying overhead.

"This is great! I'm sure Shaddra and Langa have very much felt left out of our discussions," Axel said. "I asked them to look around and see if there are any potential dangers about. But they may be back by now. Should we have them come down and join us?"

All agreed to the suggestion and, after a brief discussion, decided to call the new construction "Clara's Meeting Place."

While Axel was gone, everyone else moved out to the awning. "Look at these support beams," Jarrad said to Eleth, with a strong element of pride in his voice. "No windstorm is going to blow the awning away, and no winter storm is going to bring it down.

"Now, watch this demonstration," he said to everyone around the table. He opened an almost hidden, wide door to expose a large wood stove, set just inside. This stove looks like it was placed to warm up the outbuilding, but by simply opening the door and setting the awnings on their hooks, it is possible to warm up the Meeting Place. He went into the outbuilding and carried out three large and thick candles with multiple wicks. He hung them from hooks on the support beams, lit them, and set glass chimneys over them. These will make certain we have ample light."

Axel returned in minutes, followed closely by two dragons. The humans sat in the chairs around the table, while the dragons found comfortable spots under the awning to rest with their heads close to the table. "I've summarized to Shaddra and Langa everything we've spoken about so far," Axel said. "But they seem to be more interested in wedding plans than anything else right now. Perhaps Clara ought to fill them in before we go any further."

"Ten minutes later, all the females looked, as one, over to the menfolk, indicating that it was time to move on."

"If we are ready to talk about non-marital issues," Axel said with a brief cough, "let's talk first about the Coops. There are a number of very significant issues that need to be addressed."

"Very well," Jarrad said. "But there are bound to be many points made, and we should record them. Clara, do you have ink, quill, and paper?"

"Yes, I'll be right back with it."

"All right, Axel," said Jarrad, when the supplies were handed to him, "you talk, and I'll write."

Actually," Axel said, "I think Eleth should do the talking."

"What me?" Eleth cried out in total astonishment.

"Yes, you. It's about time you started pulling your weight around here."

"You oaf!" Eleth blurted out. "Who put you in charge of everything?" She stood up and, looking like she was going to do some physical harm to Axel, she rushed around the table trying to get within striking range of the boy. "I'll show you what I *can* do!" she cried as she ran.

Both Jarrad and Clara stood and rushed to intercede, but not quickly enough. Eleth came upon Axel's chair and put up an arm ready to swing when she suddenly rested it on Axel's shoulder and gave him a quick kiss on the forehead.

"You know," Eleth said, "I think Axel is perfectly correct. It's about time I, uh, what did you say, Axel? Oh, yes, it's time I started pulling my weight around here."

Clara looked curiously at Jarrad. Then she looked at Eleth, who still stood at Axel's right shoulder.

Eleth broke out in a laugh that was quickly picked up by Axel. Jarrad and Clara both smiled weakly in their direction until Axel said, "Eleth and I talked about the raid on the Breeding Coops on the way up here. It became quite clear that Eleth is in the best position to plan that task, despite her separation from the Valley and the Free Colony; she is here in the center of the Breeding Coops and knows all about them. Hope you don't mind the little joke we played on you two. The dragons were already in on it."

Jarrad ran his hand through his hair and started shaking his head. But Clara put on a big smile and said, "That's the best joke anyone has put over on me in memory. But I've forgotten so much, lately, that I could be wrong."

"Ah, yes, Clara," said Eleth. "You're as sharp as a sengel's claw and always will be."

Once everyone was properly seated, Eleth said, "Now, is it all right if I start by summarizing the basic issues? We can, then, proceed to determine what we know about each one."

No one objected to this approach.

"The first question is how we should deal with the guards. The second is how we find the jewels for the hens so that they can become free. The third issue, and perhaps the biggest, is how do we transport a number of large dragons that cannot fly, along with any younglings or eggs that go with them?

"Clara, what can you tell us about the guards?" Eleth asked.

"There are three shifts of twenty guards each. Five are dragonriders, who work only the day shifts. They are armed with crossbows, swords, knives, and, sometimes, axes. Each shift eats a meal in the common room immediately prior to their shiftwork, after which they separate out to the various gates. Guards rarely come into the coops themselves.

"Coopers bear responsibility for security within the coops, in addition to seeing to the daily needs of the dragons. Senior Coopers do little of the actual manual labor, such as providing feed, cleaning stalls, bathing the dragons, and so on. The senior coopers are like overseers and often act more like guards, but they are never armed with anything more than a club.

"Lastly, there are the midwives, who are responsible for taking care of the dragons during the time just before egg laying and while the young remain with their mothers. All midwives report to me."

"Who prepares the food for the guards?" Axel asked.

"It's prepared by the wives of some of the Coopers who live nearby. They have special wagons and containers that they use to bring the food in through the main gate."

"Is there some kind of a room where coopers and midwives could be locked up for a time after we leave?" asked Jarrad.

"There is a large storage room with only one door, but it doesn't have a lock. The door does open outward, however, and could be blocked by something large and heavy."

"I have all that down," Jarrad said. "That's enough on question number one for now. We need time to think about this. Let's switch to question number two. Eleth, you said that the second item involves finding the Bechars for the breeding hens."

"Yes, the jewels. The thing is that we cannot free the hens unless we can find their Bechars. I assume they are all kept together somewhere within the coops, but where?"

"I know the answer to that one," Clara said with a sigh. "They are kept under lock and key in the main guard room, near the front gate."

"That and the fact that all the dragonriders will be wearing their own Bechars," said Jarrad, with a small shake of his head, "should be all that we need to mention, right now, about the jewels."

"One question," said Langa. "Do you think a dragon could break into this guard room and, if so, could that dragon break open the container housing the jewels?"

Clara shook her head. "I'm afraid I don't know. I have never seen the guard room, nor the box that contains the jewels."

Jarrad looked over at Eleth. "Okay, so moving on, the last question was transportation. Can you break it down any better than what you said so far?"

"The problems here are easy to describe but difficult to find solutions to. First, none of the hens in the coops have flown in years, if ever. The muscles in their wings and legs will have atrophied to practically nothing. That means they won't be able to fly unless we can find a way to exercise their wings for orais every day and for at least a Kivan or more before the journey. They won't even be able to walk unless we can have them exercise their legs. Second, we have the draft dragon problem again, but this time with mothers who are bigger than any other type of dragon. Third, if there are any younglings or eggs, we won't be able to guarantee their safety on the journey."

Jarrad rested his chin on the fingers of one hand and spoke as if reading his thoughts out loud: "With the kind of load that needs to be transported, we can forget about flying them all out. We'll have to use some form of ground transportation."

"Oh, I can just see that happening," said an exasperated Axel.

"I wouldn't suggest ruling out the improbable in this case. But it's our only alternative to the impossible."

"All right, have it your way. How do we go about transporting nearly a hundred dragons on the ground when they can't walk?"

Jarrad ran a hand through his hair. "I don't know how. But I know where to start the process that will eventually lead to knowing how."

"And where is that?"

"Maps!" he said with a satisfied smile on his face. "Maps tell us what the ground looks like and much more. Are there any maps of this area?"

Clara affirmed that she doubted even the existence of rudimentary maps for this area, let alone all the way over to the Mysura Valley. "We might be able to locate a map or two of the area between here and the escarpment, but the western side of the kingdom is so lightly settled," she said. "I doubt any serious effort to make maps has ever been undertaken."

"Then, I guess we'll have to make them. Shaddra, will the dragons help me and others I recruit to make maps?"

"I'm afraid I don't even know what a map is. Dragons travel using our memories as guides. But we will be glad to help if it is important."

"It is important, very important. Remember when Axel drew a diagram representing the Upper Mysura Valley on the ground near my house?" Shaddra nodded her head. "That was a map. But we need maps covering more areas and all on paper so more people and dragons can look at them. We can discuss the process of creating the maps later, however."

"What else should we know right now?" he asked, turning to Eleth.

"There are a few daunting questions that are still big and needing answers, such as how are we going to break into the Breeding Coops in the first place."

Jarrad looked at Axel and Eleth, seeing how drooping eyelids betrayed their physical condition. He drummed his fingers on the table and said, "You two younglings and the dragons, too, need some sleep or you won't be any help whatsoever in planning this mission. Go get some rest. We'll talk about it again in the afternoon or the evening."

"I guess you are right there," said Eleth.

Axel waved his hand as he stood. "No dispute from me. We'll see you again in a few orais."

The dragons bowed their heads briefly and went back to the campsite for their rest.

***

Everyone gathered again under the awning at mid-afternoon to continue discussions.

Langa opened the discussions with a surprise. "Eleth was talking to Konnor on the flight down to Tarfal and discussed the idea that, if we are going to raid one of the king's reserves, why stop there? I would like to add my opinion that including the other reserves is more than a desirable thing—it is a necessary thing. If we cannot significantly increase the number of dragons in the Colony soon, the king will eventually discover our existence and gradually eliminate us until we become extinct. The same may be said about the population of the Mysura Valley; only their end may come all the sooner without the protection of a sufficient number of dragons."

"Wow!" Jarrad said, with his eyes wide. "That just changed things a lot. But Langa has a point."

Langa continued by saying, "There is little difference in what must be done if we were to raid the Reserve for Young Dragons and the King's Cadet Dragon

Reserve, in addition to the King's Reserve for Dragon Breeding. They are all close together; they have roughly the same kind of protection schemes; no one would be expecting them all to be raided at the same time; the king's dragon forces available for tracking down the escapees would be spread all the thinner; and the prospective return to us, in terms of freed dragons, would be tripled."

"Since we're on the subject, now," Eleth interjected, "just what would change?"

"Let's see," said Axel, pursing his lips, "first we would have to triple the number of dragons and humans that are involved. We know very little about the other two reserves, so we must increase our spying operations. Perhaps we could set up three separate joint operating teams. Each team would have both dragons and humans working together on just their one assigned reserve. There ought to be many crossover ideas that could be shared between the teams, but each team would concentrate on resolving specific problems relating to its own particular assignment."

Axel heard Shaddra grinding her teeth, which is something special when the one grinding her teeth is a dragon. "Yes, Shaddra, I believe you have something to say."

"Before we can even think about raiding any of the reserves, we must address the one problem that everyone seems to be ignoring. In the Breeding Reserve, you'll have at least a hundred mother dragons who cannot fly, plus their hatchlings and eggs. In the Special Reserve for Young Dragons, you'll have, roughly, a hundred young males and females who have not yet even fledged, and in the Reserve for Young Dragons, assuming you were able to crush all of their Bechars, perhaps another hundred, all of whom will be within their first year after fledging. Yes, they can fly, but only for short distances before needing a rest, and then it would be like herding snakes because they would all have the confusion caused by just coming out of slavery."

"You are quite correct, Shaddra," said Axel. "Every one of those issues will need to be addressed. Maybe we ought to have one team set up to work on that issue alone. Fortunately, we still have nearly three seasons before actions to resolve them must be implemented. We will also have the option, depending on conditions at the time, to strike at fewer than all three at one time. One more benefit is that, back home, we will be able to bring in other minds, both dragon and human, to help us find potential resolutions to each.

"Right now," Axel continued, "our task centers more on identifying the problems and starting the process going that, hopefully, will come up with the answers we need."

***

Axel ran his hand through his hair and asked, "Are there any other thoughts regarding possible raids against the Dragons Reserves?"

There were none.

"Then, I propose we switch over to the other side of this partnership, and that is the protection of the towns of Tarfal and Mikell from the king's forces. I have a feeling this may get more complicated than the first part of our discussion, and *that* is saying something."

"What do you mean?" asked Eleth. "You have your fireproof paint, and the town's people are armed with bows. Meanwhile, the Free Fragons are organizing to fight off any air attack. Isn't that right?"

Axel rubbed his chin and said, "You are correct that those are our first lines of defense against a dragon attack. But the king's dragons are trained to fight on land, too. They could destroy the towns without ever resorting to fire. Also, supposing that we win that battle, what is the king going to do? Leave us in peace?"

Jarrad took a turn to express his thoughts. "If the king loses the dragon battle, it will turn into a humiliation that he could not stand. What if word of the king's attack and defeat leaks out to other parts of the kingdom? He could face uprisings in other places. He would be considered a weak leader, and those under him may seek to overthrow him in favor of someone stronger. Face it, he won't quit. Most likely he would send cavalry and infantry up the road from the Lower Mysura Valley."

"That is a long, narrow road," said Langa, "which climbs steep switchbacks to the top of the Rim. That way would be dangerous for attackers."

"In that, you are right," said Jarrad. "There are dozens of defensible places that could be used to turn back an army many times the size of whatever force the king might send. And I doubt any of the king's forces know about the road to Blatten. That's a larger town located on a tributary of the Ibisen River in the valley just north of the Mysura. We have excellent relations with them, and they are much of the same mind as us when it comes to King Deroth. There is a secret pathway connecting the two valleys together, but it's a narrow road that is not generally open during the winter.

"Still, the king has other weapons. First, Axel says there are twenty-one children of Valley citizens remaining in the king's forces. They could be used as hostages or even worse. It doesn't take much thought to imagine what he could do with and to them.

"We must find a way to withdraw these men and women in a timely way. I say timely, because a mass desertion of soldiers originating from the Valley will likely lead to an attack, but if we don't get them away before an attack, their lives won't be worth much, either."

Axel took a deep breath and exhaled slowly. "I think we are going to need another special committee."

"The king has one more weapon that he could use," said Jarrad. "He could blockade the Valley and lay siege. Even as we may do things to keep him out, he could do things to keep us in and everybody else out. Our mines, lumber mills, and farms would have nowhere to sell their products except to ourselves or what little we could carry northward over the mountains on the road to Blatten. There wouldn't be enough trade to keep our businesses operating. We do not produce enough food on our farms to feed the town throughout the year, nor enough finished ellam wool to keep ourselves clothed."

"But what about the Free Dragons?" Clara asked.

"The Free Dragons," said Jarrad, "can become extremely useful in many ways. But they cannot bring in the food we need nor carry out iron or lumber to sell."

There were tears in Eleth's eyes as she said, "I was there for only two days, but I saw something in those people that I haven't seen anywhere else. They have strength and confidence in themselves, and they have become close to the dragons—closer than anyone ever, save those of us under this awning. What you are saying, then, is that the Valley doesn't have a chance?"

Tears were beginning to form in Axel's own eyes. "I guess that is the way it's going to b..."

The world around Axel dissolved into luminous mist. For a moment, he could see nothing but swirling light; then, shapes emerged. Eleth appeared, sunlight glancing off her hair just as he liked it, and beside him sat Jarrad. But Jarrad hadn't moved from… from where?

The mist faded, revealing the three of them still seated in their chairs, but their surroundings had transformed. Gone were their friends, the table, and the sheltering outbuilding. Now, their chairs rested on a gravel bank beside a wide, rushing river. Eleth's hand gripped Axel's tightly, her eyes wide as she took in the scene. Axel's vision blurred; he tried to remember something that felt impossibly distant. Only Jarrad seemed calm.

"Relax," Jarrad said quietly. "We are experiencing a vision like the one I had when I saw the Lady."

"I saw her too, once," Axel replied, voice wavering. "I was a child, and there was a garden… but this feels different."

Around them, the day was bright and warm, as in the middle of the season of growth. Tall mountains enclosed the valley on three sides. Axel recognized familiar peaks, but from an unfamiliar angle, as if seeing his world from a dream. Nothing was cultivated, meaning that the open bottomland near the river was filled with wildflowers and Axel could see songbirds flitting about. Beyond the flowers were forests, dense with lomas, landrins, anyus, and aldans, all intertwined with kitkis, balibis, and sokis.

"I don't see the Lady," Axel whispered. "Shouldn't she be here? This looks like the Mysura Valley, not far from Tarfal."

"That's exactly where we are," said Jarrad, scanning the landscape. "But why? Stay in your chairs. Let's watch; something's about to happen."

Suddenly, the ground seemed to fall away beneath them.

Axel stamped his foot. "Hey, we're rising into the air, but I can still feel the ground!"

"Me too!" Eleth gasped, craning her neck to look down.

Jarrad grunted. "I told you… it's just a vision. We're seeing things as if we're flying, but we're not moving at all."

Axel managed a shaky laugh. "I didn't know a vision could carry three people at once. I could get used to this kind of travel."

"My family had a vision together once," Eleth said, "but the ground definitely didn't move."

Jarrad peered out at the rolling landscape. "Don't jump to conclusions. We don't know what we're being shown."

Axel pointed downward. "There's Tarfal, to the left."

"Maybe," Jarrad said, "but look… we're turning right."

"What if I stood up and walked away?" Axel wondered aloud.

Jarrad chuckled. "No idea. But it'd be interesting to watch."

Axel shook his head. "I'll stay put, thanks."

The vision reversed, lowering them gently back to the riverbank.

"Are we just going back to where we started?" Eleth asked, frowning.

"There's purpose to all this," Jarrad replied. "Let's be patient."

The vision paused, then floated out over the river's widest span. It hovered midstream, slowly rotating in a full circle.

Axel squinted at the water. "It has a rocky bottom. What else are we supposed to see?"

Jarrad leaned forward. "It's shallow here. Look deep into the water. There's never been a ford across the Mysura near Tarfal. But this spot looks crossable for wagons, skells, anything. We'd need a new road, but this could open up the whole far side of the valley."

As the vision completed its turn, it lifted them high above the ground, soaring three hundred strides up.

"Look!" Eleth cried. "We're heading toward that canyon!"

They all saw it now. The vision was taking them up and over a twisting canyon below.

"I know this place," Jarrad said. "Bergama Canyon. See the little river down there? From the other side of the Mysura, you can see those rounded mountains. They look like someone scooped them out with a giant spoon. But the rocks below are sharp-edged. I've explored down there—the canyon's narrow, but the stream's worn the bottom flat."

Axel grinned. "Of course you'd notice that."

The vision kept a straight course, while the canyon below was tortured into many snake-like bends. Ahead, the mountains loomed, forming a high ridge dividing Sanara from the Kingdom of Mandara.

"We're in the Sudwa range now," Jarrad said. "That ridge is the border. With those remote barriers, nobody comes here."

To their surprise, the vision descended instead of climbing over the mountains. It settled at the base of a rocky wall, near a slender stream. It was clearly the Bergama's source.

After a brief pause, the vision slid forward and right, moving around the rock face to reveal a hidden cave.

Eleth blurted, "That opening's way too small for us!"

But the vision pressed on, passing them through solid stone. For a moment, all was darkness. Then they found themselves inside a vast cavern, as large as some of the smaller halls in the Free Colony, with walls twenty strides apart and ceilings twice as high.

Axel and Eleth both had to catch their breath. They glanced at Jarrad, who was now openly stunned.

"This must have been an underground river once," he said, his voice low. "Look at the smooth, gravelly floor. Wide enough for two wagons, maybe more. And that ceiling!"

"What *I'm* wondering is how you can see in the dark, Jarrad," said Eleth.

"It must be the vision," answered Axel. "This is a vision, and what we see in it is not real, but it signifies something that is real."

"Are you saying this cave actually exists?"

"Yes, it's real," responded Jarrad, "but I'm guessing it's not a cave... but a tunnel."

Axel's eyes widened. "A tunnel through the mountains? From Tarfal to Mandara?"

Jarrad blew air from his cheeks. "Exactly. However, the real question is where does it come out?"

The vision carried them along the tunnel at the pace of a running skell. Finally, they burst into daylight. Ahead was a shallow stream with a familiar, pebbly bottom, shaded by dense, unfamiliar forest. Behind, sheer cliffs soared skyward.

Jarrad looked up. "I think we crossed a divide in there. The stream flows down this side now, and we're at a much lower elevation. Look at those trees—some I've never seen before in Sanara."

The vision floated downstream, just above the water, before emerging onto a sheltered cove. A road wound through a band of forest, making its way to the shore. Beyond the cove, they viewed the open sea.

"I think it is obvious that we are in Mandara, but the question is where?"

As if in answer to Jarrad's question, the vision started rising straight up into the air. It stopped at an altitude where the visionaries could see much of the Mandaran coastline for many tondrins. Below, the sea entered into a narrow inlet, perhaps five tondrins wide at its mouth and continuing east for a distance very much comparable to the Mysura Valley in length. A large river entered the inlet at its end, with a small city-sized community lining its banks. There was a succession of widely separated coves lining the inlet all the way to its end. Some of them had piers and docking facilities, and small coastal roads reached out to all of them.

"It's quite clear," Jarrad concluded, "that we are near the north-western border of Mandara. The mountains we just passed through form cliffs, over which no one goes, and this side drops right down to the mouth of an ocean inlet. The port you see way off to the left is Bresci. It is well known as a major source of contraband goods entering and leaving Mandara. King Altrince's representatives turn a blind eye to it because most goods entering the kingdom here are things that cannot be easily found within its borders."

Axel looked perplexed. "But why is there ocean on this side of Mandara?"

"That's one I know," said Eleth. "Mandara is about half the size of Sanara, with most of its territory occupying what's known as the Shanda Peninsula. Surrounded by ocean on three sides, Mandara's only land border lies to the north—primarily adjoining Sanara, with a small section touching Kolodra to the west. To the south of that border, on the western side of the kingdom, is the Bay of Tuvira. The narrow inlet extending eastward is called the Votara Inlet, running roughly parallel to the Sanaran border for some distance.

The largest part of the kingdom lies to the east and south of the inlet—that is, all the land we see on the eastern horizon. Based on this, our current position appears to be roughly halfway west of the central point along the Mandaran-Sanaran border—and almost directly south of Tarfal."

The vision began descending and stopped once it reached ground level. Everything faded, and the three found themselves, again, looking at Clara, Shaddra, and Langa.

***

"That was interesting," said Axel, with a stunned look on his face.

"What do you mean?" asked Shaddra. Are you feeling all right?"

"I'm referring to what just happened."

"What was that? And why was it so interesting? You just stopped in mid-sentence and said, 'That was interesting.'"

"I don't know how to say this any other way than straight out," said Jarrad. "Eleth, Axel and I just had a joint vision about the Mysura Valley, and that vision appears to have solved the problem of any siege of the Valley by the king. It has also created some lesser problems of its own, but we can work on them."

"Okay," Clara said, "for those who have never been blessed by a vision, meaning Shaddra and Langa, would you please explain what a vision is? And for my own benefit also, would you please tell us what you saw?"

An orai later, after descriptions of the vision from each of its participants and after many questions and answers, everyone sat back exhausted in their chairs or on their haunches.

"In summary," Shaddra said, "the people of the Valley can go around a king's siege by making a road and finishing off a tunnel to establish economic relations with the King of Mandara, who is King Deroth's enemy."

"Not exactly, I hope," said Jarrad. "King Altrince of Mandara is every bit of a scoundrel as Deroth. He would work with us all right but stab us in the back at the first occasion where he saw a benefit, especially if it meant gaining more power or wealth for himself. The town of Bresci is a haven for smugglers, and I think the best course for the Valley is for us to set ourselves up as smugglers, too. The longer we can evade Altrince's scrutiny, the better. Once he discovers who we are, he will try to use us for his benefit against Deroth. He might consider something really stupid, like invading Sanara through the tunnel. He might also try to blockade us on that side. Face it, our other plans must be well underway and with successful results before that happens."

Axel fell back against his chair and looked up at the wooden roof above his head. "Oh, my word," he said. "We're going to be placing ourselves into the middle of a war between two kingdoms!"

Jarrad leaned over and set an arm on Axel's shoulder. "Axel, the gods didn't give us that vision to burden our minds with worry. Instead, the gods gave us a way to move forward toward the ultimate goal that you and Eleth, as well as all of us, who believe in freedom, are called to achieve. The old proverb, 'We climb the highest mountain one step at a time,' applies so very much right now. Our eyes have simply been opened as to how we can better reach the top of that mountain."

He turned to the group. "I think this day has been well spent. Perhaps we've reached the point where others need to share in what we have learned, what we've decided, and what we haven't. Two neighboring peoples are waiting for us to do that very thing. After all that has happened and after all that has been discussed, one thing is abundantly clear; neither of those two peoples can accomplish what is most important to them without the help of the other."

"Shaddra or Langa, do you have anything you wish to say at this point?"

The two dragons looked at each other and spoke to each other in their High Language. Then Shaddra took a small step forward. "For nearly thirty years, the Free Colony has done nothing but wait. We didn't even know what we were waiting for. Now that the something is here upon us, we have to admit, stepping into an unknown and dangerous future is intimidating. But doing nothing isn't an option—something has to be done. Axel was the one who gave us the answer: "Do the right thing." He meant the thing we know in our hearts is usually right. If we follow that, we'll end up with the best possible outcome, and we won't be blamed if things do not work out. Langa and I are both of the same mind and support the decisions and directions that came out of this meeting. Now, we must take this information to our peoples, and may the Great Ceragon bless our endeavors."

"In that case," Jarrad announced, "we shall adjourn this meeting, go get some rest, and prepare for the funeral tomorrow morning."

***

In the morning, the dragons carried, first, Jarrad and Clara, and then Eleth and Axel to the ground just below the veps' nest where the large white skeleton of Hukken lay undisturbed. Nothing remained of his body, other than bones, teeth, and claws. Every last scale had been consumed.

Further up the ravine, the remains of those who once opposed him lay exposed to the sunstar. In spite of the bright day, a cool wind penetrated clothing and caused those who were not working to bundle up tightly. Langa and Shaddra selected a spot on a slight rise, protruding level out from the hill. It stretched out far enough from the slope to contain the grave and allow room for those who would be paying respect to stand about it. The two dragons dug the grave, while the two men started carrying the remains up to a place beside that where Hukken would rest. They tried to keep the bones in their natural relationships, but once separated from each other, it was difficult to reform what the gods had made, especially regarding all the small bones.

While they worked, Eleth walked away for a while. When she returned, she patted Axel on the elbow. On turning toward her touch, he saw her holding four bright red jewels in an outstretched hand. He stopped his work for a few minutes to find some rocks he could use to smash the two Bechars. Once the task was completed, he held two sparkling white Minqars in his hand for Eleth to see. "Because of you and Hukken," he said, "no other dragons will ever wear these. But a great sacrifice was made to do that." He pocketed the two white jewels, gave her hand a squeeze and rejoined Jarrad at the gravesite.

As the last bones were being brought up, Eleth looked out over the scene from the hill. Below her was an open field of bracken. It looked dull and gray at that moment, but she knew, come spring, there would be green grasses, a broad variety of wildflowers out there, and a leafy green covering on that bracken. A scattering of brown and grey broad-leafed trees framed a view of the ocean on the other side of the field. She knew that between those trees and the sea would be a giant leap off towering cliffs.

This was a fitting place for Hukken's resting place, she thought. It suited his peaceful personality yet honored his righteous anger.

Hukken's bones were carefully laid into the grave. Again, they tried to maintain some sense of integrity to their order but were greatly restrained by the dirt walls. After Jarrad and Axel finished, they climbed out and joined their friends in a reverent manner. The wind seemed to hush, and the world went silent until Shaddra began to sing. Langa quickly joined in.

None of the humans present understood any words in the song, but the feelings it invoked went straight to the heart. The song continued for five minutes or so and then softly came to an end.

Shaddra, then, stepped forward and spoke, saying, "We Free Dragons have never really known death. Yes, we know it will come to us all at some time, but apart from the burials in Frithden last year and the burial of Kulek's rider not so long ago, none of us had ever needed to participate in any kind of burial service, let alone one of our own. So we discussed the matter and decided we want to seek your advice as to how we, as dragons, should proceed.

Jarrad looked down at the remains of one who had been his friend for nearly thirty years and said, "'According to human traditions, burial services are intended to make a home for the remains of individuals after their spirits have returned to the gods who made their physical bodies. The individuals no longer care about this world, but their friends and loved ones do. For this reason, we gather at gravesides to honor those who have departed and to offer comfort to those left behind. We share stories and memories of our loved ones—reminding ourselves that, although they are no longer with us, they will forever remain in our hearts. This sacred space becomes a place where we say our final goodbyes, holding onto hope that we will reunite again in the presence of our gods.'"

Shaddra nodded her head and turned to face the whole group. "In that case, I would like to tell you what I loved about my friend Hukken..."

Everyone in the circle about the grave took a turn speaking, even as did Shaddra. The time was taken up with some laughs, some tears, and, when it was over, more than anything, everyone there felt loved.

***

Back at the cottage, the group separated. The dragons returned to the clearing to get some rest before the flight home, which would begin as soon as the sunstar could no longer be seen. Clara and Jarrad went for a walk, not wanting to waste these last precious minutes together. Eleth caught Axel's gaze, which indicated that she also wanted to go for a walk. Axel readily agreed. Somehow, though neither one initiated it, their hands clasped together.

Once more, they managed to find themselves perched atop the rocky throne with a view of Dremlin Bay's cliffs. They snuggled close and wrapped their cloaks about them such that they could hold both of each other's hands.

"How long will it be before I see you again," Eleth asked.

"It's hard to say. We'll continue sending the messenger dragons as regularly as possible. Many things are going to be happening in the Valley, in the Free Colony and, here, with you and Clara. We must stay in communication and keep everyone updated. Who knows, perhaps I could arrange to catch a ride every now and then. I imagine Jarrad is thinking the same thing."

"Clara and I need to bring our dragons down to the Colony, and soon."

"Oh, so they are your dragons now and not the king's."

Eleth smiled and said, "You know they have never rightfully belonged to the king. He has taken what was never his to take."

"You realize that you must be the leading figure in the raid on the Coops."

"I still don't know how I can manage a raid when everyone participating is two-hundred-fifty tondrins away."

"The dragons of the Free Colony are going to be doing this raid blind without you. The humans participating are likely to die one way or another unless you can show them where to go and when. You are the one that needs to plan the raid, step by step, and show the rest of us the way. It may even be best if you come down to Tarfal more than once before the raid to get to know your team, have them get to know you, and finalize roles with all of the participants."

"But I've never done anything like this before! I have no training in this kind of thing!"

"Eleth, you were born with all the tools you will need in your very blood. I can tell you that based on my own experience. As I have said before, you and I are the same, except for some ways that I have truly begun to appreciate."

Eleth blushed and squeezed one of his hands. Their hands and arms were so intertwined that she wondered whether Axel could tell which of her hands did that.

"Okay, then," she said softly, "what do I do in this role?" she asked.

"I'd suggest that you prepare a map, maybe even multiple maps, of the complete layout of the caverns, which embody the Coops. Each map would be made to emphasize different things. The first map might show, as accurately as you can, the positions where guards and master coopers tend to be stationed. Mark where the gates, checkpoints, storage rooms, stairways, and everything else that could have value are found. Prepare a map to show routines for changing of the guards and routes they follow, both inside and outside the caverns. Another document would show when and where food is served for the soldiers, staff, and dragons. You might make a document to list the locations of any nearby military or police forces and routes that a raiding force may find desirable to follow. Use your dragon mind to record everything that might be important and transfer it to paper when you can.

"You might consider making two copies of everything, so you'll have one to keep and one to send down to Tarfal. Finally, don't store these documents in the house or any of the outbuildings. Find a safe and protected place in the forest. If any of these documents are found by the king's men or even discovered by another member of the Breeding Coops' staff, it will most certainly mean a very unpleasant death.

"You have gifts, Eleth—gifts granted by the gods to help you in this work. You can see and hear better than anyone else there. You may have other talents you haven't discovered yet. In the end, I think you're the best person to plan this operation and probably even lead it."

"Lead it?"

"Eleth, you were born to be a leader, as much in your life already has shown. You haven't yet had a chance to show all your talents, but believe me, they're there, and you'll need them."

"That just made my day," she said, half-laughing. "How is it that you know all of this stuff?"

"I guess I've been thinking about it, or at least things like it, for some time. I've been working on plans, some wild and some real, ever since the day my family was killed. Jarrad taught me the importance of gathering information. The most important thing I've learned is that nothing can be accomplished without knowing your enemy—knowing everything you can. Then you break the task into manageable pieces and work on them one at a time. Gathering that information is tedious and dangerous, but it's the foundation for everything that follows."

"Do I have to think about it today?"

"I see no reason for that."

"Good. So, hold me a little tighter and shut up."

Chapter Twenty-One

PREPARATIONS

The trip down to Jarrad's cottage was cold and uneventful. The dragons landed in the very early morning orais, so Jarrad and Axel had a quick meal and went straight to bed. But Jarrad woke Axel at High sunstar and said, "Something is wrong."

"What do you mean?"

"Not one of our employees is here and neither are your two apprentices."

"I guess we go into Tarfal prepared for the worst."

Axel quickly dressed, grabbed his weapons, and joined Jarrad, who had the skells ready.

When they neared the town, Axel had to look carefully to be certain it was Tarfal. A significant number of the houses and buildings now gleamed in the vivid colors he had come to associate with his bows. Some structures were even more striking, adorned with fresh window boxes overflowing with various winter-blooming flowers that thrived in this southern climate.

People were at work everywhere, painting houses and constructing things on roofs. Axel was particularly curious about the new structures on the rooftops.

The two had hardly gotten as far as the third street in the town when Bardin rode up hard.

"It's about time you got back here!" Bardin said in a chastising tone. "While you two have been on vacation, we've been working hard."

"What vacation?" Axel called back, "And how did you know we were here?"

"The lookouts spotted you coming in last night, and again when you left the house just now," Bardin said. "We know what's happening almost anywhere in the Valley and a lot of places out of it."

Jarrad frowned. "Lookouts? Who organized all this?"

"We have sentry dragons providing top cover for all air approaches to the Valley. In addition, we have spotters in strategic places along the sides of the

Valley. The ones on the ground use mirrors and a simple code developed by Fala to pass messages. Councilman Bessen and Licor developed the system, with assistance from the Community Council and the Dragon High Council.

Axel glanced at Bardin. "And where's the Councilman now?"

"Best guess would be he's in the Council Hall."

"And where will we find you and Fala?"

"We'll be in the Square making more batches of paint. It seems like half the populations of the towns are out gathering landrin blossoms, while the other half are either painting buildings or preparing food for the ones who are painting. It's a good thing that landrins bloom repeatedly and throughout most of the year."

"Bardin grinned. "Oh, and I nearly forgot—a group of our best marksmen are down in the fields south of town, training with the dragons."

Axel blinked. "Training? What sort of training?"

"Licor said, 'Our bowmen aren't worth hirvior shit if they can't hit a target as small as a man on the back of a moving dragon.' Would you believe he got together with Ketter and Rook and set up a special target range in one of the fields south of town? They've got dragons pulling targets on long lines behind them for bowmen to shoot at."

Axel shook his head in disbelief. "I'll be a coshil's watering trough."

"Let's meet with the councilman first," said Jarrad, "then you can go out and play with the bowmen."

Axel shot arrows from his eyes at Jarrad. Then, kicking his skell to catch up with his friend, who was already three lengths ahead, he called out, "It appears like the bowmen don't really need me at the moment."

Another surprise waited for them in the Council Hall. They found the entire town council gathered and standing as the two walked in. Word of their arrival had apparently come before them to this place, too.

Three large slate boards were set about the room, bearing numbered lists: obviously setting out priorities.

"Please be seated," said Axel, "and I would very much appreciate it if you didn't make the effort again. You are the honored leaders of this town. We're just the temporary help."

This caused a laugh to break out among the group. "We can only wish that we had more such temporary help," said one of the councilmen.

"I see that you have prepared a well-developed list of prioritized tasks," Axed said, pointing to one of the boards. "I note that you placed finding the twenty-one soldiers from the Valley as number one on that list. That shows you have been thinking very much along the same lines as Jarrad and me. What are your thoughts regarding that item?"

"We have a meeting with the families of the twenty-one this evening to discuss possible actions and would like you to take charge of it."

"But how did you know we would be returning today?"

"Oh, we didn't know. We simply decided to hold it on the evening of the day you returned. Word has already gone out."

Axel looked over at Jarrad, who simply shrugged his shoulders. "I must commend you and the whole town on how much progress has occurred over the short time I was away with Jarrad. leaders of this town, and you have taken the lead. You enlisted the help of worthy citizens to share the burden and ensure the completion of all necessary tasks. The fact is that Jarrad and I are only here to assist you, but we will bear whatever burden it takes to do that.

"It's especially pleasing to see that you are working so well with the dragons. Jarrad and I share a similar responsibility to help them. However, we can best assist both the dragons and you by strengthening the precious bond between the Valley and the Free Colony.

"Prominently listed on your prioritization of important questions is one showing that you recognize the danger of King Deroth blockading and laying siege to the Mysura Valley. Of necessity, we must first prepare for and survive Deroth's initial assaults. After that, a siege is almost certain. It's clear; you know we have to prepare for that, too. At first, Jarrad and I were at a total loss about how to address this grave threat. But now, we have discovered a method to defeat King Deroth's attempts to blockade the Valley and even grow stronger as a result.

All at once, the room filled with looks of incredulity and loud questions directed at both Axel and Jarrad. It took several minutes for Axel, who was holding up his arms as a sign to quiet down, before he silenced the councilmen enough for him to continue.

"You all have known Jarrad for more than two dozen years. Over that time, he has constantly been a support and an advisor to you and many other citizens of Tarfal and Mikell. Please, listen to him explain what we've been able to learn over the last while. If you can find him an empty slate board, he will show you how the Valley can counter, if not defeat, the might of Sanara."

After the meeting with the council, Jarrad and Axel took Councilman Lang Privas aside for a private consultation. "Councilman," Jarrad said, "we know that as the owner of the largest lumber mill in the Valley, you have a great many friends and contacts across the kingdom. You've traveled and continue to travel much across the land. We would like to ask you if you might take on a tremendous responsibility on the Valley's behalf."

"Jarrad, stop with the Councilman thing. Please call me Lang. That's enough. Now, what might this heavy responsibility be?"

"We would like to ask you to be the head of a secret committee tasked with getting word of the Valley's plight out to the people of Sanara."

"Why is this committee secret?"

"Because anyone caught by the police even talking about Tarfal and Mikell outside of this valley is likely to be imprisoned or worse."

"How do you propose that this task be undertaken?"

"That is going to be your second task—deciding on a plan."

"All right then, what is the first task?"

"Getting a bunch of people with skills like yours to help."

"What do you see as the ultimate goal of this committee?"

"The goal is to ensure that people throughout the kingdom understand the truth about why the Crown might attack the Valley, rather than believing the King's misinformation. Oh, and do it without getting anyone killed."

"Just so you know," Axel added in. "With the dragons' help, we have ways to get people in and out of the Valley without being observed."

"I'll keep that in mind. At least you decided to give me one of the easy tasks," Lang said with a wink and a smile. "But I like challenges, especially when they are for a cause I believe in."

***

That evening, just as the sunstar set, the relatives of the twenty-one children of the Valley, who remained under the control of the King, met in the Council Hall. The Hall was built as a meeting place for the Community Council but also as a courthouse and a place where citizens could meet to bring up grievances or discuss matters concerning the towns. It was not built to hold large crowds, but tonight, citizens packed the room to its capacity. If the guards had allowed them to pass, many non-relatives would have attended. meeting would be for presenting and approving secret measures to family members only on how to accomplish one crucial task.

Axel began the meeting by saying, "You are all aware of the status of relations between the Valley and the Kingdom of Sanara. You are also aware that the Valley is in danger of attack by forces of the King at any time. We already know that the king's secret police are watching who goes in and out of the Valley.

"Your family members in the military are particularly vulnerable. Many of you have reported that you don't have any idea where your relative is stationed. Others have told us that all letters have ceased coming from your children, apart from a very few, which have literally been secreted out to reach you.

"I would like to give you a warning. Everything that we talk about this evening is secret and must not be shared with anyone, including close family members who don't happen to be with us tonight. Failure to keep these things secret may result in your child or family member being held as a hostage, being tortured, or killed in any of several brutal ways. I hope that makes the situation clear enough for everyone to understand."

The crowd gaped as Axel stepped down. Many had startled or angry looks on their faces. People raised their voices, questioning or claiming that insufficient measures were in place to safeguard their children.

B O N G!

Axel had arranged to have the giant gong, used in the town-wide meetings held in the Market Square, brought into the Council Hall just in case. Here inside the hall, its tremendous retorts echoed off the walls in a nearly deafening manner. Everyone went silent, immediately.

"I'm sorry we had to do that," Axel said to the group, "but we cannot afford to waste time on activities, that do not help the plight of your children. We know you are greatly worried for their safety, and so are we. Now, if you will let us proceed, allow me to introduce Councilwoman Marta Regen to you. As most of you know, she is the mother of Alasha Regen, a soldier whom we buried hardly a sycle ago. If there is anyone who understands your plight, it is she, and she will be leading the effort to save and retrieve your children. From now until the crsis is all over, her sole responsibility is to bring them home alive and well."

The crowd remained hushed and respectful as Councilwoman Regen stepped to the front of the group. "We have a basic plan," she said, "for rescuing every Valley citizen in the King's forces whom we can locate. To achieve this goal, we will need your assistance in locating them, as we can only rescue those we are able to find.

If you can gather every letter or other evidence of any kind you have received from or about them, we will analyze those pieces of information, not just for what was said, but for what kind of paper it was written on and what kind of ink. We'll check registration marks for items that went through the mail, and we'll determine what other hands may have helped in delivering letters that didn't go through the mail. We need you to tell us anything else you can about what kind of facilities they were stationed in, what functions they were trained for, and the names of anyone else whom they may have worked for or with."

"How will knowing the name of someone he worked for help us find him?" someone called out.

"We are making a record of the complete organizational makeup of the King's forces," the Councilwoman said. "We want to know the name of every military unit and the names of every leader in each one. We are sending spies to learn each unit's location, duties, and main assignments. If we know the name of a unit, we can find out where it is stationed. If we know what kind of barracks your relative slept in, it might help us track down where it is. Even things you believe to be unimportant may prove valuable.

"If you gather what you can, we'll take over and do whatever is possible to find them.

"The next thing you must do is write a letter to your children," she said, "asking them about how things are in their lives and to tell you about conditions they work in. Since this letter must be written very carefully, we will provide you with assistance on what you should say."

Another voice called out, "But you said that the secret police are reading all mail from the Valley."

"Indeed, they are. However, we will send these letters by dragon to someone friendly to the Valley, who is living down in the lowlands. Our friend will mail the letters and receive the replies on our behalf. Hopefully, this action will help us trace the locations of more of your children."

A woman in the front waved her hand determinedly. "What if you find them? How are you going to bring them back?"

"We have friends and allies who are able to penetrate even the king's strongholds, if necessary. If it is at all possible to get them out, by the gods, we will do it."

"What happens if you can't get them out?" said another from the crowd.

"Then we will send them into hiding, somewhere in the kingdom. But know this: if we are blockaded by the king's forces and a Valley son or daughter is offered as a bargaining chip, there will be no negotiating to save anyone. The best I can say is we won't let them be tortured to death."

"That's not very reassuring," said a woman, who had tears running down her cheeks."

"That's why we need your help to find them before the Valley is attacked."

Neither Axel nor Marta mentioned a word about the Special Action Force, now organized under Axel himself. The purpose of this force was to conduct activities of a specialized nature outside the Valley and, if necessary, perform small-scale offensive operations wherever needed.

***

The very next day, the Council dispatched a team on skellback to assess the feasibility of constructing a road up Bergama Canyon. Simultaneously, a group of mining and explosives experts flew on dragonback to the Sudwa tunnel, tasked with evaluating the challenges of widening the tunnel's entrance on the Sanara side of the Sudwa Range.

By nightfall, both teams had returned, reporting that a serviceable road could indeed be built—extending up to and across the Mysura River, through Bergama Canyon, and into the tunnel—all within a single sycle. Of course, they noted, ongoing improvements would certainly be necessary to ensure the road's durability and safety for future transport and exploration activities.

"My, my," Councilman Bessen remarked, a broad smile lighting his face. "I believe we should send an exploratory party through the tunnel as soon as the opening is widened and we have secured the proper torches for the journey."

Fortunately, two years prior, one of Bessen's mines had to be abandoned shortly after operations began, when oil began seeping in through a long fault in the rock. The oil flowed slowly from the mine and was contained by an earthen dam. As it pooled, the heavier pitch settled at the bottom, while the lighter fractions rose to the top and gradually evaporated. The pitch proved valuable for waterproofing buckets, watering troughs, and the few boats that crossed the Mysura. Meanwhile, the lighter oils made excellent fuel for long-lasting torches and lamps, casting a bright, steady light. Unfortunately, these torches could not be used underground, as they quickly fouled the air. However, the exploratory team reported a steady breeze flowing through the tunnel, ensuring fresh air for travelers along its entire length.

***

The next morning Axel paid an obligatory visit to Doc Netton's place. He'd made a promise to visit Flin Milfort after his return from the north. He found Flin in bed on his side and propped up with his back against a wall. In one hand he held a drawing board and was diligently scribbling on a project with his free hand.

"I thought you were supposed to be working on getting better and not becoming some kind of artist," Axel said, breaking Flin's concentration.

Flin jumped, dropping both pencil and drawing board to the floor. "Oh, you gave me a start!" Flin said, but quickly recovered. "I am so glad to see you!"

"And why have I become so highly placed on your 'must see' list?" Axel asked as he picked up both board and pencil to restore them to their original positions.

"I've been working on drawings of fortifications for you."

"You what? How is that going to make you well?"

A voice, unmistakably belonging to Doc Netton, drifted in from the adjoining room. "All I can say is that giving that young man a purpose has worked wonders. And whatever your friend Eleth did—it's clear both have played a major role in his recovery."

He entered, holding a small whetstone and a surgical knife he'd clearly been sharpening. "I'd give anything for a chance to work alongside her, even if just for a few Kivans. Thanks to her, we might actually save Jenner Apeldorn. When I first saw him, I thought he was lost for sure, but now he's making an impressive recovery. He's even woken up a few times and taken some food."

"I am really hoping that you find just such an opportunity to work with Eleth."

Axel turned back to Flin and said, "I came to talk with you as promised, but you seem to be rather busy."

"I'm busy doing exactly what I wanted to talk with you about. Go look at those drawings on the table in the corner and you might get an idea."

Axel moved as bidden and immediately looked shocked. "These are maps... and... fortifications! Intricate plans! How could you do these here? For that matter, how could you do these at all without flying over the Valley Road on a dragon?"

"I have an excellent memory, and, if I can see an object from two or three angles, I have the ability to imagine how it looks from a different angle, such as from the air, and I can apply drawings of what I propose over those."

"But I recognize exactly where these are on the road, and I *have* seen them from the air. This is precisely how the places look!"

"I've been up and down that road many times and have it all practically memorized. Oh, the ones on the bottom are the defensive structures I'm proposing; at least the ones I've worked on so far."

"These are incredible."

"The best thing about them is that they can be built in a reasonably short time yet provide maximum protection against any weapon the king has. The canvas bags, filled with dirt or sand, will make it possible to put up a basic redoubt anywhere in about a day's time. With your new paint, I also hope to make them impervious to dragon fire."

Axel drew in a big lungful of air and blew it out in short bursts as he thought. "Would you mind if I take these over to the town council? They really need to see what you've put together?"

"Not at all, but I wonder if you would drop by to see my dad first. He's the best mason in town and could answer any question as to how these are built. There's something else he wants to bring up with you. He's expecting you at High Sunstar."

"How does he know that I'll be able to see him at High Sunstar?"

"He was here an orai ago and said you were on your way. He checked with the Town Watch, which keeps an eye on you wherever you go, and with the Town Council, where they have a complete schedule of your planned activities."

"Do they keep a record of when and where I plan to find an outbuilding?

"I wouldn't be surprised."

"Hmm. There's someone at the Council Hall I need to have a chat with."

"Okay, but don't forget my dad at High Sunstar. Our house is by the forest in the northwest corner of town. Dad tells me he's painted it brown."

Since one look in the sky told Axel it was close to midday, and he really did not have anything else on his schedule for that orai, he decided to go visit Flin's father. He hoped the man had something important on his mind.

Axel reached the house precisely on time and knocked on the door.

"I'm over here," came a voice from the forest side of the house. Axel looked over that way but saw no one. "Hello," he called back.

"Thank you for coming on time," said the voice.

"You're welcome, but where are you?"

"I'm standing right in front of you, about twenty strides away."

"That would put you right in front of the trees. I've got pretty good eyes. Why can't I see you? Are you a friend of Shaddra's?"

"Who is that?"

"Never mind, where are you?"

Suddenly, a figure moved, right in the place the voice had described. But the figure stopped and seemed to disappear again.

Axel walked over to the spot where the voice had originated and only recognized that a man was standing there when he was fewer than twenty strides away.

"What in Etmar's Garden are you wearing?"

"Hello, Mr. Daimon, sir; my name's Rollo Milfort. This here get-up is a way to keep animals or other people from seeing you when you're in the forest. We didn't know what to name it, so we just call it 'masking.' My boy and I developed this technique to help us when hunting. You see, we really like the taste of kota meat, but they're so darn hard to see because of their coloring and even harder to get close to in the forest without being gored. We use a little of their medicine to sneak up close enough so we can get a good bowshot or even hit one with a spear."

"Interesting. Tell me, what are you wearing and what's on your face?"

"I hand dyed my clothes, and even my boots and hat, in irregular patterns using mostly shades of brown, green, and black. I used colors specifically designed to match the colors of our forests around here. I made this floppy hat with special bands around it to hold small branches and leaves from the trees in our area, but occasionally I use bunches of weeds, again from the area I'm in. The paint on my face and hands is a special paint made from pigments mixed with daewol oil. I try to match the colors of the clothes. It's all to eliminate my human outline, which is what both animals and humans look for out in the wild. The oil also helps to eliminate the human scent, which can scare prey away. I don't know, but maybe it might even prevent a dragon from smelling me."

"Mister Milfort..."

"Oh, please, just call me Rollo. I don't know that other person very well."

"Um, yes, Rollo, you've provided a truly excellent demonstration, but how do you think I might best utilize masking in general and this masking suit in particular?"

"I know you are planning secret operations against the king. Since we'll never be able to have a bigger force than he will, it means we're going to have to sneak up on them, in which case, masking would be particularly useful. This masking can also work to hide fortifications, especially from dragonriders. You can use fish netting with special strips of colored sackcloth woven through and tied into the netting to do that."

"Mister... uh, I mean Rollo, I hope you don't mind, but I'm going to send some friends of mine, named Ketter Harbert and Rook Dermin, over to have a long talk with you. Please tell them everything you just said to me and give them a demonstration. I think they would be fascinated."

"I'm always pleased to speak with new people about masking and, especially, if they're friends of yours."

"Wonderful. I might even join with them as you talk about your ideas, combined with some of theirs."

***

Early in the third Kivan of the year, a man walked up to Councilman Bassen, who was standing out in front of the Council Hall and asked if he might volunteer for service to the people of the Mysura Valley. The councilman glanced down at the man's obvious peg leg and answered, "We can always find ways for people to serve. I am Councilman Kiel Bessen. May I ask who I am addressing?"

"My name is Sonder Arhus from Blatten. Formerly, I was Regimental Commander Arhus of His Majesty's Fourth Cavalry Regiment, so I have some skills to offer."

The councilman looked down again wide-eyed at the man's wooden leg below the knee and asked, "You say you are from Blatten? How did you get over the Yakuta Mountains?"

"Oh, I can't ride skells anymore, so I walked over the mountain road."

This answer caused the councilman to step back in wonder. "What would make a former ranking officer in the King's service, bearing such an impairment, want to help us so badly that he would walk twenty-one tondrins of that frozen mountain road to work with us?"

"First, I have to admit that I did not walk the entire distance. A farmer gave me a lift after I had covered only about nine tondrins, but I would have walked the whole way if I had to. Still, my whole life, I believed the Tarfal Trail to be a track that was only two strides wide. While on that road, I stood amazed to learn that it not only permitted wagon traffic, but also, in places regularly spaced, had room for two wagons to pass abreast. Additionally, all challenging-to-cross areas, such as avalanche blockages, were effectively cleared in some way. It must have required an immense amount of work. While I am thankful for the farmer, I certainly would have preferred bringing my own wagon if I had known."

"If you need transportation…," Kiel began to speak.

"No, no. Don't bother yourself. I will buy a skell and wagon here. They will provide for my needs.

"Now, as to the reason why I am here, I know about the danger you are in from Deroth's military, and I want to be of assistance. There is nothing I wouldn't do to prevent that monster of a king from killing any more of his people."

"In spite of the strenuous effort you have exerted in coming here," the councilman replied, "how can we be certain that one so long a king's officer does not retain loyalty to his former lord?"

"I understand why you must ask this question, Councilman Bessen," Sonder said. "May we sit somewhere together, where I can tell you why you should trust me?"

"Please call me Kiel," the councilman said. "We're very informal here, in the Valley. The council chamber is currently occupied. There are chairs and a table off to the side of that building. The day is sunny and warm, so please sit there and enjoy it while I have some food and drink brought over. I hope you won't mind if I invite one or two others to join us?"

"If it will be of value, I will be glad to meet with whomever you wish."

A half orai later, Sonder found himself meeting with Kiel, Axel, and Jarrad. Axel and Jarrad were introduced only as "important people in the community."

Sonder looked questioningly at Axel, obviously evaluating his youth, but quickly seemed to let the matter drop. He took a deep breath and said, "The questions you have already asked are, 'Why would I want to serve the people of this valley?' and 'How could I be trusted not to retain loyalty to the king?"

"Please allow me to share some of my background to address both of those questions. First, I must explain that my father was the richest man in not just Blatten but the entire province of Bredsten. Our family held and still holds power and close relationships with the king and other leaders in Rabianice.

"When I came of age, my father insisted that I enter the Royal Officer Training Academy in Rabianice. The school assigned me to the cavalry because of my skellmanship and leadership qualities. I graduated, became an officer, and worked my way up in rank as the years passed.

"I married, and my wife bore me a son, who grew strong and so much like me that I felt more blessed than any man had the right to be. When he came of age, he followed in my footsteps and was commissioned as a second officer in the cavalry. He was the one who helped me to remain strong and remember my responsibilities to the cavalry when my wife took ill and died.

"I became close to the people I supervised. Perhaps that was a mistake in King Deroth's military, but I was fond of my troops, treated them with respect, and they gave their hearts to me in return. I could count on them to give everything they had in a fight, and many did just that. As long as I saw purpose in battle, I aimed to win. My troops won many battles and lost rarely. I was eventually promoted to the rank of Commander, Second Level. It was only then that I began to understand why we fought the battles we did, and the answer did not please me. Far too often, the lives of noble men and women were wasted for inconsequential, even frivolous reasons.

"The end of my career came two years ago on the Mandaran front. My unit held a well-protected hill against an equally strong position controlled by the enemy, just across the valley. I didn't know it at the time, but the King, himself, visited the senior staff just behind our lines on that day. He happened to witness the enemy stretching a copy of his personal standard below the bastion at the top of their heavily fortified hill. One after another, a hundred men proceeded to urinate on the standard.

"Deroth was so infuriated by the act that he ordered an immediate all-out attack to seize that virtually impregnable hill. He didn't even wait for dragon support. Needless to say, our troops making the assault were massacred. Out of the, roughly, five hundred men in my unit, only two-hundred seventy returned alive; nearly half of that number suffered wounds of varying severity. Since we fought on ground controlled by the enemy, we couldn't bring out our wounded, and no quarter was given. Every one of our wounded who was left on the field, was brutally slaughtered to the man, in front of us.

"I managed to return to our lines, but only after receiving a deep saber slash across my lower leg. Later that day, I learned that my son had been involved in the charge, too. He belonged to the unit brought up to support our right flank and, according to a witness I later talked to, was one of those left on the field to be butchered. His body was never returned to us. I later learned that the total bill for the attack was over a thousand young men and a few young women dead and nearly half that number wounded but returned."

Jarrad looked over at Axel upon hearing the news, and Axel could read his mind. Without a doubt, these words stirred very unpleasant memories in Jarrad's mind. They were also forcing Axel to blank out some of his memories, best left buried for now.

Sonder continued his story, saying, "I lost my leg. No longer of use to the cavalry, I was released without ceremony or mention of my many contributions to the king's forces. It made no difference what I had accomplished previously, since I had failed in my final effort; the king only wanted to forget I existed.

"I went home to Blatten, even though most of the people I knew closely as a youth were gone or left so much out of touch that they were no longer part of my life. Though I received no pension, I did inherit a substantial amount of money and land from my deceased father. Overseers and trusted advisors managed everything, leaving me with nothing to do but think, which led to feelings of isolation and despair.. I considered suicide until I realized that would accomplish nothing of value. I thought about assassinating the king and soon realized he would only be replaced by someone like him—if I could do it at all. It was only when I learned of the plight of our neighbors to the south, the people of the Upper Mysura Valley, that I realized my purpose in life!"

A glow came across the man's face as he said, "My purpose is to prevent the king from destroying his people just to satisfy his own petty pleasures, and the place to begin that quest is here in the Mysura Valley. I wish to volunteer my services in any capacity that you think appropriate. I have extensive knowledge of Deroth's military forces, especially the cavalry. I also have many friends, both inside and outside of the military, who either would be willing to freely help with your problem or who could be used without their knowledge to provide enormous benefit. What's more, I could be of significant benefit in training your people in the king's way of doing things."

Councilman Kiel heaved a big sigh and said, "Let me start by offering our condolences for your loss, Commander, and for the families of the men and women so thoughtlessly sacrificed. As a small community, we all share in the grief that you are experiencing, especially since we have lost several of our own in similar circumstances."

"There is a saying that time makes us forget old wounds. But, from my experience, I've learned that the scars from old wounds do not fade as much with time as we would like. Thank you for your sympathy and your concern.

"I'd like to say," Commander Arhus mentioned upon rising, "that I'm aware that the most important question you'll be discussing after I depart this table is, 'Can he be trusted?' Since giving my word is never sufficient, I suggest contacting my relatives and others who know me in Blatten. I can also provide other references should you wish.

"One more thing," he added, "I know many people in the Silistra Valleys, including a number of leaders who share my perspective. I also know that the vast majority of Silistrans feel just as you do about the king's atrocities. If it's in your interest, I can get in touch with my friends. I understand that involving a wider circle may raise security concerns, but I believe we can manage those risks with proper diligence. Now, I've said what I needed to say for the time being. Let me simply add that I am available for a further interview at your convenience. Thank you, and I'll be off."

"Your offer is received very kindly by us," said Kiel, "but it might take a day or so for us to determine where you might be of greatest service. Can we put you up in one of our inns until we have decided on that?"

"I have already taken a room in the River Maiden, which is more than adequate for my needs. I'll wait there for your answer."

"Um, before you go," Jarrad blurted out, "please answer how you were able to walk nine tondrins on a wooden leg. The pain from that should have been unbearable."

"Oh, that," Sonder replied with a chuckle. "One of my sergeants also lost a leg a year or so before I did. He was a very inventive man and came to me saying he had found that by boiling the sap of the harda tree, one could make a strange, flexible substance, which provides superb cushioning for a wooden leg. He helped me make a mold designed to specifically fit my stump. He then filled the mold with the sap and boiled it until it reached the right consistency. It made a perfect interface between my leg and the wooden extension. My friend added a specially formed tip to the other end of the wood, made from the same sap, but boiled longer into a more solid form. That tip keeps the leg from slipping on smooth surfaces and has made the artificial leg last longer. Between the two improvements, my leg almost feels as if it is all mine. I still had to rest a lot, and travel here became difficult once I went above the snowline, but I never fell. Does that answer your question?"

"Indeed, it does," said Jarrad. "Indeed, it does."

The three men watched Sonder walk down the street and out of sight.

Axel looked off into the space at his right and asked, "What do you think, Shaddra?"

A voice answered his question from that same empty space. "I closely watched for all the signs that might indicate he was lying but saw none. I find myself inclined to believe his story."

"I knew his father, Sted Arhus, quite well," said Kiel. "I never found him to be dishonest or manipulative in anything he ever said or did. His loyalties were to his family before anything else. I think he would have been very proud of his son."

Axel put his hand on the table before him and started drumming his fingers. "Let's face it, a man with such knowledge and skills would be valuable to us in a hundred ways if we can thoroughly trust him."

Jarrad sucked on his lip for a moment and said, "I know what the trail over the Loft is like this time of year. The fact that he walked nine tondrins, some of it through snow a half stride deep or more, to get here is remarkable. I suggest we put him to work on an important but not highly sensitive project until we can learn more about him. Shaddra?"

"Yes, Uncle Jarrad?"

"Can you assign one of your messenger dragon friends to watch over him closely over the next few weeks and report back?"

"That I can do, but remember we only have limited messenger dragon resources right now."

"We know that," Axel said. Breaking into the conversation. "But if this Sonder Arhus is as genuine as he appears, he could be of immeasurable value."

"As you have requested," said the unembodied voice, "I'll find the right dragon."

"Kiel, let's identify a place for Sonder to start."

"I'll go check with the council right now," Kiel said and rose to leave.

As the councilman walked away, Axel looked over at Jarrad and said, "If Mr. Arhus checks out, I believe there is much I could personally learn from him."

"What are you thinking?"

"He's a military leader. I have no real experience in that area, but it is something I very much need to learn. Licor is a good teacher, yet his experience is limited to dragons. I need to learn how to lead people."

"You've done all right so far."

"I'm still only seventeen years old. That man has many years of real experience in the military. It's the kind of experience I need, though I've only got a short time to pick it up."

Jarrad chuckled and said, "It's a good thing you're such a sponge for knowledge."

Rubbing his chin with one hand, Axel said in a thoughtful voice, "I also wonder if Fala and Bardin might be able to design a shoe for his peg that might at least help him mount a skell again."

Chapter Twenty-Two

WAR

The attack came on the fifth day of the eighth Kivan, early in the morning, just as the first light of the sunstar began to touch the mountaintops. The dragons of the Free Colony knew about its coming as early as the day before. They had been observing the changes taking place at Dragon Force bases in Southern Sanara. They saw the integration of the Northern Special Action Group into the Southern and even witnessed the distribution of dark blue Mandaran military uniforms to the dragon-rider troops. Deroth would be sending every special action dragonrider in his military to wipe out all traces of two insignificant towns.

While it was still dark, a single messenger dragon bearing a rider, armed with two crossbows, tried to approach over the northern mountain range. Axel, riding Licor and wearing a newly designed green uniform, representing the Free Peoples, believed the soldier was sent to eliminate any escapees fleeing the burning town along the Valley Road to the east. Even though Kivan was round and nearly full, neither the messenger dragon, nor the rider, saw Licor dive from a high cover position, which allowed him to approach from above and behind. One bowshot, made from the dive, took out the rider, who fell to the length of his tether. Immediately, Kulek, who was flying nearby, dove past the messenger dragon at a different angle to snatch it from a line holding the dangling body beneath the smaller dragon's belly.

With a soldier's body in his arms, Kulek adjusted his dive, leveling off just above Licor. He released the body, which landed precisely in front of Licor's saddle. This allowed Axel to swiftly remove the Bechar from the soldier's neck and let the body fall away again. Still airborne, Axel pulled back the leather cover from a small steel anvil, its raised sides and hooked chain designed for securing the jewel. From a side pocket in the anvil's case, he retrieved a hammer and, without hesitation, smashed the red jewel between the hammer and the anvil. When he was finished, he let the hammer drop, then swept away the white shards left on the anvil. The hammer dangled safely, attached by a thin steel chain to the anvil's case, making it easy to retrieve.

"That's for Jemmy," Axel said aloud.

Kulek veered off as soon as he confirmed the jewel's destruction and passed word to Tanga, a female firedrake, to escort the now free messenger dragon to a collection place several tondrins east of Tarfal. Then Kulek and Licor climbed back up to the cover position and settled in next to Konnor. There, a flight of siris dragons, half carrying riders dressed in green uniforms, waited for the main body of the attack.

The world below started to reflect light coming from the bright skies, which preceded the appearance of the sunstar. To avoid being seen, a small flight of Free Colony siris dragons found concealment just above one of several low wisps of cloud spread about the Valley. The air was thin up there, forcing Axel to breathe deeply and more often, but the dragons seemed not to mind the rarefied air at all.

The enemy dragons' main flights crossed the mountains just north of the Rim and entered the Valley. They were still several tondrins to the east of the Free Fragons. Axel counted forty-two dragons, including thirty-four firedrakes and eight siris dragons. Shaddra was certainly correct. They brought every dragon that could be spared from Deroth's Special Assignments Forces, and a killer dragonrider sat upon each one of them.

Axel's flight consisted of six siris dragons, five of which were lined up on his right side. Three of the dragons in the flight bore a rider wearing a green uniform, and three were riderless. These dragons worked in designated pairs. The idea was for each rider and two-dragon team to repeat the action Axel, Licor, and Kulek had just completed as often as possible.

Two dragons away, Rook Dermin sat on Konnor, a charcoal-colored siris dragon with prominent white mottling across his back and wings, and two away from him, Bardin Shotley sat on Batu, a mossy-green female siris dragon, who was the near-perfect image of Hukken, at least when seen from a distance. At the sight, Axel let out a heavy sigh.

The Free Colony strategy for this engagement centered on the rapid strike capability of the siris dragons. The firedrakes would take a largely backup role this time unless an outright battle ensued.

Four of the enemy firedrakes below separated from the main group and spread out over the southern side of the Valley. Axel guessed they were tasked with picking off any homesteads found near the river or out in the middle of the Valley. Since the fire destroyed everything in this area the year before, they were doomed to be disappointed. But that wouldn't stop Axel and his friends from paying them a visit. He just hoped that none of the dark-blue uniformed riders would look over their shoulders in the next few minutes.

All six free dragons slowed down for a few minutes, then swiftly descended from their high perch to catch up to the enemy. Within two hands full of seconds, all three of the enemy dragonriders targeted were dead. Rook needed two shots to get his rider, but his second shot was in the air as soon as he realized the first would miss. The riderless Free Colony dragons cleanly picked off the dangling bodies and dropped them onto their partners' saddles. Kivans of constant practice paid off in that maneuver. Only a few seconds later, three bodies were dropped to the blackened ground below, and three jewels were destroyed. Inside of a minute, three free firedrakes, flying without riders, appeared next to three very confused-looking firedrakes to help them find their way to safety.

Unfortunately, the fourth enemy dragonrider had seen what happened to his friends and was in the process of doing everything he could to get his firedrake to catch up with the main body.

With a hand signal, Axel sent Bardin, Batu, and the riderless siris dragons to join the main fight. He and Rook would use their siris dragons to catch up and take care of the fourth enemy.

A firedrake is no match for the speed of a siris dragon, so Rook easily caught up with and passed the enemy dragon. He turned about two tondrins ahead and came back at the firedrake for a head-on fight.

The king's flying officer crouched down behind his high and wide pommeled saddle and, with little of his body showing, aimed his crossbow at Rook. When the two opponents were still half a tondrin apart, the enemy dragonrider was struck in the side by a bowshot from Axel, who had approached from low and behind, while the dragonrider concentrated on Rook.

Konnor did not even need to slow down in order to pick off the dangling rider. Five seconds later, Rook had smashed the rider's jewel and brought the morning's tally to five newly freed dragons. Two firedrakes, Torkar and Goran, would take this one to the mountain pasture where freed dragons were being comforted and cared for by some of the colony dragons.

Licor knew exactly where to go next. Ahead, the flight of thirty-seven remaining enemy dragons had reached the towns. The group split in two to attack both Tarfal and Mikell simultaneously. Just over half of each troop peeled off in line to descend and make their first runs, while the remainder kept top cover, circling overhead, waiting for their opportunity to help burn the towns to cinders.

At this point, Axel noted a third flight of siris dragons rising from hiding positions near the tops of the Yakuta Mountain Range, forming the northern border of the Valley. About a quarter of these dragons carried riders dressed in green uniforms and wearing armor, two of whom happened to be Fala Prudo and Ketter Harbert.

This dragon flight attacked the enemy's top-cover dragons. Those teams, with a rider, would approach a target from a blind side and strike first with a bow at the king's rider, dressed in dark blue.

The teams without riders used a different tactic. One of the dragons would attack the enemy rider with its claws and try to tear him from his mount. The second dragon served to catch the falling rider in its claws but would be prepared to back up the first dragon in case the strike resulted in a fight. If the second dragon managed to capture a falling body, then it would drop that body in a prearranged and out-of-the-way spot, where townsfolk were ready to take jewels from the riders and smash them. In the latter case, the first dragon would support the second in the fight, which would undoubtedly take place as the king's dragon struggled to retrieve its stolen master.

From his position on the eastern side of the valley, Axel counted thirty-six free dragons going after the nineteen dragons in the top cover group. Not all of the attacking force were siris dragons.

A second group of free firedrakes guarded the drop zone to protect the citizens breaking Bechars. They would also help lead the newly freed dragons from the battlefield.

Less than a minute later, he saw some bodies begin to fall from the melee, and dragons were picking them out of the air. But Axel also witnessed a dozen air-to-air battles taking place. He was too far away to determine which dragons were free and which not, so he prayed to the gods to protect his friends, both dragon and human.

On Axel's left, he saw an enemy siris dragon dart away from the melee with two free siris dragons close on his tail. Axel spoke to Licor, saying, "Looks like that one is coming out to greet us. Shall we go say hello?"

"If he gives me a chance," Licor responded, "I'll say a lot more than that."

Licor promptly steered a course that would put the two of them directly in front of the fleeing enemy. The rider had obviously been looking back more than to the front, so he did not see Licor until he came to a point where barely half a tondrin separated them. On seeing Licor, the enemy rider pulled his dragon to a near stop, looked back, and then forward. With little hesitation after that, he jerked the Bechar off his neck and threw it as hard as he could. His abrupt stop, however, allowed the dragons behind to get within range, and one of them sent a very accurately aimed fireball to turn the rider into ash instantly. Fortunately, the scaly armor of the rider's mount protected the dragon.

"Do you see that Bechar?" shouted Axel.

"Yes, I do!" replied Licor, as he dived to intercept.

"Let's both keep our eyes on it and grab it before it hits the ground! If it lands in that forest, it's a goner."

"There is not a lot of altitude to work with here," called out Licor.

"Then go faster!"

The distance to the Bechar was shortening fast, but so was the distance to the ground. "Remember, we'll be going down when we catch that thing. We've got to allow enough room afterward to avoid striking Tamerel."

"Are you trying to tell a dragon how to fly?" snapped Licor, his focus solely on the Bechar falling ahead of them.

As they closed in on their target, the ground seemed to rise up at an alarming speed. Axel glanced down and felt a surge of panic as he saw just how close they were to crashing into the thick forest below.

"I'm going under it!" Licor suddenly shouted, changing course in a risky maneuver. Axel's heart pounded in his chest as he held on tight, knowing they only had one chance to capture the Bechar before it was too late.

"Oh, I wish I had a butterfly net!" Axel yelled out in frustration, bracing himself for impact.

With precise timing and skill, Licor managed to bring Axel right where he needed to be to grab the falling Bechar in mid-air, which he did, barely. But Licor couldn't gain enough altitude afterward to avoid colliding with the trees. Licor struck two trees; the first one snapped cleanly in half, but the second one did not break cleanly, causing Licor to tumble head-first into the ground, bounce, and then be flung through branches and brush until he finally came to a stop amidst a tangle of mostly smaller kitka trees.

Axel groaned as he slowly regained his senses, grateful that he was still alive. But then he heard the sound of breaking branches and looked up just in time to see several large limbs hurtling towards him. He squeezed his eyes shut and braced for impact, but thanks to his protective armor, he escaped with only minor injuries.

Axel sat, not moving for a time. He was the first, however, to open his eyes. As he looked around at the aftermath of their crash landing, he couldn't help but think that the event was one of the most terrifying experiences of his life.

Immediately, he checked his hand and saw the red Bechar. He wasted no time in smashing it and brushing the remaining particles to the ground below. His next thought was for Licor. Quickly as he could, he unbuckled his tethering belt and looked for Licor's head. He found it in a pile of shorn kitka branches. The dragon's eyes were open and moving slowly but in an uncoordinated way.

"Licor! Licor!" Axel said. "Can you hear me?"

Licor's eyes gradually focused on Axel. In a quiet voice, he said, "I never had to go through this kind of thing when I worked for the king!"

"Oh, Licor, Licor, I love you!" Axel said and gave the dragon a big kiss on the forehead."

"Ouch!" said the dragon. "Haven't I been through enough already?" But on his face was a big smile.

"You just about gave everything," said Axel.

"It was a good thing that most of your momentum was used up by the time you hit that last big tree. Let me check you out for serious injuries. Meanwhile, don't you go pulling a Hukken on me. We're running short enough on siris dragons without you doing a martyr thing on us."

"I would certainly prefer not to."

Axel looked closely all over the parts of Licor's body that were visible. When he returned to give a report, he said, "I can't tell how you are underneath until you are able to stand. You appear not to be bleeding, but there is no question that your right wing was broken when you struck the second tree. It's pretty bad. Now, you've got to be hurting all over, but is there any place that may be hurting a lot more than it should be under the conditions? I'm especially concerned about internal injuries."

"A siris dragon's armor is pretty tough and tends to spread the effect of a blow over a wide area. I think I am all right, except for my wing."

"Honestly, I don't see how you can stand the pain from that wing."

"Did I say that I was standing it?"

"I'm sorry, Licor. It's just that a human would be much more vocal about that kind of pain."

"I am not a human. But I really do hope you can find some pain medicine very soon."

Axel looked up at the sky in every direction and saw nothing but the tops of trees. He then looked around Licor's body and tried to remove all the broken logs and other debris, which could be causing Licor pain. He was beginning to worry that help for his friend might not arrive for a while.

Help did not come soon, but eventually a cry came from above in High Language. "Down here, Konnor!" Axel shouted.

A crashing of branches and tree trunks sounded as the siris dragon dropped into a relatively open area a landrin away. After that, Konnor just started pushing trees over until he could work his way over to Axel and Licor. Rook jumped down from Konnor's back, and, taking a long look at his two friends, he said, "What are you two doing lying on the ground when there's work to be done?

Alton returned a sarcastic smile and simply said, "Can you tell us how goes the battle?"

"From what I can tell, the battle is virtually over. Don't you keep up on things?"

"Ketter, when we get out of here, I'm going to nail your hide to a..."

"Tut, tut, tut. No need to be rude. I'm just glad to find you two are alive. I saw the fall you took. How's Licor?"

"He has a broken wing, at least, and he's in a lot of pain."

"I apologize for taking so long to get to you. There was one last body to chase after.

A high-pitched sound told Axel that another dragon was close by.

"Kulek is above us," Axel said. "Konnor, would you please ask him to go fetch the Doc as quickly as possible and bring a lot of pain medicine? Oh, and ask him if he knows anything about casualties."

A High Language message was immediately transmitted, and a response returned.

Kulek called down in a loud, deep voice, "We don't know the number of casualties in the towns, but we'll try to bring more complete news and find the doctor as quickly as we can."

"Looks like I'd better arrange for a reception area," Konnor said to his rider. "You might want to hop down, Rook. This is going to get bouncy."

"I've learned to take your advice when given," said Rook. "Half a moment and I'll be off."

While Konnor began pushing trees over and out of the way to make a small clearing, Rook came over to get a closer look at Licor. "You know you could have saved us a whole lot of work if you had crash-landed over on the road."

"If I had done that," Licor interjected, "maybe I wouldn't have this broken wing."

"Okay," said Axel. "Next time we have to chase a Bechar to the ground, I'll remind you to crash on the road."

A familiar voice shouted down from somewhere above.

"Over here Bardin," Axel called back.

Bardin was riding Ayger, a male siris with marbled gray coloring. The dragon landed in the clearing, still being formed, and Bardin rushed over. "I can see that you look okay, but what about Licor?

"He had an argument with a kitka tree, and the tree won."

"You can make jokes about me now, Axel, but you had better watch out when I get out of this forest."

"Nothing would make me happier than to see you free from this forest and healed from whatever injuries you might have."

"Now," Axel said, looking pointedly at Bardin, "what … about … the … battle?" He put emphasis on every word of that sentence."

"Oh, that. I, uh, think we won."

"Yes?"

"I guess you know what happened down here," Bardin said, looking over at the swath of trees cleared out by the crash-landing siris dragon.

Axel returned a glare at him.

"I caught the latest news only minutes ago," Bardin said. "Fala gave us an update on our way here. She said that the king's dragons divided into two groups in the air over the towns. Our force attacked the top covers and took out all the riders except the one you chased, meaning, we got all of them. One rider tried pulling the same trick as the one you faced, but the Bechar he dropped, landed on the Mikell Road, and was easily found. None of their riders survived.

"The group that hit the towns was totally shocked when they saw that their fire strikes were duds against the painted buildings, so they, of course, kept trying to do more of the same. Talk about stupid. You'd think they'd learn a lesson. It seems they were so busy looking down that they didn't see the battle happening above when the riders in the top cover were taken out.

"Would you believe five riders in the attacking group were downed by arrow shots from the ground? I'm sure that when we get back, half the people in the towns will be claiming those shots to be theirs. Some of the rider's bodies tore through rooftops, but I don't believe anyone got hurt in those homes.

"When the force hitting the towns finally came up from below, they tried to get into fisticuffs with our side; they found themselves heavily outnumbered and outmaneuvered by Licor's tactics. Fala said the king's riders fared poorly in that battle, too. Our dragons and riders received some minor wounds, and one rider was wounded seriously enough to leave the battlefield. I don't have anything like a casualty report as yet, nor do I know who that rider was."

"There's another affirmation of what you have done for our side in this battle, Licor." The dragon simply returned a scowling smile.

I want a list of all the wounded as soon as I can get them," Axel affirmed to Bardin, "and a report on how serious their injuries are. Would you have Ayger pass that request up to Kulek?" He looked pensive for a moment as he examined the damage to the forest around him and then, looking about at his friends, said, "Am I right in thinking we increased the number of dragons in the Colony by almost a third?"

Both Rook and Bardin just shrugged their shoulders in a "Don't ask me!" response and hopped down to where Konnor was working.

Konnor, the charcoal-colored dragon, approached them after making a considerable clearing and said, "Can you walk, Licor?"

"I'm afraid I haven't tried," the amber-brown dragon replied.

"It could have been worse," Konnor said. "You could have landed on your back."

Axel made a face like he had just bitten into the sour fruit of the kisu tree and shook his head. "If he had done that, you'd be scraping me off of this saddle."

Grimacing deeply, Licor shakily rose up on his hind legs, then followed that up by very slowly rising onto his forelegs. He folded his left wing across his back but made no attempt to move the right.

"If the wing can be splinted," said Konnor, "and we break down some more trees to make a road, it looks like we can at least get you out of the forest. After that, we shall see. I'll go get some more help from the dragons."

"Get more information on the casualties in the Valley, too," Axel asked again.

Suddenly, Licor let out an ear-splitting roar and bared his fangs in extreme anger!

Everyone looked at Licor in alarm.

"Where does it hurt?" yelled Axel, staring over at the wing.

"Archos' excrement!" the dragon shouted. "I won't be there for the raids!"

Axel's eyes widened in total amazement, but he found it nearly impossible to keep from laughing a second later. "It's really too bad," he said, shaking his head. "You're irreplaceable. But we'll do them anyway. You know, I think that hurts you more than the broken wing."

Licor didn't respond. He just looked away with another big scowl on his face.

"It's a sure thing you're not going to make it all the way up to the Colony in this condition. Why don't you stay with Jarrad and me until you're ready to fly again?"

Licor still did not respond.

"I have to admit, you big, tough guy, that you had the whole Colony prepared for today's battle and ready to support the upcoming raids. None of it could have been done without you."

"It seems it's going to be done without me just the same."

"You know what I mean. The Colony needed a drill sergeant to work them into shape, and you did that. The Colony needed someone to plan and train for the dragon reserve raids, and you've done that. When Deroth attacked the Valley, we were ready, and when he brings his ground forces this way, we'll be ready for that, too, all because of you, and you might even be well enough to see some action then."

"Are you trying to make me feel better?"

"No, I'm trying to make you feel loved."

"In that case, keep going; I'm getting to like this."

***

Before the next orai ended, there were twenty firedrakes, led by Torkar, clearing a road through the forest from Licor over to the Valley Road. Doc Netton came in for his visit on Konnor, alongside Rook Dermin. Axel promptly asked Rook whether he had final news regarding the success of the action.

"I think so," he said. "Our side captured and broke a total of forty-three Bechars; unfortunately killed one firedrake; captured one messenger dragon, eleven siris dragons, and thirty-one firedrakes. We suffered one human severely wounded in the air and a number on the ground, but you should ask the Doc about them."

Doc Netton reported that, as far as he knew, Tarfal suffered eight of their people burned. "Three were bowmen or their spotters," he said, "who didn't get to shelters in time, and five were people caught out in the open on the ground. Unfortunately, they are all dead. I don't know their names yet. Mikell had some casualties, too, both dead and injured, but I don't have a count on those. A crossbow bolt struck Tolby Ranel, one of your dragonriders. The bolt struck him in the pelvis, but fortunately, it any arteries. He will live but might limp for the rest of his life. The midwife is taking care of those injured until I can get back over there."

Torkar, who had been listening in, interrupted here to say that the dragons had suffered several wounds, mainly lacerations caused by the claws of other dragons. "The Daughter was wise enough to leave us with a substantial supply of her special medicine, and we have been able to treat our wounded."

"I'm sorry to hear that you have wounded," said Axel, "but I am glad to hear that you can treat them, Tokar. I would like to go up to the Colony and visit those dragons who are wounded."

"That can be arranged," Torkar responded.

***

A half-orai later, Doc Netton expressed his amazement at what it was like to make this most unusual of house call, and to work on the most challenging of broken bones in his life.

Fortunately, he was aware of all the necessary steps; he just required three dragons to assist him in setting the bone.

"You know," he said. "I can't say I've ever set a broken wing before, especially one as large as this. Also, it's going to take up a huge part of my supply of papola seed oil to treat Licor's pain. My, this day is bringing on some of the most amazing things."

Fortunately, the wing break occurred in a place that would allow the wing, once firmly splinted, to fold back. Acting skillfully under the doctor's direction, the helpers securely tied the wing against Licor's body. He gingerly walked out to the road, and because no better means of transportation could be found, he walked all the way, though somewhat drunkenly at first, back through Tarfal and over to Jarrad's place. When he ambled through the streets of the town, everyone turned out to give him a loud reception.

"Never in my life could I have imagined this kind of reaction," Licor said to Axel, who was walking beside him.

"You are getting this reception because you deserve it, and everyone in town knows why."

When they reached the cottage, Licor settled into the conference center, which Jarrad had cleaned out for him.

***

The bodies of all the king's dragonriders, that could be found, were buried unceremoniously in an outlying corner of the town cemetery, but the dragon that died was buried, not far from where he fell, in a ceremony attended by all of the recently freed dragons and some of those who tried to free the one who died. All of the newly freed dragons were well acquainted with and respected the deceased but were grateful for what was done to try to save him. As with Hukken, the dragons began to sing. First, one began to sound off in a wordless, mournful tone, then another joined in, and another after that, until all the dragons present were united in song. Then, of a sudden, the song ended, and silence reigned.

Chapter Twenty-Three

A CHANGE OF ORDERS

On the eighth day of the eighth Kivan, three days after the attack on the Mysura Valley, two immaculately dressed officers of the King's Personal Guard rode into the makeshift encampment, currently under the charge of His Majesty's Ground Forces Adjutant-Commander Danli Graca. Graca held the honor of leading the special unit tasked with conducting the move of the King's Dragon Breeding Reserve to its new home. The somewhat overweight commander invited the two officers into his office, which was actually the living area of a home commandeered for the duration of the time necessary to assemble the conveyances and supplies required for the upcoming move.

The two officers stood at full attention, while the senior of the two gave a crisp salute and extended his hand bearing an official-looking paper. "Commander Graca," he said, "I am tasked by a directive from the king to deliver this urgent message to you."

Graca took the paper from the officer, checked the seal of the message, ascertaining that it came directly from the king himself, and then opened and read his new orders. When he laid the letter down, he puffed up his cheeks and stared at the paper for a few minutes. With a brief look at the visiting officers, he reached for a small bell on the corner of his desk and gave it a ring. Graca immediately inquired about the whereabouts of First Officer Major Capal. The orderly explained that the major was out overseeing completion of the last few special conveyances required to haul well over one hundred dragons of varying ages and sizes. The commander nodded and instructed the orderly to locate the major and deliver an order for him to report to the commander immediately. The orderly performed a crisp salute and left the building.

"Please sit, gentlemen," he said to the visiting officers, "while we wait for my first officer."

When the two members of the king's personal guards sat stiffly in the chairs designated by Commander Graca, he said, "I hope that you and the king appreciate the enormity of the effort we have been undertaking on his behalf. Even though three-quarters of the dragons to be moved have wings and are typically capable of flight, virtually none of them can actually fly for more than a landrin or two. They would hardly be able to walk the same distance, because for kivans and often, for years, these hens have been sitting in nesting boxes with the sole responsibility of producing offspring. Their wings and even their legs have significantly atrophied. For that reason, we have constructed approximately eighty-five flat-bedded conveyances and appropriated other heavy-duty carriages, which will be pulled by a herd of over a hundred draft dragons. Most of the conveyances are rigged to resemble nesting boxes so that eggs and hatchlings can be taken care of without fear of them falling off onto the road. We also have somewhere between sixty and seventy wagons being pulled by draft skells to haul the breeding coop staff workers, and supplies for the care and feeding of all the dragons, skells, and men.

"We are almost entirely self-contained and will have to do very little purchasing of supplies as we travel. That is because we would rather not do anything that may slow our travel and provide an opportunity for enemies of the kng's to find an advantage. A dragon squadron has been ordered to provide cover for the entire voyage to ensure safety from air attack. The Northern Dragon Command will handle this duty for the first half of the trip but will be replaced by a force from the Southern Dragon Command at approximately the half-way point to give the first shift a rest.

"To avoid having to transport supplies for the dragon escorts, ground escort duties will also be transferred at the half-way point to a unit based closer to the endpoint on the route of march. The draft dragons and skells will not be exchanged, so we will have to ensure adequate rest and provender for them along the whole route."

At that moment, Major Capal appeared at the door and gave a crisp salute.

"Sit down, Major," said the commander. "It seems we have a significant change of orders. The king has just sent a message stating that dragons from the Kingdom of Mandara have attacked the towns of Tarfal and Mikell. Since it looks like Mandara and Kolodra are teaming up to invade Sanara, the king has decided to speed up the plan to move the entire Dragon Breeding Reserve to the new location in central Sanara. The king also intends to disrupt any attempts by his enemies to attack our convoy during the move. If, in spite of our security, word of our timetable has, somehow, leaked out, then our adversaries will be left looking for us long after we've left them behind. We are to get the convoy moving as soon as possible."

"But Sir," protested the major, "some of our special transports aren't yet fully assembled!"

"Then get them assembled and make certain we have enough draft dragons to pull the entire lot! Impress whatever support is necessary from the local communities to get the job done. We must set out for the Reserve no later than tomorrow morning, or I'll have the entire unit flogged, twenty-five lashes for each day of delay!"

"Now, as for you two gentlemen," Graca said, looking at his visitors, "will you be returning, or do you require quarters?"

"I'm afraid we have been commanded to leave immediately upon fulfillment of this task," replied the senior of the two. "We must depart forthwith to deliver messages to other units involved."

"Then I will wish you a safe journey, and please deliver my guarantee to the King, when you return home, that his orders will be strictly obeyed."

The two guards officers stood, saluted, and left the commander's office, heading straight for the skells that brought them.

Graca grinned and turned to Major Capal. "Finally! Finally, we will be able to get rid of this chuda excrement of a job and get back to doing what soldiers are meant to do! The day we turn those beasts over to someone else cannot come too soon."

***

Later that day, just as the sunstar settled into the line of trees on the horizon, a stern pounding on the front door of the cottage sent Eleth scurrying to answer. Two men dressed in the King's livery stood waiting. One of them handed Eleth a rolled paper and announced that all staff of the Reserve for Dragon Breeding must be packed and ready to leave for the new location by the next morning. Families would be transported only after actual workers were in place and functioning in the new location.

"Why so little warning?" Clara asked from behind Eleth.

The solder offered a crooked smile and said, "I'm afraid they don't bother to trust us with that kind of information, ma'am. All I know is that there will be a wagon here tomorrow morning by the sixth bell to pick up your things, and you must be ready to go with them. You are to expect to spend three nights on the road."

As the door closed, Clara looked ashen-faced over at Eleth. "This is so much sooner than we expected. What do we do? Does this situation mean our plans are ruined?"

Eleth clasped her hands together and rubbed her lips with her thumbs to keep them from trembling. "What can we do? I think, for now," she said, "we have no choice. Others have set our course for us."

Right on schedule, a wagon arrived the next morning to collect their belongings. Soon after, a second wagon appeared, this one furnished with padded, shaded seats. Two of the other midwives, already seated at the front, waited patiently for Clara and Eleth to join them.

It was clear that preparations had been underway all night. Supplies and equipment had been steadily loaded, while the process of moving the dragons onto specially designed conveyances—massive wagons drawn by sturdy draft dragons—had been ongoing for hours. The scale of the operation suggested that planning had been in motion for weeks. Workers, sourced from somewhere, bustled about, hauling every imaginable bundle through each of the five gates that led out from the breeding caves.

The nesting dragons managed to shuffle the short distance to their waiting transports, moving with careful, deliberate steps. Thankfully, not a single egg required relocation to the new nesting boxes. There were several younglings among them, most able to walk and travel beside their mothers to the transports. Their implanted jewels ensured that none of the youngsters strayed too far from the group.

Packages of food and water were passed out to all the wagons. The cooks must have been working all night on preparing the bread, cheese, and salted meats in special paper-wrapped bundles. Water came in large, stoppered flasks. Clearly, it would be a while before the procession stopped for another meal.

By midway to High Sunstar, a line of vehicles and animals stretched a full tondrin along the narrow roadway that had served the Breeding Caves for over a century. Yet, despite the growing impatience, no progress had been made. Drivers jostled their wagons—some drawn by draft dragons, others by massive skells engineered for heavy loads—each vying for any scrap of advantage.

Eleth, seeking to grasp the scale of the congestion, leapt from her carriage and walked the entire length of the procession. She was determined to appreciate firsthand both the sheer number of travelers and the vast space they occupied. Three times, soldiers intercepted her, sternly instructing her to return to her assigned conveyance. She rejoined Clara just as a courier raced past on skelback, shouting a warning: anyone needing the special voiding conveyances should use them now, as there would be no stops for several orais.

Her excursion proved highly informative. She counted exactly eighty-six conveyances drawn by dragons, sixty-three wagons pulled by skells and estimated the accompanying military force to be the size of a large company—about one hundred forty soldiers, all mounted on skelback.

An orai before High Sunstar, the procession finally began to move. Eleth was taken aback by the remarkable pace they managed to maintain. She realized their speed was made possible by the more than one hundred draft dragons, who hauled their burdens with effortless strength. Eleth had never witnessed draft dragons at work before, though she'd heard many accounts praising their power and swiftness. Now, watching the massive creatures pull heavy loads with such ease, she had proof of at least one legendary quality attributed to them.

What would it be like, Eleth wondered, if these draft dragons were free—able to choose whom they worked for and even receive compensation for their labor? Perhaps dragons never considered payment for the work they performed, but Eleth thought people would certainly reconsider their reliance on such strength if they had to pay for every task the dragons completed.

The train moved at a speed, which Eleth calculated to be about six tondrins in an hour on good roads but half that on rougher roads. Every time the train approached an intersecting road or crossroads, cavalrymen from the accompanying troop would race forward to set up roadblocks, which would keep locals off the route of march and waiting for up to an orai while the procession passed. Few passengers on the train could hear comments from those waiting for the road to clear. But Eleth heard, and she saw the subdued anger in their faces.

Flights of two to four dragons of varying types would pass overhead every half orai or so, making large circles to closely examine terrain to the front and sides of the train for possibly armed forces and likely ambush sites, and to ward off any potential attacks from the air. Eleth estimated their numbers as those of two squadrons, which Licor told her would each include from twenty to twenty-four dragons.

Not long before night fall, the train was guided off the road onto a guarded pasture. Word came down the line that blankets were being distributed, and everyone was to find themselves a place to sleep, whether on or under the wagons or simply out on the grassy field. Mercifully, the skies were clear, and the temperature was bearably cool.

It was agreed among the women on the wagon that the older of the four would sleep on the wagon benches. The younger two would have to fend for themselves. The meadow was covered with thick grass, which, by good luck, readily crumpled down into a bed, somewhat softer than the bare ground.

A rider brought word that hot food was on its way and would be provided in the morning, too.

When the sunstar rose the next morning, riders were sent along the train to make certain everyone was up and teams were getting hitched and made ready for the upcoming ride.

Clara groaned loudly as she climbed down from the wagon. "My back is in so much pain, I don't know how I'm going to make it through the rest of the day, and I slept on the wagon seat. How did you sleep, Eleth?"

"Oh, I'm afraid I didn't get very much rest last night. It wasn't the ground so much as all the things I had spinning around in my brain."

"I can imagine what you mean, what with this change disrupting all the Free Dragon's plans for the raid. I was so hoping we would be able to give the hens the same kind of freedom we are giving to some of their hatchlings."

Eleth sighed in a big way. "Don't worry Clara. The gods will show us the way."

The food arrived as scheduled and turned out to be acceptable, though not very inspiring. After the meal, everyone loaded up on the wagons, and the column started off again. The scenery passing by the column proved to be beautiful, but monotonous. The women in the wagon spent orai after orai watching a wall of mixed trees, interrupted only occasionally by planted farmers' fields. Not even the numerous small streams, needing to be forded, offered any visual stimulation. The planners of this move had taken care to line the bottoms of the fords with flat rocks to ensure nothing would hinder the column's movement.

An orai before High Sunstar, the line of wagons and conveyances stopped for a brief rest in another large pasture. No meal was provided, but the passengers were allowed to exit their wagons to rest or even take brief naps, but keep all teams hitched, for departure orders could come at any time. Food would be provided a short way down the line.

"Well, that will give me some time to work out the kinks in my dear old back," Clara said with a weak grin.

Eleth wasted no time, however, in moving some distance away from the wagons to walk parallel to the train and stretch out her legs. Her behavior seemed a little strange to Clara, who watched her closely. She was certain that Eleth was talking as she walked.

When the call came for everyone to return to their wagons, Eleth took Clara aside and said, "Shaddra has confirmed that a dragon attack was directed at Tarfal and Mikell, but the Free Peoples were prepared. All of the king's dragonriders were killed, and nearly a hundred enslaved dragons were freed, but one firedrake was also killed. The towns suffered no significant damage because of the fireproof paint, which had been applied to all the houses; however, a few of the townspeople were killed."

"Ahhh," Clara said. "No wonder the king moved our timetable up after taking a loss like that. I am sorry, though, for the one dragon who died."

Less than fifteen minutes later, the column was again underway.

Four more orais had passed when word finally came down the column that another rest stop would be made in a pasture similar to the ones previously used. The real purpose of the stop was to conduct a changeover of the accompanying military units, both on the ground and in the air.

Hot food had already been prepared and was waiting for the travelers at the rest stop. People would be allowed to lie down and relax on the grass in the shade of the wagons. This time the food was of much higher quality, and the travelers ate heartily and stretched themselves out on the grass to sleep off the effects of overeating.

***

Just as the women were finishing up their meals, a wagon pulled up to a place not far away from the one in which Clara and Eleth were to board. A soldier on a skell was accompanying the wagon, and he moved his mount closer to speak with Clara..

"You two are the chief mid-wife and her assistant, correct?" he asked, not bothering to dismount.

"Why, yes," answered Clara. "Those are our positions in the Coops."

The soldier's mount moved about in a spirited way, such that it was challenging for him to keep the animal close by the wagon. "I'm sorry," the soldier said, "but we need you to help with a problem. Would you please get on this wagon? The driver knows where to go."

Clara glanced over at Eleth and then back at the soldier. She could not help but pass a worried expression onto Eleth in so doing. "If you need us, I suppose we should go," she said to the officer. "But what about our things? They are in the wagon behind us."

"Point out which items are yours, and the driver will move them over. If you have no other questions, I'll leave you here and join you later."

"As you wish. But why do they need us...?" The soldier left before Clara could finish her question.

"I guess he wasn't very serious about that last sentence," Clara muttered.

The driver of the other wagon was a friendly young man who eagerly jumped off his rig and moved to transfer the items, which Clara and Eleth pointed out. He helped the women to climb into the new wagon, which was considerably more comfortable than the one they left.

The wagon, carrying Clara and Eleth, proceeded right up to the front of the entire caravan, where they happened to move alongside the officer in charge, who was riding a skell. Clara took one look at the man and nearly fainted.

"Jarrad! What are you doing here?"

The man on the skell shrugged and said, "Hey, I wasn't going to hang around the house while everyone else was running around like kiplans being chased for supper! I had to have something constructive to do! You don't like this?"

"Like it? I think you're crazy for risking your life. But I've always thought you were crazy, you wonderful man!"

Jarrad dismounted to tie the reigns of his mount to the rear of the carriage. Then he hopped onto the seat next to Clara.

"Hi, Jarrad," Eleth said in greeting. "Have there been any problems so far?"

"So far, things have gone so well that I'm beginning to get worried about what lies ahead."

"Jarrad," Clara asked, "what have you been up to, and why are you wearing that Sanaran officer's outfit?"

"Actually, I'll have you know, I am Adjutant Commander Orten Kelby, and I took over this column at the orders of the king himself. Well, to tell the truth, the king doesn't know about it, but that's just tough for him. In reality, I am serving under the orders of Eleth Keiron, who's a lot prettier than the king and nicer too."

Just then, a soldier rode up to the leaders of the column. He gave a salute to Eleth and a wink to Jarrad. "Ma'am."

"All units have reported." The soldier said. "The changeover has proceeded without a hitch."

"Thank you, Tarak, that sounds good," Jarrad replied. "Are the drugs taking effect?"

"Yes, we managed to get them secretly placed into the food pots just before the individual meals were prepared. Your food, of course, was prepared separately. We've told all the wagoneers and passengers to go ahead and take naps if they wish. We said we would be here somewhat longer than originally supposed. Even most of the draft dragonriders are dismounting and finding places to lie down."

"That is very good," said Eleth. "One of the reasons we chose this site is because the grass makes for soft places to nap. I suppose our people are already making certain that no one remains awake, including any drivers or soldiers who didn't change out at the last stop?"

"Yes, in a little while, we'll be giving everyone a needle prick to ensure they're out, and then we'll be on our way."

"Make certain that all Bechars are collected," Eleth said, "that the scouts are in place on all sides, and coordinate with Brot to confirm the skies are clear."

"Just finished coordinating with the assigned teams but will follow up to be sure everything stays covered." With that, Tarak turned his mount and headed back down alongside the conveyances.

That reminds me," said Eleth, "Jarrad, did you take control over the Bechars belonging to the breeding hens?"

"The changeover took place exactly as planned. All that remains of the Bechars in the former commander's safe is, now, little more than a pile of sparkly dust. We even found a substantial supply of jewel pairs, which were to be used on the next batch of hatchlings."

"May I offer my congratulations on a job well done?"

"Certainly, if you will accept my congratulations on a job well planned and prepared."

Clara reached out to take hold of Eleth's shoulder, turned to face her head on, and said in a commanding voice, "Why didn't you tell me?"

Eleth pushed back to the edge of her seat and said, "I, uh, told you lots of things."

"Just not the fact that you have taken charge of this raid?"

"Oh, Clara, you're such a worrier. I've been in charge since the beginning. If I told you what I was doing, you would have fretted so much that you couldn't do the job you're best at, which is caring for your dragons. Also, this way you acted much more naturally than otherwise."

"Are you saying you don't trust me?"

"No. I'm saying I know you better than you think I do."

"I simply don't understand," Clara said, shaking her head, "how you could do all this work from our house in the north when all the activity appears to have been taking place in the south with Jarrad and all the others. Yes, you went south with the dragons a few times, and we were visited by messenger dragons at least once a sycle, but could you be a... a commander without being there?"

Eleth smiled weakly and said, "I guess it all started in the twelfth Kivan of last year, on a typical working day in the firedrake coops. I was in the middle of a post-hatching examination of old Orfa's young male hatchling when I suddenly realized that, if the rumors of the Breeding Coops being moved to a new location were true, the king or his assigned manager would already have a plan for moving all the dragons. All we needed to do was replicate his actions, or even take over his entire operation. There had to be a way to do it. Thereafter, I put all my thinking into what his planner would do and how we could steal it away from him.

"I mentioned my idea to Shaddra on her next visit, and she agreed this was the way to approach our raid on the coops. Together, we made a basic list of the kinds of information we needed to collect to pull the operation off. From that point on, I became the chief spy in the Coops, while Shaddra went home and organized the biggest spy operation ever among the messenger dragons."

At this point, Jarrad joined in. "When Eleth presented her idea to the combined high councils in Tarfal on her next visit, she received unanimous support to undertake planning for and commitment to just such a raid on the Coops. The decision was also made to conduct simultaneous raids on the other two Dragon reserves, if feasible. Both High Councils unanimously decided to place Eleth in charge of the Coops raid, in spite of her physical location, because that location and her superior insight offered more benefits than disadvantages."

Jarrad smiled deviously and said, "Everyone knew old Deroth was concerned about Kolodra or Mandara raiding the Breeding Coops. Strangely enough, since our new plan required his move to actually take place, we simply fed those fears by providing new dragon sightings in the skies above and around the Breeding Coops."

Clara looked down and, putting a finger on her lower lip, thought for a moment. When she raised her head, she asked, "I have to ask, how did you cause the dragons to not have any eggs at the time of the move? That was you, wasn't it?"

Eleth laughed and said, "You are very perceptive, Clara. I knew from the medical training I received from my father that the juice squeezed from the stalks of the ganan plant would prevent pregnancy in humans for a time. I didn't know whether it would work with dragons or even how much I should use, so I secretly fed some to our three most prolific layers. I discovered that it required only a small amount to prevent a dragon from laying any eggs at all. I also discovered that the new medicine did not otherwise affect their health, at least in the short term. My father did say, however, that extended use in humans had some nasty side effects."

"Is that the plant with the tiny pink blossoms you collected so much of three or four Kivans ago?" Clara asked. When Eleth responded by pasting on a weak smile and nodding her head, Clara said, "I've never known a pretty little plant like that to have a more pungent smell. I almost asked you to take your work to the outbuilding."

"It was pretty strong, wasn't it? Anyway, once it was confirmed we would be moving at the end of the sixth Kivan, I simply arranged for the juice to be placed into the feed of all the dragons, beginning two Kivans in advance. It worked perfectly. But I have to admit you gave me some very confused looks at times."

"You little demon!" Clara exclaimed. "All that time, I wondered whether our dragons had come down with a terrible sickness but could find no outward signs."

Jarrad put his hand lightly on Clara's knee and said, "I'm sorry we had to keep you in the dark, but there was so much going on that we had to maintain the strictest security with everyone not having a need to know."

Clara's face went red as she looked down at Jarrad's hand, but when realization set in, she placed her own hand on top of his, sat back, and smiled.

Jarrad extended an open left hand in an emphatic gesture. "The messenger dragons, under the direction of Langa, learned that High Commander Kalow had been placed personally in charge of the move by King Deroth. That made it easier to know where to look for key information regarding the move. This discovery made it easy to find out where the king intended to relocate the Breeding Coop operation, which in turn led to determining when and how the move would occur. Later, with help, our dragons learned how to move the breeding dragons, the route, how to feed them, and how to care for the hatchlings.

"In the process, Langa's team learned which military units would escort the procession, what kind of overhead dragon protection was planned, which dragon units would be involved, and their planned changeovers to other dragon units.

"There were many others involved in the planning and preparation for this raid," Eleth said. "The dragons brought their information to both High Councils, Axel and Jarrad and to Ketter Harbert, who was to lead the Young Dragon raid.

"Licor, Torkar, Ketter, and Rook Dermin were placed in charge of training," Jarrad said. "To accomplish what they needed to do, they had to be given up-to-the-moment information regarding which units were to be used, where those units were based, how those units marched and gave commands, what uniforms they wore, and the most difficult thing—how did they conduct unit changeovers? Most of this information could be obtained by having the messenger dragons watch those units and listen to their conversations, but some details could not be gathered this way.

"That's where one of our biggest blessings came into play," he said with a grin. "A former high-ranking officer in the king's cavalry, by the name of Sonder Arhus, dropped by and simply asked if he could help. We were very suspicious of him at first, but the messenger dragons, which he knew nothing about, were used to double-check his background. In conjunction with Lang Privas' information-gathering unit, the dragons facilitated a background investigation in his hometown of Blatten and among men of his old cavalry unit, all of which he passed gloriously. He also soon allayed our doubts by providing insider information of the highest quality, and a lot of it. Right away, he gave us names of important contacts that we were able to put to use in many productive ways.

"Arhus helped us train our false king's cavalry unit in how to wear the uniform properly, how to give and react to orders, and how to conduct skell parade and drill, which our artificial soldiers practiced until they could act with a precision that would fool the king himself. He also trained our men in unit change-over procedures, something that we could acquire nowhere else. As you saw, our troops performed without flaw when we took over from the king's own. Lastly, Sonder is now a member of the Lang Privas' organization of spies and information gatherers."

But Clara protested, "There still must have been many little things that you didn't know or special papers that needed to be prepared or many other things that could give you away if not done right."

"Since we had good inside information," Eleth answered, "we discovered there were necessary things that couldn't just be stolen. All official documents coming from the King needed to bear his seal, and there was no way for us to sneak that away from him. But one intrepid messenger dragon managed to steal a document bearing the mark of the King's Golden Seal. We used a Mysuran artist to study the mark under a magnifying glass and create a very precise drawing. After that, we found a metalsmith in Mandara who could use the drawing to create a reverse replica of the seal and with precisely correct dimensions. He was expensive but worth it since he used bronze with an iron core, and it turned out to be an almost perfect fake. We've been able to use it more than once for important work.

"Also, in the fourth Kivan, the messenger dragons managed to place the same Mysuran artist, all dressed up in a masking suit, in a tree next to the king's own parade ground. From there, he could view Deroth's personal guard in action and draw their uniforms in precise detail. After that, seamstresses made nearly perfect copies of the King's Personal Guard's uniforms from the drawings. They also made all the gray Sanaran uniforms you see here."

"We enticed a few people," Jarrad pointed out, "who were good actors to go live in Bresci for a while and learn how to speak with a Mandaran accent. If things went well, we could blame the raid on the Mandarans.

"Finally, as you know, the Minqars the dragons wear do not prevent them from speaking to other dragons in High Language. Accordingly, we were able to get many of the king's dragons, who were still wearing jewels, to pass on to our messenger dragons incredibly sensitive information about when and where they would be going on this move and what the units would be composed of. The fact is, we almost had more information than we could possibly process and evaluate."

"Unfortunately," Jarrad added in with a sigh, "there is always the possibility of last-minute changes or accidental encounters, which can foul up everything we've planned on. We can never be totally prepared for the unexpected."

"That's all pretty amazing," Clara said. "But where do we go from here?"

Jarrad grimaced when answering this question. "We've had a team making maps, with an emphasis on finding routes we can take to get all these dragons home. The king was kind enough to bring the dragons almost halfway there. While we have tentative routes planned for our next steps, a great deal of what happens from this point on will depend on plain luck."

***

When the Breeding Coop caravan began to move, Clara and Eleth were the only members of the Breeding Coop staff to remain on any of the vehicles. The caravan's drivers and support staff, who initially joined, had all departed. Not a single soldier from Commander Graca's fine cavalry unit accompanied the train. Not a single dragon, flying cover overhead, wore a red-colored jewel. Everything in the string of strange-looking vehicles was, now under the control of a ragtag group of country folk from a southern mountain valley, all dressed in uniforms of the king's army. Nevertheless, Eleth knew that control would not last for long if they stayed on this road.

Tarak again appeared at the side of the command wagon to report that everything in the column was proceeding according to plan after having departed the rest stop.

"Excellent, Tarak," Eleth exclaimed after returning his salute. "Are the forward and rear screens in place?"

"Yes, Ma'am.

"How long do you estimate until the forward edge of the caravan reaches the bridge?

"We should be there sometime after nightfall."

"We're on a good road. Let's try to maximize the pace of our travel, without overtaxing the skells and draft dragons. The sooner we get off this road the better."

"I'll pass the word to our drivers," Tarak said with a salute and turned his skell toward the rear of the column.

"I'm no strategist," Clara pointed out as the soldier departed, "but it doesn't take a genius to figure out that the sleepers left in that field will be discovered soon enough, or something else will go wrong and the military will find out that their caravan of precious dragons from the Coops has been kidnapped. What's more, we've been traveling on the Grand Trunk Road. There will be hundreds of witnesses along this route to point out where we are and where we are going. The king's troops and dragons may experience a delay, but they will undoubtedly reach us within a day. That is, unless you have a way of making us disappear."

"Clara," Jarrad said with a smirk on his face, "you are soon to witness the greatest disappearing act in history!"

Tarak came up to the lead carriage roughly two orais later to give a report. He saluted Eleth once more and said, "We have had one of the dragon conveyances break down with a broken axle. We used draft dragons to shove it off to the side of the road, where it can be repaired."

"How long is this issue going to delay the caravan then?" Eleth asked.

"Fortunately, the King's planners have done well at their jobs. We have all of the necessary repair materials on hand, and the train will simply keep on moving without delay. Hopefully the broken conveyance will simply drop back into formation at the back of the column once it is fixed. It was very clever of you to include a blacksmith and a wainwright in the company. They are already half-way into the repair."

"Excellent, Tarak. Your diligence is appreciated. Can you provide any kind of update on the status of the bridge?"

"The bridge is secured on all sides, and the dragons in the covering team are on the alert for any traffic in the nearby woods or anywhere from which the bridge may be observed. We are taking great pains to prevent anyone from witnessing the crossing. The setting of the sunstar will soon bring darkness, making our task easier. I should also add that the wooden planks are already in position on the far side of the bridge."

"Then let's proceed with the offloading as soon as we cross the bridge. Make certain that counts are kept for each section."

***

Ahead, lay one of the few bridges of any size in the entire kingdom. It crossed over the wide and muddy Ibisen River. In the darkness, no one in the command wagon, other than Eleth, could see it at the moment. It would mark the point where members of the raiding party she commanded and the dragons they escorted would separate in a half dozen different directions. A troop of soldiers could be seen off to one side lighting dozens of torches, then walking out onto the bridge to nail them on either side of the roadway as guides.

Once the command wagon reached the far side of the river, Eleth ordered the wagoner to pull off the road about one hundred strides from the end of the bridge. She and Jarrad left the carriage and walked back to the bridge to observe how the separation transpired.

All wagons maintained a prescribed distance from the next wagon in front to prevent the weight of the vehicles from overloading the bridge's capacity. The special conveyances each stopped at the wood plank trail, which had been laid down from the road to the river just on the opposite side of the bridge. Once the conveyances stopped, the dragons on board exited with significantly greater agility than they had when climbing onto them and walked down to the river. A free firedrake, already standing in the water to serve as a guide, sent reassuring messages, via High Language, on how to walk down the planks and join her in the water.

Clara noticed the strength and confidence demonstrated by the hens as they descended from the conveyances, entered the river, and began to walk upstream. "Eleth," she said, "it looks like the exercise program you introduced to the hens in the coops has paid off. Look how our hens are moving into the river."

"What was that about?" Jarrad asked, looking at Clara.

"Eleth knew the hens would have to fly or walk most of the way to the Colony, so she invented an exercise program for the hens in the coops to use in developing their walking and flying muscles. The hens worked diligently to strengthen their legs and wings every time members of the coops' staff were out of sight. There was not very much that a hen could do to develop muscles in such a confined space, but what they could do, they did." Clara looked down, shaking her head, and laughed at the memory of seeing a giant room full of firedrake hens flapping in place, getting in each other's way, or trying to lift themselves up to the high ceiling without crashing into a neighbor who was doing the exact same thing. Eventually, they counted off numbers, and every odd-numbered hen would work out while the even numbers rested. Then they simply reversed the process.

Once empty, the conveyances on the road moved forward another hundred strides and stopped to allow some humans to remove the harnesses connecting two out of every three *draft* dragons to the conveyances. This permitted two draft dragons to exit on the right side and enter the river.

It was fortunate that messenger dragon spies had determined the king's forces had placed special hitches on the front and rear of each conveyance to permit linking them together. When free of the dragons, so much of the weight was removed from the conveyances that it became possible for one draft dragon to pull three empty conveyances linked together. As each group of three was assembled, a free dragon in front would direct the, still attached, draft dragon to start moving along the main road to the point where another free dragon would show where it should turn east onto a side road.

Similarly, once a group of about six dragons, whether hens from the coops or draft dragons, entered the water, a free dragon would direct them to start wading westward up the river, staying close to the banks. Fortunately, dragon spies determined, some weeks ago, that the muddy river was shallow near its banks for many miles and had a firm bottom composed of pebbly rocks. The high runoff of the spring season had cleared most of the mud from the river's edges, allowing it to easily support a dragon's weight.

Eleth, Jarrad, and Clara watched this process continue for the better part of an orai, with at least one-third of the vehicles remaining to be unloaded, when a siris dragon descended from the sky and settled into the space next to the command carriage.

"Commander Eleth," it began. "You may not remember me. My name is Karu, and I am part of the overhead protection group."

"Yes, said Eleth, "I remember you from my visits to the Colony. Your mate is Ansa, and you have a female youngling."

"You remember correctly, Commander. I have come to report that one of the drivers from the Breeding Coop staff, which was left at the first rest stop, has managed to make his way to the headquarters of Commander Graca. I believe he stole a farmer's cart and skell to do it so quickly. Both Graca's men and their skells are worn out, having had little opportunity to rest. Nevertheless, he set up an investigatory force of about two-hundred cavalry and sent a message to the dragon base from which the original dragon escort came. Graca's force is well armed with crossbows and swords and has departed in this direction with the purpose of finding us."

Eleth looked intensely over at Jarrad and began running her tongue back and forth behind her lower lip.

Chapter Twenty-Four

OTHER RAIDS

The way flying dragons entered the Command Complex for the King's Cadet Dragon Reserve was a wide tunnel bored through the side of a high rocky hill. The dragons landed on one side of the opening and took off from the other. Hallways dug out at intervals led off to large stalls where guard dragons were billeted and where quarters for flight officers, miscellaneous workrooms, and one hall leading to the Reserve's Command Center were located. This was the place where Adjutant Commander Aran Calda, the Commander of the Dragon Reserve Cohort, oversaw all the complex operations found in the reserve.

He had subordinates who took care of managing the staff workers in the Reserve, managing the care and feeding of guard dragons housed in the Command Hill, or observing and managing the health of the two hundred fifty or so young dragons now residing throughout the Reserve. His subordinates lived in compartments set up below the flight center. The Commander, himself, took direct responsibility for all the flying officers who guarded this reserve against any who might threaten the upcoming generation prepared for the Kingdom's dragon air and ground forces.

The High Command had recently discovered that dragons can see and function in the dark. Nevertheless, he did not trust sending out any of his twenty-four officers and associated dragons, on the mere belief that the beasts could follow commands properly if not clearly verified by their flying officers. With Kivan only providing a large smile of light tonight, he did not send his dragons out on patrol. Patrols would begin at the first glimmer of morning, some three orais away. Still, he insisted that the Command Center itself be manned, at least minimally, around the clock and with minimal lights to maximize the night vision of his men. Tonight, he was undertaking a surprise inspection to make certain his people were on their toes. His second in command accompanied him only a step or two behind.

***

Kivan, failing in its duty to light any part of the night due to a blanket of high clouds, made approaching the entrance to the tunnel very easy for the free forces. Shaddra glided silently toward the opening, virtually invisible, due to her near-black color adopted for this mission. Axel, riding on Shaddra's back, appeared only slightly more visible, due to his black masking suit and black painted face and hands. Even the saddle had been dyed black.

Both Axel and Shaddra kept their eyes glued on the two protected sentry positions at the mouth of the tunnel. At this distance, the sentries were quite visible to the invaders' dragon eyes, but both sentries, exposed from the waist up, appeared to be looking straight out into the dark with unfocused eyes. When the messenger dragon reached a point approximately fifty strides away from the opening, Axel loosed two arrows in quick succession. Each arrow, carefully constructed with a small bag of wet sand in place of the usual arrowhead, struck its target hard in the chest. The arrows did not penetrate the heavily mailed armor of the sentries, but the shock waves they started penetrated each sentry's iron mail and wool gambeson (worn underneath to cushion shocks) to momentarily stun the muscles of their diaphragms. Both sentries immediately fell to the ground, unable to speak, unable to move and concerned only with getting every possible wisp of air into their lungs.

Shaddra landed in the flyway and hastily moved aside to allow Torkar to make his landing, too. Axel jumped off Shaddra and headed for the left-most sentry, while Rook leaped off Torkar and ran to the right. Three minutes later, the two sentries were trussed up, gagged, and still gasping for air, though not quite so desperately as before. In rapid succession, four more firedrakes landed on the flyway, each as concerned for silence as the first two dragons. These did not stop, even to offload their riders, until they had reached the passages leading to the dragon pens and the quarters of flight officers. Another firedrake turned around at that point and watched the passages to the headquarters and supply areas. The dragon's riders ran down the flightway to incapacitate any guards stationed at the other end or in between. They then lit the torches in the flight center near the entryways to the officer's quarters.

Axel did a run-through of his mental checklist: Shaddra now watched the entrance to the dragon pens. Using their night vision, Torkar, Goran, and Arnal watched the three rooms used for flight officers' quarters, and Sental watched the opening leading to the HQ and the supply rooms.

A messenger dragon suddenly appeared from nowhere to indicate that all quarters in the level below the flightway were under control.

Next, Axel checked his riders, who were all armed with bows. Upon receiving a 'thumbs-up' from each of them, Axel and two of the riders quietly opened the doors to the flight officer's quarters and placed shims along the door bottoms to prevent them from being closed again. At this point, Axel caught the eyes of all the dragons again and nodded his head. Four firedrakes suddenly roared in unison, loud enough to shake the stone walls about them.

A crowd of the king's dragonriders raced out of their quarters only to stop abruptly when they saw what was waiting for them.

Stepping forward, Axel shouted, "Don't touch your Bechars! If we see even one dragon poke its nose out of the pens, the next communication you'll hear will be the blast when you and everything in your rooms, except your Bechars, of course, are incinerated.

"You should be plenty awake now. Follow my next instructions carefully, or you'll make my dragons mad. Everyone return to your quarters!"

Axel gave them time to disappear and then announced, "I will say 'right,' 'center,' and 'left' in that order. Each time I say one of those words, one and only one of you will come unarmed out of the doors from your quarters and from my point of view. You will walk five steps forward, lay your Bechar on the floor, and return to your room. Any appearance of a weapon or disobedience to a command will result in a firestrike. I will announce the next room as soon as the hall is clear. After that, everything will be repeated again and again until all of you have had your turn to walk out and greet us. Honestly, we don't want to hurt you. If we did, remember it would be easiest for us to just toast you and pick your Bechars off the floor."

Axel heard a familiar thunk. Without thinking, he turned and loosed an arrow at the sound. He watched his arrow fly only a short distance to strike a man in the center of his chest. The spent crossbow the man was holding dropped to the floor, followed swiftly by the man's body. Another man, standing next to the shooter, dropped a crossbow and threw up his hands. The fallen crossbow fired, but the quarrel slipped off the string and went nowhere.

Without looking, Axel knew the first quarrel had struck his side and penetrated his armor. Rook was there in an instant, lifting Axel's armor, gambeson, and tunic and wrapping bandages around his chest to take care of the wound. He had a very surprised look on his face but said nothing. Axel could tell the quarrel likely struck a lower rib just behind his left shoulder and bounced off. The rib might be broken. This was going to hurt... a lot.

Axel turned back toward the room and glanced at Shaddra. She gave him an 'okay' signal. No dragons had ventured forth from their stalls. "Sorry for that diversion, everyone. Someone tried shooting me with a crossbow, and I had to kill him. I hope he wasn't a friend of yours. Now, let's start. Left," he called out loudly and firmly."

A young man walked stiffly out of the left barracks room, looked over at the body of his commander, and then over at Axel, who had nocked another arrow to his bow. The man placed his Bechar on the floor and backed up into the same room he came from. Rook rushed to pick up the jewel and place it in a bag.

Why did Rook have that surprised look? Axel thought. He glanced down at his wound, which was now bandaged and covered by his black tunic, but on the floor were large drops of blood. They didn't look quite right. The light from the wall lanterns was not bright; still, with his dragon eyes, he could tell. The blood had a definite purple color, but it seemed to be turning red along the outside edges of the drops! How can that be? *Better not think about it now.*

"Center," he called out. As before, a man came out of the center room and left his Bechar. Once more, Rook rushed to retrieve the Bechar after the man vanished back into his barracks.

"Right." This time a woman walked out of the right-most barracks door. *Ah, yes,* he wondered. *Just how many of the king's dragonriders were women? He remembered that he, himself, killed one when...* He quickly decided to drop that thought. *Yes, the quarters on the right side are where the female officers sleep.*

"Left."

So, the cadence continued, 'left, center, right, left, center, right,' until someone from each barracks announced, "I am the last."

"It's strange that the women's barracks should announce that all there have surrendered their Bechars," said Axel. "I count five Bechars, which have come from that barracks. But I am certain that as little as fifteen minutes ago there were six women. If I don't see that last Bechar within thirty seconds, I'll have my dragon friend scorch the room and we'll worry about who was the offending officer later."

Right on cue, a red-faced and obviously, angry woman stepped out of the barracks to place her Bechar on the floor.

"I'm glad you found your senses, ma'am. It would displease me greatly to dispatch five innocent spirits because of one unbending heart."

Axel spun on his heel to face the officer who had dropped the crossbow. He took a deep breath and let it out slowly; that little movement hurt a lot. All the while he stared into the near-panicked officer's eyes. "I'm sorry about your commander's unfortunate death. He didn't need to die, you know, and you don't have to either. Let me think, you are Captain Menek, right?" A widening of the officer's eyes confirmed to Axel he was correct.

Axel walked over to the commander's body, bent down, and removed a chain from around the man's neck. "Captain, would you please accompany me into the commander's office or, perhaps, I should say, your office since you obviously take up the acting role of commander in the event of his, er, unexpected absence?" Axel also nodded at one of the firedrakes and walked into the headquarters area without looking back. The acting commander and Torkar followed behind.

Axel did not stop in the main headquarters area but proceeded directly into the commander's office. There, he removed a picture of the king from the wall, revealing a safe, and placed his key into one of two obvious keyholes in the safe's door. He turned around to face Captain Menek and stepped to one side. "Now, if you please?"

Menek looked over his shoulder at the menacingly close firedrake and, obediently following Axel's implied instructions, used a second key hanging from his neck to unlock and open the safe.

Axel called for Rook, who stepped into the office, opened the safe and started pulling fistfuls of Bechars from the shelves inside.

"Okay, then," Axel said, "you know what to do. Be sure to send the message."

***

Rook Dermin stood on the edge of a large mead at the base of the rocky foothill, which contained the Command Complex for the King's Cadet Dragon Reserve. Not far away stood six firedrakes and two siris dragons; in the dim light from Kivan, more dragons could be seen approaching. All were ridden by Mysurans who volunteered for this mission. Rook held out the chain from which the approximately two-hundred-fifty red Bechars hung suspended. In a loud commanding voice, he called out, 'Find me!'

For many sycles, Axel, Eleth and Jarrad had pondered how to gather the two hundred-plus fledglings that were scattered about the Cadet Dragon Reserve with little luck. It was only when Eleth suggested that the young dragon should have some way of being ordered to come to the one who possessed their Bechars that Axel remembered something important. His GranDa, a former flying officer himself, had taught him about the Code of Orders that every flying officer needed to know. GrandDa never really went into a lot of detail about them, but he figured out that 'Find me' meant come stand on my right side so I can mount you. 'Present me' meant to stand for inspection. The phrase 'Protect me' signified safeguarding the rider through the specific techniques that would follow. 'Take me' meant literally to take the rider somewhere. Finally, 'attack' meant attacking something as directed and by using whatever technique is provided next.

It was only when Eleth suggested that there had to be a way for the Bechar to find its assigned dragon that Axel remembered the Code. He decided that "Find Me" did not mean "come stand on my right side so I can mount you." Rather, it meant "Come from wherever you are and find me." It meant just the opposite of Eleth's thoughts, in that the Minqar was finding its Bechar." Rook was, now, using the Code of Orders to call all of the fledglings for which he held a Bechar. They should soon be coming from wherever they are in the reserve.

Rook was surprised at how quickly they started appearing. The mead was covered with low grasses and bracken of light color, so once the small dragons started landing, it was easy to see them, but he quickly lost count, and they were followed by much larger, but not yet adult, dragons.

After half an orai, Rook turned to Sental, a free firedrake who volunteered to work with the young dragons. "Sental," he said, "I have two-hundred-fifty-three Bechars in my hand. Can you tell, using your High Language whether all of the dragons associated with those Bechars have arrived?"

"Rook," Sental answered in a voice filled with great pleasure, "We have two hundred twenty-nine dragons on the field before us. Twenty-four draft dragons are yet to arrive. It takes them longer."

"Wonderful," Rook said in response. "As soon as our wayward dragons arrive, will you please give me a sign?"

"I will indeed."

About half an orai later, Rook saw Sental point to a small group of obviously fatigued draft dragons settle into the cluster gathered in the meadow. A nod from Sental indicated these were the last.

Rook took a deep breath and shakily blew it out through a fist he held up to his mouth. "May I please have your attention," he shouted. "To make certain that all of you hear and understand my words, my good friend Sental, who is a firedrake, will translate everything I say into High Speech. If, for any reason, you cannot hear or understand what we say, please step forward."

There was no movement from the crowd of fledglings.

"Okay," Rook continued, and Sental translated. "Off to our right and left is a group of free dragons. When I say 'free,' I mean that either they have never worn a jewel in their necks or they have had the force commanding the Minqars in their necks destroyed. By that, what I really mean is the Bechars that have enslaved them for most of their lives have been destroyed. Now, all of the dragons beside us have the power of 'free will' and can live their lives as they wish. We would like to offer you the same opportunity. These dragons would also like to offer you a place in their Colony of Free Dragons, where you would be completely free from human control."

Remembering Axel's words—that he should not give the young dragons any choice, for they might fear losing their freedom—Rook carefully arranged the Bechars in a row across several large, flat rocks, bought specifically for this purpose. He laid them gently on the ground at his feet. At his nod, ten young men stepped forward, wielding rocks and hammers, and began smashing the Bechars. In a swift moment, they were reduced to shimmering piles of white, glittering sparkles that scattered across the ground.

"What you are feeling right now," Rook said, "is the removal of a yoke of bondage. You are no longer beholden to me or any other human. Take care to guard your freedom with all your might, because someone, whether human or dragon, may someday try to take it from you. Always be on the alert, because there are still many dragons out there who are under the control of a Bechar and would likely try to take your lives."

"Now, the dragons that you see next to us are here to guide you to the Free Colony. Because of the weakness that still lies in your wings and legs, this process will take some time. Sental will lead the dragons who, will help you to find resting places and food on the route to your new home. Follow their instructions and they will lead you step-by-step to your future."

At that point, the dragons began to divide into smaller groups, first based on whether they were flyers or draft dragons, and then according to their strength and ability to fly or walk. Every group had adult dragons, similar to them, to serve as protectors and guides. Pre-positioned sites were already set up to ease the way of their travel and keep them hidden from enslaved dragons as much as possible. No two groups would follow the same route of travel, and the draft dragons would have mounted soldiers following behind, with the task of masking tracks and preparing miscues to divert any king's troops trying to follow.

"I wish you all a safe and successful journey. You may leave as soon as your guides determine you are ready."

***

Axel stood on the lip of the flightway into the Command Complex, watching the departing groups of dragons down on the plain below. His dragon sight gave him a clear view of how things were progressing, and he could tell that Rook was definitely in control.

He turned around and addressed the dragons and humans from the Free Colony grouped behind him. "I have received messages saying that the other raids are proceeding, so far, as planned," he announced. "Once the last group leaves the plain below, we will depart for our secondary objectives. You should all have no doubts about your specific next assignment. If you are taking our new friends from the Reserve Guard Detail home, please set a good example for them."

Preter Odif, a man, in his thirties or so, approached Axel and stopped, coming to a crisp attitude of attention. "Commander Axel," he said, "all the king's soldiers are, now, locked in the largest barracks room. It should take them an orai or two to break out."

"At ease, Preter. We don't need to be quite so formal when by ourselves."

I know, sir. But making a good habit now prevents mistakes later on."

"Oh, yes. I've heard that somewhere, too."

The man smiled and backed off, knowing it was one of Axel's favorite aphorisms. He, in turn, had picked it up from Sonder Arhus.

Axel looked back to the plain and thought how nearly every grown dragon down there, now working with the young dragons, was a slave only two sycles ago. Training the fifty-odd new dragons, which had come from the recent large battle, had been a huge task. Now, the Free Dragons and their human allies were working to bring on as many as four to five hundred more dragons of varying ages. Oh, what were they getting themselves into?

***

The headquarters for the King's Young Dragon Reserve was simply a building attached to a row of other buildings. There was nothing fancy about any of them. They just held the quarters for the various workers who kept this operation going and, of course, the butcher shops, too. The facility didn't directly rank protection by even one of the king's dragons since there was a Dragon Force Base only four tondrins down the road. A dragon could fly that distance in less than ten minutes, so why bother?

Even the commander of this complex held only the rank of captain. That was because the job was coonsidered a mere caretaker's role. Watching a bunch of near-adolescent dragons was as exciting as tending a herd of ellams. At least a herd keeper occasionally had to fight off a killer beast. But no killer beast ever came here. Simply put, the job was boring.

Captain Embar wondered why anyone even bothered to hang around these little beasts, other than to feed them and clean out their pens. Overseeing the work of this camp was definitely not a job for a King's officer. His commander, over in Rabianice, had not appeared for an inspection tour in two years. The few officers stationed here were not even allowed to share in any of the cuttings from the butchered dragons. Only individuals of high influence in Rabianice earned that privilege.

After waking in the middle of the night on the eighth day of the sixth Kivan, Embar dressed quickly and walked out to the pens. This activity was not his normal practice, but he was not sleeping well, and he needed something to do besides stare at a dark ceiling. The first light from Kivan was only just beginning to show itself in ruddy-colored reds and grays. A platform on one edge of the large pens would give him the best view once there was a little more light reaching the facility.

The pens were huge to fit the more than approximately two hundred dragons held here, aged between three Kivans and five years. Made of vertical and horizontal iron bars, a finger thick and suspended from tall wooden poles placed liberally about the compound, the main pens covered an area of two hundred strides on a side and ten strides high and were divided into four separate sections to keep males and females separate from each other, as well as the more recently arrived separated from the nearly fledged. Walkways around the outsides provided access to each of the pens separately.

Because it was never a good idea to mix flying dragons with non-flying ones, one more pen, off to the side, held nothing but draft dragons. Its size was a quarter of the area found in the main pens and rose to only half the height, but the bars were twice as thick. About thirty-five draft dragon younglings made their home in that pen.

Fortunately, Embar only managed operations here. An actual caretaker's job was always risky. For that reason, the workers all wore heavy protective clothing to avoid receiving wounds from the fiendishly sharp teeth these children of Archos had in their mouths and the claws, which grew ever sharper as the beasts aged. Even so, the medical staff stayed busy, and the number of staff losses due to wounds stayed high. They were fortunate that dragons don't develop the ability to throw fire until they reach five years of age.

When Kivan brightened enough so that Embar could see into the pens, he blinked hard. The night haze hid things from view, but he should be seeing movement out there. The little miscreations of the gods were always moving, night or day, kicking up dust. But, tonight, there was no movement, no dust. In fact, the pens... were empty. *The pens were empty*! How could two hundred odd animals varying in size from that of a coshil to a yolka just disappear overnight?!

Captain Embar raced back to his headquarters to get messages off to the Flying Corps, and his commander as quickly as possible. As he raced along, he did not notice in the dark that on five separate corners, several wooden support poles had been literally pulled out of the ground.

When he reached his office, he threw open the door, ran to his desk, and, without sitting down, automatically reached for the alarm bell, only to find that it was not in its usual place in the corner of his desk. A special raised mounting used to keep the alarm bell ready at hand was, presently, empty.

A soft click sounded from the direction of his door, betraying that it had just been closed. The noise made him look up. In the dim glow of the room's sole candle, he saw four soldiers—all clad in the dark-blue uniforms of Mandara—standing before him, each with a loaded crossbow leveled at his chest.

"If you wish to live beyond the next minute," said the closest of the soldiers with a strange accent, you will open the safe containing the Bechars of your dragons."

"I... I can't do that. The king has entrusted me with...."

A fifth soldier came up from behind, and thrusting something into Embar's open mouth, he securely tied the gag down with a cloth strip. Embar also felt his hands being grabbed and securely tied behind him.

The soldier who spoke before said, "I'm afraid you misunderstood what I told you. I wasn't giving you a choice."

Embar found himself placed against the wall, facing the four soldiers armed with crossbows.

The soldier spoke again, saying, "When I give the command, one of these men will shoot a bolt into your right leg. If you haven't indicated you will comply with my order by then, you will be shot in the left leg. If you haven't satisfied me by then, you will be shot in the right arm, and the process will go on until I am satisfied. I'm sure we can find enough places to go on shooting you to keep the game up for some time. Do you have anything to say before we start?"

***

The ability of young dragons to follow instructions without complaint or objection remained a total surprise for Ketter Harbert. Ketter stood next to Arad, his assistant commander on this raid, watching a queue of nearly two hundred young dragons obediently, if not patiently, waiting for their turn to load into special belly baskets worn by a line of firedrakes. The charges over which he and Arad had taken responsibility were not draft dragon hatchlings, which meant two and sometimes even three of the small dragons would fit into a single basket. Conditions in the baskets would be cramped, but Arad assured Ketter that no complaints would be heard during the forty-minute ride to the first stopover along the way to the Free Colony.

A set of seventeen Firedrakes had the difficult task of moving the draft dragon younglings. Only one youngling could be carried at a time, so each dragon would be making two trips to the stopover place reserved for the draft dragons—the first stop on their journey home.

Thirty firedrakes took their turns at landing, loading the other young dragons and taking off for their first stopover, which lay in a narrow, heavily forested valley thirty tondrins to the west. The young dragons were quickly offloaded and directed by free dragons at that location to places where they could find food and cover. The firedrakes immediately returned to the Young Dragons Reserve to pick up another load. Round trip, the journey required less than an orai. Ketter and Arad followed the last flight from the reserve, which took off just a little more than four orais after the first had left.

Thirty tondrins separation was not enough to ensure safety, Ketter knew. But, when the king's forces finally arrived at the reserve, sometime in the morning, they would find only about thirty members of the human staff, of which none could provide concrete information as to what happened. They could say that an unknown number of men in dark-blue uniforms took over the operation; the leader spoke with a strange accent; something tore holes in the fences surrounding the young dragons, and all of the young dragons in the reserve escaped into the night.

What concerned Ketter more than anything was that enemy dragons might appear before he could get all of his charges off to the second way-stop on their very long journey. The king's dragonriders would have some idea as to the limitations involved in transporting two hundred non-flying dragons. He wanted to get as much distance between his charges and the Reserve and well before any serious threats arrived. He took some small hope in the fact that the king thought less of these non-flying dragons than he did for any of the others.

Chapter Twenty-Five

DECEPTION

Eleth glanced down the long line of dragons still in conveyances, all needing to be offloaded, and then at Karu, a male, golden-brown colored siris dragon. "Hmm," she said, "if Graca's force were in good shape, I would expect them to reach the Ibisen bridge in about two and a half orais. Since they are tired, it will take a little longer."

"Am I correct in thinking there are no dragons available to him anywhere nearby?" Eleth asked.

"Yes, Commander," the Karu answered. "Graca has sent messengers out to the Northern Special Action Group's headquarters and Garrison Woolwell for assistance. As you already know, there will likely be little or no assistance coming from either of those sources. As I said, he has also sent a messenger to the dragon base near Sinegor, where the original escorts were stationed. It will take the messenger as much time to reach that base as for the mounted regiment to reach the Ibisen Bridge."

"Jarrad, how much time will be required to finish offloading?"

"I believe it will require at least two orais and that is assuming no problems arise."

"If we can get clear of this place, the passage of their two hundred skells would only serve to help hide our tracks. The dragons could be a very real problem if they arrive soon thereafter. Maybe you ought to see what you can do to hurry things up a bit, Jarrad."

"Yes, Ma'am!"

Jarrad leaped off the carriage rather nimbly for a fifty-some-odd-year-old man. He loosed the reins of a skell, tied to the rear of the carriage, and turned its head back to the column of vehicles.

When the last of the special dragon transportation conveyances had been unloaded, Eleth ordered the draft dragons, pulling empty conveyances, to make all possible speed toward the prepared position on the seacoast. Meanwhile, the wooden planks were pulled up from the roadside and set adrift down the river from the middle of the bridge.

The Mysuran cavalry made every possible effort to disguise whatever signs of the unloading remained at the bridge. This included removing the torches, scratching out tracks with leafy tree branches, spreading mixed small gravel and sand over the larger indentations, and running large numbers of the skells stolen from Garrison Woolwell over the road and much of the roadside repeatedly.

Using less care to hide their tracks, the draft dragons, still pulling conveyances and most of the remaining wagons, headed east twelve tondrins to a small but deep ocean inlet. Here, Mysuran carpenters had been at work for days making simple but strong landing piers big enough to serve very large ships. All of the draft dragons were released from their burdens this time after separating the conjoined conveyances and parking their loads in an organized manner. They made many tracks from the conveyances to the docks, which extended out to deep water. To make it appear that even more dragons were involved, they raised their tails and carefully walked backward to the conveyances to do it all over again.

Some of the top cover dragons also landed to mingle their tracks with the others. Once a sufficient number of tracks were laid across the breach, the draft dragons carefully entered the ocean and began walking south, precisely at the level where their tracks would be quickly washed away by waves and the incoming tide.

The skellmen rode their steeds and wagons over the beach to make the scene even more confusing, many of them riding up onto the docks, then stepping into the ocean off low platforms, which were then removed. In the end, all ended up marching, or swimming, into the rolling waves and joining those headed south. They would turn to the west again in the shallows of one of the many smaller rivers flowing into the sea. After that, they could split up and travel again on roadways.

Various tactics were used to confuse those pursuing from behind, including creating false trails and using decoys to mislead pursuers. Some of the skellmen changed to their civilian clothing right away and broke off into groups of two or three riders. Military markings were removed from saddles and other equipment that would be retained. All wagons not required for further use by the Free Peoples were abandoned further down the beach, and their teams were set free.

Some stayed in groups of twenty or so riders for a time before dropping their military disguises. These acts caused witnesses along the way to gain conflicting understandings of what they saw and of what they could report.

***

One dragon remained on a conveyance near the beach to climb down last. On Eleth's instruction, the driver of the carriage carrying Eleth, Clara, and Jarrad moved his vehicle to join old Orfa, who was just stepping down to the sand. The old firedrake turned her head when she heard the wagon's approach. "You have come to give me my medicine, haven't you?"

Both Clara and Eleth climbed out of the carriage to place their arms around the old hen to the extent they *could* reach. Patting Orfa's side Eleth said, "I have some medicine for you, but I would rather find a way for you to not take it."

"Don't be silly, girl." the dragon said. "I have lived a long time and have finally come to an end, even as we all must. The place you go is too far for me, yet I have the honor of not only dying free, but also of helping others to win their freedom from the tyrant. I will not enter ashamed into whatever lies beyond."

"That you will not. At least one of your children is now free, and by spreading your tracks across this beach, you will help a hundred more to find safety.

"Oh, Orfa," Clara said, with tears running down her face in rivulets. I have known you for almost as long as I have been working in the Coops. I don't know what life will be like without you."

Eleth also cried, silently, but with many tears. "I will miss your wisdom and miss playing with your tiny hatchlings," she said.

"Please do not worry for me, Daughter of the Great Ceragon. You must take care of yourself. I foresee life will be good for you, but it will be filled with dangers. You were born for that. It is your destiny to fulfill the words of Ceragon, himself. Go join hands with the young man, who waits for you, and free the world. I will be happy knowing I filled my small part in the foretelling. Remember, I will be watching you. Of that, you may be sure. Now, off with you and let me do my part in peace."

Eleth walked over to one of the conveyances and laid a package on its wooden deck. She looked back a long time at Orfa before letting go of it and then returned to her carriage. Orfa watched her movements the whole time with sharp eyes.

Checking to ensure everyone was on board, the driver gave a shrill whistle, causing the two skells to carry the wagon off into the surf and turn south to follow the draft dragons.

For the next orai, Orfa carefully made sets of tracks to look like many hens had climbed down from the conveyances and marched to the docks. She used every clever trick she could think of to hide the fact that all the tracks came from simply one female dragon. Once satisfied, she went to where the paper package lay, put it into her mouth, and swallowed. She looked down the beach in the direction her friends had departed, sighed heavily, and found a comfortable place where she could settle in and enjoy the ocean view.

Before leaving the road, one of the humans had told her the tide would be coming in, which would help hide their footprints. She did not know what a tide was and looked out into the ocean for anything that could be a tide but saw nothing. The ocean waves were lapping at her forefeet, and she liked the feeling of that. There were a lot of spider-like animals in the water. She would stay here and watch them for a while.

Off in the trees, a man on skelback waited for the dragon to die. He would be as patient as possible, but the dragon's white jewel must be retrieved and smashed before he rode out on his trip south.

***

King Deroth paced back and forth in front of five men, all sitting chained to their chairs. In passing each man, the king firmly placed his swagger stick under the captive's chin and brought the man's head up so Deroth could glare into his eyes, as if this act would reveal all the information the king needed to know.

"What has happened to you five? Until this year you were all my most trusted, reliable officers. I could once count on you to do anything I asked for, and it would be done immediately! But this year, this year! You started out by losing six dragons on ordinary missions, and then, I asked you to destroy two little undefended towns, and you not only failed in your missions, but somehow... *somehow* you managed to lose *every* dragon in the attacking force!

"At least we found two bodies from the first six that went missing. It's been more than a full sycle since the attack on the Valley, and you've found nothing else!" he shouted, with his whole face engaged in a sneer. "You even lost the six dragons sent to learn what happened to the first forty-one!

"Now, in just the first half of this day, I am getting reports that all three of my special dragon reserves have been raided and every one of the dragon residents has disappeared, including most of the guard dragons. It's early, as yet. Perhaps these reports are in error. However, I may find out by nightfall that *all* my dragon armies have disappeared!

"Why didn't you see this coming? You were the ones in charge. High Commander Kalow, why weren't you prepared for this, the most disastrous day in my entire reign? Let me tell you the truth; if we can't discover where these dragons have gone, it will take a year or most likely more for our forces to recover.

"Graca, you had charge of the breeding hens. Archos' excrement! They couldn't fly and they couldn't walk, yet they simply disappeared from your watch.

"As for the rest of you, and all of you, if we manage to locate our dragons in good condition, you may yet live. But, right now, your future prospects aren't looking very bright.

"Guards! Get these idiots out of my sight!"

Once the room was cleared, Deroth turned around and looked Brasa, the Intelligence Adjutant, in the face.

"What is happening, Brasa? Who has done all this work? Was it the Mandarans? Soldiers were seen wearing Mandaran uniforms and they are closest to the Mysura Valley. But how could they expect to pull it off?"

"I'm afraid it could have been either the Mandarans or the Kolodrans, or even the two working together. We just don't know. However, we can speculate about the possible reasons for these events.

"The most likely purpose is to occupy the Sanaran ground and air forces while our enemy launches an invasion. Such an invasion could happen in either the south or the north. If there are no signs of military moves associated with an invasion within, say, a sycle, then this option falls to the bottom of the pile.

"The second most likely option is to steal or destroy as many Sanaran dragons as possible, whether they be young or of fighting age, and thereby reduce the availability of dragons to the Sanaran military in the future.

"Our forces are already on the alert throughout the kingdom," Deroth said. I assume your analysis means we should organize for a cross-border attack?"

"Yes, but that may swiftly change as we learn more. We definitely must retain sufficient force to conduct a kingdom-wide search for the dragons and also for a small army of humans, soldiers of some kind, based on their training."

"But, if we do that, we must take at least some forces away from the borders."

"Correct, Sire. But we can do it in secret, with only minimal numbers coming from any one unit. We want neither our people nor our enemies to know what has happened or is happening. We could also take more dragons from the remote areas of the borders, where attacks are extremely unlikely."

"As for the Mysura Valley attack, it never happened."

"All right, see to it. Oh, and kill those incompetents that just left. I have no further purpose for them. Place Zadar Beorg in charge of the military and promote the other men's seconds-in-command as replacements. Give them all the number one priority of finding my dragons. Of course, for some of them, that won't start until we can be assured there will be no invasion in either the north or the south."

"As you wish, sire.

"You are dismissed."

"Yes, Sire"

Since most of the dragons removed from the reserves could not fly, and nothing could be done about the dragons that may have been taken away by ship, Brasa determined he would instruct the new commanders in the middle of the kingdom to concentrate their efforts on ground searches conducted along logical escape routes. Perhaps some of the stolen dragons could yet be recaptured.

Chapter Twenty-Six

THE TIVERTS RIVER ROAD

On the fifteenth day after the raids began, Shaddra and Axel landed at the Free Colony flightway an orai before the first light from the sunstar made its appearance. Having finished a night of searching for teams of walking dragons, the two went immediately to Kulek, who was acting as the coordinator for all the teams. Kulek and his staff, which included two firedrakes and seven humans (five of whom were female), were still compiling reports from all sources and aligning them with the chart of planned groupings and routes. They looked exhausted but relieved. Obviously, the night was going well.

Kulek looked up from his reports when he heard Shaddra and Axel approaching. "I am so very glad to see you two," he said.

"We are glad to see you also," Axel responded. "How many teams have not yet reported?"

"Three teams of walking dragons and two teams of Mysurans."

"What about Eleth? When did she come in?"

"I thought she was with you."

"What? She's not with us. Where and when was she last seen?"

Kulek turned back to one of his human assistants and talked for a moment. The woman ran to a pile of papers and started sorting through them. A quarter way through the stack, she grabbed a sheet and handed it to Kulek.

"We have a report saying she joined Tarak Ranel's team about eight orais ago. That's all I can say for sure."

"What does Ranel have?"

A troop of twenty-five Mysurans. They were assigned final cleanup duty behind the last of the walking teams."

"Do you know where they are right now?"

"Unfortunately, that was our last record of Ranel."

"Eleth's still out there, and it's getting light," Axel said. "Where was she when that report was made?"

"At the confluence of the Silistra and Tiverts Rivers."

"That would put them, perhaps, twenty tondrins east of Blatten now," Axel thought aloud.

"Eleth knows how to take care of herself, Shaddra interjected."

"Yes, if she was by herself. But she's apparently with a group of twenty-five of our people, and that's a bigger target. I'm sorry, my excellent friend, but I have to go out again. I'll go find a messenger dragon who is more rested." He turned toward the group of dragons gathered a short distance down the hall.

Shaddra placed a large hand on Axel's shoulder. "Axel, she said, when it comes to Eleth's safety, you know that I am your partner, even as I am your partner in all things."

"Sometimes I think you give too much, my friend."

The dragon grinned and shook her head. "You and I have been working together on this project for more than a sycle. What have I done that you have not?"

Axel grimaced, reached up to pat the messenger dragon on the shoulder, and said, "As you wish, Shaddra. Let's go."

Acting on a hunch, Axel grabbed a bag of the throwing knives Eleth preferred and a large bundle of arrows, which he tied to Shaddra's saddle before leaving.

After crossing the mountains into the next valley northward, Axel requested that Shaddra check out the roads to the south, leading to the convergence of the Silistra and Tiverts Rivers for any signs of the missing soldiers. Unfortunately, there were several roads in that area and no way to know which one the Mysuran troop would be taking.

Shortly after passing the town of Blatten, they passed over a group of eleven siris dragons and firedrakes walking along the road beneath them. The group was turning onto a less-well-used road, which would bypass the town and lead toward the Loft.

"A messenger dragon is ascending to meet us," said Shaddra. "I believe she is Tistra."

Axel peered down in the direction of the dragons on the ground and searched about for a moment or two before he noticed an ascending light brown-colored dragon. "I think you have eyes that are better than any dragon I know," he said.

When the messenger dragon approached, she exchanged words with Shaddra in High Language.

Shaddra translated her message. "Tistra says the hens she is accompanying are exhausted and suffering from sore feet and muscle problems, but still determined to reach their goal."

Axel waved at Tistra and shouted, "Tell the hens they are less than half a day away from the check-in point. Their journey is almost over!"

Tistra called back in human language, "Thank you, *Son of Ceragon*. Your words will inspire them all the more!" and she banked off to the south to rejoin her group and pass on Axel's tidings.

A dark, overcast sky threatened rain and limited the altitude at which Shaddra could fly while still retaining a view of the ground. That, in turn, limited the amount of ground they could observe at any one time. Since the hens were found on a road linking to the Silistra River area, they started by observing the Silistra River Road and its offshoots.

After nearly two orais of looking at roads near the Silistra, they approached that river's junction with the Tiverts River, which came from the north. Shortly thereafter, Shaddra called out, "A black-colored messenger dragon with a rider is rising from those trees four or five tondrins to the east. Shall we check it out?"

"Please, let's do."

When Shaddra reached the point where the dragon first appeared, it became obvious what it had been up to. Below them, a troop of about one hundred gray-clad soldiers was already on the road and moving at speed toward the west.

"Shall we go for the dragon?" Shaddra asked.

"Yes," Axel replied. "It's too close to home to have unfriendly dragons flying about, and we need to learn what it knows."

Shaddra used an elevation advantage to race down to the messenger dragon. Still in her invisible mode, it would have been difficult for the dragon to spot Axel, even if it were looking in his direction. Neither the dragon nor its rider glanced back as Shaddra slipped in behind, close enough for Axel to get off a bowshot. Only one arrow was needed to drop the rider, and two additional arrows managed to make a slice through the tether. After that, it turned into a race for the ground.

The rider's body struck Tamerel before Shaddra could reach him. Axel jumped off his saddle only a second or two later and raced after the Bechar. Meanwhile, Shaddra turned to fend off the attacking messenger dragon, who was diving closely behind. They collided twenty or so strides above the ground but came out of the tangle of dragon wings, tails, and heads with little apparent damage to either side. By that time, Axel had crushed the Bechar. Immediately, the other messenger dragon fell back on its haunches in a state of total confusion.

Axel walked up to Shaddra, who was panting heavily, and patted her on the shoulder. "Are you okay, my friend?" he asked with genuine concern.

Shaddra looked around her body, shook a limb or two, and replied, "There is no damage I can determine."

"I'm surprised you didn't come out of that with serious wounds," Axel said. "Sometimes, I think you're a little too ready to sacrifice yourself."

"I do what I have to do."

"Just remember you're too precious to lose."

The dragon merely looked back at Axel with a blank expression.

"Well, uh, unfortunately," Axel said, "we don't have time to babysit this one. Can you give it instructions and send it to the check-in on its own?"

"I'm afraid that will have to do."

Shaddra walked over to the new dragon's side and asked him his name.

"My name is Surad."

"What did your rider tell the soldiers that you visited five minutes ago?"

"He said there was a group of enemy cavalry soldiers ahead on the Tiverts River Road, and they were resting in a vulnerable position. The enemy appeared to have wounded individuals with them in a wagon, which prevented them from moving quickly without abandoning those who were injured. "Thank you, Surad. You must be feeling very confused right now. That is because you have been freed from the slavery of your jewel. There are free dragons waiting on the other side of the pass at the end of that valley over to the southwest, between the two white peaks. You need to go there. They will help you to clear your head and feel better."

"Surad," Axel added in. "Please tell the dragons you meet that we require dragon support down here. Where there's one enemy dragon, there will be more. Have them send at least two dragons and tell them to look for Shaddra and me or a group of about twenty-five Mysuran cavalry."

Surad agreed. He stood up on all fours and tested his legs, after which, he tested his wings. He quickly looked back at Shaddra and leaped into the air, flying toward the two white peaks.

"Let's go find Eleth and the others," Axel said with a grim look on his face.

Fortunately, no one in the company of cavalry pursuing Ranel looked up as Shaddra passed above them. Shaddra maintained her invisible mode and flew over the soldiers at a very high altitude to reduce the risk of Axel being spotted.

At this point, Axel asked Shaddra to take a wide turn to avoid passing again over the King's troops and head north, this time over the Tiverts River.

After flying for a little more than half an orai, Shaddra was able to point out a spot some fifteen tondrins south of Blatten, where at least a score of men were hidden in the brush next to the road. They had a wagon with them, however, and that was not so easily hidden.

"It looks like they do have wounded," Shaddra said. "Just as Surad said."

"Yes, and Eleth is with them, too."

Shaddra and Axel drew near Ranel's team, but Shaddra veered sharply to the right to hide their approach. Descending to the tops of the forest, she spoke something in High Language to give Eleth warning of their coming.

When Shaddra appeared over the trees, now in her visible form, half of Ranel's team was already out in the road looking skyward. Shaddra settled in on the road next to Eleth, who ran over and threw her arms, as best she could, around the messenger dragon's neck.

Eleth stepped back and shouted out, "Hey, everyone. Look who's stopped by for a visit!"

Axel jumped off Shaddra in his usual way and shouted out in a volume to match that of Eleth, "Unfortunately, we aren't bearing good news."

Ranel came over to join the little group and asked, "What's up?"

"Hello, Tarak," Axel answered. "Have you been taking care of my friend here?"

"It's more like she's been taking care of us, really. She heard a cavalry troop approaching well before any of us and gave us time to prepare to meet them. They regretted that encounter, but we took two casualties in the process. It's fotunate that Eleth is a doctor, or we might have lost them, too."

"I haven't done that much, really," said Eleth. "Tarak was the one who devised that masterful ambush."

"Why are you on the Tiverts Road," Axel asked, "when we saw the team of hens you're assigned to on the upper reaches of the Silistra Road?"

Eleth answered, saying, "We couldn't have that cavalry troop we ambushed following them. We figured the rain, which should start up at any time, would wash out their tracks, so we turned in this direction at the crossroads. It's better that any enemy troops coming up follow us rather than the hens.

"That's logical, but it puts you in danger."

"We're here to keep the danger away from the hens," said Tarak. We can take care of ourselves. So, what's the bad news?"

"You have a large company-sized group of cavalry following you. Eighty to ninety men, I'd say. They know where you are from information supplied by the rider of a messenger dragon."

"Yes, we saw the dragon, but there was no way to hide the wagon with such short notice. How far back is the enemy company?"

"About six tondrins and they're pushing hard."

Tarak cursed and started pacing back and forth across the road, pounding one fist into the open palm of the other hand. "They'll be on us soon enough, and there are no trails or roads in this river valley for us to use in throwing them off."

He looked over at Axel. "Did you see any routes we could take to get away from their trackers?"

"Unfortunately, we did not follow the Tiverts Road to get here."

Tarak sucked hard on his lips and thought for a moment. He looked up at Axel once more and asked, "How long do you think it will take the soldiers to reach us?"

"At the pace you can travel, they're an orai and a half behind; perhaps a little more."

"Then, there's no choice but to fight them or melt into the forest. However, the forest here is filled with killer beasts. Our men would be picked off by them one by one.

"We can try to find a spot for an ambush, but the country doesn't suit it, and they're sure to have scouts running ahead, looking for ambushes."

"Yes," Axel said, "nevertheless, I saw something from up above that might make an ambush work very well for you."

Tarak suddenly stopped and put on a sour-looking grimace. Rubbing a whiskered chin, he said, "I'm afraid that the last fight left us rather short on arrows."

"I just happened to find a bundle of arrows tied behind my saddle," Axel responded and pointed over at Shaddra. "There should be a little over a hundred in there, with mixed heads. Will they help?"

"Has that dragon blood of yours also turned you into a foreseer?" Tarak said, laughing and shaking his head.

"No, I just thought you might need them."

Axel looked over to his dragon-sister. "I have a gift for you, too."

When she looked curiously at him, Axel moved over to Shaddra's saddle and reached into a saddlebag. He pulled out a canvass sack and threw it to her. She caught it easily, in spite of its weight.

"I hope whatever this is, it's edible. We're really short on food right now."

"Unfortunately, it's not edible. But, knowing you, it may prove useful in that way."

She opened the sack and reached in to pull out a throwing knife in a small sheath.

"Oh, my, how many of these did you bring?"

"Don't know for sure, but, from the weight, I would guess twenty or so. Jarrad has been collecting them for some time, just for you."

"That man deserves a kiss for sure."

"Hey, wait a moment! I was the one who brought them to you!"

"Hmm. Well, maybe that's worth a peck on the cheek."

"Oh, my heart is breaking."

"Let's get out of here and, perhaps, I'll reevaluate that reward."

"At least, there's hope."

"All right, all right, break it up, you lovebirds," said Tarak. "Axel, where is this ambush site you saw?"

***

When Axel, who had been riding in the wagon, called the group to a stop a half orai later, Tarak looked around in surprise.

"This is it?"

"Yes."

"There's nothing special about this location to make it good for an ambush! I see a slight bend to the left and thick outer forest on both sides. There's a fair amount of cover on both sides of the road. That's it."

"You see correctly."

"If I put soldiers on both sides of the road, we could end up shooting our own people. If I put all my men on one side, the enemy soldiers who survive the first volley of arrows will take cover on the other side, and they will still outnumber us by more than two to one. After that, their numbers will give them sufficient advantage to flank us."

"Again, you see things correctly."

"What am I not seeing?"

"Perhaps I'd better explain," said Axel.

Satisfied with Axel's plan but still somewhat leery of it, Tarak had the four skells unhitched from the wagon and led to an area out of sight in the forest to the left of the road. Then the troop manhandled the wagon between the trees to a place not far from the skells. All of the troop's skells were securely tied to trees, and a guard set about them. One other man stayed to watch and care for the wounded, if necessary. Once satisfied with the wagon's placement, Tarak assigned several of his men to cutting away at the base of a tree, which would only be allowed to fall once the king's men arrived. It would completely block the road. Then he started concealing his troops for a surprise attack from the left.

Axel sent Shaddra up to pinpoint the locations of other forces in the area. She returned to say the cavalry troop was, perhaps, half an orai away at their current speed.

Tarak sent out orders for his little company to add more masking and cover to their positions, if possible. After that, everyone settled in to wait.

The anticipated drizzle of rain started to fall while they waited.

The first three enemy soldiers to pass were, obviously, scouts. They were widely spaced and kept a wary watch on every rock and tree that could hide an enemy. Behind them came another three scouts, also spread wide apart. The main body followed fifty strides behind. They looked exhausted yet maintained a state of diligent wariness. Still, a slight relaxation seemed to show on their faces, because the ground they were passing over and through was certainly not best for an ambush. They changed their minds quickly when the tree suddenly fell in front of them, and the arrows started to fly.

The first volley took out twenty-seven enemy soldiers, counting the four scouts who fell from Axel's shots. The steady rain did not hinder the performance of the Mysuran bows at all but did tend to make arming and firing crossbows more difficult. Still, more than sixty king's men remained, compared to Tarak's twenty-three serviceable troops, plus Axel and Eleth. Eleth used one knife, though she preferred reserving them for critical minutes.

In a flash, the cavalry company commander evaluated the source of the attack and ordered his men to the right side of the road and to continue returning fire with their crossbows. That commander could tell from the rate of fire directed toward his men how many enemy troops they were facing and quickly devised a plan to outflank the Mysurans on both sides with a pincer movement.

Axel, now standing behind the lines, picked up a fistful of dry dirt from under a bush and watched as he let it fall to the ground. Then he mounted Shaddra, who, in her visible mode, jumped into the air and flew to some distance behind the Sanaran troops.

The enemy troops watched the jump, and, in so doing, many of them exposed themselves to fire from the Mysuran bows. Still, the Mysurans were outnumbered at least two to one. The enemy commander finished outlining his plan to his troops and gave the order to commence.

At that moment, the first hairy head poked its way through the trees and became visible to the Mysurans. The hirvior's eyes stood as tall in the air as the head of a man, but its hump was half again taller. It carried a thick, dark brown mane of hair all about its head and neck, while its face was mostly an elongated snout, with long, sharp canine and incisor teeth. Saliva dribbled in long streams from its mouth.

Then came the first scream.

When Shaddra and Axel flew down to the Mysurans on the road after freeing Surad, they saw, in the distance ahead, an unusually large herd of hirviors on the valley's northern edge, less than half a tondrin from the road. After studying the shape of the road, Axel determined a different kind of ambush was feasible there.

When he dropped the dirt from his hand, he was checking the direction and speed of the wind, which he put to use upon making the jump to the opposite side of the road. Shaddra landed just on the other side of the hirviors, and the wind carried the scent of both Shaddra and Axel into the herd of killer beasts. The two split up to maximize the spread of their scent and to direct it into the herd at the proper angle. All killer beasts are afraid of dragons and will flee the smell of them every time. In this case, they fled directly into the cavalry troops and another smell having a lot of meaning to a hirvior—the smell of blood. With several of the cavalry troop wounded by arrows, there was blood enough to encourage the hirviors to break out into a feeding frenzy and start attacking anything living.

The troops being, to a man, city-bred and raised, knew little about killer beasts in general and hirviors in particular. When the beasts started attacking, the troopers reacted by shooting the hirviors with their crossbows, but not knowing exactly which parts were vulnerable, they only succeeded in making the hirviors mad.

One scream led to another and to another and another. The air was so heavy with the sound of fear and pain that the Mysuran troops clasped their hands to their ears to keep that noise out of their heads. Axel wanted to do the same but knew he was responsible for this slaughter. He needed to hear and own every scream so that he never grew to enjoy this.

No hirvior crossed the road. A hail of arrows quickly downed all that tried. But there really was no need to cross the road, with plenty of flesh right where they were, consisting of men, skells, and wounded hirviors.

One of the two surviving scouts had turned back to help his friends, but upon seeing the carnage, spun his skell around and headed back up the road. He traveled perhaps two hundred strides when, suddenly, a huge black beast charged out of the forest, using an unusual gate to take down both man and skell. It was a chuda probably attracted by the same smell that was driving the herd of hirviors crazy.

When they saw what happened to the scout, all the Mysurans clustered into a circle with bows facing outward to protect against any other beasts wanting to join in the party.

***

Once Axel determined enough damage had been inflicted, he set his mind on finding Shaddra and rejoining the Mysurans. However, having just made a turn towards the road, he saw a Sanaran soldier, five strides away, aiming a loaded crossbow straight at his heart. In an automatic reaction and knowing full well he would be too late, he drew and was on the verge of firing his bow, when something big and black crashed down in front of him so fast there was no time to even think what it was. Immediately, after recovering from the shock of whatever the thing was, he loosed his arrow, striking the Sanaran in the center of his chest.

Only at that instant did he look at what had crashed into the ground before him and saw, to his horror, what it was.

"Shaddra! Nooooo!" he wailed.

In what seemed only a few seconds, Eleth was there at his side. She heard his cry with her dragon ears and, heedless of anything else, ran to where she knew she'd find both Axel and Shaddra. As she ran the hundred strides separating them, she went directly through the Sanaran line, or what was left of it. She passed two troopers struggling to aim weapons at her but dropped them both with knives as she pushed by. The last one fell with a knife protruding directly out of his eye socket.

Shaddra had landed on her feet and was facing the enemy, where she stood to take his shot. At this range, her armor provided no defense. The bolt struck her in almost the same position as it would have struck Axel.

Neither of the two young people needed more than a single look to know Shaddra had only minutes to live. Eleth knelt and cuddled Shaddra's head in her lap. Axel knelt beside Eleth and clasped Shaddra's paw to his chest.

"Shaddra," Axel said, with tears flowing freely from his eyes, "you saved me when I thought my life was over. You are my longest and dearest friend. I would trade my life for yours, right now, if I could."

Shaddra gazed steadily into his eyes and said in a low, steady voice, "That is not for you to decide, Son of Ceragon. From the moment we first met, my life has been devoted to serving and protecting you—I was born for this purpose. It could never have been otherwise."

She turned then to Eleth, her expression softening. "You and Axel are destined for something greater: a task of immense importance lies before you. My role has only ever been to guide and aid you on your journey. If you love me, then do not fail."

"Shaddra," Eleth whispered through her tears, "we do love you, and, while we will accomplish our task for all dragons, it is you who we will be keeping closest to our hearts."

"I vow to see the *Great Foretelling* fulfilled," said Axel, "and will do so in your honor."

"Axel," Shaddra said weakly, "I am grateful for the first day I met you, and every day since, and every day yet to come."

The messenger dragon looked once more at Eleth and back at Axel. "Axel," she said weakly, "Eleth was born to be your mate." She looked once more at Eleth and said, "Eleth, Axel was born to be your mate. Together…, no force will be able to stand against you for long."

With one final look at the two Children of Ceragon, Shaddra closed her eyes, exhaled once, and breathed no more.

Eleth looked up from her reverie and quickly ascertained the need for action. She stood and placed a hand on Axel's shoulder. He looked up at her as if through a cloud. "Shaddra's gone," he said in a whisper.

"Yes, and we need to be gone, too. Get up. It's time to go. We need to remove her saddle and get out of here."

Axel first shook his head, then stopped and nodded. He stood, and the two unbuckled Shaddra's saddle then walked back to the team. Hirviors and other killer beasts with fresh blood dripping from their mouths made way as they passed, but no human stood to greet them until they reached the encircled men of Tarak

Ranel's team. They had all gathered around the wagon holding the wounded. That ring was, in turn, circled by a ring of dead and dying killer beasts. Still more were coming through the trees, but now, a very familiar and fearsome smell kept them at bay, so they avoided the group of humans.

Eleth looked around and could not see the team commander. "Where's Tarak?" she asked. A soldier shook his head and pointed behind her. When she turned, she saw Tarak lying on his back with a crossbow bolt in his forehead.

Eleth's hand went to her mouth, and her already wet face was bathed in tears again. She took a deep breath, let it out, and said, "Let's load him and any other dead or wounded into the wagon and get it back on the road. We need to leave immediately."

Eleth's orders were crisply obeyed. With some effort, members of the troop pushed and pulled the wagon back to the road, while others manhandled the tree obstacle out of the way. Tarak's second in command called for the skells, which were again harnessed to the wagon. Then the team added two dead and three more wounded into the box in the back and set the dragon saddle across the sideboard. Eleth joined them there in the cramped box to do what she could for the wounded. All the enemy skells were long gone, most likely claimed by the hirviors, but the skells ridden by the Mysuran dead and wounded remained.

Axel grabbed two unclaimed skells and set the remaining riderless skells free to give them a chance to survive. After tying one of the two to the back of the wagon, he climbed aboard the other. Only a few minutes later, the group departed in the direction of the Loft.

Axel rode up beside Eleth and said over the side of the wagon, "Shaddra's body should lie there undisturbed until she ends up like Hukken. No flesh-eating beast will go near the body of a dragon.

"I couldn't do it, but we'll have to send someone right away to make a cut in her neck as if a jewel had been removed. We can't let her body provide evidence of the Free Dragon's existence."

***

The group rode on for another orai. Axel rode in the lead, keeping a sharp lookout ahead. His heart weighed heavily on him and, perhaps that was why he did not see the approaching dragons first. A cry from Eleth made him look back, and he saw her pointing to the eastern horizon. "Two firedrakes are coming at us from behind!" she called out.

As he watched the oncoming dragons, he saw them dip down to the ground.

"Two enemy dragonriders have discovered the battlefield we just left!" he shouted to the troops while turning his skell back toward Eleth and the wagon. "They are riding Firedrakes."

Eleth looked down the road and noticed the dense broad-leafed forest lining both sides for as far as her eyes could see. "Lieutenant Witt," she yelled out, "disperse the men into the forest on both sides of the road. Have them spread out as much as possible to find shelter underneath the densest trees. The dragons will find us by smell, but the trees will shield us from most of their dragon fire. If they come into the forest after us, we can strike out at the riders. Axel, you, and I need to move these wounded over into the trees."

Everyone hastened to obey her orders without question and scattered about in the forest.

"You know we're in deep trouble," Axel said as the two carried their wounded comrades under the trees. "Those two dragons have enough firepower to burn through the canopy if they keep at it."

"Don't tell the others. Just take a shot if you can find one."

"I don't think a firedrake's sense of smell can help it pinpoint prey in these woods…especially in this rain." Axel said. It will only be able to target areas where the smell is strongest up there"

"That's what I thought, too. Let's hope we are both right."

The two friends disbursed the wounded into places where the canopy was thick, then sought an open place where they could keep an eye on a reasonable piece of the sky. Their scent would not likely be targeted by the dragons above.

Eleth suddenly started climbing a landrin tree.

"What are you doing?" Axel called out.

"I'll serve as spotter and tell you when something you can shoot at is approaching."

"You are a crazy woman!"

"I'll take that as a compliment!"

She reached a solid branch with a view and tried to settle herself in where only a small portion of her face could be seen from above. "I see them coming. They'll be here in a few minutes," she shouted down. "They're staying high, so I think this pass is just for a look."

Axel peered up through his small view of the sky and saw one dragon pass along the edge of the leaves.

"They're making a wide turn that should bring them back this way," Eleth shouted. "They're coming on more to the south than before and much lower. I don't think you'll get a shot at them. Take cover, everyone!" she bellowed at the top of her lungs.

A sudden blast of heat and bright light penetrated through the canopy, but the attack seemed to be aimed at least two landrins away. Someone started screaming, and the screams lasted an agonizingly long time.

Axel paced back and forth trying to find a place where he could maximize his view up through the trees. Smoke now rose thickly to further block his view.

"They must have smelled us. They're turning and coming back," Eleth shouted, "and I think they are coming straight at you and me. I'm coming down!"

Eleth expertly dropped from branch to branch until she struck the ground and rolled. Fire billowed down from the tops of the trees not far behind her but never reached the ground. The firebolts, which had been sent at an angle, seared across the branches above, lighting fires all about them, in spite of the wet leaves in the canopy. The riders were having their dragons clear away the cover protecting the Mysurans.

"A terrible gust of steam, created by the superheated rainwater on the tree leaves, roared down upon them, burning their ears, noses, and any other exposed skin. Axel, holding his breath, ran to Eleth and threw himself over her until the heat wave passed by. He then got up and said, "I can't see anything here! I'm going out onto the road. Maybe I'll find an available shot over there."

"But you'll be a perfect target on the road!"

"Maybe they will be, too!"

He started off through the trees at a run. Eleth rose and followed twenty strides behind.

When they broke out into the open, they saw the two dragons lining up for another run. One rider adjusted his dragon's course to turn in their direction. Axel drew back on his bow and aimed.

Suddenly, two black bird-like objects dropped out of the clouds and, flying faster than Axel believed possible, swooped down on the unsuspecting dragonriders. Striking the firedrakes like a flat stone skipping on water, the two siris dragons bounced off their upper surfaces and kept on flying, each holding something in their forearms.

Axel lowered his bow in utter amazement. "Did you see that?" he called back to Eleth.

"I certainly did. Two siris dragons just nipped the riders off their dragons like arrows knocking globefruit off fence posts! What are they doing now? The siris dragons are flying away!"

"They're leading the firedrakes away from us!"

Indeed, the two firedrakes swiftly changed their course and struggled to give chase to the siris dragons carrying off their riders.

Eleth ran over to Axel and placed a hand on his shoulder. "Where are the Free Dragons going?" she asked.

"I think they'll fly a wide circle and build up some distance between themselves and the king's dragons. They'll be back here in no time with Bechars for us to break. Quick, find some rocks!"

Eleth ran to the shoulder of the road and soon came back with two hefty rocks the size of cobble stones. Meanwhile, Axel kept an eye on all the dragons, at least to the extent that they stayed in view above the line of trees.

Minutes passed before Axel shouted, "Here they come. See, there, to the west; it's Konnor and Kulek. They have a pretty good lead on the firedrakes and have separated themselves so they can come in one at a time. That's good. You grab the Bechar from each rider after it drops to the ground and smash it. Be careful. The bodies might bounce and travel some distance. I'll watch for the pursuing firedrakes and shoot them down if they get too close."

"Looks like Kulek is coming in first," Eleth said. "We'd better keep the road clear for him."

Kulek swooped in swiftly and low, threading his way through the gap between the trees. As he approached the two young people, he flared his wings and began to ascend. Nearly coming to a halt, he released the body he carried from a height of no more than ten strides. With a powerful flap of his wings, he surged upward, generating a fierce backdraft of air that buffeted the two teenagers. The dragonrider must have been killed or knocked unconscious in the initial strike, because he neither screamed nor flailed about as he fell. Eleth had no more than a couple of minutes to find the Bechar and smash it. She did this smoothly, as if she were long experienced. Axel did not need to shoot at the oncoming enemy dragon, since it veered off quickly as soon as the Bechar was broken.

When Konnor approached for his turn, he had a good lead over the pursuing firedrake, but they were both approaching at a very fast speed. He came in much lower than Kulek had and released his burden over the muddy roadway about thirty strides to the west of Eleth. The body fell, showing no signs of life on its way down, and struck the ground at high speed. It started bouncing and rolling, coming to a stop only three strides away from her.

"Do it quick!" Axel shouted. "That firedrake is coming fast!"

Eleth fumbled with the broken body, trying to reach the Bechar. She secured it after a few seconds and ran with it to her rocks to smash it into pieces.

"Duck!" Axel shouted in almost a scream.

Eleth threw herself flat to the ground as the huge firedrake flew right over her head, missing her by only a stride. It crashed into the wet road with a tremendous noise, spraying mud and water in all directions, then rolled head over tail until stopping a hundred strides behind her.

"When Eleth looked up, Axel was kneeling in a puddle of water beside her, reaching for her arm.

"I'm okay," she said, then looked at her clothes, which were soaking wet and covered with muck. Well, mostly okay, I guess."

Axel helped her to stand and together, they turned to look at the firedrake.

"Think he survived that?" Axel asked.

"Firedrakes are pretty tough," she replied.

"I almost shot him. But I saw you broke the jewel in time."

"Barely."

"That was one determined dragon. I hope he survived. That's the kind we need."

Kulek settled softly to the ground nearby and asked, "Are the Son and the Daughter all right?"

"Yes, Kulek," Eleth said. "But it was close."

Konnor dropped down next to Kulek.

"I am so sorry to have let go of that rider this way. I put you in danger. If anything had happened, I would never..."

"Relax, Konnor," said Axel. "Everyone is just fine. Well, except maybe that one. He pointed at the firedrake. Oh, and where is the other one."

Kulek raised his arm and pointed up. He's flying circles overhead. I'll go bring him down." He lifted off, almost vertically into the air.

Pointing over at the prone firedrake, Eleth said, "Maybe we'd better go check on our new friend over there. He may be injured."

"I can't imagine a firedrake being too bad off after a simple fall like that," Konnor said.

The three walked over to the slime-covered dragon, which opened its eyes as soon as they approached. "What would a siris dragon know about a firedrake, anyway?" he said.

"See, I told you he would be okay," said Konnor.

Eleth stepped closer and spoke. "Are you injured, dragon? May we help?"

"I don't know about my body, but I think I have suffered severe damage to my pride." The dragon slowly raised himself up and looked at those about him. "Who are you anyway?"

Konnor stepped forward and said, "My name is Konnor, and I am a free dragon of the Colony. These humans are the *Son and Daughter of the Great Ceragon.* They have just freed you from slavery to your jewel."

"Surely this story is some kind of jest."

"Would you have said those words if you were still under the control of your jewel?"

"Interesting thought. I would never have said anything in human speech if I were still commanded by the jewel. What did you do?"

"Look over there," said Eleth, pointing at the two rocks she had used to break the jewels. "Those sparkly bits are all that remain of the Bechar your rider once wore. The red Minqar in your neck is now white and clear as the bits you see before you."

A sound in high speech interrupted the conversation, and everyone looked up.

"Kulek wants to bring his new friend down for a visit," said Konnor.

Axel waved an arm up at Kulek, and the humans, plus Konnor, all shuffled back to give the two newcomer dragons space to land.

Once the two were on the ground, Kulek said, "May I present Tilak, a firedrake, once of the Southern Dragon Command.

"Tilak, may I present Konnor, a free dragon, and the *Son and Daughter of Ceragon*? Please introduce me to your new friend, Konnor."

"I don't know yet whether he is a friend," said Konnor. He turned to look at the mud-covered dragon in an expectant manner.

"Are these two humans really the *Son and the Daughter*?" said the as yet unknown dragon.

Konnor said something in high speech and the slime-drenched dragon stepped back and fell solidly on its haunches. He immediately rose to his feet and bowed."

"Oh, please don't do that," said Eleth. "We are only servants. No one should ever bow to us. But, please, tell us your name."

"I apologize for being so discourteous. My name is Aykal, and I served in the same unit of the Dragon Corps as Tilak."

The sound of shouts and someone crashing through the underbrush came from the forest behind Axel. A man suddenly appeared and just as abruptly came to a stop. He looked up at the four huge dragons and started to back up.

"Wait, Lieutenant Witt!" Eleth called out to him. "These are all now free dragons."

"Free or not," the lieutenant answered, "we have three new wounded men. All burned, one severely. We need your help."

"Lieutenant, show me where the men with burns can be found. Then I would like you to assign five others to gather landrin blossoms, as many as they can, and bring them to where your wounded are lying. Okay? Oh, and have someone fetch my medical bag from the wagon."

"Yes, Commander Keiron. This way, please."

Eleth ran off, following the lieutenant, while Axel turned back to the dragons."

"Tilak and Aykal," he said, "are there any more of the king's dragons likely to come upon us in this location?"

The two firedrakes looked at each other and communicated in High Language.

"It's not very likely until we are reported missing," said Aykal in human speech. "We were due to report before the setting of the Sunstar. Even then, our home unit would not know where to look for us. That means there should be no dragons in this area before late tomorrow."

"It also means we can take some time to treat the wounded before leaving," said Axel.

He sighed deeply, then addressed Konnor and Kulek. "I have some very sad news to give you before you return to the Colony...." He stopped speaking and tried to swallow but found the simple task very difficult to perform.

Konnor interrupted him and said, "Shaddra is like your shadow, yet you are alone here. I believe I know what you are trying to say."

Axel had never seen a dragon shed tears, but Konnor appeared to be on the verge of crying. Kulek also looked stricken.

Kulek now spoke up. "Why don't I escort our new friends to the Colony and bear this unhappy news to Torkar? Konnor, I suggest you stay here with the *Children of Ceragon* to serve them in any way they might have need. I know you have a special attachment to the daughter."

Konnor looked embarrassed but nodded his head. "I will stay."

Kulek turned once more to Axel. "Where does the body of Shaddra now lie?" he asked.

"Tilak and Aykal," Axel said, looking over to the firedrakes, "when you investigated the battlefield to the east of here, did you find the body of a messenger dragon on the field's northern edge?"

"Yes, we did," answered Aykal. "We thought it belonged to our missing messenger dragon. The body was of the same color."

"No, unfortunately, that messenger dragon was Shaddra, one of ours. It appears that Surad should be safe and has found the members of the Colony waiting for him at the checkpoint on the Blatten Road. Will you please tell Torkar, when you see him, where the body of Shaddra may be found?"

"If Kulek leads us to Torkar, we shall indeed pass on that information."

"Thank you all for your help. Kulek, you should be on your way."

Kulek led the two firedrakes down the road some distance, where Aykal shook himself to rid himself of as much of the mud as possible, then the three stepped into the air in a steep climb.

Heaving a big sigh, Axel looked over to Konnor and said, "We still have more than a full day's travel before us and should get the troop going as soon as possible. By the way, how are you at finding game?"

***

The Loft check-in site was situated a short distance away from the road in a cave. The cave was large enough to comfortably accommodate a dozen dragons or, perhaps, a hundred humans. When the troop, which once was led by Tarak Ranel, reached the check-in, they discovered all the groups arriving ahead of them had already proceeded down into the valley. This meant the entire troop would fit in the cave, where food and blankets were set about to provide a meal and rest for the men. There were also provisions for dragons and extra skells if needed.

The dead were removed from the wagon to give the wounded more room. The dead would be transported to the valley on a later run. Eleth quickly arranged for fresh skells to be harnessed to the wagon, a new driver, blankets to make the wounded comfortable and food for everyone who just arrived. They were then shipped off to the valley where they could get better medical care.

Axel went over to see Licor who was now manning the check-in station, his right wing all bundled up in a tightly wrapped sling. "Are any teams still out on the roads," he asked.

Licor beamed and said, "All the teams, both dragon and human, have checked in."

"Have there been any losses?"

"Licor sighed and said, "Apart from Shaddra and the five dead humans from Ranel's team, we lost Orfa, a hen from the coops, and two young males from the Cadet Reserve. The strain of the flight here proved to be too much for them."

"All their Minqars were destroyed, I assume."

"Oh, yes. Orders for destruction of Minqars were obeyed to the letter."

"It's hard to believe that the three raids all turned out so well. Everything seems to have succeeded beyond our most optimistic dreams. So how does this success translate into the number of dragons arriving here at the check-in?

Licor sucked on his lips in a very human gesture and called for an assistant to look through the records. "I happen to have a man who is an expert on that subject," he said.

The assistant turned out to be Sonder Arhus. He saluted upon first seeing Axel and smiled broadly. Axel returned the salute and then extended his hand. Arhus accepted the hand and shook it hard, smiling broadly as he did.

"I see you have a new pair of boots," Axel said and pointed down at Sonder's left foot.

"Oh, you noticed. Isn't it wonderful? I mounted and rode a skell up from the valley without receiving any assistance at all. Fala and Bardin are among the finest craftspeople I have ever met."

"So, what do the records tell us about the dragons who have arrived?"

Sonder looked at a stack of papers in his hand and said, "The first groups to arrive were adult dragons, formerly serving as guard dragons at the Cadet Reserve. They included seventeen firedrakes and seven siris dragons. They stopped only briefly and then moved on.

"Two teams of hens capable of moderate flight came through four days ago. They performed quite well despite the need for frequent rest stops, Sonder said. "They included the strongest of the hens, and while they were capable of some flight, they mainly walked since departing the train. Of course, these groups still required numerous rest stops. In total, 36 firedrakes, 21 siris dragons, and 18 messenger dragons from these groups met the challenges of the loft in this manner. Not one was lost."

"What about the king's dragons? Did they run into any of them?"

"The groups traveled only at night, which reduced their speed considerably, and every rest stop during the day had to be thoroughly masked to prevent discovery.

"Flying patrols of free dragons closely guarded the Loft and the various routes through the Silistra Valleys, so no enemy dragon patrols were able to penetrate that far. There were, however, several air clashes with king's dragons, and some injuries were given and taken in those battles. One more enslaved dragon, a firedrake, was killed."

"What about the young draft dragons?"

"They were divided into seven separate small groups to spread out the risk and make them easier to hide. As the days passed, more and more enemy dragon patrols flew above them. That always made foraging for food more dangerous, even though the Free Colony dragons and their human assistants had placed large piles of the green food the draft dragons appreciated at each rest stop. Unfortunately, they reported it was never enough. The constant travel used up a lot of energy, and the dragons always found a need for more than they found at the sites. On the fortunate side, free messenger dragons kept a lookout in the skies during the days to provide warning when patrols approached, and whenever one of our patrols appeared on the scene, the king's bravest always fled. It seems our dragons have developed a reputation. It all just took time for the draft dragons—a lot of time.

"During the latter stages, the drafts frequently found themselves walking up the middle of small streams until they became too rocky to permit travel at any reasonable speed. The dragons then found themselves using small roads until they reached the Loft itself.

"Flying patrols of Free Dragons closely guarded the Loft, so no enemy dragon patrols were able to penetrate that far. Since no dragons wanted to be discovered crossing the Loft, the final leg of their journey was never attempted until every dragon in the group was thoroughly rested and fed. There would be a dash to begin after the setting of the Sunstar. It would last nearly until morning."

"After that, scattered groups of cadets began to arrive, starting with the best flyers who accompanied those with weaker flying abilities whenever possible. Their arrivals were scattered over the next three or four days. Unfortunately, we lost two of the weaker cadets who just couldn't handle the long flight. We received a total of 249 cadets between the two groups.

"Eventually, 109 adult draft dragons made the trip on foot in four larger groupings. They walked, but they made the trip quickly. Their journey was made simpler by the fact that it was easier to provide food for this group, as they were able to forage along the way and share resources among themselves.

"The next groups involved free dragon firedrakes carrying underbelly baskets full of the youngest dragons. We counted 145 youngsters. They stopped for a brief rest and some food, and were then on their way."

"Okay, Sonder, what about the other teams?"

"The last of the walking groups consisted of hens from the Coops, who were draft dragons with weak legs, or flyers who could not regain sufficient strength in their wings to fly all the way to the free Colony. Most of the 200-odd men and women who volunteered to make the raids come about also reported in at about the same time. They had been following behind to cover tracks.

"The hens, basically, followed the same kind of routes as the draft dragons but more slowly. They lacked the strength and speed of the draft dragons but lacked nothing in doggedness. In the end, there were 33 firedrake hens, 23 siris dragon hens, and 27 draft dragon hens, but no messenger dragons, which was not a surprise to anyone knowing much about messenger dragons."

"You know so much about messenger dragons already?" Axel asked.

"Licor has proven to be an excellent teacher. Since we were both physically encumbered, we have developed a natural friendship."

"Those men and women on skellback or in wagons, crossed in small groups as best they could. As you know, they preferred not to be seen as a migration heading over the Loft, so they tended to remain in small groups and take on the loft at night. They had the same challenge as the dragons when it came to hiding from the dragon patrols. Fortunately, no enemy patrol of humans would chance attacking even one large dragon. Tarak Ranel's group was the only one attacked by enemy forces. As you are aware, you folks got struck both by cavalry forces and dragons. The only losses by Mysurans and by the Colony occurred in that group."

"So, what do these figures total up to?"

"The totals equal 291 adult dragons, of which 158 are hens who are weak, but can regain their strength within a Kivan or two, 24 are mature military-trained dragons, and 109 are mature draft dragons, capable of either carrying burdens or fighting on the ground.

"We also have 394 young dragons of all types, ranging from those in their first year to those nearing young adulthood at 15 years."

Axel stood straight and stared at Sonder in surprise. He blew air out of his mouth and said, "All that's going to change the makeup of the Colony a bunch! What do you think, Licor?"

"I am not a member of the Council," the dragon replied, "but I wager these numbers will cause them a headache or two."

Chapter Twenty-Seven

WARNINGS

The Free Dragons could not bear the idea of mutilating Mother Shaddra. Therefore, they implored Axel and Jarrad to find a way to bring her home. With some serious thought and help from Axel's apprentices, a thick canvas sheet was reinforced along the edges and special ring mounts put into its corners and sides. Sturdy ropes were tied to the ring mounts, and the whole assembly was tested using logs for weight and firedrakes for lifting. It worked, but the dragons needed to exert special effort to keep the weight from pulling them together and causing a collision.

While this effort was under way. A team of human guards scoured the two battle sites with the enemy cavalry to find and remove as many other signs of who was involved in those fights as possible. The team concluded, however, that it was impossible to recover all arrows. A thorough search by the enemy is bound to discover some that were missed.

Shaddra's body was moved at night to avoid detection by the enemy. The four firedrakes, the lookouts, and the official representatives of the Colony decided to call themselves Shaddra's Honor Guard. Axel, Eleth, Jarrad and Clara were also present in the company. This was the first time that Clara had ever ridden a dragon.

With meticulous care, Shaddra's body was rolled onto the canvas and lifted over the mountains to a high valley, not far from the Colony. Nearly every dragon in the Colony was there to welcome the arrival of Shaddra's honor guard. The valley was wide and green with meadow grass, spotted with wildflowers and crossed by a lively brook. A grave had already been prepared, and the Honor Guard only had to lower their beloved mother gently into her final resting place. The ropes on the tarp were cut and the ends draped over Shaddra's body before the earth was placed over her.

Everyone waited a short time for the sunstar to rise over the mountains and bring glorious daylight to the valley. When all was in readiness, Torkar stood at the head of the grave to speak to the very silent group of over five hundred dragons who filled the valley.

"We stand here today," he said, "to honor our most beloved mother, Shaddra, who was first among us in so many ways: first to take flight; first to be led to the home, made by the gods for our benefit; and first to introduce us to the *Son and Daughter of the Great Ceragon.*

"Death is something, that we of the Free Colony have little experience with. While Hukken became our first honored martyr, his burial occurred far away, and few of us were able to participate in the service honoring him. It is fortunate we can all be here for this special service today in a cemetery, which now holds the remains of Shaddra, who was first in our hearts.

"I would like to quote the words of someone who is an adopted member of our community, because they help us understand why we do these things.

"'Burial services are intended to make a home for the remains of individuals after their spirits have returned to the gods who made their physical bodies. The individuals no longer care about this world, but their friends and loved ones do. For this reason, we gather at gravesides to honor those who have departed and to offer comfort to those left behind. We share stories and memories of our loved ones—reminding ourselves that, although they are no longer with us, they will forever remain in our hearts. This sacred space becomes a place where we say our final goodbyes, holding onto hope that we will reunite again in the presence of our gods.'

"In this case, this gravesite will serve as a place where we can come and, without fear of being disturbed, remember Shaddra and Hukken as they were when they walked and flew among us. Unfortunately, we know that Hukken and Shaddra, and now, Orfa, will not remain as our sole martyrs for long. Until the fulfillment of the foretelling of Ceragon, Tamerel will remain a dangerous place for our kind, as the ongoing threats from the dark forces that seek to harm us continue to grow. This place will be where we can come to remember those lost, no matter where those losses may have occurred."

Torkar softly started to sing. In a matter of seconds, others joined in and then more until the voice of every dragon present merged into the sweet and sad refrain. The song lasted about five minutes before slowly diminishing to silence.

Torkar bowed his head and said nothing for a few minutes. Then, he looked up and announced, "I will now give the opportunity to a few who knew them best to share their memories and to tell us about the greatness that was in the hearts of Hukken, Shaddra, and Orfa."

Several dragons took turns coming to the head of the grave to speak. Jarrad, Axel, Eleth, and Clara stood by to listen but did not venture to speak. Though tears flowed freely down the faces of all four humans, they knew this event was something for the dragons to cherish. These humans would be content to remember Shaddra and the others in their hearts.

***

Two days later, the High Councils of the United Peoples of the Uplands, known as the Upland Alliance for brevity's sake, met in Jarrad's meeting tent to discuss and evaluate the operations conducted and decisions made over the previous weeks. This meeting involved a larger group of leaders than had originally been anticipated. In addition to officials from the Free Colony and the Mysura Valley, there were council leaders from Blatten, Pepirin and Thun, all located in the valleys of the Silistra and Taiverts Rivers. There was no way that nearly two hundred dragons could have moved through those latter valleys without their residents knowing about them, so their leaders were given warning. Yes, only a few hours in advance for some, but it was warning, nonetheless. Now, the three new townships had become entirely integrated into the Free Peoples of the Uplands, and, for the most part, were thoroughly glad of it.

Kiel Bassen opened the meeting by extending a special welcome to the new members of the Council, which included Eston Kielder from Blatten in the Silistra River Valley as well as Verna Willer from Teperin and Andros Ripton from Thun. Teperin and Thun were the two largest towns in the Tiverts River Valley. Together, the three communities accounted for a population of roughly 9,000 inhabitants.

"I would like to point out," Councilman Kiel said, "that, prior to extending the invitations for the three new communities to join our new Upland Alliance, leaders of the Mysura Valley closely monitored the voice of the people in the Silistra Valleys to determine whether they would fully support joining and preserving such an alliance with their very lives if necessary. The answer came back with a nearly unanimous voice of approval."

"The leaders of the Mysura Valley communities then met extensively with leaders of the Free Dragon Colony to discuss both advantages and disadvantages of such a move and especially to address potential security issues. We are fully aware of the virtual certainty that this move, along with some other items of very sensitive information, will be reported to the king by informants. The key piece of such information would be the fact that the Free Dragon Community exists. We must all understand that disclosure of those secrets was inevitable anyway within a short timeframe." Here, Kiel nodded toward the three dragons sitting with their heads under the tent and continued, "The dragon leaders understand the issues and have enthusiastically approved the creation of the Upland Alliance."

Each participant was given an opportunity to report on their own activities and to provide input regarding the current situation. The reports and discussions lasted many orais.

One very intriguing report came from Lang Privas, who told of how word of the recent dragon attack had been received in communities outside of the Mysura Valley. "As you all know, delegations from the three largest communities in the Silistra River Valleys have now joined us." Other towns and villages," he said, "especially those in or near the uplands, are angry with the despicable acts of the king's secret police among their populations and the king's high-handed treatment of their citizens. They are looking to the Mysurans as leaders in opposing Deroth's tyranny and murders. We have several secret communications from community leaders saying unrest is widespread and they are seeking advice regarding how to organize to resist his majesty's forces at every level possible.

"While, in many ways, these communications are good news, we must remember there are significant dangers in conducting a secret resistance and, especially, in setting ourselves up as leaders of such a resistance. That said, we all know how our necks are already stuck out so far; there is no chance of ever bringing them back in.

"I will soon seek your individual counsel on how the people of this valley can assist at-risk communities in joining our resistance efforts." Also, I will wish to discuss how we can prevent the king from using those communities to spy on or threaten us. Thank you."

As the final speaker in the meeting, Axel stood and walked to the speaker's platform wearing a grave face. "I must congratulate everyone," he said, upon taking his place, "on the success of the three raids. Their achievements went way beyond our expectations, and our losses, though still grievous to our hearts, were minimal. Over these last few sycles you have been able to save the people of the Valley from annihilation, multiply the size of the Free Colony by a factor of five, strengthen the bond between Free Dragons and the Upland Peoples, and put the

King of Sanara in his place. We must thank the members of the special committees, the Valley Protection Force, and other organizations who worked so diligently to make our victory possible.

"Our defense is the item that I wish to talk about right now. I dare say that our actions have awakened a monster, for a monster is what Deroth truly is. There can be no question the king will seek revenge for what we have done. We have made him look foolish in the company of the other kings on this continent. We have stolen hundreds of his favorite toys and weapons of war. We have, unfortunately, been forced to kill too many of his soldiers. We have weakened his ability to expand the kingdom by attacking his neighbors. He will be determined to find us and destroy us in any way possible.

"Unfortunately, he already knows that the people of the Valley are his enemies. He will use our lost arrows to connect us with the destroyed village of Frithden and my family. He is probably even now putting his military mind to work at finding a way to penetrate our mountains and valleys and overcome the other secrets that protect us here. We, the people of the Mysura Valley, have been aware of this situation for some time, and we have adapted our lives to coexist with the constant threat while devising new methods to ensure our protection. The people of the Silistra Valley have now joined us. I suspect that the king's agents will shortly become aware of that relationship, too. We must, therefore, look to the protection of the Southern Uplands as a whole and very likely an even larger area in the not-so-distant future. We are all fortunate to be living in a region that has so many natural features that can be used to help us in a defense against attacks from the lowlands.

"The Free Colony dragons have, to this time, been able to keep themselves in near-perfect anonymity and live their lives without interference from the king or anyone outside of the Valley. That is about to change. In all that we, dragons and humans, have done together over the last few sycles, there are bound to have been numerous clues left behind. Those clues will certainly make the king's military aware that the Free Dragons not only exist but have also joined the peoples of the southern uplands in declaring war on the king—as indeed we have.

"We can no longer live the way we did not so very long ago. We must always be alert. We must always look to expand our influence to other parts of the kingdom and even neighboring kingdoms. We must ever be seeking new tools to accomplish our objectives, all while ensuring the survival of our communities.

"I wish to propose the creation of the first tool we will use to ensure our survival. Those of you who spend a lot of time in the higher mountains know about the hamaret plant. It is a tall bush that sprouts long, straight branches covered with thorns half a thumb in length. The thorns are sharp enough to pierce thick leather easily, and when any thorn gets broken, it readily releases a highly acidic sap capable of causing extreme pain on any living tissue that happens to come in contact with it or, worse, happens to have the acid injected beneath the skin by a puncturing thorn. Even chudas avoid this plant out of natural instinct.

"The plant is used by hunters and others in the hills who wish to create a barrier that cannot be penetrated by any killer beast. Base camps and ellam paddocks are often surrounded by walls of hamaret thorns for protection both day and night.

"I propose we build a wall of hamaret about our communities. This particular hamaret will not be made from plants, but from the combined might and minds of the human and dragon peoples of the uplands. It will be an armed force of citizens who will keep watch over our enemies and come together in force when called to defend and protect. While almost everyone will be trained to fight, beginning as early as age 12, responsibilities will be rotated to make certain that as many of our normal activities as possible go on as before, ensuring that the community remains engaged in daily life and that the burden of defense does not fall on a few individuals.

"The Tamerel of tomorrow will be filled with surprises, both good and evil. That means we have no way of knowing what will come next. However, we will meet those surprises by being prepared for just about anything and everything we can. We must think both offensively and defensively. It will demand work, innovation, caring for each other and caring for our neighbors outside of the valleys, who are potential friends, and it will require dedication to a goal. That goal can only be the fulfillment of the *Foretelling of Ceragon*, to bring freedom and justice to both the dragons and the humans of Tamerel!"

The meeting concluded with expressions of steadfast resolve to do what must be done and planning as to how a new defense force, to be called the "Hamaret," could be assembled.

***

On the first day of the tenth Kivan, Jarrad and Clara were joined as man and wife on the Tarfal Common Green, with many citizens of the Valley and the Colony watching on.

After the ceremony, the residents of the two human communities occupied themselves with much feasting, dancing, and general merry-making. All the while, the visiting dragons looked on in a sort of benign amusement of their own.

Eleth and Axel approached Langa during the celebrations.

"I gather that dragons don't celebrate much when they choose their mates," Eleth asked their good friend.

"You are quite correct in that assumption," Langa replied. "The High Language helps us to truly understand those who are potential candidates for mating. It is a matter of simply finding the perfect fit. When we find our proper spouse, we make an agreement to become mates, and we announce this to the Colony. That is all there is to it."

"I'm afraid I like our way better," Eleth said, "but then, we have no High Language to help us see into each other's hearts."

"Your way certainly involves a lot of other people. It is as if you use the ceremony as a reason to celebrate widely."

"Oh, that we do."

The dragons left soon after that conversation, whereupon the two young people walked to Harbor Valley and over to Axel's newly completed house on the far side of the meadow. They sat in some chairs set out under the trees for shade, but the sunstar was setting behind the mountains and darkness was already coming on. The sky above them changed in hue many times while they sat, eventually turning a dark blue rimmed in brilliant reds and golds along the western skyline. A full Dragon Moon appeared far to the east even before the sunstar set. The eye looked as if it might be staring straight down on them.

Axel reached out and clasped Eleth's hand. She blushed but clasped his in return. They looked out at some of the folks from the towns who were gathered around a brilliant bonfire in the meadow between the two houses, and a smaller group was dancing merry steps to the music from a pair of fiddlers.

"I think it is time for the two of us to have a serious conversation," said Axel.

"Uh, oh, what kind of trouble am I in now?"

"A great deal of trouble."

"Oh, you mean like always."

"I suppose, yes... and no."

"Stop being so secretive and come out with it."

"You and I are different from other people."

"Is this supposed to be news?"

"No, but it's an important clarification that needs to be made before I go on. You remember how I told you that my blood first appeared purple when I was wounded in the side during the raid on the Cadet Reserve?"

"Yes, but you said the drops on the floor dried red like normal blood."

"Yes, they did. It's the final proof that we two are half-dragons."

"That's a little blunt, but I suppose you're right."

"The fact that we're half-dragons is important here. It is why we're stronger than our completely human peers, why we think faster and remember better than they do. We are even somewhat larger than others of our age."

"Where are you going with this?"

"I'm trying to say that while other humans are considered mature when they reach eighteen, I believe that our maturity sets on earlier than it does for others. We're, now, both seventeen, and I think we need to take that into consideration in our decision-making."

"I'm listening."

"Since we are the only two half-dragons on Tamerel that we know of, I think it is time that we remember the words of Shaddra in her final minutes of breath. She said we're destined to become each other's mates. Face it, the *Great Foretelling* already joins us together. To make a long story short. Eleth Keiran, I love you and I would very much like you to become my wife."

Eleth's free hand rushed to her mouth, but in her heart, she knew Axel's request did not surprise her. To be honest, she had considered the idea of marrying him many times before. She loved him and could imagine being with no one else.

"Others," she said, "will tell us that seventeen is too young."

"Since when have we let others make our decisions for us?"

"I have to admit," Eleth said, raising her hand to Axel's cheek, "that I feel we're destined to be bound together forever."

He took her raised hand and kissed it. "I've thought the same. So, will you marry me?"

"She smiled broadly, and her hair flared fiery red in the last rays of the Sunstar. "Axel Daimon, I will marry you. But when should we be married?"

"Is right now too soon?"

"Yes, much too soon."

Axel leaned forward in his chair and stared intently at Eleth, looking concerned.

"You and I are destined to be together," Eleth said, "but until the coming war is settled, we cannot be married. This is not because I don't want to marry you. Rather, it is because children would be inevitable. With both of us heavily involved in the resistance to Deroth, our children would be left in the care of others far more than we could tolerate. They may also be the targets of an attack, which could put their safety and well-being at risk in a time of conflict. They deserve a better family life than that. Besides, the words of the prophecy do not guarantee either of us, or our children, will survive."

An angry expression crossed Axel's face, but it softened after only a moment. "That is going to cause me to work all the harder to finish this effort."

"Me, too," she said.

Axel gently placed his hands on either side of Eleth's face and drew it to his own. Their kiss was soft but long.

THE END

This story will be continued in the

The Isle of the Cursed Stones

The final volume

of the

Prophecy of Ceragon
Trilogy

by Terry Brewer

About the Author

A LIFE IN MANY WORLDS

Terry Brewer is a lifelong book lover and history enthusiast whose rich and varied career brings unique depth to his writing. With a distinguished record spanning business research, military intelligence, and diplomatic security, Terry has cultivated a wealth of experiences that inform his storytelling. He served as an intelligence officer in both the U.S. Air Force and the U.S. Army, ultimately retiring as a lieutenant colonel. His civilian roles have included management positions in marketing research and data analysis, and he notably supported the U.S. Embassy in Moscow, Russia, as part of the U.S. Bureau of Diplomatic Security.

An avid traveler, Terry has journeyed across the globe, fueling his fascination with diverse cultures and people. These international adventures, combined with his military and diplomatic background, lend his novels a sense of authenticity and detail that transports readers to worlds both real and imagined.

Together with his wife, Judeen, Terry has co-authored two captivating fantasy books: *The Protector of Central Park* and *Revelations at the Snakebite Café*. He has recently released two new titles under his own name—*Under a Dragon Moon* and *The Children of Ceragon*—with a third installment, *The Isle of the Cursed Stones*, completing the trilogy in the coming year.

www.ingramcontent.com/pod-product-compliance
Lightning Source LLC
LaVergne TN
LVHW010628110826
845149LV00014B/2806

* 9 7 8 0 9 8 4 8 0 6 1 5 7 *